TWENTY–SEVEN STORIES

by Pearl S. Buck

TWENTY-SEVEN STORIES

by Pearl S. Buck

ORIGINALLY PUBLISHED IN
The First Wife and *Today and Tomorrow*

THE SUN DIAL PRESS
Garden City, New York

1943
SUN DIAL PRESS

Author's Note

Since I came home to America I have not ceased to follow China's changes and struggles with unending interest, sympathy, and implication, and from time to time this implication has expressed itself in stories. This volume contains a group of such stories, written during the past several years, some of them during the past few months.

The least extraordinary in incident are purely imaginative, if by that one means the absorption of facts until they are an atmosphere of truth. The most extraordinary incidents, such as those in "Tiger! Tiger!" "Golden Flower," and "The Face of Buddha," are based upon true happenings, some of them told me by Chinese who have come to see me straight from the scenes of which I have written in this book.

I hope that the reader will feel as I do the continuity in these stories. It begins with the older Chinese and traces their increasing contact with this terrifying new age, and it goes on to the immediate moment of Japan's war upon China. If I have at all portrayed what I feel so deeply, the tough resistant indomitable quality of the Chinese people, then I have done what I wished to do.

P. S. B.

Acknowledgment is made to the editors of the following magazines in which certain of the stories in this book originally appeared: *Asia, Colliers Weekly, Cosmopolitan, Ladies Home Journal, Pictorial Review, Saturday Evening Post, This Week, Woman's Home Companion.*

THE
FIRST WIFE
AND OTHER STORIES

CONTENTS

FLOOD

INTRODUCTION

INTRODUCTION

⚛

ALTHOUGH by nature and choice a novelist above
all else, Pearl S. Buck has written a great many
shorter pieces. No one has been aware of the
number and variety of these. Even the author herself had
forgotten two or three which have been brought to light by
earnest search, and it is by no means sure that some do not
remain hidden still. For many of these writings have been
in the true sense fugitive. The earliest was more than ten
years ago. Several that rank with her best work came
before her name had been widely noticed. Even today she
is often to be found in obscure corners of the strange wide
realm of print. If a topic is of concern to her she will write
about it, in the place that seems to her most fitting, without
thought of the payment or of prestige.

Her fame as a novelist has tended to draw attention away
from her short stories of distinguished quality written
both before and since her books were published. The present book brings together her short fiction, omitting one
story not set in the Chinese scene, and omitting also certain sketches that lie on the border between fact and fic-

9

tion, a border which in her field is more than usually dim and hard to fix.

The stories in the first group for the most part tell of the clash between the old and the new, between the firm traditions of the East and the urgent ideas of the West. "The First Wife," which opens the volume, is of such length and breadth and depth that it might well have stood alone between covers as a lesser novel. Another of the longer stories, "Repatriated," is one of the few in which the author writes from the point of view not of a Chinese character, but of a foreigner. "The Frill" is notable for its fine scorn of a certain type of white resident in contact with the Chinese. "The Rainy Day," a story which first appeared in 1925, has been somewhat revised for this volume, and may be regarded as introductory to the stories of revolution.

Of the four tales of revolution which make up the second group, "Wang Lung" is of special interest. Those who read this story when it appeared in *Asia* in September, 1928, under the title "The Revolutionist," met then the character whom so many more were to meet two and a half years later in the pages of "The Good Earth," and they saw in vivid detail a looting scene which became the basis of a similar scene in that famous novel. When Mrs. Buck began "The Good Earth" she turned back to this story for her chief male character; indeed she wrote the novel with the name of Wang Lung in mind as title for the book, and it remained so until after the manuscript reached her publisher. Anyone who wants to know how Wang Lung really looked may turn to the file of *Asia* and see the photograph of a sturdy smiling farmer, come into the city to peddle his produce, a picture chosen by Mrs. Buck herself as the very figure of the man she put into her novel. "Father Andrea" is another story in which the point of view is that of a non-Chinese—in this case of an Italian priest, who is a type of the Jesuit missionaries who have so long served in China. The locale of "The New Road" is Mrs. Buck's own city, Nanking.

In the third group are four sketches of the tragic effects of the Yangtse flood in 1931. This flood swept over a cultivated area of fourteen and a half million acres and bore upon the lives of twenty-five million farm people, as many as the whole farm population of the United States. Three of the sketches here are chosen from a set of five which were written not for sale, but to help in getting relief for victims of the disaster. Through the body known as Flood Relief in China, the stories were sent gratis to newspapers in all parts of the United States, and one was read several times over the radio. There is no record of where they were printed but they were beyond doubt the greatest single influence in raising a fund of more than two hundred thousand dollars. The final story, "The Good River," also deals with the flood and closes the book on the appropriate note of American sympathy with China.

These last stories are perhaps the only ones which Mrs. Buck has ever written for a purpose or with intent to serve as interpreter between China and other lands. She has often said that she has no sense of mission and that she writes of China only because that is the place she happens to know best. "My chief pleasure and interest," she says, "has always been people and since I live among Chinese, then

Chinese people. When I am asked what they are like I do not know. They are not this and that, but people. I cannot describe them any more than I can my own blood kin. I am too near them and have shared too closely their lives."

Yet it seems clear that no native Chinese, however schooled in English prose, could have written of his own people as Mrs. Buck has written of them. Born in Hillsboro, West Virginia, in 1892, she drew from her American origins certain qualities that shine through her work. Her father's forebears came to America before the Revolutionary War, and her mother's somewhat later, having left Holland and Germany in quest of religious freedom. They settled in the South, where many of her father's family, the Sydenstrickers, became distinguished in the professions. In a talk on race relations Mrs. Buck has said, "Neither of my grandfathers, although they were landed men, and men of some wealth and position, was ever willing to buy or sell human beings. Indeed, my paternal grandfather seems at times to have been considerably persecuted because he made it a principle that he hired men irrespective of whether or not they were colored or white, and he paid them equal wages for equal work. So from my ancestors I have the tradition of racial equality."

Her parents, who were missionaries, had spent the year 1892 in Europe and America, after a long period of hardships in the far interior of China. So it happened that she was born in America. At the age of four months she was taken to China. There, she has said, "I grew up much alone. My parents lived in many places but when I was a child moved to a city on the Yangtse River called Chin-kiang. There I spent my childhood very quietly in a small bungalow built on the top of a hill which overlooked the great river and the crowded city whose tiled roofs overlaid each other as closely as scales upon a fish. On the other side of our house there were low mountains and lovely gardened valleys and bamboo groves. At the foot of the hill where we lived was a big dark temple where lived a dour old priest who used to chase me with a bamboo pole if in my wanderings I came too near the gates. I was deliciously afraid of him."

She learned to speak Chinese before English, although when it came time to read and write she studied English rather than the difficult Chinese characters. For the first direct literary influence upon her we may look to her Chinese nurse, whom she has herself described in an article in the *Country Gentleman,* from which I quote at length by permission:

"She is one of the two clear figures in the dimness of my early childhood. Foremost stands my mother, but close beside her, sometimes almost seeming a part of her, I see, when I look back, the blue-coated figure of my old Chinese nurse.

"She was, even at this earliest memory of her, already old. There had been other babies before me and none of us ever had any other nurse. But death had been to our house before I was born and had taken the two babies, very close together, and so when I came the old nurse received me with a tenderness which made me her own. . . .

"'And what stories can I tell, who am only an ignorant

13

old thing and I never learned the name of a letter in my life?' the old nurse would exclaim, squinting at the toe of the perpetual stocking she held over her hand to darn.

"This remark we both knew to be merely polite, and I answered, in like terms: 'You do know more stories than any woman in the world!'

"It was true she had an inexhaustible supply of tales of magic, which she had heard chiefly from Buddhist and Taoist priests. The Buddhist stories were about wonderful daggers that a man could make small enough to hide in his ear or in the corner of his eye, but which when he fetched them out again, were long and keen and swift to kill. Or they were tales of this god and that and what they did to men. Heaven and hell she told me about, too, the horrors of the Buddhist hell, and what heaven was and what the wheel of life was that carries us along whether we will or not. I spent many an hour lying under the bamboos, trying to think what I would like to be born into next time after I died.

"But I liked the Taoist tales better, really. They were tales of devils and fairies, and of all the spirits that live in tree and stone and cloud, and of the dragons that were in the sea and the dragons in the storm and wind. There was a pagoda toward the east and I knew there was a dragon's head pinned under there. If ever he managed to wriggle loose the river would flood and swell until we were all drowned. But there was no danger, for it was a great, strong, beautiful pagoda and there the dragon was, imprisoned and helpless.

"Many and many a time when I was surfeited with

14

magic I used to beg my old nurse: 'Now tell me about when you were a little girl!'

"This demand I made continually upon my father and my mother, too, and from them I heard the brave stories of early pioneer days in my own country, the country I had never seen, tales of fearless undertaking, of heroic religious independence, of a stern and god-fearing morality. Now I listened with equal interest and belief to the story my old Chinese nurse told me of her childhood, and of how, in the very days when my parents were growing up in a little Christian village, going to church on Sundays, learning their catechisms, she was living in a great old Chinese city upon the Yangtse River, going to the temple to worship, having her feet bound, thinking of marriage. . . .

" 'There, it is enough for today!' she ended suddenly. 'Go and read your book now.'

"This was the usual ending to any period of play or idleness, for my old nurse, although she could not read a word herself, was inordinately proud of the fact that, although a girl, I could read as well as my brother. True, she did not consider it important until I began to go to a Chinese school and learned to read Chinese. Then she used to boast proudly to her friends: 'This child of mine, although she is only a girl, has her stomach full of good Chinese characters!'

"If I dallied and complained over my book as often I did, being an extremely willful child, she would turn very serious and admonish me: 'You shall learn to read! Here am I all my days like one blind, and if I want to write a

15

letter to my son, even, I must go to the public letter writer and he puts in so many words I did not say that I can make nothing of it even when it is written.'

"But I muttered willfully that I wished I were a little Chinese girl and need not learn, and well I knew I would like to be ignorant. At this she made her eyes so wide at me and thrust out her lower lip so far that I was awed and fell unwillingly to my book again.

"In many other ways she spoiled us badly. My mother deemed it wise that I should learn to work, and she set for me the task every day of sweeping and straightening my own room and of making my bed. My nurse muttered: 'And why should this child work, seeing she is to be as learned as a boy?'

"Immediately I was comforted, knowing that the old nurse had her ways and means. So it came about that many a time when I went upstairs after breakfast to my task I found my little room spotless and my bed made and my old nurse whispered to me always: 'Child, put but a little more time on your book and I am paid.' . . .

"But when her old body had been laid most tenderly into its coffin and the coffin sent away to be buried with her husband, the house was very sad for a while, and empty of a tender presence. Yet even though we grew used, and grown up, we know quite well and to this day that she left her share in us, her white children. Part of her went into us, as mothers are part of their children, so that now and forever her country is like our own to us, loved and understood, her people our own kin. And some essence from the gods in whom she believed lingers in our hearts still, and keeps us, when we think of our old nurse, too large for disbelief, too humble for any scorn."

The child's father went on frequent journeys into remote parts, and brought back tales of his own adventures, some of which took him close to death. And her mother talked to her for long hours, mostly about her own childhood in West Virginia, so greatly different from all that the daughter knew. "My mother taught me everything and made alive for me music and art and beauty. Most of all did she teach me the beauty that lies in words and in what words will say. Other American children have community and school and church and all that makes their varied environment. I had my mother and missed nothing. From my earliest childhood she taught me to write down what I saw and felt and she helped me to see beauty everywhere. Not a week passed without my giving her something to read that I had written and she was fearless, though kind, in her criticisms."

Soon her mother began to send some of the little pieces to the *Shanghai Mercury,* an English language newspaper which had a weekly edition for children. There many of them were printed, during a period of several years, over the signature "Novice." There are American writers who remember with pride their first appearances in the well-loved columns of *St. Nicholas.* Mrs. Buck's recollection is less of pride than of the prizes which the *Mercury* paid in cash and which she won so often that she came to look upon them as a regular source of spending money.

When she was fifteen she went off to boarding school in

Shanghai, her first formal schooling, and at the age of seventeen came home to America—"in spite of our living in China our mother always taught us to call America home"—to enter Randolph-Macon College. She says, "I did not enjoy my life in college very much. It was too confined. I did not know of the life of which the girls talked so much, and my life was as remote from them as though it had been on another planet. I soon learned, however, to show myself, superficially at least, as much like them as I could, for if any heard from whence I came she would exclaim and make round eyes, and this was very irritating to me." Nevertheless she became a leader in college, and president of her class. She wrote for the college paper and in her senior year won two literary prizes, one of which was for the best short story.

"At the end of the college life I went to my home in China to find my mother seriously ill. Two years I spent in taking care of her, finding my only recreation in long walks and in talking with my Chinese friends, but this was my pleasure.

"Then I married a young American and my mother being recovered we went to a town in north China where his work was and there we lived for nearly five years.

"These five years were among the richest as well as the hardest of our life. Part of the time we were the only white people there in that town and countryside, and at no time were there more than six of us. But my life has always been among the Chinese, and here I went about among the people and came into the closest and most intimate knowledge of their lives. As a married woman I had more freedom than I had ever had to come and go among them and Chinese women would talk to me as woman to woman and friend to friend. Some of my best and closest friends were made in those years and I have them still.

"Outwardly our life was exciting enough. We had a famine, with all that means; we had battles between bandits attacking the city and bullets flew thick as flocks of birds over our little Chinese house which clung to the inside of the city wall. Sometimes we went into the country, walking sometimes and sometimes, if it were far, I in a sedan chair and my husband on his bicycle. We went into places where white women had never been and I furnished topic for conversation for weeks, I am sure.

"Then we came to Nanking, my husband to take the department of Rural Economics in the University of Nanking. Here life was different again. We came out of the country and from country people into student life. Here during these ten years we have watched the nation in revolution, have seen the old day defeated and the new day, struggling and weak, but living, come to birth."

She knew always that one day she would write. But for some years she was busy with the care of her home, her children and her parents, with her strong interest in her husband's researches in Chinese farming, and with her own teaching. As part of her job as a Presbyterian missionary, she taught English literature in the University of Nanking and in the Southeastern and later Chung Yang University.

Though there was no time to write, while her hands

were occupied her mind was framing stories. In 1922 she found her first spare moments. At that time the *Atlantic* was disturbed about the younger generation. Reading some of its articles on this subject, Mrs. Buck looked about her at the young Chinese whom she knew. With her daughter playing in the room, she wrote an article and mailed it to distant Boston. It was the first she had ever sent to any magazine, and the *Atlantic* lived up to its rôle as "the amateur's paradise" by prompt acceptance. The article appeared under the title "In China, Too" in the issue of January, 1923. In form and manner it shows the touch of the writer of fiction. At the time only thirty years old, she cast herself in the part of an elderly woman for purpose of contrast with the young people whom she was discussing. An excerpt: "I am rather breathless over it all, having had my main outlook on life the last quarter of a century from this quiet corner of my veranda in a little interior city of China. We are really very conservative here yet, the rare visitors from an outside world tell us. Vague rumors of coeducation, of men and women dining together in restaurants, of moving pictures, and even imported dances, float in from the port cities. I know that I sometimes see the inhabitants of such places pass through the abominably ugly railway-station, which has just been foisted upon our old-fashioned little old town; and they look scandalous women to me, with their wide, short trousers and short sleeves and tight coats; but I suppose I am behind the times. I confess that I like my old Chinese friends better, with their courteous speech and gracious manners. I dislike the acquired abruptness of these young creatures. I dislike the eternal cigarettes, and the blasé, self-sufficient expression on young faces, which I am accustomed to seeing timid and reverential."

Seeing the *Atlantic* article, the editor of the *Forum* wrote to the unknown author asking her to write something for him, and she sent a piece entitled "Beauty in China," which appeared in the issue of March, 1924. Here are found some of her early glimpses of America: "In such a mood as this I crossed the Atlantic, and was thrown straight into New York. Who except one accustomed to the leisurely traffic of trams and rikshas and wheelbarrows can realize the astounding activity of New York! Where one dodged one vehicle, a thousand sprang up to take its place, and crossing the street was a wild adventure, compared to which bandits in China are a mild affair. There was the bewildering clatter of elevated railways to dizzy one's mind, and subterranean roars within the yawning earth, which swallowed up people by the hundreds in one spot, only to vomit them up, restless as ever, miles away. Personally, I could not commit myself to the subway, and clinging to a trolley strap, thought regretfully at times of jogging peacefully along on a wheelbarrow, watching the lazy ducks swimming in the ponds by the roadside and stopping to pluck a wild flower for babies tumbling brown and naked in the dust.

"But if New York shook me out of my quiescent dreaming, even New York did not prepare me for the shock of the American woods.

"A week later I found myself walking through a wood in Virginia. How can I put the excitement of it into words! No one had told me how paganly gorgeous it would be.

Oh, of course they had said, 'The leaves turn in the fall, you know,' but how does that prepare one? I had thought of pale yellows and tans and faint rose reds. Instead, I found myself in a living blaze of color,—robust, violent, vivid beyond belief. I shall never forget one tall tree trunk wrapped about with a vine of flaming scarlet, standing outlined, a fiery sentinel, against a dark rocky cliff."

A third article, in the *Nation,* October 8, 1924, on "The Chinese Student Mind," had some of the author's experience in teaching Chinese students: "I stand sometimes before one of my classes of ninety-odd Chinese college students and am almost convinced that they are a band of young Gideons. I seem to see unquenchable fires in their eyes and a determination in their young faces which warms my heart, cold after so many years of contact with Oriental habits of squeeze and face-saving. I find myself repeating that old Israelitish war-cry: 'Surely the Lord and the sword of Gideon can do it.' . . .

" 'Oh, if you can teach us this term, teach us something to make us hopeful!' cried a young woman in one of my classes in the large government college here. It is the wistful cry of youth; a heartbreaking cry to those who hear it, for who has a right to hope if youth has not? And we who come from that West which has done so much to take away their hopefulness must give it back again in a courage strong enough for life as it must be lived in China today."

In 1925 Mrs. Buck came to America with her husband on furlough and took up study at Cornell for the master's degree. Her dissertation was on the English essayists, and she won the Laura Messenger Prize in history (although herself in the English department) on the subject, "China and the West." This study was so soundly built that the author was able to use a large part of the historical matter seven years later, in an address before the American Academy of Political and Social Science, at Philadelphia, April 8, 1933. This address will be found in the Annals of the Academy.

On the ship bound for America in 1925 Mrs. Buck had written the story which grew into her first novel. Of this she has told in *The Colophon*. The editors of *The Colophon* have courteously granted permission to include the article in full:

"When I began to write 'East Wind: West Wind' it was certainly not with any idea in my mind that later it might be put between the covers of a book. I wrote it in mid-Pacific, in the writing room or in odd corners of the lounge of an Empress liner. I was quite shut off from the world, for there is no more delightful privacy than the isolation of an English steamship, where each passenger fears equally speaking to or being spoken to by another, lest in such an act a fatal social mistake be made.

"In this privacy the slender tale wove itself out, my first attempt to write anything longer than a little sketch. At its conclusion at the end of about fifty pages, I put it away and did nothing more with it until some months later when a valued friend asked with urgency why I had nothing written to show him. Ashamed of my delinquency, for he was ever urging me to write, I brought forth my story, written with the utmost illegibility upon ship's note paper.

"After he had deciphered it, with pains, I am sure, although he was too kind to say so, he persevered until he had made me promise to type it and then I sent it to *Asia* magazine. It was accepted and appeared as 'A Chinese Woman Speaks.'

"After its publication a well-known New York publishing house wrote to me—I had then returned to China—asking me to enlarge the story into a full-length novel and offering to publish it. Meantime I had written another story, in the nature of a sequel. I examined the first story again with some interest, naturally, but I decided that to enlarge it was to put too heavy a burden upon its frail structure. It was necessarily a delicate, limited tale, because I had unconsciously chosen in the first place that very limited point of view, a young girl's mind.

"I wrote the publishers, therefore, that I could not with honesty enlarge the original story, but I offered the two stories together. This arrangement they refused.

"The manuscript lay then for a year or two in a drawer, and I forgot it until one day a man said to me of it, 'Why do you not put that story of yours into a book?'

"I remembered it again, and I fetched it from its drawer, read it, and decided its chances were so slight that I could not trouble to retype it. Nevertheless, I decided that I would send it to some literary agency and if a publisher could be found it would be well, and if not, then nothing was lost. I chose at random the names of three such agencies out of a handbook for writers I happened to have had given me. Two of the agencies replied saying they preferred to handle nothing from China, since editors and publishers were not interested at all in such material. The third agency wrote me that they would be glad to handle material dealing with China. I sent the manuscript to them and it was accepted. I forgot it again in the series of exciting events in China. Mr. David Lloyd, my agent, will have me believe that its fortunes until it found a publisher were exciting to him. It seems to have been well read before publication, as it was on offer, Mr. Lloyd says, from one October until the next September through a period of forty-seven weeks. 'Despite a prejudice,' if one may quote one's agent—

"'Despite a prejudice among those who publish books and sell them, we put our best Chinese foot forward about your manuscript from the start. The original selling memorandum (a direct yet delicate portrayal of the new and the old in China) still seems to fit aptly, and foretell the spirit of its successors. For its readers, we chose successively publishers we knew were accessible to its flavor and authentic substance, and—always up to a certain point they responded to these temptations—editors of established lists, publishers later in the field but not behind in reputation. It was the sort of manuscript such men are reluctant to decline, a mental state often mistaken by inexperienced writers for an editorial affectation. In one office everyone would agree that the book was delightful, in another, one convinced champion would fight for it as a thing of beauty, in a third, five or six excited judges could compose the different bases of their interest only in respect to that well-known prejudice (it was believed in, only three short years ago) against Chinese books. In the Paget agency itself we had to save our face as business men and women by conferring on the question whether to go on offering a book by Pearl S. Buck! We went on. In the forty-seventh week, on the seventh day of the month, to borrow the accent of Noah in his Ark, the book found its imprint. Richard Walsh and his associates, perhaps not without some prayer and fasting of their own, decided to plump for it.'

"We made in that year (1929), however, a hurried business trip to America, and while we were there a letter was forwarded to me from China, whither it had been sent by my agent, saying that the John Day Company had made an acceptable offer for the book and would I cable concerning certain matters. At the instant of receiving this letter I happened to be but a few hours from New York; I had so completely forgotten the whole matter that I had neglected to tell the agency of my change of continents.

"When I could, therefore, I went to New York and to the John Day offices, and found that the title I had given the manuscript, 'Winds of Heaven,' was not liked. We compromised, therefore, by using the sub-title. I found also, that in my effort to write English that would be usual enough to be acceptable to English-speaking people I had used a number of trite phrases, which I had remembered from English books I had read. In Chinese it is good literary style to use certain well-known phrases previously used by great writers. I now learned this is not true in English, and it is best always in writing this language to use one's own words. Therefore I went over the manuscript again, deleting the phrases I had so painfully put in.

"But it was worth the effort, for the little book made its way. Before 'The Good Earth' was published, ten months later, 'East Wind: West Wind' had become a successful book in its own right, and was in its third printing.

"So runs the slight story of 'East Wind: West Wind.' The book is of value to me chiefly because it gave me confidence to go on writing, since now I had found a publisher who could be interested in what I wrote, even though I, knowing nothing else well, could write only about China."

This account has brought us to May, 1930, when "East Wind: West Wind" was published. In the meantime, however, there had been other incidents of bibliographical interest.

Upon her return to China in the autumn of 1926 Mrs. Buck began to write constantly and in earnest. She took up as a major project the history of the Chinese novel, and she wrote what was to have been her own first novel. But in March of 1927 the Communist soldiers entered Nanking, looting and killing foreigners. By the narrow margin of ten minutes Mr. and Mrs. Buck and their children escaped. They heard the door of their house battered down. Throughout a day of terror they stayed hidden in the hut of one of their Chinese neighbors, just beyond their own garden wall. This is one of the incidents of which she has said, "I have had that strange and terrible experience of facing death because of my color. At those times nothing, nothing I might have done could have saved me. I could not hide my race. . . . The only reason I was not killed was because some of the others in that race knew *me,* under my skin, and risked their own lives for me." When on the following day the members of the white colony were taken off by an American destroyer, they left behind everything except the clothes they had been wearing when the looters came. Thus was lost the completed manuscript of Mrs. Buck's first novel. When she came back, after a year spent in Japan and in Shanghai, it was to find the house gutted by fire.

Her observation of this and other scenes of revolution is to be traced in the second group of stories in the present volume and also in her short book "The Young Revolutionist." The latter was written at the request of the Missionary Education Movement for use among young people in the churches and was published as a minor work in May, 1932.

The course of "The Good Earth" is too familiar to need much reference here. Completed in 1930, it was published on March 2, 1931. It was hailed in chorus by the critics and for twenty-one months it stood on the list of "best-sellers," a record made by no other book since "Quo Vadis," thirty-five years earlier. It was awarded the Pulitzer Prize for the best novel of its year by an American author. The sequel, "Sons," published in September, 1932, has been characterized by William Lyon Phelps as "one of the outstanding works of our time."

In addition to her stories, she has contributed important articles to various magazines. In *The Saturday Evening Post*

(April 22, 1933) she described the Chinese war lords, on the basis of personal acquaintance; in the *Yale Review* of April, 1932, she gave a searching analysis of "The Foreign Chinese"; and in the *Cosmopolitan* (May, 1932), a bold and loyal treatment of the conflict between China and Japan, entitled "China the Unconquerable."

Upon her arrival in America in July, 1932, for the first time in nearly three years, Mrs. Buck found herself in demand among editors. She was also called upon for various addresses, some of which have come to publication. One of these, given before an audience of Negroes in Harlem, in December, 1932, was a deeply moving discussion of race relations and race pride. At its conclusion Mrs. Buck, with simple generosity, handed the manuscript as a gift to the editor of *Opportunity,* the journal of Negro life. Published there, it has also been reprinted in a leaflet.

Her address before a large body of Presbyterian women in New York, on November 2, 1932, has been given permanent form as a John Day Pamphlet entitled "Is There a Case for Foreign Missions?" Attacks upon Mrs. Buck's doctrinal beliefs as set forth in this address led to the acceptance by the Presbyterian Board of her resignation as a missionary.

She now gives her whole time to writing and research. Her fourth novel, "The Mother," has been completed. She has also finished her largest single undertaking, the translation of one of China's most famous novels, "Shui Hu Chuan," to which she has given the English title, "All Men Are Brothers." This translation was an outgrowth of her study in the history of the Chinese novel. Beginning in

Shanghai in the autumn of 1927, she worked upon it almost daily for four and a half years. During these years she has kept a routine of spending the morning hours at her original writing, and the afternoons in research and translation. Like every sincere scholar, she feels the need of working with a continuous interest at a long project, of a certain steadiness of purpose. Therefore she has now taken up once again her history of the Chinese novel, which will probably occupy her for some years to come.

Yet we must end, as we began, with the recollection that however devoted in scholarship, however skilled in the art of the short story, she thinks of herself as above all a novelist. And so perhaps she will forgive me for closing this introduction, which has already drawn so heavily upon her own words, with a quotation from her remarks about the craft, as made in a lecture at the Columbia School of Journalism:

"I do not consider either writing or reading novels one of the necessities of life. Millions of people in China, at least, exist intelligently and happily without reading novels and certainly without writing them, and I have the greatest admiration and respect for such persons and even at times the greatest of envy.

"For I must confess that I happen to be a somewhat peculiar person, not at all to be taken as typical of human beings in general, and certainly not desirable as an average, because the truth is I cannot be happy without writing novels, quite irrespective of whether they are read or not. I am, I regret to say, one of those unfortunate creatures who cannot function completely unless he is writing, has written, or is about to write, a novel. . . .

"Never, if you can possibly help it, write a novel. It is, in the first place, a thoroughly unsocial act. It makes one obnoxious to one's family and to one's friends. One sits about for many weeks, months, even years, in the worst cases, in a state of stupefaction. Even when from sheer exasperation and exhaustion one lays down one's pen, the wicked work goes on in one's brain. The people there will go on living and talking and thinking, until one longs, like Alice in Wonderland, to cry out, 'You are only a pack of cards after all!', and so brush them away and wake from the dream to find only leaves gently falling upon one's face; wake again to real life and people.

"For the man or woman obsessed by these dream people can never be a very happy person. He lives a thousand lives besides his own, suffers a thousand agonies as really as though they were what is called actual, and he dies again and again. He is doomed to be possessed by spirits until he cannot tell what is himself, what are his real soul and mind. He is thrall to a thousand masters. He is exhausted bodily and spiritually by creatures alive and working through his being, using his one body, his one mind, to express their separate selves, so that his one poor frame must be the means of all those living energies. It is no wonder that much of his time he sits bemused, silent and spent.

"If you would be yourself, therefore, free and unpossessed, never begin to be a novelist."

31

On the matter of personal freedom only the author herself is competent to speak. Certainly the world at large has passed its judgment that the creation of Mrs. Buck's novels, and of her shorter fiction as well, far from being unsocial, has been a social act of a high order. Few modern writers have done so much to further the common understanding of the human heart.

Richard J. Walsh

OLD AND NEW

THE FIRST WIFE

THIS was the day on which the tea merchant, whose surname was Li, expected his only son home from foreign parts. Seven years the young man had been away, and now here in his home they were awaiting him, his father, his mother, his wife, his son and daughter. Seven years these all had not seen him, and each in his own way longed for the hour when the young man might arrive. The exact time when he would come could not be known, since this town where they lived was not on the coast nor near any place where the railway ran. It was a small, quiet city in the midst of a wide plain where farms were set closely beside a slow and shallow river. On both sides of this plain mountain ranges rose, at first gently in foothills, and then abruptly to high and misty crests. Upon these foothills were planted the thousands of tea bushes which made the region famous for its tea.

In winter the river was very low, and the people were quite cut off from every part of the world—except such travelers as came horseback or by wheelbarrow over the rough country roads. But this was now the end of summer;

abundant rains had fallen, and the river ran high enough for small junks to come up from the coast a hundred miles away. It was on such a craft that the tea merchant expected his son. Even so, the hour could not be known, since all depended on winds and on the tide that filled the lower reaches of the river near the sea; nevertheless, it was probable that he would come at some time in the late afternoon or evening of this day. Yet, lest there should be unexpected winds and his travel be quicker than they thought, they had all dressed themselves early in the day and for hours had sat waiting.

There the old father sat, a gentle old man of the town, who had inherited from his forefathers much of the good rolling land to the south where the best tea grew, and he had the tea shop as well, where for hundreds of years the same great square pewter tea canisters had stood on shelves, each with its own tea. He was a man respected and listened to if he spoke where men were. He sat now in his accustomed seat to the right of the table placed in the center against the inner wall of the central room of this house. Today, because his only son returned, he wore his best robe of a deep plum-colored satin and a sleeved black satin jacket, flowered in an old-fashioned circular design. He was thin and pale with the pallor that opium gives, and it is quite true that the tea merchant had smoked opium ever since he had been a young man, not heavily nor greedily, as coarse men will, but a little at a certain hour every day, delicately mixed, and only the same amount, unless he had a pain of some sort, when he allowed himself a little more. Thus opium had not made him sere and emaciated, but it

36

had only hollowed slightly his temples and cheeks and had taken every ounce of superfluous flesh from his bones and had yellowed his skin softly and smoothly.

Across from the seat in which he was, his wife sat, the mother of his only son. She had had four children, but there was only this one left, the youngest one of all, whom they loved surpassingly. It would not have occurred to the old lady that her son could have been refused anything. This would not have been fitting, and anything unfitting would have been impossible to her. At the same time she was possessed of some temper, as could be seen from her very black and piercing eyes, and, if she yielded to her husband or to her son, it was not always without some struggle. Nevertheless, at this moment, as she sat in a chair exactly like her husband's except that it was in a place lower than his, she sat in the properest silence of wife before husband, as one who does not speak first. An old servant almost as old as the lady herself stood to one side and held a brass water pipe in her hand for her mistress. When her mistress lifted her hand, the old servant blew into flame a brown paper spill she had, and with it she lighted the tiny ball of tobacco she had already rolled and thrust into the bowl of the brass pipe, and then she handed the pipe to the old lady. The old lady took two puffs each time, and then she gave the pipe back to the servant, who prepared it again in the same way, without sound or weariness. If a little ash fell upon her mistress's gray satin coat, the servant brushed it away most carefully with her shriveled old finger.

In a lower seat, below the old lady, sat the daughter-in-

37

law of this pair and wife of their only son. She was a woman less than thirty years of age, a woman neither pretty
nor ugly, with small, neat, regular features and exceedingly
beautiful hands; in her hands she now held a piece of
pale-pink satin on which she was embroidering very minute
crimson flowers and a small green bird on a bough. Every
now and again she bent to whisper to a little girl, some ten
years or so of age, who sat on a stool beside her also embroidering, but slowly and painstakingly, upon a piece of
cotton cloth. Every now and again this little girl looked
with longing out into the court where a robust lad of seven
played with a little white kid. His long robe of bright
peacock-blue silk was caught up under his scarlet sash so
that he could have greater freedom of movement. He was
teasing the kid, laughing and holding out a handful of grass
to it, and, when the kid, still clumsy upon its high legs, tot-
tered toward the grass, the lad jumped back and then
shouted with laughter to see the kid's idiotic amazement.
At every burst of this laughter the little girl looked up and
smiled longingly, and each time her mother said in a low
voice, "My child, attend to what you do." The mother's
feet and the grandmother's feet were bound into tiny flowered satin shoes, but the little girl's feet were left free, since
the child's father had written it must be so.

Yet in this quiet room that appeared so peaceful this mid-
afternoon there was no peace at all but only intense waiting,
the father and the mother for the son whom they had not
seen all those years, the wife for her husband. Each waited
in his own way. The father sat with his eyes fixed on the
romping boy, but the stillness of his face showed that in

his mind there was no thought now of the child. The old mother turned to the servant and said, "Did you tell the manservant to buy duck for the meal tonight?"

The wife looked up quickly and said in a soft, even voice, "I have seen to it, my mother, that there is everything he likes best."

Then, seeing that the old lady's tea bowl was empty, she rose and felt of the porcelain pot on the table to find out if it were hot, and then she poured out tea and presented it with both hands to the old lady and emptied the chilled tea from the old gentleman's bowl and poured hot tea in freshly. Then she sat down again to her embroidery.

No one could have seen from the steadiness of her lovely hands nor from the serene folding of her small lips that she was in any inner excitement. No, she sat there in the afternoon light that fell upon her from the open door, so quiet that she seemed too still, her face smooth and colorless. Even her satin coat was of a blue so pale it seemed gray. But her eyebrows were beautifully marked against her pale skin, shaped like two narrow willow leaves set there in black above her black eyes, and her black hair was oiled and smoothed back immaculately into a round, netted knot at the back, through which she had thrust a plain gold pin to hold it firm. She wore very small plain gold earrings, also, and her ears showed small and precisely set against her head. From time to time she moistened her lips with the tip of her tongue, very slightly and delicately.

Once, when the boy slipped and fell in the court and lay waiting to be picked up, his face all puckered with weeping, she rose quickly and went out and helped him to his feet and dusted off his garments. At this moment her face could be seen to change in small ways, and she held the child a moment to her and said in her even voice: "Do not cry. Your father will be here at any moment, and what a thing it would be if he came in and saw you crying! Why, you were but a month old when he left and you were crying then, too, and he will think you have cried the whole seven years he has been away!"

The boy began to laugh at this in the midst of his weeping and rubbed his sleeve across his eyes, and she took a kerchief she had in her bosom and wiped his eyes for him and led him into the room where the others were and gave him a drink of tea. The old gentleman looked at the lad and smoothed down his scanty beard, smiling a little, and he said in the gentle way he had: "My son will be pleased with you, my daughter, for such a son as this you have for him, and be sure we shall tell him everything of what you have been to us, the best and kindest daughter and the carefullest of mothers, and everything a daughter-in-law should be in the house. A good day it was for us all when we betrothed and wed you to our son, although we did not know how good, then."

"But we knew her family was a good gentry family in the country," said the old lady quickly. "I always said I would have a maid from a good landed family for him and not one of these townswomen who are so proud and willful. No, I came myself from a good landed family in a market village, and they are the best, and their girls are the best taught of any."

"That I know who have been wed to you these thirty-five

years and more," said the old gentleman, smiling; "and the only fault you have had is that you did not keep all your children alive, and I do not blame you for this, either, since there is an end to every life, some soon, some late, and we can do nothing to mend it when the time has come for each of us that has been fixed by destiny."

The old lady sighed and she answered: "But the youngest one was the best of them all, and he has lived and has had such honors as would in the old days have bought him a governor's place. But I do not know what these new days are."

"My son Yuan will not need to fear," replied the old gentleman with certainty and pride. "With all his learning he need not fear anything. East and West, he has it all."

No sooner had he said this than they all heard a voice at the gate and the commotion of men carrying boxes and loads. The voice was that of the old manservant whom they had sent to meet Yuan. Then another voice came, the one they knew and for which they listened, but deeper, too, than they remembered and somehow strange.

"Ah, I am home!"

The old gentleman, hearing this voice, rose, and then, remembering what was fitting, he sat down again and waited. The old lady folded her hands tightly upon her lap. The young wife called quickly to her daughter and, rising, took her position just behind her mother-in-law, and the little boy was suddenly frightened and ran in and clung to his mother's hand. The little girl stood with her sewing still in her hands, her eyes wide and shining and fixed upon the gate. But the young wife did not look up at all. She fastened her eyes steadfastly upon a crack between the tiles of the floor and stood motionless.

Then the gate opened suddenly, and she heard him come in—very hard, firm footsteps. He was wearing some sort of leathern shoes. His feet clattered upon the flagged courtyard. He came nearer, into the very door of the room. He had come to his father. Out of the corners of her eyes the young wife could see the old gentleman rise, and she heard the young man, her husband, cry out, "My father, my father."

"After seven years—" said the old gentleman, and suddenly his voice cracked, and he began to weep a little.

"Sit down, my father," said the young man, and, laughing unsteadily, he poured out a cup of tea for his father. "I am home again from across the seas—your son, safe and well, home again! My mother, here I am!"

The old lady rose trembling and laid her hand wonderingly upon her son's arm. "But, Yuan, my son, you seem taller," she said. "You look strange to me, you look so much older."

"Seven years do not leave any of us the same," said Yuan in his quick clear way, and he poured out tea for his mother also.

Now it was her turn who was his wife. He stood before her, and she did not raise her eyes. No, she knew what was proper; she had been very well taught, gently bred. But he stood there upon the very spot at which she had been looking so steadfastly, and she saw now the leathern shoes upon his feet and the thick dark stuff of his trousers,

42

made of some foreign material she did not know, unshining and coarse.

"Ah?" he said, his voice distant and respectful. "The mother of my son is well, I hope?"

"The best daughter-in-law to us, Yuan," said the old gentleman, suddenly voluble, "never forgetting any of her duty to us or to your children, always careful in the house, just to the servants—"

"Ah?" said Yuan; "and where is my son?"

"Here am I!" said that small one loudly, and he stood and stared at his father with eyes as round as dollars.

Yuan laughed and lifted him up and cried merrily: "So this is what you have done in seven years! You have changed yourself from a crying month-old, red as a radish, into a goodly tall man!"

She could look at him quickly now, when he was turned away from her, absorbed in the child. Yes, he was changed, he was matured. Her eyes could see the difference. He had been slight and young when he went away at twenty-four, in spite of his cleverness and great learning. But now he had thickened somewhat, grown a little taller, even, and there was another look in his face. Seven years in a distant country had changed him. He had always been confident, assured, quick to laugh, to speak, but in those other days there had been something young and willful about him. Now he was no longer a youth; he was a man and her master. She was suddenly very shy, and she felt a little warm pink begin to creep out from under her ears. Still speaking no word, she pushed her daughter forward.

"Speak to your father, my child," she said in a whisper.

43

But the little girl hung her head, smiling, until the lad cried out, "There is my sister, too!"

Then Yuan turned and was kindly to his little daughter, and he took her small, needle-pricked hand and he said, "And what are you making, my Siu-lan, shoes for yourself, or a pillow or something?"

"She is ten years old now," said the old lady, "and she is old enough to begin embroidering her marriage clothes. Her mother knows all the good and proper old ways to teach a maid, and so Siu-lan is practising the stitches for her wedding skirt."

The little girl listened to this with some unspoken impatience. Her under lip pushed up against the upper one and she looked down, and it seemed she was about to speak, except that her mother suddenly put her hand firmly on her shoulder, and so she said nothing after all.

As for the young father, he did not answer his old mother. He opened his mouth, and then he closed it again, and, after a strange pause—as if each listened for another's voice—he said, to put aside the awkwardness of the moment: "Ah, it is good to be home again! I must go to my room and wash and refresh myself after these three days on the river. It seemed slow after the Western ways of travel—a hundred miles in three days!" He laughed and went out.

The old gentleman stared a little. "Three days is not slow," he said to his wife. "The winds must have been good enough. If the winds had been adverse and if men had had to pull a boat, five or six days would not have been enough."

"I went to the temple every day," answered the old lady

44

gravely. "I went and prayed for good winds for him and spent two pieces of silver for incense and tea money for the priests. It would have been an ill thing if the winds were not good after that."

The old gentleman looked tolerantly at his wife. He himself did not go to temples nor believe in these gods, being a follower of Confucius and leaving gods to women and children. "It is the season for winds, now," he said mildly.

At this the old lady looked up with some spirit and cried: "Ah, you never believe, but I have tried it again and again, and the gods do hear, and, if I had not gone to the temple regularly, what evil might have come to our son on those great seas and in those strange lands no one knows!"

"Ah, well, and well," said the old gentleman peaceably, as if this were an old argument between them. "Worship your gods, and, if you will only ask for things in their proper season, I am sure you will have them."

But that night, when the evening meal was over and the young man had taken out the presents he had brought for each of them, the young wife went into the room which she now would share with her husband. While he was gone, she had not slept there because the night seemed too lonely. In the daytime she kept the room brushed and dustless, but at night she slept in a smaller, adjoining room with the two children. Sometimes she had come and sat in that other, empty room with her embroidery, but, except for this, it had been unoccupied. Now she sat here again, waiting for him to come.

45

He would be late; for his friends had heard of his coming, and they were there in the outer room, making merry over his return. The old father had commanded wine to be heated, the mild rice-wine that was made in this region, and she could hear the young men calling out to one another, drinking to Yuan and calling out: "To the bottom of the cup now; this time, a clean cup everyone!"; "Drink to Yuan, drink to his new place in the new capital, drink to his son, drink to his many sons to come!" A great laughing broke at this last toast, and she smiled somewhat painfully there alone in the dusky room, and she felt the warmth of blood begin under her ears again. Then she heard meats being passed and the foods that men use with wine, and at last there was the shouting of farewell. Merry calls of future meetings floated through the courts, and above them she could hear Yuan's laughter.

Then, in the sudden quiet of the house, she heard him return from the gate. She heard him say, half-laughing: "With all this wine I shall have a headache tomorrow. I have not drunk like this since I left!"

"Do they not have wine in foreign parts, then?" asked the old gentleman, surprised.

"Oh, yes," said Yuan carelessly. "But it is thick stuff, and I did not drink it. I had to have a clear head and must still, for that matter, since I have an important post in the new capital. But I shall talk of that tomorrow. It is time for sleep."

"But you will not go at once to your position, my son?" said the old man. "You have been away so long. I know it is honorable to work in the capital, and I shall not hold you back. But you have been so long away, and we fain would keep you at home a little while. Moreover, there is your young wife, so good all these years, in the prime of her youth—and you have been away seven years!"

What would he answer? The young wife leaned forward suddenly to listen. Only the silk curtain hung between this room and that. The door was not closed. What would he say? He said nothing for a time. Then he said, as one who has but just remembered an obligation: "I have a letter to write before I can sleep—I had forgotten it. I will leave you now, my father. Lean upon my arm, and let me take you to your chamber."

There was the sound of their footsteps, one soft and feeble in velvet shoes and the other clear and hard. The room was silent, and she sat waiting as the wife should, until the husband comes. Then she found the matches on the table and lit the candle and sat down again and waited, her eyes fixed upon the floor. Her hands were cold, and she pressed them together.

When he came in, he came quickly and carelessly as his way was, and he seemed surprised to see her. "Ah, you are there still? Do not wait," he said. "Go to bed. I have a letter that I must write before I go to bed."

He seated himself at the desk at the far end of the room, the desk where he had been wont to sit and study years ago when he was fitting himself for the examinations which, if he passed, would take him across the seas. During the seven years, she had often seemed to see him there. Now he searched hastily for paper and for a brush, and he pointed his brush swiftly upon the wetted ink block.

She sat on quietly. In a moment he threw down the brush with a movement half-petulant, half-laughing. "I have forgotten how to use the brush," he said. "I have written so long with a foreign pen." And he brought a strange metal pen out of his pocket and began to write with it. He looked up again and saw her. "Do go to bed!" he said, and his voice even sounded half-angry. "Do not make me feel you are there waiting. I dislike it." Then his tone changed again quickly. "I am sorry—I do not mean to be rude. I appreciate your proper attention. But surely we may dispense with form in these days. Sleep—" He paused, hesitating.

Just at this moment there was a sudden cry from the little boy who lay in the other room. The young man's eyebrows lifted, alarmed.

"He is dreaming," said the young wife. "He is accustomed to my sleeping with him all these years, and he misses me."

The young man's face lightened. "Ah? Then go to him. I shall be late tonight. I have my affairs to note in my book. Do not let me disturb your habits—not tonight."

He rose with greatest courtesy. She looked at him quietly. A moment of hesitation hung between them, delicate, difficult. Then she put her hands into her sleeves as women do, and she bowed slightly, saying, "Pray seat yourself, my lord."

In her silent, gentle way she moved about the room with movements that were at once graceful and yet swift and economical of effort. She felt the teapot and blew into life with a breath or two the charcoal embers in the little brazier under it. Then she spread the quilt upon the bed and folded it over and dropped the bed curtains of white linen out of the brass hooks that parted them. Then, since the pot was hot, she poured out a bowl of the steaming tea for him. He nodded a little, smiling, busy with his eyes upon his paper. She went out in her perfect stillness.

In this silence she undressed herself to her white linen undergarments, washed her face and hands and rinsed her mouth. Then, before she lay down, she went to the bed where the little girl lay, a small curtained bamboo bed in the opposite corner of the room. She drew aside the curtain and felt of the child's hand as it hung over the edge of the bed. It was warm, but not too hot. She listened to the child's breathing. It was regular and subdued. She took up the candle from the table and searched carefully in the curtains for mosquitoes, found one and pinched it between her fingers. Then she fastened the curtains carefully together and went to her own bed, where her little son lay, naked for the heat except for a little square of red cloth over his belly and fastened about his neck with a silver chain. With the gentlest, stillest care she moved his legs inch by inch, laid his chubby arm against his side and made a little space for herself. She lay down so gently one would not have said a mouse moved, but the child stirred, and she put out her hand and patted him rhythmically, and he, feeling the accustomed touch, fell asleep again, and more deeply.

But the young wife lay motionless and awake. She listened to every sound from the next room. For a long time there were but the rustlings of paper, the pushing of a drawer into its place. Once an ink block fell on the floor and broke, and she heard his hasty exclamation in a foreign

49

word she did not understand. Before she lay down, she had put out the candle made of cow's fat lest it burn down in the night and make a vile odor, and she had lighted instead a small bean-oil lamp. Ever since he had gone away, she could not bear to have the room wholly dark, and now, although he was back, it was not the same as it had been before. But the light made by the lamp was very feeble, and the strange, brilliant light of a waning autumn moon came suddenly from over the courtyard wall and poured into the room, and the lamp was suddenly meaningless.

"It must be near dawn," she thought at last.

Then she heard him give a loud sigh, and he rose and walked to his bedside. There were a few minutes of quiet. She listened acutely. Would he call her now? But she heard him stretch out upon the creaking wooden bed, a great carved bed two generations old, and again he sighed that loud sigh. She heard no other sound, then. He was asleep. As for her, she lay as she had these seven years with her arm curved about her little son.

The next morning she rose as usual an hour before the others and slipped noiselessly out of the bed without waking the child. By the light of the rising sun she unbound her long straight black hair and combed it through and through with a small comb of white bone. She sat before a little toilet table whose mirror lifted up out of the top and stood at just the height of her face. It was the usual table that in those parts a bride brought with her as part of her personal belongings, and, since her father had not been a poor man, the table was made of good wood, and the drawers had brass handles. Like everything she had, it was cared for and dusted. When her hair was smooth and glistening, she divided it, tying one part with a cord while she coiled the other part. Then she brought the two parts together again, weaving it all into a neat oblong knot about her gold pin. Over it she slipped with her adroit fingers a net of fine black silk thread. Then she took a little brush from a pot of a certain wood oil that stood upon the table and smoothed back the already perfect smoothness of her hair.

There was a cough at the door, and she went to the curtain and received a brass ewer of hot water from a servant there and set it upon a stand made to receive it. The water was very hot, and she wrung a towel out of it and washed her face and arms and her beautiful hands. Then, with the lightest touch of powder upon her face, she was dressed. She had fastened meticulously every button of her thin, gray silk coat and beneath it had girdled her loose trousers neatly about her small round waist with a white silk strip. She wore plain black shoes, since she was not a woman given to wearing flowery things, and, where another woman would choose gems set in gold, she would choose plain metal and the smallest ornament. With all this plainness she was still youthful-looking, being slender-boned and small and delicately shaped. One would not have said she had ever borne children, so slight was her bosom, so straight her body. Yet she was not beautiful. There was some vivacity lacking in her, and she was too quiet, too much the same.

Now, being dressed for the day, she went out into the kitchens and saw that the maids there had begun the fires and that the rice was simmering in the caldrons for the

51

morning meal. "We will have the salted chicken this morning," she said to the elderly woman who controlled the two country maids under her—one to stoke the brick oven with grass and the other to wash the meats and vegetables and rice and both to be at beck and call.

"I will slice it, then," replied the elderly servant. "Is there any other dainty for the young master?"

"He likes the red bean curd better than the white—the curd with red pepper. Have the red today and the best tea."

At this instant the old maidservant who had stood behind her old mistress the day before came near with two clean towels, a cake of red soap and a brass bowl of very hot water. One of the kitchen maids followed with a pot of fresh tea. "Shall we go now, young mistress?" asked this old servant.

"Yes, Wang Ma," answered the young wife, and she preceded the servants to the door of her mother-in-law's room, and there she paused and coughed delicately.

"Come in!" called the old lady, and they went in.

"My mother, I hope you have slept well," said the young wife in her subdued voice, and, taking the teapot from the maid's hands, she set it upon the table and poured a bowl of it and stood before the closed curtains of the bed, waiting. A small thin yellow hand came out and took the tea. The young wife poured another bowl, and this was so received, also. Then she went to the table, and from the receptacles there she mixed a little opium and lit a small lamp to burn under the bowl of the opium pipe that was there, and this the skinny hand received also into the closed curtains. Then the young wife and the maid withdrew, leaving the old servant to await her old mistress's pleasure.

Every morning the young wife performed these rites in exactly this order. Then she usually returned to her own room to help her children rise. But this morning there was yet another to whom she must go. She had as a matter of course formerly so brought tea to her husband. But somehow this morning it seemed difficult. He was so changed. It would be like going into a strange man's room. Nevertheless, it was still her duty. She called to the maid, "Fetch another brass bowl of hot water and a fresh pot of tea— the best pewter and the new green tea."

She waited, and, when the maid returned, she lifted the lid of the freshly infused pot of tea and sniffed it delicately. Then she went to the door of the room where her husband slept and coughed, the maid waiting behind her. There was no answer, although she listened with her ear to the silken curtain. Then she felt behind the curtain. He had closed the door. She patted it gently with the flat of her hand.

"Who is it?" her husband shouted suddenly.

She was appalled by this suddenness. She had forgotten what it was like to have a young and vigorous man in the house. Seven years is a long time, and she had been living wholly alone with the two old people and the children. Since her own father and mother were dead, she had not even visited her old home. She had forgotten what a young man's voice could be when it shouts out.

The door opened abruptly, and Yuan stood there, his eyes heavy with sleep and his stiff black hair awry. "What is it?" he asked in a voice somewhat ill-tempered.

53

"Your tea," his wife faltered.

"Tea!" he exclaimed. Then he smiled and rubbed his hand over his spiky hair and yawned. "Ah, well, bring it in! I had forgotten tea. I have not had it these seven years so early." Then his eyes fell on the brass bowl. "I shall want more water than that," he said with decision. "I have the habit of bathing all over in the morning."

His wife looked at the maid in consternation.

"It would take a great deal of water—men usually go to the bathhouse to wash themselves all over," said the maid bluntly; she was newly from the country and did not know how to be polite, even when she did not wish to offend.

But this bluntness did offend the young mistress, and she said with dignity, "Certainly the young master can have what he likes in his own home." And to Yuan she said, "The water will be here soon."

"Ah, if it is trouble in the house—" said Yuan carelessly.

"How can it be trouble when you have been away seven years?" she answered simply.

He looked away at this and busied himself with pouring another bowl of tea, and, when she saw he had nothing more to say, she turned and went away to see to the heating of the water.

Yet it seemed to the young wife that surely this first day her husband was back must be different from the seven quiet years when he had been away. The greatest events in all those hundreds of days had been his letters. The old gentleman read them aloud to all of them, to the two ladies sitting in their places and the two children sitting upon their stools. Yet there was no great variety in Yuan's let-

54

ters—study, an occasional strange sight seen, sometimes a command given, as when he wrote, "My daughter's feet are not to be bound," and when he wrote, "My son is to be sent to the modern state school, and he is not to learn the Four Books as I did. It is not necessary in these days."

Both of these commands had given consternation when the old father read them aloud. He had paused and looked over his great brass spectacles at the two ladies who sat listening.

"If the girl's feet are not to be bound, how will she get a good husband?" said the old mother, astounded. Her own small pointed feet were crossed before her on a brass foot-stove wherein were coals, since, when this letter came, it was winter.

They had not accepted the command at once, and the old father had written to his son, pointing out the difficulty. The reply was speedy—it came in little more than two months—and it was as emphatic as ever. "I am to be obeyed in this. I shall be extremely angry if I am not obeyed," he wrote.

This had nettled the old gentleman somewhat, and he said with gentle heat, his eyes rolling a little, his hand trembling and stroking his gray beard quickly: "I hope my son does not forget that while I live I am the one to give final directions to the family. No, I hope my son does not forget this!"

In the end it had been Yuan's wife who said in her soft firm way, "I had better obey my husband. Let it be as he says." And so she had not bound the girl's feet, although it had been a sorrow to her, too, to see them lengthening beyond all hope of change, and at least she had the girl's shoes made as narrow and firm as possible.

But, when the matter of the boy's learning had come up, and this was but recently, since the lad was so small, it was the old gentleman who was sorest disturbed, and he said in his distress: "But not learn the Four Books? But not know the sayings of Confucius the Master? What will he study, then?"

For the old gentleman was a student of all the books of Confucius, and he believed that in these books only was rectitude to be found. He was himself careful to do all he could to conform to the behavior that Confucius sets forth for the conduct of the superior man. Thus the old gentleman went to excess in nothing; in all he observed the golden mean. It was therefore of the greatest moment to him that his son and his son's son should know the Way. For women he did not consider that it mattered. They were simple and their minds concrete, and he believed that they might be allowed to worship the gods which can be seen. Women are so made that all must be plain and visible for them.

"My grandson will grow up without virtue," he said solemnly.

But there was not time to reach Yuan with a letter, and so they waited.

These had been the questions of greatest moment when Yuan was away, so smoothly had seven years slipped past. As for the young wife, her father had died of a summer flux one year, and the next winter her mother had died of a strange illness none knew, and the land had gone to her four brothers. The old spreading house was divided among the four growing families, and the young wife had no desire to return to it any more, since it was no longer her home. Instead, she had buried her life with deeper devotion in this house where she was wed, loving well these old two who were very kind to her.

She could never be grateful enough that the gods had given her so good a mother-in-law. When she went with the old lady to the Temple of the Three Buddhas, she gave thanks before the god who makes marriages, he who, with his silken, scarlet thread, ties two lives together before ever they are born into this world. Well she knew, as all maids know, that some mothers-in-law are cruel and jealous of their sons' wives and make their lives worthless. But hers was a mother to her. They suited each other well, this quiet girl and the gentle, unworldly old lady, who lived so much with the gods, who believed so deeply in the need for every kindness to all living things that for many years she had not touched a bit of flesh of any kind in her food—not even an egg—which might give life. If a moth fluttered in at the window, she would not have it killed. No, she bade a maid catch it and hold it gently and release it into the night again, and, even if the night were windless and hot, she would have the papered lattices drawn, so that no moths could flutter in and be burned in the flame of the candles.

Yes, the young wife could love and serve two like these. The old gentleman was as kind to her as if she were his own daughter. Every morning he went to his tea shop for a little while to see what the clerks did and how the stores of tea were. When he came back, his garments slightly fragrant with the tea, the young wife was swift to fetch his teapot and, if it were summer, his fan, or, if winter, his foot-stove. She learned how to mix his opium as he liked it best, and she kept the books in his study dusted and set in order the small collection of old fans he had for his pleasure, since these were too ancient and frail for a servant's handling. And he was not like some fathers-in-law who receive the services of their sons' wives as a right and so it ought to be. No, he had an eye quick to notice the small things she did for him, and he would thank her with such courtesy and praise that his praise was the sweetest thing in the world to her. So she builded herself into this house, and she prided herself on the care she gave to it.

It was not as large a house as some, since it also had been divided in the last generation, but there were three courts, the peony court, the bamboo court and the chrysanthemum court; and, since the old gentleman loved flowers, there were peonies and, under the bamboos, lilies and, in autumn, chrysanthemums. The gala day of the spring was when the first thick red shoots of the peonies thrust themselves out of the black soil of the peony terrace. They all went to see this, and the only time the young wife had ever seen the old gentleman forget himself in anger was when his little grandson had reached over and had wantonly broken off a rosy shoot. The old gentleman without a word had bent and slapped the child's round cheek with his bony old fingers, and they stung and left four red marks on the child's golden skin. For a moment the boy's face was transfixed with surprise; then he burst into a mighty yell of terror.

The old gentleman turned very pale. "I have forgotten

myself," he muttered, and he went away quickly to his room, and he sat there alone in meditation for a long time.

In the evening the young wife took her son by the hand and led him to his grandfather and made him kneel and knock his head before the old man in sign of his sorrow at what he had done. Then she herself made apology for her son thus: "I do not know why my son is so mannerless, my father. I am ashamed and grieved, and I ask forgiveness from you because I have not been able to teach him better."

The old gentleman raised the boy tenderly and held him in the circle of his arm and said: "It is true that it was wrong to touch the peony and cut off its life. Now there will never be the beautiful bud and the ferny leaves and the full flower. No, that shoot is cut off as if one died young." Then he paused and said with effort: "But he is only a child. I am an old man, and I have for many years followed in the footsteps of my Master, and I thought I knew something of the Way and that nothing could betray me into anger any more. I thought the coarseness of anger was impossible to me. I see I am not so far as I thought."

He sighed and was so sad that his daughter-in-law could not bear it and she said gently, "You are the most perfect man I have ever seen and the kindest father to me always and to everyone."

He smiled at this and was comforted a little, too, although he would not show it, and he turned to his book again, and the young wife led the child away.

With such small things the greatest events in this house

—and not even feast days too marked because Yuan was away—the seven years slipped by almost like dreams. Summer slowed into autumn. The chrysanthemums glowed in the courts a little while; and then it was winter and the scarlet berries of the Indian bamboo glittered against shallow snow in the courts, and then spring came again in the small pale lilies and the leafless flowers of plum against black branches. And so it was, year after year.

In the young wife's own life the greatest events were but two, after the birth of her son. The first was his weaning, which she had not completed until he was four years old, and the second was the swift illness he had had one summer two years ago. That swift illness stood out for her as the sharpest fear she had ever had. In the morning he was well and merry, and by night he was nearly lifeless, seized with such vomiting and flux and fever that in a few hours his body was shrunken and dried to his frame. They had all been beside themselves, and the old lady had rushed on foot to the temple, she who scarcely walked about the courts even, and she had promised silver enough to fill her two hands brimming if the child did not die. She flung herself down on the reed mat before the mother goddess, and she knocked her old head again and again on the tiled floor, and she lay there in such sobbing and prayer as would have moved any heart, even of gilded clay. Even the greedy priests feared she might die from such anguish, and they came to lift her up, saying: "Lady, you have prayed, and the goddess will hear. Go back—he is better."

But, when she reached home, the child was not better,

and he was blue about the lips and his finger nails were black and he was gasping.

Then Wang Ma, the old servant, who had seen seven of her own children die in the days when she was young enough to bear them, cried out and said: "His spirit is wandering. Quick! We must win it back!" And, lighting a paper lantern, she ran out, calling to the young mother to follow her with the child's coat, and they sped over the cobbled streets, going here and there and everywhere.

Wang Ma held the lantern high, and at every step she called, "Child, come home—come home!" And the young mother held up the little red coat the child wore every day and most commonly, so that the wandering childish spirit might recognize its garb and see where it belonged. How many times had she not heard this call of other people, other mothers, and shuddered and held her own child close, and now here was she! Passers-by cried out to see them and said, "Ah, may the child live!" And the young mother who in her proper seclusion never passed beyond the gates of the house now ran upon her small feet over the round and slippery stones, seeing nothing of all the strange sights of the city, seeing only the pallid, dying child who was the only son she had borne to her husband.

But it had served. When they returned, exhausted, they found the old grandfather by the bedside and a maid standing with a bowl of hot broth, and the old grandfather slipped spoonful after spoonful into the child's mouth. The boy's eyes were still closed, but he could swallow. The spirit had returned.

The child grew well almost as quickly as he had fallen

ill. But the others did not so quickly recover from the terror of the night. No, the old grandfather was pale for days afterwards, and every now and again he would call the child to him suddenly and feel the small body rounding again and quick with life once more, and he would laugh gently and say, "Well, you are my own, and you are whole again, my child!"

And the old lady said again and again, "If I had not gone as I did to the temple and if the goddess had not had mercy and spared him to us, what else could have saved him, and I count the silver well spent!"

As for the young mother, she woke still sometimes in the night, wet with a chill sweat because she dreamed she was stumbling again through the dark streets, holding the little red coat for the child's escaped spirit to see.

So the seven years had passed in deep, narrow, peaceful living in this house. All their dreams centered in the return of the one who was away. The old father dreamed of his son's coming back to an official position and becoming a noble statesman, such as there had been in the past history of the family. There had never been a fighting man from his family at the courts of the emperors; there had been those far more honorable, advisers, viceroys, even a prime minister. The family had not always been merchants, although there was always one merchant to look after the tea lands and to provide the money necessary if a change in dynasty meant that for a time a statesman must go into retirement. Therefore the old gentleman had no higher dream for his son than this, that he might serve as an official in some high place.

It is true that now the times of the empire were passed and the affairs of the nation were changed. But government is government, and, when his son came and begged to be allowed to go to foreign countries to study, the old father was moved most when Yuan said: "I cannot hope to achieve any place in the affairs of state now, unless I have Western learning. Either I will give up my studies and come into the tea business with you, or I must go abroad."

"And are the Four Books to be nothing?" replied the old gentleman with mild heat. "I have taught you them well, and you went also to a scholar to learn and also to the schools of Western learning that foreigners have on the coast."

But Yuan had answered firmly, "The Four Books are nothing today except old and curious books, and they will not put a man in any place at all."

This had been more than the old man would believe, but still he let his son have his way.

But it was the old mother who was most stubborn, and she would not give her consent. "No, and not till you have a son, Yuan," she said with the gentlest voice but with her eyes very bright and hard.

"Now how can I make a son?" he had answered, trying to be good-humored with his mother, but impatient, too, and his face reddening quickly. "Suppose she has girls and nothing but girls, as some women do! Am I to give up all hope of advancement because my wife has no sons?"

"We must have a son, Yuan," said the old lady, drawing a little harder upon her pipe than she was wont. "If you die in those wild lands, we shall have your flesh and blood here still." Then she said in her calm way: "I will help you this much. I will pray double what I have been praying for a son for you, and I will give more to the goddess of sons than I have!"

"For that inclination I thank you, my mother," said the young man, laughing shortly. "I wish I could be as sure as you that I shall have a son."

To this his mother replied with great gravity, "My son, we are taught that if we believe in the gods we shall receive from them."

But Yuan said no more. He never dared to tell his mother that he did not believe at all in the religion to which she clung. No, not since he was a little boy, frightened and timorous before the fierce faces of the warrior gods, clinging to her hand when they went to the temple, not since those early days had he believed. But neither did he tell his old father that he believed no more in the Confucian principles in which he had been reared.

No, the heart of this son of theirs, if his parents had known it, would have stricken them; for it was full of belief, it is true, but belief in strange vessels of war, such as they had never seen, and in mighty guns and in well-trained armies and in force and might of every kind. What he dreamed of secretly was that one day for his country he would make such guns and a gun for every man to carry and great ships of steel carrying huge cannon and ships in the sky such as his parents had never even heard of, carrying the death that drops on the people below on the earth. For this he had spent his seven years, learning how to make such things as these against a certain day about

64

which he and his friends talked often enough. Thus he had busied himself, while his old father read his books and studied his old fans and pottered among his flowers and while his mother watched lest a moth be burned and while his young wife cared for the home.

Now, although these seven years were over and he was back among them as he used to be, they were all aware that he was not as he had been among them. Before the second day after his return they all knew that Yuan was somehow changed. His heart was elsewhere, and he seemed, even when he laughed and talked, to be thinking of another place, some other life.

He was very busy writing letters. Three letters came for him in one day, each marked with a great seal. He took them in silence and told no one what was in them, but, when the third one came, he left his desk and went to his father, who at that hour of the day, just after noon, sat in a reed chair under the pine tree taking a little sleep. His large handkerchief was over his face to keep the flies away.

Yuan coughed, and the old gentleman peered out from under the handkerchief. When he saw it was his son who coughed, he struggled to his feet, a little confused with his sleep.

"Yes—yes—" he said.

Yuan began to speak at once. "My father, I am called to go at once to the capital. I cannot wait beyond today. I must leave at dawn tomorrow. I am sorry; for I had planned to spend a whole month here with you. But there are developments—international developments—" Yuan hesitated.

65

"Yes—yes—" said the old gentleman vaguely. He wiped his face with the handkerchief and passed his hands over his beard and opened and closed his mouth, dry with his sleep. "International?" he repeated. This was a new word he had never heard before.

"With foreign countries," said Yuan.

The old father cried out in consternation, "You do not mean you are going again to foreign countries!"

The young man pressed his lips together a little to control some inner impatience. Then he answered: "No, no, not that. But there is some talk of war with the country to the north of us. I am needed."

"Ah," said the old father. He staggered a little and laid his hand on his son's arm. "Well, if you must go, you must go. But do not have anything to do with wars, my son. Wars are evil and are entered into only by coarse and low persons."

Yuan's lips twitched slightly. "No, my father," he said with great gravity, and, measuring his steps to the old father's, he went with his father into the house.

But to his young wife Yuan made not even these explanations, since he felt she was a woman who could not be expected to understand anything outside her home. But he was very kind to her and he said: "I regret that I cannot have the month at home which I had planned. I have scarcely seen my children. I have many plans for them. I can stay longer at the New Year, perhaps."

All the day Yuan was away seeing this friend and that. He did not even come home for the noon meal, and at night he went to a feast to which he was invited. When he went, he said to his wife: "Do not wait for me, if you please. I prefer not to be waited for. I shall be late tonight, and tomorrow I start at dawn."

His wife answered nothing at all to this, merely standing before him and holding ready for him the curious curved stick he now used when he walked out. It would not have occurred to her not to wait for him, since this was her duty.

Therefore on this night, when she had done her usual tasks, she went into Yuan's room and sat upright upon the chair by the table, the candle lighted beside her. For a long time she worked at the embroidery she was making for the ends to be set into a pair of round pillows for her daughter's marriage bed. But at last she grew a little weary of the intricate pattern, and she laid her work aside, folding it up neatly, and then she sat with her hands folded over each other in perfect stillness. They were such hands that, when they were seen thus in repose, one might have thought them carved or painted they were so perfect in their shape and paleness. Thus she sat.

When at last she heard the sound of voices at the gate, she rose and blew into life the embers under the copper teapot and stood waiting. There were merry voices of men shouting to each other and Yuan's voice bantering and answering and bursting into laughter. Then footsteps sounded, and the gate was barred.

An instant later Yuan came into the room, his face still in smiles from his laughter. There was a deep red about his eyes and cheek bones, the red that wine sets there, but still he was not drunken since he knew exactly how much he

67

could drink, and he had been well bred, so that he was not drunken as common persons may be. That this red had come into his face showed he had been more merry than usual, since for a gentleman to say, "I have drunk enough; if I drink more, my face will be red," is excuse enough even to a friend.

He started when he saw his young wife standing there, quiet as a shadow in the dim room. "Ah," he said suddenly, "I did not know—you should not have waited." He threw himself down into a chair and took his handkerchief and wiped his face and smoothed his hair, still smiling. "Such a night! Every one of my old schoolmates was there—some back even from the coast city to see me. Ha, some of them come because they have heard I have a good place in the capital, and they keep friends with me for the hope of a rice bowl! Well, we shall see. I shall not serve any who cannot serve me." He yawned mightily and stretched out his arms. "Ha, how sleepy I am! And I must rise before dawn, too! Do not wait longer, I beg. I must get to sleep at once."

There hung between them again that delicate, poised moment of silence, and she was the first to shatter it, as she had been the night before. She put her hands into her sleeves, bowed and went softly away. He stared after her as she went and then called out suddenly, "Do not get up in the morning! It will be too early, and besides there is no need. I have told the manservant what to do."

She paused, the curtain in her hand. "But I shall get up," she said in her soft, definite voice. "I shall get up and see to your breakfast."

"No, no!" he said impatiently. "I forbid you; I cannot eat so early."

She paused; then said, "As you will, then."

Nevertheless, when he rose in the morning, the table was set with his chopsticks and with the bowls of salted dishes, and the closed rice pail of polished wood was there. In it was steaming rice gruel. He had thought he could not eat, but the smell of the food was good to him, the pungent smell of the salty foods that taste well upon a winy tongue. He sat down and ate quickly and heartily. From behind a curtain his wife watched him, although she did not appear before him, since he had told her not to rise. But her hands had set the table and chosen the dishes that might tempt him.

When he rose to go, his old father came to the door with his robes girdled about him, and Yuan bowed and said: "You should not have risen, my father. It is too much for you. Go back and rest. I shall return soon."

"You must care for yourself, my son," said the father, laying his old yellowed hand on his son's arm. "Care for yourself and come back quickly. Tell the Governor who is above you that you are your father's only son, and he will understand. Only two days after seven years!"

"Yes, my father," said Yuan. He was impatient to be off, but he stayed himself respectfully until his father took his hand away. Then he bowed again and was gone.

When the gate had closed behind him, the young wife came out and began to collect the dishes on the table very quietly. The old man watched her closely, but she was apparently intent upon this task, and there was nothing to be seen from this face of hers. It was pale but not more pale than usual, and, although it was so early, she was dressed as she always was, and her hair was smooth. Suddenly the old man struck his two hands together.

"We forgot to ask him about the Four Books for the child," he said. "Run, my daughter, and see if he is gone out of hearing!"

She ran obediently and opened the gate and looked down the silent, unlighted street, on either side of which the closed houses could now be faintly seen in the coming dawn. But she could not see Yuan at all, except that at the farthest end of the street there was a small light. It was the light of the lantern the servant carried to guide his master to the river's edge where the junk lay. She went back to the old man.

"It is too late; he is gone," she said.

The old man's face fell a little. Then he said: "It does not matter. He will be back this time very soon. At worst he must be back in time for the New Year, and that is less than six months away. Six months is nothing after seven years!"

The young wife smiled faintly in answer. Nevertheless, it seemed to her suddenly that this six months would be longer than all the seven years had been.

Now the days were exactly as they had been, except that the letters Yuan wrote were not stamped with the strange figures they once were and they were not filled with the accounts of his studies. Instead, he spoke of conferences, of great men he met and dined with, and also of great ladies.

At first this mention of ladies had made the old gentleman somewhat stiff in his manner as he read the letters aloud to the old mother and to Yuan's young wife. Indeed, he omitted the lines in which Yuan said, "Last night I dined with Madame Ching." This the old gentleman did not read, because he supposed it must be some light woman, and it would not be respectful to the two ladies of his house to mention such a person to them.

But another time Yuan said, "Tonight I am to dine with Madame, the lady of the Prime Minister." Then the old gentleman, feigning not to see a character clearly, hesitated, while the two ladies waited for him to go on. The truth was he was suddenly dismayed. If the ladies of the chief ministers of state were persons like this, what of the state then? Therefore he omitted these lines and read on, and, when the letter was read, he rose and went into his own room, drawing his curtain over his door so that anyone seeing it might know he was not to be disturbed.

In his room alone he seated himself by his old polished desk that stood under the lattice, and with great care he began to mix the ink upon the block. When it was exactly the consistency he liked, he pointed his brush in it extremely fine and began to paint upon the paper the letters for which he was really somewhat famous among his friends in the tea business. But these letters for all their beauty were sharp in their meaning. They said: "My son, take care how you entangle yourself with women in high places. It is better to rise more slowly and to rise without

71

the help of women." Then he signed and sealed the letter and sent it at once by messenger. When this was accomplished, he lighted a candle and burned to the last scrap the letter which Yuan had written.

But, when the answer to his letter came, it was evident that Yuan was at pains to set his father right. It was a very long letter, and it was fortunate that the servant had brought it when the old gentleman was alone since, when he had read it, he decided it was not such a letter as he wished to read aloud. No, it was full of a great deal that he had never heard before, and in his room with the curtain drawn he read it over three times and burned it at once. True, he was the only one in the house who could read, but still it was better to burn it. It was full of such phrases as these: "In this new day wives should stand beside husbands as equals"; "In this new day we men cannot be satisfied with the old standards of wives who are part servants, part mistresses"; "Not to have an educated wife is my great handicap. I have no one to keep such a home as I must have and to entertain for me, to be a companion to me. I am anxious even now because my children are not taught as they should be."

The old gentleman sat quite rigid for a long time after reading this letter and after it had become ashes. He felt somewhat faint at last, and he clapped his hands. His daughter-in-law heard the sound and, when a servant would have run to him, stayed the maid and said, "I will go myself, since the children are playing with their rabbits and do not need me now."

When the old gentleman saw her come in, he stared a

little, and his eyes grew moist. "I am glad it is you," he said. "I feel a little faint. I should like my pipe."

Then he went and lay on a long carved couch where he usually smoked his opium, and he watched while his daughter-in-law's slender figure bent over the mixing of the stuff. Her small, smooth face was wholly intent, and she took great care that the opium was exactly as he liked it. He never took his eyes from her at all so long as she did not look up.

When she brought the pipe to him at last and lighted the little lamp under its bowl, he said, "Child, how old are you?"

"I am twenty-seven, my father," she answered in great surprise.

"And you were married ten years ago," said the old gentleman slowly.

"Ten years," and her voice was like an echo of his, but it was not sad, only patient and mild.

"We have been wrong," said the old man suddenly. "My son's mother and I are wrong. We have grown so to lean upon you and to need you about us, so much our daughter are you, that we have not realized that we have deprived our son of his wife. While he was in foreign countries, it was impossible for you to be with him. You could not go there with children, certainly. But now he is in his own country. He has his house there in the capital, and there should be a mistress in his house to see that his feasts are given properly and that the servants do as they should and that he has what he likes."

"You mean, my father—" said the young wife, and her

73

pretty eyebrows that were like willow leaves seemed to flutter above her eyes.

"I mean you must go to Yuan," said the old man.

The opium began to be hot and its sweetish smell crept through the room and hung upon the air, heavy and sweet. Since the old gentleman was not smoking yet, the young wife turned the lamp flame a little by waving her graceful hand gently in front of the flame. She dropped her eyes to this task, and so he felt free to look at her again—in the school in which he had been bred no gentleman stares into a woman's face if he respects her. He saw the pink flush creep out from beneath the lobes of her ears.

"You would like to go?" he said kindly.

She did not speak for a moment, pondering, the eyebrows moving a little above her eyes. Then she said, "I do not think I should go unless there was someone here with you, my father, and with my mother."

"We have Wang Ma," said the old gentleman. "We can manage. Truly we should miss you. It would be like our hearts gone—and the children, the house would be empty without them. But I must think of my son first. I have not done well by my son. I have thought much about this. You should have gone with him when he went to the capital."

"He went so quickly," she murmured.

"Ah," said the old gentleman, "too quickly. I shall write him."

Then he began to smoke, and the gentleness of his face deepened into absorption and settled gravity, too deep even

74

for ordinary sleep. His daughter-in-law stood there until she saw he had no need of her, and then she went away.

She went then, this young wife, into the middle room where she had been sitting with her mother-in-law, since it was afternoon, and she took up the embroidery she had laid down. The green bird was finished now, and she was working on the spray of plum blossoms beneath its feet. Ten years from now her daughter would be sleeping as a bride above these symbols.

At this moment there was a cry heard from the court, and the boy burst in, holding a wriggling white rabbit by the ears. He complained loudly: "My sister says this one is hers, but it is mine! I know it is mine!"

The mother rose and went to the door, holding the child's fat hand in hers. He was pouting and crying over and over, "I want it for mine—it must be mine—" The little girl was out in the court, bent over a rabbit hutch as if she did not hear, thrusting cabbage leaves into it.

"My daughter!" called the mother.

Then the little girl turned and looked at her mother with a direct, rebellious gaze. She was a handsome child, with her mother's regularity of feature, but she had some fire that her mother had not.

"It is truly mine," she said in a quiet, perfectly firm voice.

"My child!" said the mother again and paused.

The girl stood erect, threw down the cabbage leaves she held and bit her lip. She said in the same hard voice, "It is a strange thing that I must always let him have his way."

"But, my child!" the mother said again for the third

75

time; and the girl burst suddenly into sobs and ran past her mother into the room where she slept.

"It is mine, then!" said the boy triumphantly.

"Yes, my son, it is yours," said the mother quietly, and she left him and sat down again to her embroidery.

The old lady had listened to all this, and now she sighed a little. Then she said: "It will be well when you have another son, my daughter, with whom this boy must share his goods, even though he is the eldest son. I perceive he is very willful by nature."

The young mother did not answer. She was listening to the sounds that came from the inner room. They were deep sobs, buried and softened by something held over the girl's mouth. At last the mother rose, unable to endure this sound any longer, and with that peculiar stillness which was her chief characteristic she went into the room and approached the bed where the little girl had thrown herself. The child lay under the quilt. The mother drew it aside, and, when the girl turned, her face was red and wet with weeping, and her eyes were hard. Her mother said nothing but began to smooth away the fringe of black hair that hung over the child's brow. It was the softest, smoothest touch, and the girl's hardness faded gradually under it, and her face took on a plaintive look. When the mother saw this, she began to speak in a low voice that was almost a whisper.

"My child, I did not even ask whose rabbit it was. I must teach you somehow to learn submission. Submission to father and to brother, then to husband. If your brother says it is his wish to have the rabbit, you must defer to him."

"But why?" the child wailed suddenly. "It was my rab-

76

bit! I know it because it has one black whisker. And he pulls it so by the ears!"

"You learn submission by submitting first to your father and to your brother; then you will know how to submit to your husband," the mother explained patiently, as if she repeated a thing she had heard and had said many times. "A woman must learn to obey. We must not ask why. We cannot help our birth. We must accept it and do the duty that is ours in this lifetime."

But her smooth, light hand never ceased its movement on the child's head, and this touch seemed to bring some calmness that her words could not. Indeed, it was true that she had said these words many times before, in this long training she must pass on to her daughter even as her own mother had passed it on to her. They were not new words, being many hundreds of years old. But the regular, soothing touch was the direct, mute message she had for her daughter, and the girl received it and for this once was comforted.

A few days later, when they were all seating themselves about the table for the evening meal, the old father looked with gentle pleasure at his daughter-in-law and smoothed his beard and cleared his throat. There was a mild sparkle in his eye which betokened something unusual in his mind. When she had put before him the broth that he liked and the small balls of pork and had set before her mother-in-law the vegetable dishes prepared for her without even the oil of any flesh, the old gentleman cleared his throat again.

With the fingers of one hand in his beard he said, brightly: "My daughter, I wrote today to Yuan to say

77

you were ready to come to him at once with the children. It is true what he said in one of his letters—a man should have a mistress in his house, and for his servants. I said, if he could beg a few days' leave and come to fetch you, that would be best, but, if he could not, the journey is not difficult, and the old manservant can take you. He is old and faithful, and I can escort you to the junk here. There are but three days by sea, and surely Yuan can come to the coast to meet you and accompany you on the land journey, which is less than one day. Even if he cannot do this, you are safe with the servant, since he used to travel that road often with Yuan when he accompanied him as a youth to school. It is very simple. And true it is that a man needs his wife in his house. Yuan is right."

Yuan's wife said nothing to this, because there were several thoughts in her mind. First of all was the warm, secret pleasure she had because she heard that her husband had written that he needed his wife in his house. So, then, the vague feeling she had had that perhaps he was changed to her was a foolish one. He needed her still—had written that he needed her. Her hands trembled a little as she stirred her chopsticks in the central dish of chicken and mushrooms for the titbit that her son was demanding noisily.

"There, my mother—that piece, the white bit! No, that!"

"It is what my grandfather likes best," said the little girl accusingly.

The young mother paused. "So it is, my son," she said gently. "It is your grandfather's favorite bit."

The boy pressed his full lips together hard, and his eyes grew very wide and bright as if he might begin to weep.

The old gentleman leaned over at once and picked up the titbit with his chopsticks and placed it on the child's bowl of rice.

"It is for you today, little one," he said, smiling, and the child laughed suddenly.

"Thank your grandfather, my son," his mother said gravely.

The child stood up, willing enough now that he had his way, and he bowed.

The grandfather put out his hand, smoothed the boy's golden cheek and said in a soft, regretful voice, "Ah, if you go with your mother, my man—"

"Am I going somewhere?" exclaimed the child in sudden excitement. "On the boat?" He leaped up, tipping over his rice bowl and the meats upon it, and he cried out again, heedless of what he had done: "Mother, when shall we go? Where are we going?"

But his mother had begun at once to repair the damage the child had done. "Hush, child," she said. "It is too soon to talk of it. It is whatever your father says."

"Ah, he will write you are to come at once," said the old gentleman quickly. "Let us count the days. Today and seven days, and we shall receive his letter—say perhaps a day or two more because of winds, and we shall have it."

"I do not see how I shall manage without my daughter-in-law," said the old lady suddenly, perceiving what all this was about. She had been supping her soup of cabbage hearts with a porcelain spoon, since she had only a few teeth left and loved soup best of all foods. Now she stopped and put her spoon down upon a little saucer and looked around at them all. "I am used to her, and it is hard for a person of my age to be without her daughter-in-law. I cannot undertake the management of the servants as I did when I was young."

"There will not be much management with only the two old ones of us here," said the old gentleman.

"But—" the old lady began once more. Then, glancing at her husband, she saw a look on his face which for one so mild was terrible in its command for silence, and in some alarm she began to sup her soup again hastily.

"Yes, she must go," said the old gentleman again. "And you must go, my little one, also."

"And I?" asked the little girl, who had been listening intently to all this, her eyes very wide.

"Yes, perhaps you, too," answered her grandfather, "although, if your grandmother misses you too much—"

The little girl's face turned pale, and she put down the chopsticks with which she had been eating. "If I cannot go, I shall die," she said positively.

At this the old lady looked up in great irritation. "Do not, my child, use words like 'die' and 'death' so carelessly! One never knows what spirits—"

The young wife spoke. "If my mother can spare us and we must go, I should like to take both the children, since it is the time now when my daughter must be taught many things. But of course I am not to decide. It is true that my mother at her age cannot control the maids. They are good if controlled, but otherwise they will yield to opportunity, and there will be laxness in the house."

"We will manage, we will manage," said the old gentleman heartily. "Wang Ma shall control the maids, and she can mix the stuff for my pipe and go with her mistress to the temple. We will manage!"

But the young wife, who now said no more, could scarcely for all her stillness wait until the meal was over. With her usual swift motions, she saw to it that each one had what he liked, that the tea bowls of the two old ones were filled with the red tea the old father liked and the green tea the old mother liked. She did scrupulously all she did every day, missing nothing; and after the table was cleared and the old pair sat drinking their tea she led the children to them, each in turn, and then she washed the boy while the old woman servant helped the girl, and so they were put to bed.

Only then did the young wife not do what she usually did. She went into her husband's room instead of returning to her parents-in-law, and she sat there in the darkness in his chair, and she began soberly to think of what this future might mean to her. She could not imagine what it might be to leave this house. She thought of every separate part of it over which she guarded. Who would see to it that the three courts were kept in order, that the young bamboo shoots were protected in spring—the largest left to grow, the small ones cut to eat? The servants left to themselves would pretend each year that there were no shoots and would never bring one to the old pair to eat. Servants were so. Who would dust the old gentleman's fans? His own hands were too trembling now to do it. These and a hundred other small duties that filled her life occurred to her now and seemed to lay on her invisible bonds that she could not easily break. They were duties that had become habits, the mute needs of inanimate things—certain bits of carving that she alone dusted, with a feather dipped in oil, the rolling of certain scrolls that hung upon the walls at certain seasons and the hanging of others in their place, the cleaning of the four ancestral tablets that stood in a niche in one of the outer rooms, the preparation for the obeisances to be made and the sacrifices to be burned at the family graves on the day in spring when it was proper to do these things. The fulfillment of all these duties—the rites of family life, which make a house entire and cared-for and full of well-being—depended upon her, seeing that none save her so belonged to this house, as daughter and wife and mother.

Yet there was her husband. He needed her also in the house where he lived. It was not to be hoped that he could again live as he had when he was a boy in this small old city, where there was nothing for such a one as he to achieve. With all the languages he had on his tongue and all the other things he knew, it was necessary that he should live in the capital. They could not spare him there, doubtless. She sighed a little. It did not occur to her that there was anything she could not do there that she did in this house or that there could be anything about a home which she did not know. If she went to her husband, doubtless there would be a house like this one but somewhat smaller. She would see to the kitchen as she did here, herself cooking the special dishes he liked or the dishes for a feast not large enough to be sent in by professional cooks. She would see to the wines as she did here. There would be furniture to keep clean, a court to be persuaded into bloom, her daughter to be taught as she was now, the son to nurture. No, there was nothing she did not know about a woman's duties.

The old gentleman coughed suddenly at the door, and she rose and went out. The old lady had retired. The old gentleman stood there alone. He said: "I have decided you are to go, my daughter. So prepare your boxes for your possessions and the children's, also, if it be that you still feel you must take the little girl; for you shall go to be with your husband."

She bowed her head slightly. "I do what you command, my father," she replied. "I take the little girl only because it is the time when she should be preparing for her life, and there is much I must teach her for the future, and my mother is so old it would be hardship to her."

But, after all, it seemed the young wife was not to go. Just as she had come to think of her going with secret, sweet excitement, not one sign of which she allowed to escape her outwardly, a letter came, and the old gentleman did not read it to them. No, he was so disturbed when he read it that they did not know what to do for him. He was scarcely calmed with his pipe, and he would not eat. He sat staring at his son's wife, and they all waited for him to speak. But he did not speak.

At last the young wife could wait no more, since she was frightened, and with a boldness that was wholly foreign to her she entered the old gentleman's room on a pretext of some service, and she said, "My father, if it be so that you can tell me, tell me then when I am to go, because there are certain things I must see to in the house first, the winter clothing and the furs to sun, so that my mother will be spared the superintending of the task."

The old gentleman coughed then, and he coughed longer than he needed, as if he did not know what to say, but at last he spoke: "Child, there is the strangest letter from Yuan, and I cannot tell you what he said. But I must go and see for myself what his life is. Then, when I come back, you must be ready, and you shall go."

Now, the old gentleman had not been away from his home since he was young, and the two ladies were in consternation when they heard this. To the daughter-in-law it seemed impossible; for how could he bear the journey and who would see to his pipe and to the things he liked to eat? The old wife was distracted, and each lady begged in her own way that he would explain what the matter was and if Yuan were ill or not. But the old gentleman was stubborn and silent as he had never been before, and he would say nothing except, "No, he is not ill; no, I must go myself and see to it—I must go and see for myself."

So they could do nothing except take care that there was every change of garment he might need in his boxes, and the young wife herself put in garments suitable to every season, since who knew what the winds were in that northern place where Yuan lived? And she put in his favored tea in a lacquered box; for well she knew he could not drink such coarse tea as is sold commonly to travelers. And she put in boxes of delicacies, so that he need not be dependent on the wretched fare that travelers must eat. And they sent with him two servants, one of them the old man who traveled with Yuan. Then, when they had seen the old gentleman into his sedan safely, his hands shaking with excitement but his eyes bright and hard and his lips set together in his beard, the two ladies could do no more than go again into the courts where their life was and wait.

So the young wife waited the days that the old gentleman was away, and on the fortieth day he returned. They had not known on what day or at what hour to expect him, since he had not written a letter, because there was no one who could read it if he had and it is an ill thing to take a letter to a professional reader if there is anything private in it. Therefore the old gentleman was at the gate before they knew it, and he came into the court staggering, as if he were very weary, and he scarcely lifted his eyes. He smiled so wearily that the two ladies were frightened, and the old wife went after him into his room, and the young wife of his son hastened to prepare the best chicken broth that could be made, to restore him.

Three days he lay in his bed in silence. He groaned every now and then, and he said nothing except a word of thanks for some service, and they waited and knew some dreadful thing was on his mind, but they did not know what. On the third day he rose and dragged himself into his usual garments and sat on his chair by his desk, and he called for his wife and for his daughter-in-law, and the two of them came in. Well they knew he had something hard to say to them. The old mother was frightened lest it concern the health of her only son, and the young wife thought of her husband. Each thought of the same thing, whether he had an illness or not, or even if perhaps he were dead. But

85

neither of them had thought at all of what the old man was to say, and he said thus:

"I went to that new capital, and I saw my son and his friends. I was there twenty full days, and I saw such things as I have never seen. I saw high houses, and I saw machines that run alone, and I saw many wonders, but these I will not speak of now because they are nothing to us. I saw what Yuan meant when he spoke of the women of that city. It is true that they were to me the strangest things of all. They go everywhere alone; their hair is cut off like men's hair; they are like men. At first I said, 'These are evil women, and my son is lost among them.' Then I saw that they were not evil. No, I have heard that women are changed in these days, and it is true. I had not believed it, since in this quiet place they are as they have always been." The old gentleman paused as if at some painful recollection, and he stared down at the floor.

"But how changed and by what changed?" asked the old lady, who had been listening to all this in the greatest astonishment.

"They have been to schools such as we sent our son to," said the old man simply. "They read and they write, and they have even gone to foreign countries. Yuan saw them there. I would not have believed it otherwise. But I went with him into a house of a friend of his, and the wife of his friend was such a one as I tell you about, and at first I feared to look at her lest she were an evil woman. Then she spoke so gently and she was so courteous, and I saw her four children and they were courteous and clean also, and the house was in order although strange—but still ordered

86

and clean—and I saw she was not evil at all. No, Yuan told me she could teach her children to read and to write and many things in books. I have not seen women like that before. Yet she sat there talking and laughing with the men, and they respected her. I could see they respected her."

The two ladies listened to this in perfect silence. The young wife as she listened grew very pale, even more pale than she usually was, and she began to moisten her dry lips with the tip of her tongue.

The old gentleman went on in his gentle, hesitating way: "Yuan lives in a house alone. It is not like this house. It is the strangest house—one house piled on top of another and full of glass windows!" The old gentleman stopped again, and at last he continued with increasing agitation, "I said to him, I said, 'Yuan, your house has no mistress'; and I said, 'Yuan, your wife shall come to you when you say, because we can manage, your mother and I'; and I said, 'Yuan, she is your wife.'"

The two ladies now sat perfectly motionless, their eyes fixed upon the old gentleman's downcast face. His yellow, thin old hand hovered incessantly over his beard, and he crossed and uncrossed his velvet-shod feet.

"What did he say?" asked the old lady, unable to bear the silence.

The old gentleman coughed and said in a sudden loud voice: "He said, 'My father, you see for yourself! How could she manage a house like this, how be the sort of wife to me that I need? She cannot even read and write. I would be ashamed of her before my friends and their wives!'"

At this the young wife's face became as fixed as stone, and

she did not move at all. Her eyes dropped to her hands folded in her lap, and so she sat motionless.

The old gentleman looked at her secretly and sighed heavily, and then he said: "I could see what he means. Yes, I can see what he means. And yet I said also, and I still say again, Where is there a woman like you, my daughter? You have been incomparable in our house." Again he sighed, and then he added in a bitter voice such as no one had ever heard him use before: "But you cannot read and write! It seems that in these days women must read and write."

There was a loud cry from the little boy outside in the court where he was playing, a cry of rage and disappointment. If it had been a usual moment, his mother would have been instantly beside him. But she did not move. It was as if she did not hear him, even.

The old lady began to speak quickly and loudly: "But what does he mean? But what does he expect? No, I know what all this fault-finding is. He has found one he likes better; that is all! I know, I know! I said there would be ill out of all this going into foreign places."

The old gentleman raised his hand to command her silence. "You do not understand, Mother-of-my-son," he said. "If there is such a person as you say, I did not see her. No, he even suggested a way. He said, 'Let my wife go to a school for three years, a foreign school in the coast city where I know the foreign principal. I will write a letter there for her, and they know me and will receive her for my sake, even though she is not a usual pupil. There she could learn to be more like the other women here. She will

88

learn not only reading and writing but something of how to teach her children what they should know.'"

At this the old lady began to laugh, a delicate, brittle, bitter laugh. But a pink flush rose in the young wife's face. She looked up suddenly, and it could be seen that her whole face was rosy, and her eyes were full of tears.

"It is true, I do not know anything," she said humbly. "Yuan is right. How am I fit for him? I will go to school if he says I must—as soon as I have sunned the winter furs and made things ready against the coming cold, I will go." Then she added in a small, breathless voice, "Well, I will go, if he must have me like others!"

But how can a mother of children go back and be a girl again? When she had torn herself away from the crying children and had looked back to see them leaning out of the gate calling after her, their arms outstretched, when she had set out upon her journey, the astounded old manservant beside her filled with disapproval of this strange adventure, when she had entered the schoolhouse and had taken her place in a row of beds in a dormitory and at a desk in a schoolroom, how could she forget what she was? True, there were those to be kind to her, even the strange pale foreigners who filled her with repulsion at their whiteness, but she had to sit in a room where little girls were, and she had to pore with them over books of big characters. She set herself to do it, her heart hard and aching, determined to do it all quickly. But, when she tried to fix her mind upon these letters, it would fly of its own accord to her home, and she could think of nothing else. She could only wonder if they had thought today to put warmer coats upon the children since the wind blew so chill, and she fell to thinking of her duties in that house and whether they were done or not, and suddenly the hour would be gone and she had not learned what she ought to have learned, and the teacher was impatient and she was ashamed.

When night came, it seemed dreadful to her that she must unclothe herself and lie down in a room where there were so many who were strange to her, and, when she did do it somehow and crept into the narrow, iron bed, she lay sleepless, longing for the little son with whom she had slept all his life. And the three years she must spend at this school were forever to her.

Thus it went day after day, and she could not fix her mind. Many began to think her stupid, and one day she heard two teachers talking, and one of them said, not knowing she was near: "She cannot learn. It is a shame, when her husband is so clever and learned. She is stupid by nature, and it is hopeless." And the other one said regretfully—for they all liked the young wife—"It does seem quite hopeless."

At this moment the school was called together to listen to a certain great man, who talked to them about the Revolution and the Three Principles of the People and about the new times that were come everywhere, and the young wife sat there among the others, her heart very sore at what she had heard the two teachers say. And she looked about the room suddenly, and she saw all the girls listening to the great man with keenest attention, and she looked especially at the oldest ones, already past the age that she was when she married, and far they were beyond her, how many years beyond! As she looked at them, it came to her that these were the women of whom Yuan spoke. They could read and write as quickly as men. They understood perfectly what this great man told them, although she herself had no faintest idea of what he meant when he said such words as "economics" and "equilateral treaties" and many other words and phrases she had never heard. Yet she was ashamed to ask their meaning, because there was so much she did not know.

Then it came over her with a great despair that it was all no use. She could never become like these, no, not if she put her whole life to it. She could manage the old home and care for her children and for the parents of her husband, but this other thing she could not do. No, she must go home. And, as the man went on in his loud clear voice, she sat with her head down, thinking, planning, giving up. For in renunciation she saw a way for herself.

She said in her heart: "I will go back to my home, and I will take care of my children and of the old two as I have done always, and I will ask my father to write to my husband: 'I cannot be two women for you. If it be you must have the other kind also, then, although it breaks my heart in two, take one of that sort to be with you where you are; as for me, I will stay at home and care for your parents and take care of the children!'" When this came into her mind, although she was filled with a deep sadness, it was a quiet sadness, and she could bear it better than the despair, because she saw a way in which she could go home.

Immediately after the man had finished and the pupils

were released, she went to the principal of the school, and she said: "I think I must return to my home. My mind is continually on the children, and it is true I cannot learn anything here."

Then, since this principal was a very kindly foreign woman, although too busy to think much of one student only, she said kindly enough: "Perhaps you are right. Perhaps it would be better for you to go home. I am sorry." And, although she smiled, it could be seen from her smile, even, that her mind was on other and more important things.

Then Yuan's wife set about putting her possessions together, and there was not a single person to mark her going away although she had been two months in this school, so entirely had she been outside the life of all. No, she put her things together and tied the strings of her bundle and paid what money she owed, and she went out of the gate and hired a passage on a boat that went up the river to that city where her home was. Although she had never been anywhere alone before, she did this all so steadfastly and quietly that no one looked at her, because she seemed so usual.

On the fourth day she entered the gate of her home once more, and they were all in the court of the peonies, and the old gentleman was directing the fertilizing of the roots before winter fell too cold. They looked at her in silence for a moment, scarcely believing it was she, and she began to speak quickly, lest one of them might say something before she told why she was come. She spoke in a voice at once pleading and firm, and she said, looking at her husband's father:

"I must give him up. I do give him up. Let him take a second one, of the kind he likes. Only let me stay here with you and with my mother and with my children as ever I have. I cannot learn anything at that foreign school. I tried, but my heart was continually asking my mind, 'Have they drawn the curtains close about the children's bed—they are so easily chilled.' Or, 'How does my son sleep without his mother—he stirs so much in his sleep—and will his sister wake to cover him when she is only a child herself?' No, I am as I am, and I am only useful and clever when I am in this house with you whom I care for. Outside I am so stupid and awkward—you would not believe how stupid if you had not seen. Even the youngest ones in the school were more clever than I. It is true what Yuan says. I am fit only for this house and for you and for my children. I cannot—I can never leave here again."

At the end she began to pour out these words in a quivering, half-weeping voice not at all like her usual way of speaking, and her pretty eyebrows fluttered above her frightened eyes. The old father and mother looked at each other and said nothing, but the two children, who had not understood what their mother meant at all, now flew to her, and the boy cried out, "Now we shall have cakes to eat!"

And the little girl said coaxingly: "When you go back to school, take me also, my mother! I have always wanted to go to school!"

At last the old gentleman, seeing perfectly what the

young wife meant, saw also that she was right, and he stroked his beard and sighed and said: "My child, I can see how it has been. Therefore there is nothing to do except to write it all to Yuan. I will tell him, and we shall see if he will have mercy."

So saying, he went to his room, sighing as he went, and the old lady said nothing at all, but she took her daughter-in-law's hand and patted it very gently, and after a time she leaned over and whispered so that the children could not hear: "You are not to grieve! I myself will speak to Yuan when he comes!"

The young wife smiled sadly at this, but she did not answer. She knew there was some spirit now in Yuan which even a mother's words could not move.

But she took up again with ineffable joy the old duties of the home. In the night she woke up sometimes in terror, thinking for an instant that she was back in the school, her bed one in rows of others exactly like it. Then her little son would stir, perhaps, and, when he tossed his fat legs across her, she came to herself and held herself ecstatic and breathlessly still, lest she should wake him.

She found in these first days a score of things undone about the house. The caldrons had not been scraped of their soot in the kitchens, and the fire was thus kept from the food and the fuel wasted. The candle stands were caked with the tallow of the dripping candles. There were many such things that servants' eyes do not see, and it had been so long since the old lady noticed such affairs that she also did not see.

Day after day the young wife busied herself until the

house was as she liked it again. They never mentioned Yuan now nor talked of her ever going away any more. If she spoke—but she seldom did—it was to say something to a child or else to make a remark about some household need. The old gentleman, watching her, saw her look frightened for an instant if he began to speak unexpectedly, until she heard what he said, and he told his old wife: "We must never send this child of ours away again. You see how she is—trembling and so thin. How she has suffered!"

He did not reproach her at all. Nevertheless, he waited in heaviness of heart for his son's letter. The truth was he had not yet told Yuan that his wife was willing for him to take another woman. He was sure that he could explain to the young man once more how it was, how sheltered his wife had been in this old house, how her life had entwined itself about them all, how, although she was so swift and capable at home and made all of them so comfortable, she could not adapt herself to a change so great as the life he now lived, and how, in the presence of those lively, learned women, she would shrink and fade away and none would ever see or care what she was. No, Yuan must be content to have her stay in the old home with his parents, and he could come back when he would and spend some time himself with his friends. So the old father had written, and he waited for his son's answer.

It came very quickly, and it was not an unkind letter. No, Yuan was not unkind, and he said only this: "You have dealt so very gently with the wife you gave me and you have understood so well what her nature is that I ask only to be shown the same gentleness and understanding.

95

My father, I was eighteen when you married me to one I never saw. It was an age at which I would have taken any woman, and I was pleased enough with the one you gave me. If I had continued at home and gone into business with you, I should always have been content with her. The men of our house are not given to many women. I would have lived with this one only, even as you and my mother have lived together all these years, with increasing joy and peace as your old age comes on. But I went away, and you were willing and even ambitious for me, and I have pushed on into another life, one as remote as the stars from the quiet city in which you all live. I need a companion in this life—from which I cannot now separate myself—one who shares it and with whom I can speak. I have nothing to say to the one you chose for me—she has nothing to say to me. We have no common life about which we can talk. I could never be content again with this one, seeing what women may become in these days. I can hire a servant to give me what that one does. I want a woman who is trained as I am, who is a part, with me, of the new day. Be gentle with me, my father!"

The old gentleman did not read this letter to the two ladies, either. He thought to himself that surely he did not need his son to beg him to be gentle. He read the letter over three times, groaning as he did so, since he understood, and yet what could he do?

Being driven to extremity, he wrote again, and he said, "She is willing for you to take another after your own heart, and she will stay on in this house and care for us all as she has always." And he thought the matter ended and the uttermost done. Therefore, he was not prepared for the answer that came back.

Yuan wrote: "It is not lawful in these times nor becoming for a man to have more than one wife, and moreover the new woman will not be a second wife. I must first divorce the old one; for the new one must be the only wife. But I shall be very generous, and I will pay the old one well, and she shall not want. I do not want her to suffer at all."

The old father could scarcely restrain himself when he read these words his son had written. His eyes started, and he read it over again to make sure he had really understood it all. Then he wrote back in a great anger, forgetting himself completely: "These are strange times when a man can cast his wife off like this so that she has nothing left, neither respect nor place among men and no place in her husband's home! Better the old days when she lost nothing but her husband's favor and had all else left to her, and her life could go on in her house. My son, you have written what is unworthy of you!"

Then, pulling his straggling beard, he waited in the utmost impatience for an answer. During these days, the old gentleman grew thinner even than he was and more haggard, and he could only steep himself more in his opium than he had ever allowed himself to do before, because otherwise he could not sleep at all. When the letter came from his son, he went into his own room and he tore open the envelope, but, when he drew the letter forth, he could not read it, since his excitement made him giddy and he had to lean his head upon his hands to recover himself.

The young wife had stolen in and seen him thus, and she poured out a cup of tea. She was extremely pale, but she did not ask anything concerning the letter that lay there. Well she knew whose it was, but she would ask nothing now—only wait for what must come.

This time the letter was brief and plain. "My father, you cannot, I see, understand. We had better be perfectly open with each other. I have begun the bill of divorcement, and I am betrothed now to a young woman who was in the same school with me in the foreign country. Like me, she was betrothed to one she never saw, but she was braver than I and repudiated the bond. We are made for each other. I shall be generous in everything to the other one, but we are no longer husband and wife. Do not blame me. Remember, I tried—I sent her to school, and it is not my fault if she would not make the effort to stay. If she had cared, she would have made the effort. I do not blame myself. There are many who do what I do today. Indeed, the lot of the new women is as hard as that of any. The men whom they should wed, the men of their generation and training, are already wed, as I was, in childhood. Someone must suffer, and it is better for the country and for the children to come that the educated women be the wives and mothers. But I shall be generous to that other one. I will give her all you think she needs. Only she must go away to some other place and live there, because she has no more right in my home. When I come back with my wife to visit you and my mother, it will be an embarrassment to us if she is there."

The young wife lingered about the room, silently waiting.

She waited, hoping that the old gentleman would tell her something that was in the letter. But he only motioned to her to leave him. He would tell her nothing at all. No, his mouth felt dry, and he was faint, and he sat for a long time alone, sipping the hot tea she poured for him before she went.

Then he mixed his ink carefully and drew his brush and paper to him again, and he wrote: "My son, if it had been as it was with myself when young and my father, I would have commanded, and you would have obeyed. But well I know I cannot command; for you would not obey. No, it is I who obey now. In these days and times sons do not obey, and so fathers must not command. No, I say only this, if it must be as you say, let the poor child who has been our daughter all these years live on here. Though she be not your wife, yet must she be our daughter. We are not changed to her. We do not know this new one. We should be ill at ease in her presence. I was afraid of those swift, learned women I saw in the capital who are your friends and the wives of your friends. I am not used to these women. No, let our daughter live here with us and care for your children, and let her never know she is divorced from you. I will not tell her, and in this quiet place she need not know."

When his letter was written and sent, the old gentleman seemed more at ease again. Nevertheless, it seemed to him best that he should tell the young wife something of what had passed, but not all. Therefore he called her to him that evening when the children were asleep and when he sat with his old wife in the middle room with the lighted candle on the table between them. The young wife came in when she was called, and, as she always did, she saw to their tea that it was hot before she seated herself in her accustomed place below her parents-in-law.

The old gentleman began: "My daughter, I have written to my son, and our letters have been like birds flying north and south. The end of it all is that my son has accepted your generosity, and he does take another wife, but you are to stay here freely, my child, in this house that you know, and we shall be as we were before, except that we shall not see Yuan so often as we might otherwise have seen him, since his life is now elsewhere."

Then for the first time did this young wife begin to weep openly before these old two. "I have dealt ill with you," she sobbed. "I have repaid so badly all your kindness! It is because I am as I am that you cannot see your son so much and that he is separated from his home!"

The old lady opened her eyes very wide; for she, even, had not seen her daughter-in-law weep before—no, not in all these years, not even when the little boy was near to death. She exclaimed with mild heat: "I shall speak to Yuan myself—I shall see to it myself—I shall see if sons no longer obey their parents!"

But the old gentleman shook his head and was as patient with her as if she were a child: "No," he said gently. "No one has done wrong—not you, my child, who have always done the best you could; not Yuan, who is still generous as he ever was. No," he hesitated and stroked his beard with his pale old hand, "I cannot say whose fault all this is nor why these strange times have come when all is so changed, so that even a good wife is not what a man wants."

"It all comes of not heeding the gods," said the old lady with obstinacy. "If one does one's duty by the gods—"

The old gentleman closed his eyes, waiting for her to finish, because he had heard this many times before. Then he continued, as if she had not spoken: "But you may live on here, child, where your home is, and we shall live from day to day and watch the peonies bud and the lilies, and we have the children. There are not many so happy as we."

Thus he comforted them.

But it was not to be so. On the sixth day from this day, as they were eating their night meal together, there was an unusual noise at the gate, and the manservant cried out, "The young master is come!"

They looked up from the table, and there Yuan was, standing before them. He was weary and dusty and looked thinner than they had ever seen him. There was a constraint upon him, and he spoke hastily to his parents without noticing anyone else. It was as if he labored under some task which he hated but which he must perform and complete. He wrung out a towel from the basin of hot water a servant brought in, and he wiped his face and hands quickly and sat down to the table, and, taking a bowl and chopsticks, he began to eat rapidly. The young wife hastened to fetch hot rice and hot dishes, and this he acknowledged with a short nod. When he had eaten a bowl— for he was never one to eat much—he turned to the others who were waiting for him to finish, and he began to speak quickly and with indrawing breath, as if he knew what he had to say and must say it and yet dreaded to say it.

He turned to his father and he spoke thus: "My father, I must return at once, even tonight, and so it is better to say at once before us all what I have to say. This passing back and forth of letters is too slow. The matter begun must be finished quickly. The bill of divorcement is drawn, and it must be signed by the two of us to be divorced. My wedding is set for the sixth day of next month. It is better for this one, here, to withdraw to some quiet good place with a relative, because it will be too difficult for me to bring my wife home—I want you to see her, my father and my mother! When you see her, you will understand!"

Now the young wife heard all this, and it was for the first time, since she had not known at all that she was to be divorced. She turned a strange white face to him, and she said: "But I have nowhere to go at all. There is no relative who will take me and the two children."

Yuan had not looked at her, but, when she mentioned the children, he looked at her quickly and said, in surprise: "But naturally I would not ask you to take my children. They are my responsibility, and, when I am married, they will come to my house where they can receive the benefits of my wife's education." Then, as he saw her look, he cried out in sudden hostility: "Do not say it is my fault! I gave you your chance, and you threw it away."

The young wife continued to gaze at him as he spoke, but as if she did not know it and did not see him. Twice she essayed to speak, and her eyebrows fluttered above her eyes, but not a sound came from her lips. The old man was looking down, stroking his beard, his face as gray as ashes. The old lady began to weep suddenly and secretly.

But Yuan turned to his children and said, "Son, you would like to come with me to the new capital, would you?"

The little boy began to leap up and down crying out, in ecstasy, "I shall go on a boat—I shall go on a boat—"

The little girl asked her father, her face tense with anxiety, "But shall I go?"

"Yes, you, too," said Yuan heartily.

The little girl turned to her mother, her face flushing with joy. "Then I shall go to school," she said with grave pleasure in her eyes; "I have always wanted to go to school."

But not one of them looked at the young wife to see how she was. If they had looked, they might not have seen anything except that her pallor was deeper even than usual, and, since she was always silent, her silence was not strange. None would have seen how she trembled, unless it were the old gentleman, and he sat there stroking his beard, gray as ashes, his eyes fixed on the floor, since he would not look at her. The old lady had wept noiselessly, wiping her eyes with her sleeve, and she sat quiet, also.

Yuan was delighted with his son's merriment, and he said, "You shall go on a train, and you shall see great wide streets and automobiles and airplanes and all the things you have never seen and can never see here!"

The child could not contain himself. He began to run about in circles and to cry out: "When shall we go? I want to go—I want to go—"

The young wife looked at this son of hers and then at the little girl. The little girl caught her mother's eye and smiled dreamily and said, "I have always wanted to go to school, Mother!"

Then the young wife could bear no more. No, it was no use for her to say anything. By the grayness of the old father's face, by the old mother's weeping, the young wife knew it was no use for her to say anything at all. Yuan caught his son to him as the child ran past him, and he hugged him and smelled of his sweet flesh, and the child was delighted with his father and clung to him and looked arrogantly at his mother.

Then Yuan said to her earnestly, his cheek beside the child's: "Of course you shall never want. I shall always take care that you have plenty of money."

The young wife gave him a full, proud look. But he did not see it; for his eyes were fastened on his son again. With the fickleness of childhood the boy and the girl thought at this moment of their father only, and without their noticing it their mother slipped away from them all.

She went into the room where she had slept with the two children during all these years, and she sat down heavily upon her bed. It came over her in one complete moment what her life was, what it now must be. It did not take her one moment more to know what she must do for them all. Yes, for Yuan and for the children she must do it —for herself, also.

She rose and drew open a drawer in the table, and from it she took out a silk girdle that she wore customarily with her holiday garments. It was of soft white silk, very strong and soft. She climbed upon the massive bed, and with steady hands she tied one end of the girdle about her throat and she reached and tied the other end around the beam that ran just above the bed. From the middle room she heard her son's voice crying merrily, "And shall I ride in an airplane, too?"

The old father had begun to speak in a soft, sad, pleading voice, but she could not hear what he said. She did not try to hear. No, she tied the girdle firmly and steadily, and she took one long look about this beloved room. Then she pressed her lips together and closed her eyes. With quiet decision she thrust one foot off the bed and leaped into the air and felt the girdle tighten and jerk. She remembered one thing for an instant, one more duty. It was that she must not let her hands fly out for support. She clasped them convulsively upon her breast. The blood pounded in her ears, and her ears were filled with the roar. Like a voice very far away she heard the child say over and over, laughing, "I shall ride in an airplane!"

But this sound died away, too, and she heard no more. Her hands dropped.

THE OLD MOTHER

T HE old mother sat at the table with her son and his wife and their two children. Their noon meal was being served by the elder housemaid. The old mother sat very quietly with her hands folded in her lap, and she looked with subdued eagerness at one dish after another as these were brought on the table. There was one dish she liked especially, but she said nothing. She knew that it had not been prepared for her, but only by accident, since her son and his wife had often told her they could not eat the dishes she wanted because they were such coarse country fare. Therefore, the pepper and beans were not here today because she liked peppers.

As she gazed at this dish her mouth watered. She was very hungry. She would have liked to take up her chopsticks and plunge them in the peppers and take up all she could and pile them on the bowl of rice the maid had placed before her. But this she had been taught not to do. Yes, in the four years she had been living with her son and his wife she had learned many things. Therefore she waited with such patience as she could until her son's wife said formally, after the food had all been placed on the table,

"Mother, will you take what you wish?"

Nevertheless, the son's wife contrived, as she passed the bowls one after the other to the old mother, to emphasize the fact that there were in each bowl extra chopsticks, and she watched sharply lest the old mother forget and dip her own into the common dish. It was true it had taken a long time for the old mother to learn not to do this. All her life long as farmer's daughter and farmer's wife she had not seen it held unmannerly to put one's own chopsticks into the dish. No, her son and his wife were the only ones she knew who thought it so. They had come back together from foreign parts where doubtless the people were savage and filthy, and they had cried out in horror on the very first day when she had carefully and decently licked her chopsticks clean between her lips before she dipped them into the dish.

At first hearing their cry she had stared in astonishment, her chopsticks suspended above the bowl, and she said, "What? What?" There must be, she thought, something untoward in the dish, a shred of hair or cloth or a stick or something that even the best of cooks will drop sometimes, not knowing it, into the food as they cook it. But her son had cried out,

"You must use the extra chopsticks—you must not dip in with your own that you have had in your mouth!"

She was greatly outraged then, and she said with indignation,

"Do you think I have some vile disease, and are you afraid of me?"

When they had tried to explain about some sort of small things, too small even to be seen, but that pass from one person to another and carry illness, she sat stiff and unbelieving, and she said over and over as they told her,

"I do not believe I have these things on me. I have never seen worms on myself."

When they answered, "Ah, but they are too small to be seen!" she had said in triumph, "Then how do you know I have them on me if you can not see them?"

This she had thought victory, but her son had said as firmly as though he were his own father,

"There is no use in discussing this matter. I will not have these untidy ways in my house. I will not have it!"

The old mother was very hurt then and she sat in silence and ate nothing at all but her rice, refraining from every bowl of meat and vegetable, although she suffered cruelly in doing this, for all her life she had a good and hearty appetite for her food, and now that she was old her meals were her chiefest pleasure.

Nevertheless, she had had to submit. Once she even saw her son's wife do such a thing as this. The maid had brought into the room one night and placed upon the supper table a bowl of very hot melon soup, a dish the old mother loved, and she was overcome with pleasure at the sight. She forgot all else and she plunged her porcelain spoon into the soup and supped up the delicious brew and dipped her spoon in quickly for more. Instantly the son's wife had risen from her seat, and taking the soup she went to the open window and poured it out into the garden. There was the good soup gone!

When the old mother stammered in her astonishment, "But why—but why—" stammering and wondering, the son's wife pressed her thin lips together and answered very quietly,

"We do not care to drink after you."

Then the old mother grew angry. Yes, she had dared to be angry in those early days. She cried out stoutly,

"I shall not poison you, I daresay!"

But the son's wife had answered yet more quietly and very cruelly,

"You do not even use a toothbrush."

At this the old mother replied with great dignity,

"I have rinsed my mouth all my life in the way I was taught, when I rise in the morning and after every meal, and in my day we never considered that this was not enough."

At this her son said contemptuously,

"In your day! Do not speak of your day, if you please. It is such a day as yours that we must change altogether if this country is to be considered less than barbarous among other nations."

But the old mother had no idea what her son meant by such talk as this. At first when he made such remarks she had laughed in her big country way, and it seemed to her he was like a little boy talking high words he had heard somewhere and did not understand himself. But when she saw his cold patience with her and his gravity when she laughed at him, and when she saw the respect

that visitors to the house paid to him, and how they but
tolerated her for his sake, she ceased her laughing without
knowing she did, since it is very hard for one person to
laugh alone when there are only grave faces everywhere
about.

Yes, she had learned to eat in silence and to wait until she
was served. She did so now, and when she had eaten a bowl
of rice she rose silently and went to her own room across
the hall. But there at the door she paused. The truth was
that she was still hungry. Her years on the farm had made
her used to her three bowls of rice at least, and she felt
empty and weak with the one scanty bowl in her. They
had used big bowls on the farm, too, big blue and white
bowls of pottery, but her son had the little fine bowls city
people use. Yes, she was still very hungry. But she did not
dare to eat all she wanted lest her son say in his half-
sneering way, as he did sometimes,

"You eat what laborers do! I never heard of a lady who
ate like this. What do you do that you need so much as
this?"

Yet he did not begrudge her the food, that she knew. No,
how could he, since he earned every month for his teaching more than his father and mother had earned in a whole
year on the land? No, it was because he was ashamed of
her. She knew he was ashamed of her. When they invited
guests to dinners they made excuses to have her eat in her
own room. Well, at least she could eat as she liked there.

But now she was still hungry. She turned and crept noiselessly down the hall and out of the back door, across the
court, to the kitchen. She went in smiling timidly at the

servants, and she took a bowl and dipped some rice out of the half-emptied caldron where it was. Then she went to the table where the left-over foods were for the servants to eat. The dish of peppers was there also, but she did not dare to touch them, for there was but a little left, and the servants would not be pleased if she took it. She helped herself therefore only to some of the cabbage, of which there was plenty left. Then she went back to her room, not daring to glance at any of the maids as she went, and frightened lest she meet her son or his wife. As for the servants, she knew they did not like to share their food with her thus, but still they pitied her somewhat, too, and were tolerant of her, while they scorned her, taking her side against their exacting mistress.

Once in her own room the old mother closed the door softly and slipped the bolt. Then she sat down to enjoy the food. She ate it greedily to the last grain of rice, and rising, she washed the bowl and chopsticks in her wash basin, so that no extra trouble might be given the maids.

When she had eaten she went to a small tin box that stood among several others on her table and opened it and took out of it a little piece of cold rice. This she had saved from yesterday. Now she ate that also, munching it in her jaws. She kept all bits of food she could get in these little boxes lest she be hungry out of meal time. Then she sat down and picked her teeth with an old silver pin she wore in her hair.

After the old mother had sat thus awhile she rose and opened her door and peered out. She did this to see if either of the two children were about. She was afraid to call them to her since her son's wife did not like her children to come into their grandmother's room. She said, when the old mother reproached her for this,

"You never open your windows and the air in your room is unhealthy for them. You will keep those old musty clothes, and there are mice everywhere because of those bits of food you hoard."

"Those coats were my own mother's and far too good to be thrown away," answered the old mother. "One can not throw away good things, not clothing and food, surely! If you were as old as I am you would know that poverty comes suddenly, and when one does not expect it."

But to this the son's wife had only smiled her little chill smile. Nevertheless, she called to the children to come with her for some cause or other if she saw them go to the grand-mother's room. Therefore it became one of the pastimes of this old woman's life to leave her door open and see if she could entice one of the children to her. Besides, they were such dear little things, so fat and so fragrant. She loved to nuzzle her old nose into their little creased necks and make them laugh helplessly.

When these children were born she was very glad. She had always loved children, and although in her early youth she had married a poor man, a man who must earn their rice by extreme labor on the land, still she welcomed every child that came to her. Yes, even the girls she welcomed and she kept every one except the one her mother-in-law had commanded must not be saved because it was so poor a year and so without harvests that they did not know what death lay ahead for any of them. It was true that many had starved that year, and all had come too near it.

But to this day the old mother remembered with sorrow the little girl she had seen but the moment it was born, and never again, and she counted it as one among the four she had lost altogether. Yes, she counted it as one among the four the gods had taken from her.

Of her three children who had lived to grow up, this son was the only son left, for the eldest had died of a cholera eight years ago in the very midst of his manhood. The third was a daughter whom she never saw now, since the woman lived in another village than her old one, and was married to a poor man, and it is not to be expected that a daughter's husband will welcome his wife's mother when she has a son to care for her.

Therefore she had only this one son left, but she and her old husband had always considered him the finest they had. Yes, when this son was a baby he was the cleverest and the most willful child of all. From the first they had said to each other that they must give this child more than the others and make a scholar out of him, and so her husband had taken him to a foreigners' school in the nearest city when the boy was not more than ten years old, and they had left him there for ten years. This was because the learning was good enough there, and they did not mind, as some did, that he had to learn a foreign religion of some sort with his other books, because the tuition was very little, and after a year or so when the boy did very well, nothing at all. Yes, those foreigners gave him everything. At first the boy had come home for New Year holidays and in the summer, but after a few years he did not wish to do this, because he had become so fine a scholar he was not comfortable any more in the earthen country house. Well, those foreigners put it into his head even to go to other countries to study even more, and they gave him some money to help him, but not enough either. She remembered that very day when her son had come in unexpectedly and said to her and to his father while they were planting the rice in the water beds,

"Mother, I am going away to foreign parts to study more. The foreigners will give me some money, but not enough, and I want to ask you and my father for all you can give me, and in your old age I will care for you uncomplainingly."

At first it had seemed the wildest thing for him to do, but she and her husband had talked here and there with everyone about it, and there were many who said,

"We have heard that if men go to foreign parts they get such learning that when they return they make vast sums of money every month. If you let him go you will not need to work in your old age."

Yes, so they heard, and they let him go then, seeing that at that time they had their good elder son, who was a small shop-keeper in the nearest market town, and he did enough business to care for himself and his wife. They let this boy of theirs go without betrothing him, even, before he went, because he was so lordly and so willful with all his learning, and they so much more ignorant than he that they did not know how to force him nor even answer all his great talk.

Well, he had married himself in the new way that men

did nowadays, without asking his parents. He married himself while he was in that foreign country, not to be sure, to a foreigner, but she was the same as a foreigner, this pale, finicky woman who spread woolen cloth on her floors and hung cloth at her windows, and who would wash her children all over every day, as though such dear little things could be so dirty!

Well, when her son's return was yet two years off, her good old man died. A lusty, hearty old fellow he was, and yet he died all of a sudden one cold winter, and he died of a pain in his chest and a fever, and before she could call a doctor, thinking it would right itself and he unwilling to go to the expense. There he was, dead, and she had to pay for his coffin and his funeral, and there was nothing for it but to sell some of the land, because they had kept themselves so pinched to send money to the boy in foreign parts.

But she was a woman alone now, and she could not till all the land, anyway, and so she had sold a good big piece, and the old man had a good coffin. Yes, and she was glad she had bought him a new blue coat to lie dead in, and it was better than any coat he had ever worn in his life.

That very year in the autumn her elder son died, too, and since he had no children, his wife went back to her own people, and the old mother had no one left except that son in foreign parts. No, she had only him left, and so when he wrote for more money and he must have more money, she sold the land to the last foot and gave the silver to the foreigner to send to her son. Once an old neighbor said to her,

"It is better not to sell all your land, for even sons do not love so well a mother who brings them nothing."

But she was not afraid; she answered,

"He is a good son, and it is all his land anyway, now, and if he needs it, let him have it. As for me, I am not afraid. He has said he will care for me without complaining, and I am not afraid he will not have a place for me in his house." She laughed as she said this, for she was sure of her son.

But now she sighed as she thought of this answer. Well, here she was in her son's house. It was a very fine house. Every visitor who came exclaimed how fine a foreign house it was. There was a top floor above this one and a stair going to it, but they let her have this room on the lower floor because she could not climb the stairs, or if she did manage to get up somehow, she must be led down again. But when they wanted to be rid of her they took the children and went upstairs and sat there and left her alone. Oh, she knew them very well! Although they thought her so old that she did not see through them, yet she saw.

Suddenly the two children came, fresh and rosy from their sleep, into the room across the hall from her open door. She saw them sit down to play with a toy. Both of them were little girls. When the younger one was born the old mother had cried out to her son,

"This one should have been a male!"

But her son had replied very stiffly,

"We do not feel in this way any longer. In these times sons and daughters are equal."

The old mother laughed noiselessly and contemptuously

117

to herself as she thought of what her son had said. Yes, but suppose everyone gave birth to girls; who would father the next generation? There must be both male and female. Fools!

When she turned again, she saw the younger child looking at her, and she smiled at her. It was true that these were the sweetest children, and of the two she loved the baby better. She longed suddenly to hold the little round thing in her arms. Yes, she must have her old face there in that sweet soft spot beneath the baby's chin. She clucked softly and cautiously with her tongue to the child and the child stared back at her uncertainly. Then the old mother thought of something. She rose and went to one of her many little tin boxes and opened it. In it she found a little sweet nut cake that she had put there ten days or so before. It had a film of mold over it, but this she blew off and wiped the cake clean with her hands. Then she held it out silently to the baby.

The child looked at it and, having but newly learned to walk, she rose painstakingly and toddled to the old mother, holding out her hand for the cake. The old mother seized the little thing and gave her the cake and the child ate it gravely. The old mother closed the door, then, and sat down on her bed, the child in her arms, and she buried her wrinkled face in the little warm neck. She hugged the sweet morsel to her. Ah, little children—little children—

But they had already taught the children to hate her. Yes, for the older child, left alone, went and told her mother and suddenly the door opened and the son's wife came in swiftly and she said very gently, but with what cold, compelled gentleness,

"Mother, thank you, but it is time now for the child to go out into the garden." Then, seeing crumbs upon the child's red lips, she cried out, forgetting her gentleness, "What have you given her to eat?"

The old mother tried to answer boldly, for after all, how could a little sweet cake hurt anyone?

"It is only a little cake I had."

But the child's mother seized the child and pried her little jaws open.

"Nuts!" she said angrily. Then she pressed her own lips together and said no more, but she took the child in her arms and carried her away, and the child cried with fright.

The old mother sat down again in great indignation. She told herself that she had done nothing wrong—nothing at all wrong. Nevertheless, she had been so subdued by these four years that she felt a vague guiltiness within herself. She sat muttering in her room. Yes, a little small sweet cake such as all children love, and it is called a crime! Poor little things that must be fed on such pap as their mother gave them!

Then as she sat there muttering she heard a noise. At the door stood the elder child. The old mother forgot the cake and the trouble it had brought her, and she smiled and reached out her hand to the child. But the child shook her head and backed away from her and the old mother's hand dropped and she murmured in a whisper,

"They have taught you, too, haven't they?" And she smiled painfully.

119

But the child only stared at her half afraid, and sat down again to play, with her back to the old woman. Every now and again she turned and stole a glance at her grandmother.

Nevertheless, that night the younger child became ill. Whether it could have been the small nut cake or what it was, the child fell ill. The young mother tended the child through the night, and the son was sleepless also, but by the next morning the child was over the worst and could rest. The old mother when she heard this from a passing servant was much relieved, for she had been very much frightened by the bustle in the night. So therefore when she came into the dining-room for the morning meal and found only her son there, she said to him as she seated herself at the table,

"Ah, it was nothing serious, then! Children will have these little illnesses. I remember when you were small also—"

But he interrupted her. She saw at once that he had something to say to her, and that he was very pale and angry. Instantly she could not eat any more and she put down her chopsticks. She stared at him. She tried to remember that he was her son, and but a younger son, and she tried to remember him when he was a small, crying child, coming to find her breast. But she could not. It seemed to her he had always been what he was now, a very proud and learned man, dressed in these foreign clothes he wore, his gold spectacles on his nose. He was a merciless and unsmiling man, and she was desperately afraid of him. For a moment she even wished her daughter-in-law were there, for sometimes she stopped her husband when he spoke too harshly to his own mother.

But there were only the two of them, mother and son. He had even sent the maids from the room. . . . Would he kill her then—his old mother? . . . He was saying,

"I do not wish to be unjust, my mother. I know my duty and you have your place in my house. Nevertheless, if you are to be here, you must do as I say. You shall not spoil my children. I am responsible for my children. Yesterday in spite of all we have begged you before, and we have told you that you are not to give the children food, and particularly not any one of those stale bits you keep in your room as though we starved you—" He stopped an instant to control an old irritation. Then he went on very coldly. "In spite of our wishes you gave the younger child a thing she had never eaten in the best of times. Last night she was ill."

"It was a very small, good cake," muttered the old mother, still rebellious.

"But we have asked you to give her nothing," repeated the son firmly.

Suddenly the old mother gave way. She could not bear any more, and she began to weep aloud and to sob out as she wept.

"I shall go away! Oh, let me go away! I have no home here—I must go away!"

The son waited patiently until she grew a little quieter. Then he said,

"Mother, be reasonable. How can you go away? Where will you go in the whole world?"

"I can go to my daughter's house!" cried the old mother violently. "Yes, I will go and hire myself out to my daughter's husband. I am strong yet, and I can gather grass on the hills and pick up manure and look after the children and sweep the floor and burn the fuel in the oven. I could earn the little I eat!"

But the son smiled bitterly. "Do you think I have not thought of that?" he said. "Last year I wrote and offered them money, yes, so much a month if they would take you, because my wife felt it was so hard to have you here because you will not learn or adapt yourself to our house. They answered that, even so, it was more than they could do and that their house was full with their own children."

At this the old mother fell suddenly silent. It was true she had not really thought they would ever have her. But all these years it had been something to say. Yes, when she was angry at her son or his wife she would mutter to the servants behind their back, or to anyone who came to the house, or even to a vendor who was selling fish or vegetables at the kitchen door,

"I have a daughter who has land and I can go there if I do not like it here with my son and his wife!"

But now she knew she could never say this again. No, for if she did her son's eyes would fall on her with bitter knowledge. He had offered to pay out money to have his mother out of his house, and they would not have her, no, not though they were paid for it. She dropped her head and listened as her son went on.

"You see, my mother, my wife is an educated woman and you are but an ignorant country woman. I can say this since we are alone. It is right that my children should be reared in modern ways. I desire it so. My house can not be like the house you lived in. We will not spit on the floors and let the fowls run in and out, and my children can not eat this and that as your children did."

At this the last spark of rebellion rose in the old mother's heart and she cried out, feebly,

"Yet you are one of my children!"

The son said forcibly and plainly then, "I do not care to lose four out of seven of my children as you did."

At this the old mother drew herself up trembling and looked at him once more and cried out,

"Do you accuse me of killing my own children, then?"

The son said loudly, as though his patience were ended and he could not keep his voice quiet any more,

"I accuse you only of ignorance and of unwillingness to learn better!"

He rose, then. He had no more to say. Yes, he was going out and leaving her there alone with those last bitter words. She must stay him somehow. She shrieked after him in her old quavering voice,

"Well, I can die—at any rate, I can die! I can hang myself—"

Her son turned swiftly at that. He looked at her in great anger and he saw some sort of final courage and despair on that old face he knew so well.

"You say that to me!" he shouted in a sudden, towering rage. "You dare say that to me! You would disgrace me and have it known everywhere that my mother hung herself in my own house!"

He pressed a bell fixed in the wall and a maidservant came in. He strove to say in his usual voice, very cold and firm,

"My mother needs a maidservant of her own. There are signs she is failing in her mind. Hire a maid who shall not leave her day or night. I put this responsibility on you."

The maid bowed, and he went away.

It was not the first time the servants had heard high voices in this house and they could be heard even without listening at keyholes. They knew well enough what had happened today. But the maid was pleased to have it turn this way. She had often complained to her master and mistress that their old mother was more trouble than a child, and that there should be a special servant to care for her as children have. Therefore she was glad now and she had in mind a sister of hers who would be willing and pleased to have the work. But the old mother turned trembling and sobbing to the servant maid.

"He will not even let me die! I can not even die!" she wailed, and she went stumbling toward the servant as a child does who must go for comfort to anyone in its desperate need. But the servant led her to a seat and said briskly and carelessly, in haste to be away,

"There—there, Old Lady! You do not appreciate your son. He gives you shelter and food and clothes, and you really ought to try to be a little more—yes, yes, he is a very good, filial son. Everybody says so!"

THE FRILL

"MY dear, the only way to manage these native tailors is to be *firm!*"

Mrs. Lowe, the postmaster's wife, settled herself with some difficulty into the wicker rocking chair upon the wide veranda of her house. She was a large woman, red-faced from more food than necessary and little exercise over the ten-odd years she had spent in a port town on the China coast, and now as she looked at her caller and thus spoke her square, hard-fleshed face grew a little redder. Beside her stood a Chinese manservant, who had just announced in a mild voice,

"Tailor have come, missy."

Little Mrs. Newman looked at her hostess with vague admiration.

"I'm sure I wish I had your way with them, Adeline," she murmured, fanning herself slowly with a palm leaf fan that she had taken from a small wicker table at her elbow. She went on in a plaintive, complaining way, "Sometimes I think it is scarcely worth while to bother with new clothes, although they are so cheap here, especially if you buy the native silks. But it is so much trouble to have them made, and these tailors say—my dear, my tailor promises me faithfully he will make a dress in three days and then he doesn't come for a week or two! Robert says I look disgraceful and that my clothes aren't fit for a rummage sale, but I tell him if he only knew the trouble it is to get a native tailor to do anything and then the weird way they cut the sleeves—oh, dear!" Her weak voice dwindled and ended in a sigh and she fanned herself a trifle more quickly for a second or two and wiped the perspiration from her upper lip with her handkerchief.

"Watch me, now," said Mrs. Lowe commandingly. She had a deep firm voice and round hard gray eyes set a little near together beneath closely waved, dead brown hair. She turned these eyes upon the Chinese manservant as he stood looking down decorously at the floor, his head drooping slightly, and said, "Boy, talkee tailor come this side!"

"Yes, missy," murmured the servant, and disappeared.

Almost instantly there was the sound of soft steady footsteps through the open doors, and from the back of the house through the hall there came following the manservant the tailor. He was a tall man, taller than the servant, middle-aged, his face quiet with a sort of closed tranquillity. He wore a long robe of faded blue grasscloth, patched neatly at the elbows and very clean. Under his arm he carried a bundle wrapped in a white cloth. He bowed to the two white women and then squatting down put this bundle upon the floor of the veranda and untied its knots. Inside was a worn and frayed fashion book from some

American company and a half-finished dress of a spotted blue and white silk. This dress he shook out carefully and held up for Mrs. Lowe to see. From its generous propor- tions it could be seen that it was made for her. She sur- veyed it coldly and with hostility, searching its details.

Suddenly she spoke in a loud voice, "No wantchee that collar, tailor! I have talkee you wantchee frill—see, so fash- ion!" She turned the pages of the book rapidly to a section devoted to garments for ample women. "See, all same fashion this lady. What for you makee flat collar? No wantchee—no wantchee—take it away!"

Upon the tailor's calm patient face a perspiration broke forth. "Yes, missy," he said faintly. And then he pressed his lips together slightly and took a breath and began, "Missy, you first talkee frill, then you say no frill. Other day you say wantchee flat collar, frill too fat."

He looked imploringly at the white woman. But Mrs. Lowe waved him away with a fat, ringed hand and began to rock back and forth vigorously in her wicker chair. She raised her voice.

"No, you talkee lie, tailor," she cried sternly. "I know how I talkee. I never say I wantchee flat collar—never! No lady have flat collar now. What for you talkee so fashion?"

"Yes, missy," said the tailor. Then brightening somewhat he suggested, "Have more cloth, missy. Suppose I makee frill, never mind."

But Mrs. Lowe was not to be thus easily appeased. "Yes, never mind you, but you have spoil so much my cloth. What you think, I buy this cloth no money? Plenty money you make me lose." She rocked back and forth and fanned herself vigorously, her cheeks a dark purple. She turned to her guest. "I have been counting on that dress, Minnie, and now look at it! I wanted to wear it to the garden party at the consulate day after tomorrow. I told him a frill—just look at that silly collar!"

"Yes, I know. It's just what I was saying," said Mrs. Newman in her tired, peevish voice. "What I want to know is how will you manage it?"

"Oh, I'll manage it," replied Mrs. Lowe grimly.

She ignored the tailor for a while and stared out over her trim garden. In the hot sunshine a blue-coated coolie squatted over a border of zinnias, glittering in the September noon. A narrow, sanded path ran about a square of green lawn. She said nothing, and the tailor stood acutely uncomfortable, the dress still held delicately by the shoulders. A small trickle of perspiration ran down each side of his face. He wet his lips and began in a trembling voice,

"Missy wantchee try?"

"No, I do not," snapped Mrs. Lowe. "What for wantchee try? All wrong—collar all wrong—what for try?" She continued to stare out into the shining garden.

"Can makee all same frill," said the tailor eagerly, persuasively. "Yes, yes, missy, I makee all same you say. What time you want?"

"I want it tomorrow," replied the white woman in a loud, hard voice. "You bring tomorrow twelve o'clock. Suppose you no bring, then I no pay—savee? All time you talkee what time you bring and you never bring."

"Can do, missy," said the tailor quietly. He had begun now to fold the dress rapidly and neatly, his thin hands

moving with a sure delicacy. "I know, missy. I bring tomorrow, frill all finish, everything finish, very nice."

He squatted gracefully, folded the dress into the cloth
again and tied it tenderly, careful to crush nothing. Then
he rose and stood waiting, upon his face some agony of
supplication. His whole soul rose in this silent supplication,
so that it was written upon his quiet, high-cheeked face,
upon his close-set lips. Sweat broke out upon him afresh.
Even Mrs. Lowe could feel dimly that imploring soul. She
paused in her rocking and looked up.

"What is it?" she asked sharply. "What more thing?"

The tailor wet his lips again and spoke in a faint voice,
scarcely a whisper. "Missy, can you give me litty money—
one dollar, two dollar?" Before her outraged look his voice
dropped yet lower. "My brother's son he die today, I think.
He have three piecee baby, one woman—no money buy
coffin—no nothing—he very ill today—"

Mrs. Lowe looked at her caller. "Well, of all the nerve!"
she breathed, genuinely aghast. Mrs. Newman answered
her look.

"It's just what I said," she replied. "They are more
trouble than they are worth—and the way they *cut*—and
then they think about nothing but money!"

Mrs. Lowe turned her rolling gray eyes upon the tailor.
He did not look up but he wiped his lips furtively with
his sleeve. She stared at him an instant and then her voice
came forth filled with righteous anger. "No," she said.
"No. You finish dress all proper with frill, I pay you. No
finish dress, no pay. Never. You savee, tailor."

"Yes, missy," sighed the tailor. All vestige of hope had

129

now disappeared from his face. The atmosphere of supplication died away. A look of cold despair came over his face like a curtain. "I finish tomorrow twelve o'clock, missy," he said and turned away.

"See that you do," shouted Mrs. Lowe triumphantly after him and she watched his figure with contempt as it disappeared into the hall. Then she turned to her caller. "If I say tomorrow," she explained, "perhaps it will be ready by the day after." She thought of something and reaching forward in her chair pressed a bell firmly. The servant appeared. "Boy," she said, "look see tailor—see he no takee something."

Her loud voice penetrated into the house and the tailor's body, still visible at the end of the hall, straightened itself somewhat and then passed out of sight.

"You never can tell," said Mrs. Lowe. "You can't tell whether they are making up these stories or not. If they need money—but they always do need money. I never saw such people. They must make a lot, though, sewing for all these foreigners here in the port. But this tailor is worse than most. He is forever wanting money before his work is done. Three separate times he has come and said a child was dying or something. I don't believe a word of it. Probably smokes opium or gambles. They all gamble— you can't believe a word they say!"

"Oh, I know—" sighed Mrs. Newman, rising to depart. Mrs. Lowe rose also.

"After all, one simply has to be *firm*," she said again.

Outside the big white foreign house the tailor went silently and swiftly through the hot street. Well, he had asked her and she would not give him anything. After all his dread and fear of her refusal, all his summoning of courage, she would not give him anything. The dress was more than half done, except for the frill, too. She had given him the silk two days ago, and he had been glad because it would bring him in a few dollars for this nephew of his, who was like his own son, now that the gods had taken away his own little children, three of them. Yes, one by one he had seen his little children die, and he had not one left.

He had therefore clung the more to this only son of his dead younger brother, a young man apprenticed to an ironsmith, and he had three little children now too. Such a strong young man—who could have thought he would have been seized for death like this? Two months ago it was that the long piece of red-hot iron he was beating into the shape of a plowshare had slipped somehow from his pincers and had fallen upon his leg and foot and seared the flesh away almost to the bone. It had fallen on his naked flesh, for it was summer and the little shop was hot, and he had on only his thin cotton trousers rolled to his thighs.

Well, and they had tried every sort of ointment, but what ointment will grow sound flesh again, and what balm is there for such a wound? It was summer, too, when flies are everywhere and how much more do they gather about a festering open sore! The whole leg had swollen, and now on this hot day in the ninth moon the young man lay dying. There were black plasters on his leg from hip to foot, but they were of no avail.

Yes, the tailor had seen that for himself this morning when he went to see his nephew—he had seen death there plainly. The young wife sat weeping in the doorway of the one room that was their home, and the two elder children stared at her gravely, too stricken for play. The third was but a babe she held in her bosom. But this last day or two her milk was scanty and poisoned with her grief, and the child vomited it and wept with inner discomfort.

The tailor turned down an alleyway and into a door in a wall. He passed through a court filled with naked children screaming and quarreling and shouting at play. Above his head were stretched bamboo poles upon which were hung ragged garments washed in too scanty water and without any soap. Here about these courts a family lived in every room, and poured its waste into the court, so that even though it was a dry day and the days had been dry for a moon or more, yet the court was slimy and running with waste water. A strong, acrid smell of urine filled the air.

But he did not notice this. He passed through three more courts like the first and turned to an open door at the right and went into the dark, windowless room. There was a different odor here. It was the odor of dying, rotten flesh. The sound of a woman's wailing rose from beside the curtained bed, and thither the tailor went, his face not changed from the look it had borne away from the white woman's house. The young wife did not look up at his coming. She sat crouched on the ground beside the bed, and her face was wet with tears. Her long black hair had come uncoiled and stretched over her shoulder and hung to the earth. Over and over she moaned,

"Oh, my husband—oh, my man—I am left alone—
Oh, my husband—"

The babe lay on the ground beside her crying feebly
now and again. The two elder children sat close to their
mother, each of them holding fast to a corner of her coat.
They had been weeping too, but now they were silent, their
streaked faces upturned to look at their uncle.

But the tailor paid no heed to them now. He looked into
the hempen curtains of the bed and said gently,

"Are you still living, my son?"

The dying man turned his eyes with difficulty. He was
horribly swollen, his hands, his naked upper body, his
neck, his face. But these were nothing to the immense, log-
like swelling of his burned leg. It lay there so huge it
seemed he was attached to it, rather than it to him. His
glazed eyes fixed themselves upon his uncle. He opened his
puffed lips and after a long time and a mighty effort of
concentration his voice came forth in a hoarse whisper,

"These children—"

The tailor's face was suddenly convulsed with suffering.
He sat down upon the edge of the bed and began to speak
earnestly,

"You need not grieve for your children, my son. Die
peacefully. Your wife and your children shall come to my
house. They shall take the place of my own three. Your
wife shall be daughter to me and to my wife, and your
children shall be our grandchildren. Are you not my own
brother's son?—And he dead, too, and only I left, now!"

He began to weep quietly, and it could be seen that the
lines upon his face were set there by other hours of this

repressed, silent weeping, for as he wept his face hardly changed at all, only the tears rolled down his cheeks.

After a long time the dying man's voice came again with the same rending effort, as though he tore himself out of some heavy stupor to say what must be said,

"You—are poor—too—"

But the uncle answered quickly, bending towards the dying man, for the swollen eyes were now closed and he could not be sure he was heard, "You're not to worry. Rest your heart. I have work—these white women are always wanting new dresses. I have a silk dress now nearly finished for the postmaster's wife—nearly done, except for a frill, and then she will give me money for it, and perhaps more sewing. We shall do very well—"

But the young man made no further reply. He had gone into that stupor forever, and he could rouse himself no more.

Nevertheless, he still breathed slightly throughout that long hot day. The tailor rose once to place his bundle in a corner, and to remove his robe, and then he took his place again beside the dying man and remained immovable through the hours. The woman wailed on and on but at last she was exhausted and sat leaning against the end of the bed, her eyes closed, sobbing now and again softly. But the children grew used to it. They grew used even to their father's dying, and they ran out into the court to play. Once or twice a kindly neighbor woman came and put her head in at the door, and the last time she picked up the babe and carried him away, holding him to her own full breast to comfort him. Outside her voice could be heard shouting in cheerful pity,

"Well, his hour is come, and he is foul already as though he had been dead a month!"

So the hot day drew on at last to its end, and when twilight came the young man ceased breathing and was dead.

Only then did the tailor rise. He rose and put on his gown and took his bundle and he said to the crouching woman,

"He is dead. Have you any money at all?"

Then the young woman rose also and looked at him anxiously, smoothing the hair back from her face. It could now be seen that she was still very young, not more than twenty years of age, a young, common creature such as may be seen anywhere on any street in any day, neither pretty nor ugly, slight, and somewhat slovenly even on ordinary occasions and now unwashed for many days. Her grimy face was round, the mouth full and projecting, the eyes a little stupid. It was clear that she had lived from day to day, never foreseeing the catastrophe that had now befallen her. She looked at the tailor humbly and anxiously.

"We have nothing left," she said. "I pawned his clothes and my winter clothes and the table and stools and we have only that bed on which he lies."

The look of despair deepened on the man's face. "Is there anyone of whom you might borrow?" he asked.

She shook her head. "I do not know anyone except these people in the court. And what have they?" Then as the full terror of her position came upon her she cried out shrilly, "Uncle, we have no one but you in the world!"

135

"I know," he said simply. He looked once more at the bed. "Cover him," he said in a low voice. "Cover him against the flies."

He passed through the courts quickly then, and the neighbor woman, who was still holding the babe, bawled at him as he went, "Is he dead yet?"

"He is dead," said the tailor, and went through the gate into the street and turned to the west where his own home was.

It seemed to him that this was the most hot day of that whole summer. So is the ninth moon hot, sometimes, and so does summer often pass burning fiercely into autumn. The evening had brought no coolness and thunderous clouds towered over the city. The streets were filled with half-naked men and with women in thinnest garb, sitting upon little low bamboo couches they had moved out of their houses. Some lay flat upon the street on mats of reed or strips of woven matting. Children wailed everywhere and mothers fanned their babes wearily, dreading the night.

Through this crowd the tailor passed swiftly, his head bent down. He was now very weary, but still not hungry, although he had fasted the whole day. He could not eat—no, not even when he reached the one room in a court, which was his home, and he could not eat even when his poor stupid old wife, who could not keep her babies alive, came shuffling and panting out of the street and placed a bowl of cold rice gruel on the table for him to eat. There was that smell about his clothes—it filled his nostrils still. He thought suddenly of the silk dress. Suppose the white woman noticed the odor there! He rose suddenly and opened the bundle and shook out the dress, and turning it carefully inside out he hung it to air upon a decrepit dressmaker's form that stood by the bed.

But it could not hang there long. He must finish it and have the money. He took off his robe and his undershirt and his shoes and stockings and sat in his trousers. He must be careful in his heat that his sweat did not stain the dress. He found a gray towel and wrapped it about his head to catch the drops of sweat and put a rag upon the table on which to wipe his hands from time to time.

While he sewed swiftly, holding the silk very delicately in his thin fingers, not daring to hasten beyond what he was able to do well, either, lest she be not pleased, he pondered on what he could do. He had had an apprentice last year, but the times were so evil he had let the lad go, and so had now but his own ten fingers to use. But that was not altogether ill, either, because the lad had made so many mistakes and the white woman said so insistently, "You must makee yourself, tailor—no give small boy makee spoil—" Yes, but with just these ten fingers of his could he hope to make another dress in three days? Suppose she had another silk dress—that would be ten dollars for the two. He could buy a coffin for ten dollars down and the promise of more later.

But supposing she had no more work to give him now —then what could he do? What indeed, but go to a usurer. And yet that he did not dare to do. A man was lost if he went to a usurer, for the interest ran faster than a tiger upon him, double and triple in a few months what he had borrowed. Then when the coffin was buried he must bring the young wife and the three babies here. There was only this one room for them all, too. His heart warmed somewhat at the thought of the babies, and then stopped in terror at the thought that he must feed them.

He must find more work to do. Yes, there would be more work, doubtless. Surely the postmaster's wife would have more, another silk dress tomorrow for him, doubtless. She was so rich, living there in that big foreign house, set in a flower garden.

Midnight drew on and he was not finished. The worst of all was yet to be made—the frill. He fetched his fashion book and pored over it beneath the flickering light of the small tin kerosene lamp. So the frill went, here it turned, a long, wide frill, closely pleated. He folded the small pleats, his hands trembling with fatigue. His wife lay snoring in the bed now. Nothing would wake her, not even the rackety, noisy sewing machine with which he set fast the carefully basted frill. At dawn there remained but the edge to whip by hand and the irons to heat on the charcoal brazier. Well, he would sleep a little and rest his aching eyes, and then get up to finish it. He hung the dress upon the form, and then he lay down beside his wife and fell instantly into deep sleep.

But not for long could he sleep. At seven he rose and went to his work again and worked until nearly noon, stopping only for a mouthful of the food he could not eat the night before. Then he was finished. It had taken him longer than he hoped it would. He squinted up at the sun. Yes, he could just get to the house by noon. He must hasten. He must not make her angry so that she would perhaps refuse him the other dress because for the moment she was angry. No, somehow he must have the other dress. Then if he sewed this afternoon and tonight he could finish it in another day. He smelled the finished dress anxiously. A little odor, perhaps—would she notice it?

But fortunately she did not notice it. She was sitting in that strange, moving chair she had on the veranda, and she looked at the dress critically.

"All finish?" she asked in her loud, sudden way.

"Yes, missy," he answered humbly.

"All right, I go try."

She had gone into her room then, and he held his breath, waiting. Perhaps there was some odor to it yet? But she came back wearing the dress, a satisfied look upon her face; but not too satisfied.

"How much?" she said abruptly.

He hesitated. "Five dollar, missy, please." Then seeing her angry eyes he added hastily, "Silk dress, five dollar, please, missy. Any tailor five dollars."

"Too much—too much," she declared. "You spoil my cloth, too!" But she paid the money to him grudgingly, and he took it from her, delicately careful not to touch her hand.

"Thank you, missy," he said gently.

He dropped to his heels, and began to tie up his bundle, his fingers trembling. He must ask her now. But how could he? What would he do if she refused? He gathered his courage together desperately.

"Missy," he said, looking up humbly, but avoiding her eyes, "you have more dress I can do?"

He waited, hanging on her answer, staring into the shining garden. But she had already turned to go into the house again to take off the dress. She called back at him carelessly,

"No—no more! You makee too muchee trouble. You spoil my cloth—plenty more tailor more cheap and not so muchee trouble!"

The next day at the garden party she met little Mrs. Newman, sitting languidly in a wicker chair, watching white figures move about the lawn intent upon a game of croquet. Mrs. Newman's faded blue eyes brightened somewhat at the sight of the new dress.

"You really did get your dress after all," she said with faint interest. "I didn't think you really would. He did that frill nicely, didn't he?"

Mrs. Lowe looked down upon her large bosom. There the frill lay, beautifully pleated, perfectly ironed. She said with satisfaction, "Yes, it is nice, isn't it? I am glad I decided to have the frill, after all. And so cheap! My dear, with all this frill the dress cost only five dollars to be made—that's less than two dollars at home! What's that? Oh, yes, he brought it punctually at twelve, as I told him he must. It's as I said—you simply have to be firm with these native tailors!"

THE QUARREL

THE man stared angrily about the crowd in the little
street of the hamlet where his home was. There
his neighbors stood about him and about his wife,
a circle of some thirty or forty people, men and women,
their faces grave and listening. Little children, naked in the
summer heat, squeezed themselves restlessly through the
legs of their elders in order that they might reach the empty
spot in the center where the man and his wife stood, and
so miss nothing of the quarrel. The man would not look
at his weeping wife and he hung his head sullenly and so
saw these children, and seeing, saw one of his own among
them, a child of eight or nine years. Yes, and there were
his two younger ones, come also to see what was happening, and the three stared up at their parents in astonishment.

Suddenly the man could not bear it. There had been
enough else, his wife's tears and scolding all these days, her
hidden angers and suspicions which she would not speak.
The man gave a great bellow and darted at his third son
and cuffed him and roared at him,

"Get you home, you little dog!"

The child burst into loud wails and rubbed his shaven head and stood wailing, sure of sympathy from the crowd. The woman cried out then in the midst of her subdued weeping, turning her tear-wet face to this one and to that one among the crowd,

"You see how he is, neighbors—this is how he is nowadays!"

The crowd stared unblinkingly at the man and in perfect silence. They had listened to everything: to the woman's accusation, to the man's short answers, to the silences. But disapproval of him was now thick in the air, and the man felt it. He looked down at his bare horny feet, and began to scuff his toe back and forth slowly in the dust. The dust made him think of his dry fields, waiting for his watering. He muttered,

"There is all my work waiting for me and here am I wasting the good afternoon!"

This thought simmered in him awhile and suddenly his round dark face turned crimson and the veins stood out black on his temples. He lifted his head quickly and threw one furious look at his wife and he shouted at her,

"What is it you want, you bitch? Tell me and let me get back to the fields! How can I get money to feed you and all your—your—"

"You see how he is," the woman wailed. "You see how he speaks to me now! Two months ago he was the best and kindest man. Sisters, you have often heard me say how I was blessed by the gods in the man to whom I am given. Always has he put into my hand every penny he earned,

and he would come like a child and ask me for a bit to
shave his head with before a feast day or to game a little
with, or to buy some tobacco. And I was glad to give him
pleasure. Now these two months I have not had a penny
from him, no, not although he sold the rice, the last rice
we had, and sold it well, and he has not even told me what
he gained for it!"

She fell to louder weeping, her small brown wrinkled
face streaming with tears, and then she took up her blue
apron and flung it over her head and wept aloud.

Still the crowd was silent, and the children stared avidly.
The man's two younger children crept up to their mother,
and hiding their faces in her baggy blue cotton trousers
began to weep convulsively. In this silence and weeping the
man looked up cornerwise and as though unwillingly at a
certain door in the street.

Yes, there was someone standing there, a young girl in
a long green robe, such as young women in towns wore
these days, and her hair was cut short about her neck. She
had a sharp mischievous pretty face and she was smiling
a little as she listened to the quarrel, leaning against the
door frame with an indolent grace. Now when she caught
the man's stolen look she took a rounded comb out of her
shining black hair and passed it quickly through her bangs,
cut long to her clearly marked eyebrows.

But the man was looking down again. His face had
grown paler and he said in a smothered voice,

"I do not know why you want money all the time. There
is rice in the house and there is flour and there is bean oil
and we have cabbages in the garden."

The woman pulled the patched apron abruptly from her face and leaned towards him, her eyes dried with sudden anger. She put her little hard wrinkled hands on her narrow hips and leaned her thin hard little body from the waist and shouted at him shrilly,

"Yes, and is bare food clothing too? Are not the shoes gone from the children's feet? Look at me, neighbors— look at these patches on my coat. When have I ever had any new clothes? Three years ago he got the gains from that money club he belongs to—ten silver pieces he gained in his turn, and he bought two bolts of coarse white cloth of the strongest, cheapest sort, and I dyed it dark blue with these hands of mine and I cut him two suits and me one suit and the eldest boy a suit and we wear them still and I have patched and patched. Now I can patch no more— must I not have cloth even for patches? I have not shoes for my feet, and with my feet bound how can I go barefoot as the children do? Only this morning I asked him again for a little money to buy stuff for shoes, and what does he do? He cursed me and gave me naught, and he was even so angry he would not come home this noon, but went and bought some bread at the inn and all the good food going to waste that I had made for him! And he said he had no money, but he could go and buy bread to feed his anger against me—" Her anger broke into tears suddenly again. "It is not as if I asked him for money to buy a long robe such as some women wear these days. Oh, well I know he would have money to buy a long robe for some woman but not for his wife!"

At this a terrible look came over the man's face. He

leaped forward, his arm raised to strike the woman, but out of the crowd several stepped and caught his arm, and the women pulled his wife back. One of the men who held him said to him gently,

"Remember she is your wife and the mother of your children."

"I have borne him sons—I have borne him sons," wailed the wife in a low voice of agony.

At this moment a gentle voice was heard. It came from an old woman with a quiet wrinkled face, who had stood all this time on the edge of the crowd, a little apart from the others, and leaning upon her staff. Now she called out with concern,

"You two, you are no longer young. Li the First, you are forty and five years old. I know, for I was with your mother when you were born. Your wife is forty and four. I know for I was at the wedding and helped her from the bridal chair at your father's door. You have been married twenty-eight years, and you have had twelve children and there are seven of them left. Your eldest son would have been twenty and seven years old, had he lived, and you would have now been a grandfather and your wife grandmother. Your youngest child here is but three years old. Think of all these things and of all the years you have lived together upon your land and let there be peace between you now."

This the old woman spoke in a quavering clear old voice, and because she was the oldest woman in the hamlet and mother to the richest man, everybody respected her and listened to her while she spoke. When she had finished the man's wife was softened and she turned to the old woman and said with earnestness,

"Grandmother, you know I have always said my man was good—the best and kindest man. So was he ever until two months ago. Now see how he looks!" She turned her eyes on the man and all the eyes of the crowd turned to him also. The man's head drooped again and a slow dark crimson came creeping up out of his neck. "See how he looks, Grandmother! Ever the gentlest good man he was, and now always angry and sour! Yes, he can go out and smile and laugh and be merry before some, but when he comes home he is dark and silent and there is not a merry word in him and he never speaks except to blame me because my hair is not smooth or my coat not clean or some such thing wrong. And I have but this one coat to my body, and how can I be always clean? I have the house and the children and the work in the fields, and how can I sit as some women do and put powder on my skin to make it pale and oil on my hair to make it smooth?"

Suddenly the man could not bear it again. He shook himself restlessly, his strongly knit body straightening itself.

"I ask you, what is it you want of me?" he muttered thickly. "All this noise and talk over nothing—what do you want of me?"

"What do I want of you?" repeated the woman passionately. "I want this one thing. I want you to be to me as you have ever been until two months ago. That is all I ask. Your heart is changed—your heart is turned away from me! I ask but this one thing—be to me as you were!"

It was now as though the crowd were not there. There

were but the two, the man and the woman, solitary in a world beating with passion, the passion of the woman. She stretched out her little horny hands to him, hands swollen at the knuckles, the nails hard and black and split. "Oh, be to me as you were—be to me as you were!" she moaned.

A sigh went up from the crowd. The man wet his lips two or three times, quickly, and out from the edge of his stubbly black hair two small streams of perspiration began to trickle towards his jaws. He glanced again, secretly and unwillingly, at the door where the slender pale green figure leaned in the afternoon sunshine. The girl's robe was such a green as are young leaves newly full on fruit trees in spring, pale, but very pure and green. He would not look so high as her face. But he knew perfectly how her face was, her pale skin, the full red lips always smiling, her eyes black and fearless, never downcast or turned away from him. It was that look of hers that caught him whenever he passed by—he passed by often just for that look, although he never spoke one word to her. How could he speak since she was the granddaughter of the richest man in the hamlet and he but a farmer who did not even own his land but must have all he had from off the bit he rented? He had been saving these two months even for a long blue cotton gown such as most men have as a matter of course, and for a pair of white town-made stockings and a pair of town-made shoes.

When he thought of this bitter saving he set his heart against that wailing wife of his. Well, he had been faithful all these years. He was forty and five years old and he had never taken a bit of pleasure for himself, no, not once had he gone into a common pleasure house where even a poor man may go and for a little piece of silver take some joy and change. Day in and day out he had labored for his wife and for his children until now he was forty and five years old, and he had but one old robe to his body and never anything else but these old patched clothes for his labor.

Yet there was this one thing that troubled him. Did she look at all men like that, with her eyes so wide open and lingering, or was it only at him? This was what had kept him uneasy all these days and nights. How could he know if she only looked at him like this? Every time he passed the door he stole his glance at her and every time she gave him back the look, so free, so bold. He had heard men talking together sometimes as men will and he had heard them say that nowadays women were changed, fearless of any man they were, taking anyone they chose, free and enticing in all they did.

He wet his lips again and felt the perspiration down his neck. How could he know if she looked at all men so, or was the look saved and for him? Somehow he must know the truth.

"Oh, be to me as you were!" his wife whispered brokenly, and she lifted the corner of her apron to her eyes and wiped them, her anger gone from her utterly, and only agony left.

He lifted his head suddenly and looked full at the doorway. Must he not know the truth?

The whole crowd looked with him. When they saw his head lift and his eyes turn thither, they lifted their heads and looked. There the girl stood in the doorway, preening herself. She had the little white comb of bone in her hand, and her fair arm was upraised, and she smoothed back the glistening black hair from her little pale ears, where gold rings hung. The women stared at her with hostility. "That long robe like a man's—" some woman muttered suddenly. But every man looked at her in silence and in secret wonder.

Now the old lady at the edge of the crowd when she saw them all looking, she looked, too, and with astonishment. This girl to her was but her great-granddaughter and a naughty child whose town parents had spoiled her. Had she not said a score of times to her son how the child had been spoiled until she was fit for no man to wed, and that she pitied the man to whom she was betrothed? But now she stared with increasing sharpness at this girl. For the first time she saw the pretty pettish face, lit with secret wantonness and mischief, turned to someone in the crowd. The dry red came up into the old lady's wrinkled cheeks. She thumped her way to the door, her stick knocking on the cobblestones, and stared in the direction of the girl's gaze. That gaze fell straight as any beam upon a young man who hung about the door. At first he had been in the crowd, listening to the quarrel, but now he had turned his back upon it and was staring at the girl, his sheepish eyes half shamed, too, his jaw hanging, a little water at the corner of his mouth.

The old lady thumped her stick hard upon the stones. She knew that lad, son to the innkeeper who owned no land and was but a sort of public servant.

"Get you into the house, you shameless, wicked child!"

she cried suddenly, her voice very shrill and cracked, but full of such anger and authority that the girl, pouting a little, turned half away. "Into the house, I say!" the old lady cried again, lifting her staff so menacingly that the girl slipped within the shadow of the door.

But her little hand was still on the lintel, a little slender pale hand, with a gold ring on the tiny last finger. The old lady went up and struck this hand sharply and it was withdrawn into the shadow also.

"Never have I seen such a maid as this," the old lady shouted, still shrill. "Standing at the door, a betrothed maid, and staring at any man who passes! So they tell me all maids do nowadays, and what the world is coming to I swear I do not know!"

In the crowd the passion died away softly. The wife smiled a little, somehow comforted, the women were less sullen, and the men looked obliquely here and there and cast their eyes at sky or field or spat in the street's dust. A child cried and the crowd moved apart and made ready to scatter, its interest gone. Only the innkeeper's son stood still bemused, staring at the empty door.

But he was not the only one to have seen that beam-like look. The man had seen it and his wife also. Out of the man's face had ebbed every drop of blood, leaving him yellow as a sere leaf. He stood looking down into the dust. Now he knew.

But the old lady was not finished. She understood everything suddenly and she was not finished. She turned and shook her stick slightly at the man and pointed it at him.

"Li the First," she said firmly, "you are a fool. Go back

to your fields. But first give your wife that money you have in your girdle."

Slowly the man fumbled in his belt and brought forth four pieces of silver. He did not turn his head but he held the silver in his outstretched hand. Then his wife put forth her hand until he felt beneath his finger tips the hard dry palm of his wife's hand. He dropped the money there and with it all his dreams.

Then he straightened himself quickly and looked about the parting crowd, his face a little bleak, but serene again, and he spoke in his rough and usual voice,

"I do not know why my woman has made all this quarrel," he said. "All she needed to do was to tell me for what she wanted the money. As she says herself, I have ever given to her all I had."

He stooped and picked up again the hoe he had thrown upon the ground when he was called there, and shouldering it he went, without once turning back his head, to his own life once more.

REPATRIATED

—⚬—

"YOU—you— What are you—" Mathilde ground the words through her teeth. She had opened the door of the bedroom an inch or two, and she stared into the main room of the little apartment where she and Cheng had lived during the three years since they came from France to this city on the coast of China.

There he sat,—Cheng, her husband,—his black hair glistening under the strong uncovered electric light that hung above the table, his immaculate, slender shape sharply defined in the dark blue Western garments he wore, his hands moving pale and swift among the bamboo gaming-pieces. Beside him sat his younger brother who was a student at the Government university and so must live with them. He was a gangling adolescent whom Mathilde despised. Now she despised him more than ever as he sat slouched in his wrinkled silk robe. Whatever he wore seemed wrinkled almost before he put it on—he was like that—and a long black oily lock of hair was forever falling into his eyes. And there were those other two, those men who lived upstairs in that apartment—those two who seemed never to have any work to do—what were they, those two? They had sat here gambling, these four men! She had lain in the bed waiting for her husband, tossing on the wide brass bed around which Cheng would have heavy curtains hung in the Chinese fashion. She had lain awake, growing more furious every hour, listening to the gaming, until this moment when the clacking of the pieces shuffled together broke out afresh.

A moment ago the noise had stopped and she held herself taut in the silence. Let him come now—and she would not say anything before the others! No, she would be just, she would be calm—for once as calm as he would be. Let him come and she would wait until he had placed himself beside her. Heaven! If she spoke to her own husband when they were alone in the night, who could blame her? Had she not heard her own *maman* speak so to her papa in the night also? And Papa as good a man as ever drew breath in Lyons, or even in the whole of France, who never looked at gaming and whose only freedom was a little wine-drinking with his comrades!

No, she would begin mildly but firmly, reasonably, as good wives do when they upbraid their husbands a little for a fault. She would say as she had said before, only now she would not be angry,

"Cheng, I have borne this gaming long enough. You see, it is thus: you game all night and when morning comes you will not be fit to go to your office. Then what must be the result? You will lose your position—and what shall we eat then?"

And then he would doubtless answer, as he always did,

in his quiet way, "But no one comes to the office at the hour. Why should I be first? Besides my chief is my father's friend, and he would not break friendship with my father and dismiss me. Besides also you seem never able to understand, my Mathilde, that to game is not to sin, and I cannot refuse my friends, especially when they come to my own house to amuse me. One cannot refuse friends—not in a civilized country, Mathilde. Moreover, when I game, I do not lose—more often I win." All this he would say in his careful student French, not looking at her but at his hands while he spoke—his beautiful hands that were the color of pale amber. He spoke French very well. He had, indeed, been a student in Lyons when first they met and fell in love, and he had come to her papa's *patisserie* to buy the little cakes he ate with his wine. He spoke French so well, indeed, that she had not troubled herself to learn Chinese. In fact, she despised Chinese. When she heard the Chinese speaking together she would hug her arms about herself and say scornfully, sometimes even aloud, if she felt inclined,—she was afraid of no one, not of these Chinese, above all,—yes, she would say,

"What a language it is! The devil himself would not speak it!"

So she had listened, taut upon her bed, her blonde head thrown back, her gray eyes staring into the red-flowered curtains, her short, blunt hands clenched in the soft stuff of her kimono. There was a burst of laughter. She heard her husband's low, smooth voice. There was laughter again. What had he said? This was the only reason she wished she knew Chinese, that she might understand these low speeches of his which were always followed with such laughter. When she asked him afterward what he said, he answered in the smooth half-careless way he had when he spoke to her,

"You would not understand, my Mathilde—a pun—you would need to have studied our literature before you could understand."

"But I am not a fool, Cheng!" she would cry. "I can understand if you will tell me. You never trouble yourself to explain anything to me."

He smiled then; he smiled very often at her. If the mood were on him he would take her hand and pull her to him and whisper, coaxing her, "Pretty little foreigner—pretty little white thing—"

Were they beginning again? Again his voice, again the laughter, again the clack of the gaming-pieces. She had leaped from the bed, her silk kimono stretched about her small plump body, her short hair tousled. She had thrust her little white face into the crack of the door and sent the hiss through at them.

But the gaming did not stop. Her husband glanced up and smiled, and shrugged slightly his slender, sharply defined shoulders. The sallow young brother bent his head lower, as though to see the game. The other two men did not look, they made no sign, but her shrewd eyes saw a change in their faces. Ah, well, then they might see if she cared what they thought of her, or if they pitied her husband! They might see if she were afraid of them at all! No, she was not afraid, although she was the only white woman in this house or in this street or even in this whole quarter of the Chinese city! These Chinese, these—these *canaille*—even though she were afraid, she would never show it—show she was afraid, and she was lost among them! No, she had her temper and she had her good sharp tongue, and she could make them understand well enough, though she could not speak their devil's tongue! No, and she did not care how loudly she let her voice come out, even though Cheng hated her to shout; he always said, shrinking a little from the noise, "Only vulgar women shout." Yet one must keep them afraid—it was the only way for her to be safe!

"Bah!" she cried loudly, and darted suddenly into the room. Now she faced them, screaming at them, her hair falling into her eyes, trembling as she clutched her kimono to her little full bosom. Her words poured from her, streaming out in the slight *patois* of her class, "Ah-ha, you Chinese—you think I am afraid? Is this my house, I ask you? Yes, I tell you it is my house! It is my house, and I will not have you in it, you Chinese dogs! Out—out! Shall I lie awake night after night because you wish to gamble here upon my table? Gamble, but not in my house! I forbid it! Never, I say, never once more!"

She darted at them again and with her sturdy outspread hands she swept the table clean. The bamboo pieces clattered to the floor. The men sat motionless, but her husband cried in a low shamed voice, "Mathilde!"

She did not heed him. Her kimono flew wide now from her thin nightgown, but she cared for nothing. She kicked the pieces upon the floor with her bare feet.

"Have a care, Mathilde!" said her husband. But he did

not rise or look at her. He sat with his hands locked together tightly upon the table, and he looked at his hands. The young brother pushed back the hair restlessly from his forehead and ran his tongue over his full pale lips. There was nothing but silence. That silence she could not bear. She snapped her fingers loudly and cried again,

"Ha—you think I am afraid—I, a Frenchwoman?"

She seized the porcelain teapot in both hands and crashed it to the floor and after it the tea-bowls, one by one. Then she stood panting, staring from one still, yellow face to the other. At last she let her eyes rest upon her husband. But he did not look at her; he sat staring at his hands that were tightly locked together upon the table before him. His face was graven and his thin lips were pressed tightly together.

Now the two guests rose suddenly, murmuring a few words to their host. The woman they ignored as though she had been a petulant child. Delicately they stepped over the stream of tea upon the floor, careful lest they soil their black velvet shoes, and the edges of their dark satin robes. They went to the door, and their host rose quickly and followed them. He smiled a little piteously, his face strained, his eyes seeking their comprehension. It was as though he besought them, as though he said, "Women are so at best; and foreign women—"

Even Mathilde, watching him, perceived that if he spoke he would have spoken thus. Perhaps if she had not been there he would have spoken thus. Her anger burned in her, hot and sore.

But suddenly she forgot him, for as he opened the door she saw figures standing there—it was that woman from the next apartment, that woman from Shanghai. She was always there when the door opened, it seemed, but she would never come in unless Cheng were at home. Yes, and the two talked together, Cheng and this woman, and Mathilde could not understand and he would never tell her what they said. If she asked—and she always asked—he answered, "Nothing—it was nothing; it is not worth telling again."

There the woman stood now, her sleek black head shining under the bright bare hall light, her smooth long face painted as carefully as though— Yes, without doubt she was a wicked woman! There was a young man with her now as she stood wrapped in her long black velvet cape, a young man pale-skinned and long-haired, and the two of them stared into the room at the broken teapot and the broken bowls, and they smiled a little, and the woman murmured a question, her painted brows uplifted.

Mathilde watched her husband. He shrugged delicately, one eyebrow moved, and he began to answer, his lips twisted in a bitter smile. But this Mathilde could not bear. At this moment she could not bear these two to speak together in the language she had never learned. She flew forward and crashed the door shut between them and she turned to face her husband.

She was not afraid of him, she told herself, and she stood panting a little, looking at him. She was not afraid of him and yet she always watched to see what he would do when she let her temper out as she had done tonight. It seemed to her now that he must punish her somehow.

But he ignored her again. He turned, without meeting her eyes and stooping in his quick and graceful way he began to pick up the pieces of broken china, holding them firmly as he piled them and yet seeming scarcely to touch them. Then he opened a window and dropped them into the darkness. She could hear the faint crash as they fell on the heap of broken brick left from building the house and which had never been cleared away.

Then he turned to his younger brother, who had risen and stood hesitatingly by the table. "Fetch me a towel," he said, very quietly.

The young man returned with a gray towel. Cheng took it, and in silence he stooped to mop the spilled tea.

"Let me, brother," said the youth suddenly and with sympathy, his voice almost a whisper.

Mathilde watched them with sullen interest, her back still against the door. Let them, then, let them wipe it away and suffer a little, too. But she had scarcely made the thought when she seized the cloth away from the brother-in-law's hands. No, she would not have Cheng's brother sorry for him!

"Go to bed!" she said harshly. Her husband said something in a low tone to the youth. She did not understand him. Well, then, and what did she care if she could not understand? She wiped the floor savagely and when it was clean she began to pick up the bamboo pieces, fitting them into the polished wooden box with trembling hands. The room was very quiet. She looked up suddenly. She was alone. The brother-in-law was gone. Through the open door she could see her husband preparing himself for bed. He had taken off his coat and collar and she saw his slender, erect back, the smooth nape of his neck where the black shining hair met the golden skin. A faint stir rose in her heart; the tears rushed into her eyes, tears half of dying anger and half of a strange shame. Why should she be ashamed? She would not be ashamed. She had borne more than any woman could bear. She must bear no more; she must keep them afraid. She had not a friend—nowhere a friend. The tears began to run down her cheeks. But she wiped them away with energy upon the sleeve of her kimono and she closed the box and set it upon the narrow mantelpiece.

When she parted the curtains of the bed he was asleep. But she could never tell if he really slept. He could seem to be asleep when he was not, his slender body relaxed, his breathing even. She saw him lying so now upon the hard Chinese pillow beside her soft one. His breath came and went, sighing through his slightly parted lips. The light fell upon his smooth oval face, still and pure and waxen. He looked very young. Though he was five years older than she, he looked younger. Her body was more square than his, her face more ruggedly shaped. She knew this, and looking down upon his calm face she told herself she did not love him any more.

And now this very calmness infuriated her. She could not bear his eternal calmness. She had never broken through it, never. No weeping, no temper, no power that she had could break through it. Even when his mood was on him, when for a time he loved her, even passion could not break through this calmness. She shook his shoulder violently. He woke as though from a dream, saw her, smiled a little, and closed his eyes again.

"You shall not sleep!" she whispered intensely, shaking him again. "All these hours you have made me stay awake —and you shall not sleep either, until we come to an understanding! You hear me, Cheng? I say we shall understand each other!"

He woke then, so completely that she was sure he had not slept at all. He had been deceiving her—and her heart grew more hard. Yet he always waked like this, suddenly and completely.

"Can we ever understand each other?" he asked gravely, his eyes narrow and shining black between their lids.

"What do you mean?" she asked quickly.

"I mean," he answered slowly, "I mean only that men and women can never understand each other—never, except when they draw near at the moment of passion, and how short a moment it must be!"

He glanced at her and suddenly he sighed and rubbed his hand over his face, his slight hand that always shamed her somehow because it was narrower and more feminine than her own. She struggled with her direct *bourgeoise* mind to understand what he meant. Now why did he look at her so and why did he sigh? Whenever he spoke in that smooth learned way she did not know what he meant. If he would only be angry with her sometimes,—simple and angry as men ought to be with their wives,—if the temper would fly out of him honest and hot and frank, if he would sometimes even beat her, she could understand him. Men in her street in Lyons did sometimes beat their wives. Her own father had often threatened it. If she had married that big Pierre who worked in her father's *patisserie* he would have beaten her, she very well knew, if she had thrown the dishes on the floor and broken them in a temper. Yes, he would have put out his great arm and seized her and held her fast and slapped her well, if she had shamed him so before his friends. That would have been to be married to a man, then!

But this—this one—he was never angry like a man. He only spoke gently, half smiling, or he sighed like this and turned away; and she could not understand him, though the words seemed plain enough. If she grew angry at last, he bore it as though her tempers might be some illness she could not help and which had nothing to do with him.

"You are vile!" she cried loudly. "All you Chinese are vile! You think women are for nothing but your—your—for when you need them. You never think of me, never, when the moment is gone!"

He smiled bitterly without looking at her and lifted his eyebrows.

"How well you understand me, after all!" he murmured.

She paused again, baffled. What did he mean now? Ah, just how could she hurt him?

She sat down on the bed and pushed back her rough hair.

"You have deceived me," she said heavily, staring down at him. "In Lyons you told me many lies. I asked you, 'What is your China like?' You told me, like France, but better and more beautiful. Yes, you said this the night I ran secretly out of my papa's house to meet you, and we sat in the park behind a tree. I was only eighteen and I believed you! We sat in that beautiful park, and we looked at the streets through the plane trees, and the comfortable kind people came and went. And you said, 'My country is like

163

France, but more beautiful and the people are more kind. There is everything in my country. There are pagodas and there are great handsome buildings. You will lack nothing. You need never do any work again. There are servants to do everything for you. I can give you what that Pierre will never be able to give you all his life long working in that little shop of your father's. In my house you shall be a great lady, living as you please. You shall have everything!' Yes, Cheng, you told me this, 'I will give you everything!' But—"

She thrust out her hands and shrugged herself violently. "I ask you, Cheng, where is this *everything?* There is nothing here—nothing, nothing! These small filthy streets—the beggars—these filthy crowds who screech at me and laugh and call me 'foreign devil'—yes, and I have been spat upon, *I!* And I cannot buy myself a hat or a little dress or shoes—there are no shops that can be called shops; there is not a theater, for I will not call that shrieking place where you go, a theater—I do not know what that place is. And that one old pagoda—crumbling to pieces, and what is there beautiful in it? And look at my house! I am ashamed to write *Maman* that for a house I have four little cupboards and for a kitchen a little stinking smoky hole! You said I should have servants, many servants. Where are they? I ask you, do you think this is a servant, this old fool of a countrywoman who will not learn of me, who does not yet know how a *ragout* is made, and who will not even listen to what I say without looking at you to see if it is to be done? No, I know you will say again that she does not understand me, but she does very well understand, if she likes! You have lied to me, you have lied to me!"

She burst into noisy weeping. "You never told me that I must have that dirty brother of yours here; no, nor that so much of your wage must go to your father and to your old uncle—but I spit at that uncle of yours! If he comes again as he did once and seeks to live here in my house and smoke his vile opium pipe, I will throw him out of the window with my own hands! I can do it! I am not afraid of any of you! I despise you all—I am a Frenchwoman!"

"That is where you are mistaken," said her husband suddenly. He sat up in bed and looked at her now with earnestness. "It is because you are forever saying to yourself, Mathilde, that you are a Frenchwoman, that you are unhappy. The truth is you are Chinese now: you are Chinese because your husband is Chinese, and you can only be happy if you will forget you have been French—"

"No—no—no!" she shrieked, shaking her head.

"You must, indeed," he said with fresh gravity. "As for deceiving you, remember you have never been willing to go and see what my home is. It *is* beautiful. My father was once a wealthy mandarin. We are poorer than we once were, as who is not in these times? It is right for me to send him money now, and to help my younger brother. But our city is set in the hills of Hunan, and in our home there are a hundred courts. Our house is older and more beautiful than anything in Lyons. Do you think it can compare with that poor house of your father's, or with the workingman's house that must have been yours if you had married that Pierre you will not forget?"

He leaned forward in his earnestness, and when she drew back from him, shaking her head, he cried out more passionately than she had ever heard him, "Ah, I know you do not forget him! But do you think I do not know I have married beneath me? I know it very well. I knew it even when for a while I was a fool over your fair skin. You are the daughter of a little shopkeeper; I am the son of a viceroy. Your father reads the newspaper and is content. My father is a poet and a scholar. If you were willing, you could go to my home and see such beauty as you have never seen. But you will not go. You are determined to stay here in this coast city, in this hideous foreign house. You will have everything as you have been accustomed; you even try to make me into a Frenchman—you keep me in the garments of your people, you make me speak your tongue, lest haply you perceive that you are married to what I am proud to be—a Chinese!"

She listened against her will, frightened, for she had never seen him like this. She had broken through the calmness she had hated, and now she was dismayed. She listened unwillingly, struggling to find a foothold for herself in his quick, even-flowing speech. When he spoke of his home she remembered her old grudge, and forgot everything else.

"No," she said quickly. "No, I will never go to your home, never! How do I know you are not deceiving me again? I see no houses anywhere such as you say there are. Besides, even though there were a hundred courts, it would still be my prison. I should be the only white woman

166

there. No one would speak my language. There would be a thousand miles between me and the sea. No—no—I must live on the sea so that I may know France is just over on the other side from me!"

"You do not trust me," he said. He lay back on his pillow again. He drew the quilt to his throat and lay looking up into the curtains, his face once more a mask.

But she cried out most passionately, "You are not of my blood—how do I know you will always treat me well? I do not know what you are!"

"You do not trust me," he repeated, and he turned his face to the wall and closed his eyes and would speak no more.

She began to weep again, and after a while she laid herself down beside him, exhausted. But she did not touch him. Soon she was not there. A sea rolled between them, and her whole heart had sped across it to France.

"Never!" she whispered with soundless passion into the night. "Never! I am French—I am French!"

Did not the very law also recognize that she was French? Yes, she knew that. She could never forget the first night she had learned it, and how she put the knowledge in her heart and kept it. It was that night of the dinner her husband's chief gave to his secretaries and their wives, and among these there was another white woman, a Frenchwoman also. But she was older, very sophisticated, a Parisian of the world, one could see. She had laughed at Mathilde's little short figure in the childish pink dress.

"What an infant!" she had murmured. Mathilde had not known what to say to her.

She had smoked many cigarettes, that Parisian, and she had laughed with the Chinese men and drunk with them and danced with them, so that the silent Chinese wives along the wall sat speechless and enraged, watching her half-naked body as it writhed and turned in their husbands' arms. But once more the Parisian had come deliberately to where Mathilde sat among the wives, speechless also, for she did not even know the English that some of them did. The Parisian had laughed and said,

"So you are Su Cheng's little French wife? How old are you—twenty, perhaps? What a child!"

Then she had begun to speak lazily, smoking her cigarette and dropping one to light another, "I also—I am married to the chief secretary in the bureau. My third marriage, child! I was dying of ennui—I said, it will be amusing perhaps for a while to be married to a Chinese.—So then, it is very amusing. I find it amusing for the time. Do you not also, child?" She rose to meet a polished young Chinese in shining evening garb. She laid her hand upon his arm, gave herself to his embrace, and then turned to say again to Mathilde, "But never forget, child, if it ever ceases to be amusing for us—and is there anything that does not cease to be amusing?—then we may go to the consul. France repatriates us when we are no longer amused with our Chinese husbands!"

She glided away, smiling at Mathilde, not seeming to see any of the Chinese women who stared after her. One of them, a young creature lovely as a water-lily in pale green satin, sighed and gazed with wistfulness at the Parisian woman. She turned and laid the painted tip of her finger upon Mathilde's arm and asked a pleading question. But Mathilde drew away and shook her head. She did not understand.

But this one thing she had not forgotten, although she had never seen the Parisian again: *"France repatriates us."*

"So I could never leave the coast," she thought to herself, beginning to tremble a little in the bed as she lay. "It would be to cut myself off forever from my France, from my *maman,* my papa—from them all. How could I ever get to the coast and to the consul, if I went inland so far? It is a thousand miles!"

And after a while, lying in the darkness alone, the sea rolling between her and that other body, silent and alien, she suddenly confessed to herself what she had never confessed before. "The truth is, I am afraid. I am afraid of these yellow people. When I go out, I am afraid of them all. I have no friend anywhere. I want to go home.—I am afraid, even of *him!"*

She planned carefully when she would tell him. She would not, after all, run away—as she had thought she would. At first in the night she had thought she would simply go to the consul and tell him she wanted to be repatriated—that is, to return to her France. Then she would go away secretly. When Cheng came home one day she would be gone and there would be the end of it.

Then he could do as he liked. His old uncle might come and live here and smoke and cough and be as dirty as he liked. Cheng could gamble also, since he loved his friends so well he could not refuse them. Or he and his brother could go home. No, but would Cheng go home? There was the woman in the other apartment—would she let him go home? She was bold—not a serious woman; she had lovers, and deceived her husband. All those Shanghai women did that—made rich old men love them and divorce their plain old wives to marry them. That woman looked at Cheng as a woman looks at a man she would like to make her lover. She, Mathilde, had never had a lover, but she knew. Any woman knows. If such a thing were to be, could she go?

Yes, she could and would go, nevertheless! What did she care what happened here when she was safe in the snug little house in Lyons again? They would be so happy to see her, Papa and *Maman* and her little brother. Was she not the only daughter? There was also the good Pierre. Later, perhaps, if she married Pierre, she would be so safe and happy, so busy going about the safe and beautiful streets, into the nice little shops, greeting her friends everywhere. She would cry to them all, "But it was impossible, *chérie!* You were so right! No Frenchwoman—" What would she care then what happened here?

So across the breakfast-table she looked at Cheng. The old slatternly serving-woman had pattered in and set the food down upon the table and gone out again. Mathilde, looking at Cheng, decided suddenly that she would tell him now, after all. Then she would know the worst he could do.

"I am going to my country," she said loudly. "I cannot live here any more. I want to go home."

Cheng stopped in his delicate, half-hearted eating and

glanced at her. He averted his eyes and began to eat again. She waited.

"It is not the first time you have said this," he answered at last, without apparent interest. She continued to stare at him steadily. It was true she had said these same words at other times when she had been angry. But she had not meant them as she meant them today. Today she was not angry. She said quickly, in the same loud tone,

"This time I mean it. I am going next week."

He did not look up. He stirred his chopsticks lightly in a bowl to find the bit of salt fish he liked. "I have not the money to spare you now," he said, speaking with effort. "It is an expensive journey. Later, I hope to be able to give you the money so that you may visit your parents again. I may even go with you. At present you must remember we are in hard times. I cannot."

He rose, and taking a cup of water he rinsed his mouth in the Chinese fashion she hated. She hated everything he did, she thought sullenly, watching him. He seated himself and picked up a small book of soft paper from the bookcase in the corner of the room. He began to read the Chinese letters, and now a faint interest showed in his face. But she knew this interest had nothing to do with her. She watched him heavily. Now she remembered something her father had said when first he found out his daughter was in love with an Oriental. Then she had not understood, but now, all at once, she understood.

"The flesh," he had muttered, looking away from her, "the flesh crawls—"

She remembered this, and she remembered that Pierre,

whose voice was always deep, had said in the strangest high voice, "He will kiss you—Mathilde, how will you bear it?"

But after all, Cheng did not kiss her. It was not the custom of his race. It remained that Pierre was the only man who had ever kissed her. Once he had kissed her when she was sixteen and they were together at a party at the New Year. He had pulled her behind a door and kissed her suddenly and hard. But soon she had forgotten it, because Cheng had come and he was so beautiful to her.

Yes, she had loved Cheng's body well, for a time. It was smooth. It was golden. In Lyons he had always been immaculate, always perfectly groomed, his hands fragrant, his hair polished into smoothness. In those days he was all that Pierre, stocky and red-faced, could never be. There had been nothing about Cheng then to turn a woman's flesh.

Yet when they had come back to his own country how quickly he had slipped into being someone else! He ate in the way they all did; he took on a score of small strange ways. His very flesh seemed to assume some faint strange reek of his own race. If she had let him wear the robes he longed to wear he would have become completely strange to her. But now in spite of his foreign clothes, the sight of him revolted her. She added this moment to the heap of hatreds she had against him, hatreds she scarcely understood.

"This time I do not need your money," she said. "This time I will repatriate myself!"

At this he put his book down. But he answered nothing

for minutes. He sat and looked out of the window at the wet blank wall of the next building.

"We have no children to bind us," he said at last. His voice was strange and thin. "You have never given me a single child."

It was the first complaint he had ever made against her. In the beginning he had often spoken of a child and longed for a child, but of late he had said no more. But even so he had never complained until now. It came to her dimly that perhaps at this moment he also was adding something to a hidden heap of hatreds of his own.

The question leaped from her lips. "Then you do not care if I go?" Strange, that she was not angry—strangely, she even half wished he would not let her go so easily!

"I have not satisfied you," he said. He locked his slender hands upon his knees and sat looking at them. He began to turn the thumbs slowly. "I know I have not satisfied you. Western women are hard to satisfy. They must be housed and clothed in the way they wish, and fed, and besides this they must be loved as courtesans are loved, even though there is no reward of a child. I have not the strength for it. Let me tell you something also. I do not complain, but it is not easy to rise in one's position in the Government when one is married to a Western woman. My friends— they distrust me. They say they do not know where my heart is. In the bureau I cannot rise."

So this was yet another thing laid upon the heap of hatreds between them. She said bitterly, "Doubtless you are glad to have me go, then. After I am gone you can marry a Chinese woman."

"No, no—" he said quickly. But after a while he added in a low voice, "At least, not soon."

He seemed about to speak more, but he did not. He continued to look at his hands. Between them the sea roared.

Yet it was soon over. She packed her box. She even put into it some silk embroideries, a Chinese coat to show them at home, a scroll, a fan. She had thought to herself that she never wanted to see anything Chinese again, but still at the end she had put these things into her box.

She climbed the gangway of the ship and at that last moment she turned to give her hand, half-hesitating, to Cheng. But he did not take it. He did not touch her. Not once in all these days had he touched her. He bowed to her and smiled and then he went back to the wharf and stood there, since there was nothing more to be said between them. Whenever Mathilde glanced at him she saw him smiling that faint, fixed smile.

But Mathilde did not smile. She was half dazed now at what she had done. It had come about so quickly, and yet it was done. She watched the crowded wharf, the shouting, sweating coolies, the noisy vendors. She looked out over the packed dark roofs of the city. Then she remembered the narrow streets, the many faces there which had stared at her with apathy or hatred. She looked quickly at Cheng. He was not looking at her. How like the many faces his was now! His face was lost among the others.

"I need never see him again—never, never!" she told herself. "I am finished with it. I am finished with them all. I am going home."

So the consul had said to her, also. He had pursed his

full lips and pulled at his little dyed mustache. "Ha, another one!" he had exclaimed. "Madame, I say to you also, you realize that it is forever? France repatriates but once!"

"Yes, yes, monsieur," she had answered eagerly. "I am never coming back!"

Now the ship pulled loose. The crowd roared and milled, and coolies leaped across the widening chasm of water and on to the wharf. Mathilde's eyes went to Cheng. In the midst of the crowd he stood motionless, looking at her now, but smiling no more. She moved her eyes away from him. She did not wish to see him. She wanted him to become altogether one of that crowd.

"Now I need never see any of them again," she said to herself over and over. "It is the last time. I am going home."

She turned and went to her cabin.

At the end of the voyage there came at last that first evening towards which she had looked with such eagerness during the long and lonely voyage. Lying in her bunk in the second-class cabin, eating silently among the second-class passengers in the tawdry dining-saloon, walking the bit of deck alone, she had dreamed of the first evening in the little parlor in the house at Lyons. Steadfastly she had looked forward to it, shunning all companionship upon the boat. She would not tell anyone about herself. Let it be forgotten now that she had been married to a Chinese.

Yes, let it all be forgotten! If sometimes what lay behind her came pouring into her memory, she pushed it away again resolutely. Cheng's golden skin—how he had been beautiful sometimes! But no, she would not think of that. Let her rather remember that gangling brother of his, snuffing his nose with his fingers. Ah, let her remember how filthy they all were, those Chinese! Let her remember only the few wretched rooms in which she had lived, the clack of the gambling far into the night, the hole of a kitchen. Above all, let her remember her loneliness, the strange language she could not learn, the hostile crowds upon the street—staring, curious, ready to laugh or curse at her. Yes, among them she was always alone and strange —although to one of them she had given herself. But better let her remember nothing now, only look forward to that little house, her own clean little home in Lyons, where *Maman* and Papa and the little brother waited, always kind, always hearty; and where Pierre waited, too.

Ah, Pierre—a good Frenchman—a true man! She would give him everything he wanted. She would say, "My Pierre, I made a great mistake. But let us count those years as though they never were. We are young, and to you I am as I was. Let us begin again together. See, I have forgotten these years away from you. I am here, your Mathilde." So she would speak to him. At the ship's rail, staring out across the gray waves towards France, she planned it so a hundred times a day. "See, Pierre, I am your Mathilde. Here—here is your Mathilde!"

Well, here she was now, the first evening. She sat looking at them all—at Papa, at *Maman,* at her little brother grown tall and shy in these three years she had been away. Secretly she looked also at Pierre, for he had come in at once to see her, as soon as the shop closed. Now he sat opposite her on a stiff-backed chair too small for him. He stared at her, his knees wide apart, his thick hands on his knees. He had grown fat and he looked strange to her, and changed; he was as silent as ever.

She sat silent too and constrained, on the sofa beside her father. He clapped his arm about her shoulders, gazed at her, and he cried boisterously across the stem of his pipe, laughing, his little gray eyes twinkling,

"This Pierre, he is not married yet, Mathilde! No, he never looks at any girl since you went away—*hein,* Pierre?"

Pierre turned a slow red, but before he could gather himself to speak, *Maman* said sharply above the stocking she was darning—*Maman* seemed not so cheerful as she used to be,

"Times are very hard, Jean! A young man marries himself with care these days. Besides, there is her divorce to manage somehow. We are respectable people, Jean!"

Pierre blushed more thickly and glanced at Mathilde. She caught the glance and turned away her eyes. She felt suddenly a little faint, filled with a dismay. Had she been dreaming of *this* Pierre? How fat his body was—his wrists and hands how coarse—how scarred the skin upon his face! She had not remembered those scars—what were they? And his eyes she had remembered so wide and blue; but they were smaller somehow, and not very blue. His garments even were not overclean! This was not the young lover she had seen in her fancy when she cried across the waves, "See, here is your Mathilde!"

As though she had spoken, Pierre muttered uneasily,

177

"I came as I was, from the shop. When they said Mathilde had returned, I came—"

"But naturally, my son!" cried her father gayly, beginning to laugh again loudly. "Who cares how an honest man looks? As for me, *Maman,* though it be hard times, it is true, yet it is not too hard for me to keep my girl—as long as I am allowed, that is!" He chuckled a little and then, suddenly serious, he took the pipe from his mouth and said with passion, "Ah, my girl, how shall I say what it is to me to have you home from that savage country? I was wretched—a thousand times, every day, I prayed the good God to bring you home to me somehow. I do not ask why, now—I do not ask how you have suffered. You are here. Some day you will tell me everything. I am glad he is not here, or I would kill him. He has tortured you!"

But she did not answer; she could not answer.

Yes, she was here. . . . She looked at Pierre; she looked about the room. Yes, she was here. How small and close the rooms were, not larger really than those she had hated! Or did they seem small because Pierre and her father—all of them—were so coarse and big-boned? Even her little brother was so. Why, her brother had the same loose adolescent look Cheng's brother had! Oh, she would never be able to tell them anything, never!—Yet what was there to tell? If Cheng had but once beaten her!—What if the things he had said about the hundred courts were true? Perhaps she ought to have— It may be she could have believed in him.

What was the matter with her? The sea which had rolled between them when she had lain beside Cheng, this sea now rolled between them in truth. Yet now Cheng was the one who seemed the most real to her—more real than these who sat here with her, of whom she had dreamed. Suddenly he was present, as he had not been when she was with him. She saw him, slight and courteous and beautiful again, as he had been used to look beside Pierre. This—this Pierre! It was true he was only a common workingman. Had she once really let him kiss her? What was it her father had said? "The flesh—the flesh crawls—"

Oh, where had her happiness gone? She had been sure for so long that it was here, in this room, with these people! She had wanted so greatly to come home, to be repatriated. . . . Now she was repatriated. Well, then, what was wrong with her? She did not know. Only everything was not as she had thought it would be, not so good as she had thought. Where could she go now, to what now could she return?

There was no return. She had cried so eagerly to the little consul, "I am never coming back!" It was true—she could never go back. They would never understand her wavering —none of them would understand. Cheng, even, would not understand. How could he, since she did not understand herself? Even if she had the money—but she did not have it; yet supposing she had the money, to return would be to give up all her pride. She would be at the mercy then of those hostile yellow crowds. Ah, would she not be at their mercy if of her own will she went back to them, knowing them? It would all be as it was before, if she went back—still the hateful rooms, that brother-in-law, still the crowds. Still she would not dare to leave the coast, still she would not dare quite to trust Cheng and all his stories of the hundred courts. Oh, she knew herself, it would all be as it had been—only worse, for France repatriates but once.

Then out of herself she knew a sudden thing. Of course Cheng would be married! Whom would he marry? That painted Shanghai woman? No, he would not marry *her*— not that one, who would give him no son. Oh, Cheng would marry a woman this time who would give him a son—she knew it. What had he said? "We have no children to bind us. You have never given me a single child." This time he would listen to his uncle, to his father. They would say, "You chose the first time, and you were mistaken. This time take the one we choose, and give us sons."

Mathilde leaned forward, out of her father's embrace, and covered her face with her hands.

"Ah, my piteous one!" her father cried. "Ah, how you have suffered!"

She did not answer. She sat motionless, her face hidden. Let them think what they would. She was in a despair of strangest jealousy of that Chinese woman. Yet why? But naturally, that Cheng would do. Could she ask otherwise, who had left him of her own will? So he would wed himself and so have the sons he wanted. Or would that woman's flesh seem to him too dark, and not so fair as hers had been against him? Would he remember her? It must be so—it must be so. She would come between him, too, and that other woman, as he came between her and Pierre. Oh, he would be spoiled, too, as she was, for any life. She knew it would be so. There was no return for either of them. They were divided in themselves—having once been united, forever divided. Somehow for the moment she was comforted a little; why, she did not know, since there was no true comfort anywhere to one so bewildered as she.

Only she must stay—that she knew. Tomorrow, perhaps even tonight, for in their kindness Papa and *Maman* would leave her alone a little while with Pierre; perhaps even tonight she must say those words to him. Well, then, she would say them; she would go and put her hand on his thick red hand and say steadfastly the words she had so often planned. She would say,

"See, Pierre. I made a mistake. Let those years be forgotten. Pierre, here is your Mathilde."

Yes, so she would speak, tonight if she must—certainly tomorrow. . . .

Suddenly her father clapped his hand again upon her shoulder and with his other hand he took his pipe from his lips to speak. But she, feeling the heavy touch upon her flesh, cried out, not knowing that she did, "Don't, Papa!"

And she moved, restless and afraid, from under his hairy hand.

THE RAINY DAY

IT was a dark and rainy day in November—so dark, indeed, that the light of mid-afternoon scarcely penetrated the rice paper of the latticed windows in the small living-room of a middle-class Chinese home. A shaft of this dull light came through the open door, and falling across the floor fell upon a pair of scrolls which hung upon the whitewashed wall above the wooden table set against it. Upon the scrolls were written very clearly and beautifully in black ink certain adages from the classics. These adages were ones well known and dealt with filial piety.

About this shaft of light sat a circle of people. At the innermost part of the circle in the seat of honor at the left of the table directly under the scrolls was old Mr. Li, Tehtsen's grandfather. He was speaking first, as was his right. He had prepared his words very carefully beforehand, and now he raised and dropped his voice in measured cadence, ending each rounded sentence with an appropriate remark based on the classics. He had begun by clearing his throat and spitting upon the damp brick floor. Then he had passed his delicate old hand, with its long yellow nails, over his beard, which spread sparsely down the front of his gown. His gown was of gray cotton, and it was spotted with bits of food dropped from his bowl of rice at mealtime. In his other hand he held a long bamboo pipe. It was black with age and when he used it, gurgled with accumulated richness.

He continued to stroke his yellowish white beard for some time slowly, while all the others waited for him to speak. Only Teh-tsen's youngest brother dared to be impatient, and to tap his foot restlessly and almost noiselessly upon the brick floor. But then he was the old man's favorite, and dared to do what others did not. As for Teh-tsen himself, he sat very carefully and correctly sidewise upon his seat in a lowly position at the end of the circle near the door. The old grandfather looked from one to the other of this family. It was evident that he enjoyed their waiting for him. But at last he began to speak, his eyes fixed, not on Teh-tsen, whom he was addressing, but upon the fringe of rain dropping from the tile eaves upon the worn stone threshold.

"You are now returned to your people," said the old man, gazing at the rain and speaking in a high quavering voice. "Four months you have been idle at home. You have not found a position whereby your industry and your Western learning, which we have given you, may support honorably your grandfather and your parents and your brothers and sisters.

"What say the Ancients? A son should sacrifice his own flesh that his parents may feed thereon. This you have not done. You have forgotten that we, your relatives, accumulated with great pain the money wherewith you were sent to the outer countries, that you might get their learning. Even your third cousin, who, as you well know, is only a poor merchant in a small shop, gave his savings, in all twenty dollars, that you might become educated in the Western manner and so rise the more quickly to a high position. To him also is due a return.

"What say the Ancients? The son who does not nourish his own family, and especially his grandfather and his parents, let him be less than dog."

The old man stopped to clear his throat. In the interval a stout man in a short black cotton coat and trousers, who sat at the other side of the table in the next seat of honor, hastened to speak.

"Not the least evil of all these things, my father, is that this unworthy son of mine refuses to marry the maid to whom he has been betrothed since he was a child, and who, as you know, has lived in this house as a daughter to us since her own father and mother died in childhood. He speaks of Western customs. We did not bid him learn the Western customs, but only the Western books, that he might find a place with higher remuneration. Now he deprives us of grandchildren. He deprives us of anyone to worship our tablets when we have ascended into heaven. He ordains, this worthless son, that we, his grandparents and parents, shall go into the land of spirits and have no one to care for us."

Teh-tsen himself listened to these words with extreme dismay. He was a dapper young man with a pale, rather delicate face, his mouth as small and pretty as a girl's mouth.

185

He wore foreign clothing, a pale gray suit he had bought in Chicago. On the street he swung a cane and appeared self-sufficient and elegant as he went down the street looking at no one. But here in this dim room among his elders in their long gowns he shrank into a rather insignificant youth, narrow-chested and timid. He sat with his hands between his knees, rubbing his soft palms slowly back and forth against each other.

He gazed from one to the other of his relatives—his grandfather, nodding his head at the father's words, his rheumy eyes fixed on the falling rain; his father, stout, impatient with much food; his uncle, a thin selfish face and nervous, slightly dirty hands; his brother, an impudent boy, eager to be away, and peeping secretly out into the street. In a corner apart sat his mother upon a stool, a somewhat bent figure in blue cotton garments. She was wiping her eyes on her apron. Behind these four figures he saw in his mind's eye many others, avaricious, greedy cousins, his crabbed old merchant uncle, all those eager to share the income he was expected to bring in with his superior education. They were hands—claws—talons—grasping for everything he could produce.

They had educated him, then, he saw now, merely because he had happened to be the brightest boy in the clan, the one with the quickest brains. They had educated him merely as an investment for old age. A furious rage filled him. A torrent of burning, reckless words rose in his throat. He waited an instant, setting his teeth sharply over them. He knew, of course, that it would be idle to speak. He had no redress from his own people. In these days they had the power over him—they could even kill him if they liked. To be sure, this could scarcely happen, but the thought reminded him of his helplessness.

Yet centuries of self-control behind him stood him in good stead now. He rose and bowed deeply to his grandfather. Then he bowed to his father, and then to his uncle. Lastly he bowed to his mother, and he knew she yearned over him secretly, although she dared not speak.

"I pray you forgive me, honorable ones," he said in a low voice. "I will try to be more dutiful."

He was conscious again of the wave of anger rising in him. He steadied himself and walked stiffly from the room and across the courtyard. He went out into the street. The rain fell in straight somber lines, steadily and drearily, and the dampness between the high brick walls on either side of the narrow way was as chill as death. The shallow gutters along the street overflowed with waste and filth so that the cobblestones ran with a viscous, black, evil-smelling liquid. It rose against his polished tan shoes and left a stain.

He uttered an exclamation of disgust. He remembered that only the week before he had called upon the magistrate of this town and asked permission to organize a sanitary street association. The magistrate had been suave, had complimented him upon his modern civic spirit, had promised nothing.

Teh-tsen looked bleakly ahead through the long straight lines of falling rain. How could his town, his country, progress with such magistrates as these? How helpless he was against all those in power—how helpless everyone was!

The rain beat upon his smart felt hat and dripped from

the brim. The hat was rapidly softening in the dampness, drooping over his eyes. His clothes were beginning to feel wet against his skin. He walked on.

Could it be that it was only six months ago he had been standing on the platform in the huge auditorium of an American university to receive his degree? He had been given a prize as well for his essay on the comparison of Eastern and Western philosophy. It had been a brilliant piece of work, so his professors told him. How proud he had been! He had been, they said, one of the best students ever graduated from the university. This was good praise when one remembered that all his work was done in the foreign tongue. But when he was graduated he had only one thought. It was to come back to his native town, to his native country, and give all he had for its development. He had come back sure of himself, glad to see his family, confident of their pride in him.

And then immediately they had fallen upon him like carrion crows! The very first night his father had talked with him concerning the salary he must demand from the local government school should he teach there.

"I should like to consider the service I can render the country first," Teh-tsen had said hesitatingly. "If the school seems the most—"

His father stared at him, his fat yellow cheeks hanging. "You think of yourself only!" he exclaimed. "I am now ready to retire from active business. The times are hard and the shop is not paying. Your brother must be cared for. Your uncle is unwell and is unable to work. Besides, there are not a few of our relatives who gave you money for your education. They will at least expect rice from you. More than that, your future wife is in the house. While you were gone all those years her parents died, and your mother needed help and there is no use in hiring an extra servant when one has a daughter-in-law. These are all dependent upon you. You are the eldest son now as I was in my time. I am weary."

Teh-tsen had been confounded. Somehow he had forgotten these things were. He had been away so long—eight years! And then he thought of the dull-faced slovenly girl he had seen about. He had imagined her a servant when he first came. His wife? A sick rebellion rose in him whenever he thought of her and his heart beat quickly. Never! He had even had angry words with his father. But it had all been to no purpose. They were determined to bend him to their will, these relatives of his, planning together to break down his resistance by sheer, ponderous immovability. He was smothering under it. Worst of all, he was terrified to feel himself weaker under the calm, inexorable pressure of family opinion. He was not so sure as he had been that he was right. His ideals were no longer as they were when he stepped from the ship's gangplank upon the coast. Those ideals—they had now become dimmed and remote, scarcely worth fighting for any more. After all, he was only one person. What could he do among so many who cared nothing for better ways of living and thinking?

He perceived now that his shoes were sticky with street filth, and his trousers were bespattered. He had come away in his haste without his top coat and the penetrating, ceaseless downpour had wet him through. He could feel the icy water trickling between his shoulders. The sky was a sodden lead color. The rain continued to fall straightly.

He shivered and wondered if there were in this whole town any spot that was warm. His own room at home was as cheerless as the rest of the house on such a day, its brick floor exuding moisture and the drops of wet standing upon the walls. Besides, meagre as this room appeared to him after his years away, he was compelled to share it with his brother, and he remembered now with fresh anger how this brother examined carelessly his beloved books, and how he left finger stains upon the white margins of the pages. Only yesterday Teh-tsen had found his most valued philosophy text book with a sheet torn out of the middle. His brother had torn it to wrap about some small coins before thrusting them into his belt. There was no privacy anywhere.

Staring through the rain, Teh-tsen wondered how he could get warm. If he were once really warm again he might find a little courage somehow to go on with his purpose. He feared more than anything that he might be weak enough to give up, to marry the ignorant woman, to throw away his life. Then a new anxiety came into his mind. He cried to himself,

"And what of my own sons, then, with such a mother, born into such a house? Shall I bring forth others to this life of mine?"

He had not thought of them before. He imagined them, their tiny hands clasped, begging not to be born. "No, no, I will not," he promised them eagerly in his heart.

A tall house loomed up suddenly before him, a foreign

house. Ah, there was where Mr. Hemingway lived, his old teacher when he had been a boy in the grammar school! He had been a kind man, a young American, full of earnestness. He would go in and see him. Perhaps he could get warm. He might even talk with Mr. Hemingway and tell him his difficulties and get a little help—a little encouragement.

He mounted the shallow stone steps to the veranda that ran around the house and rang the doorbell. Then he waited, his coat collar turned up and his hands thrust into his pockets for warmth. The vines upon the house were beaten flat with the rain, and the ground was spongy with it. Leaves were fluttering down, brown and wet. The door opened slowly. It was Mr. Hemingway. How he had aged! He was now a stooped, rather sad man, who peered at Teh-tsen uncertainly.

Teh-tsen put out his hand.

"You do not remember me, Mr. Hemingway? I was your pupil when I was a little boy. I have been away for many years. Now I come to see you again."

"Ah, yes—yes—" said Mr. Hemingway uncertainly. He had had many students, and he did not remember Teh-tsen. "Come in."

Teh-tsen stepped into the hall. Oh, how warm it was! He followed Mr. Hemingway into the study. Oh, heavenly warmth! A small stove crackled in one corner of the room. Teh-tsen stood before it, his clothes steaming.

"Dear me, I am afraid you are wet," said Mr. Hemingway, staring at him. He was very nearsighted.

"Only a little," answered Teh-tsen modestly.

"Yes, yes," said Mr. Hemingway absently. There was a high pile of papers to be corrected on the desk and he had planned for an undisturbed afternoon. He was feeling wretched today, too, with a cold coming on—this rain! If he had an assistant now—but of course there was never enough money for things as it was, and certainly not enough for these young Western-trained Chinese who demanded such impossible salaries nowadays. Here was this young fellow probably wanting a job or something. He had better see what was wanted, anyway.

Teh-tsen seated himself. He hovered as near the cheerful, robust little stove as was consistent with politeness. He stared about the bare little study appreciatively, enviously. Books—warmth—privacy; what a fortunate man Mr. Hemingway was! It was easy to be good and noble and strong in such surroundings.

He felt the delicious warmth creeping into his flesh. He began to long to open his heart to Mr. Hemingway. Perhaps the opportunity would come soon. He felt quick words begin to shape themselves in him and rise to his lips, ready to pour out.

Mr. Hemingway asked a few questions. Teh-tsen spoke politely of Mr. Hemingway's country—wonderful country, wonderful people—

"I hope," said Mr. Hemingway with a little severity, "that you will use your knowledge now for the good of your own country. China needs you— There are many unfortunate—"

Teh-tsen listened. Now they were getting to it. He could

tell his fears and longings soon. He did truly want to help his country, but—

"Still, I hope you have an attitude different from most of these young men who come back from England and America and France," Mr. Hemingway went on in a slightly higher tone of voice. He thought of the precious afternoon slipping past and the sight of the pile of uncorrected papers began to harass him. His head was aching. If only he could hire an assistant! Really it was too much to expect of a man working alone. But the scarcity of funds—

"The trouble with all of you," he continued, his irritation rising uncontrollably, "is that you think of nothing but money, you want nothing but money. You want easy jobs and no responsibility and high salaries. Nothing else will please you. Meanwhile, the hard posts where service is greatly needed for the people go unfilled. Will none of you have any courage? I must confess, Mr.—ah—Mr. Li, that I am very much disappointed in the Chinese students returned from Western countries."

The room was quiet. Mr. Hemingway played with a paper knife at his desk and glanced unconsciously at the clock on the wall. He was a good man who had borne much. He had not had a furlough in eight years, and would not go now because no one had been sent to take his place in the school, and he was tired and discouraged. Moreover, he was a true teacher who had always to work with insufficient materials and this had gradually broken him.

The rain beat monotonously against the window panes. The silent room began to fill with tense feeling. Mr. Hemingway thought of all his disappointments, and somehow this young Chinese in his smartly cut Western clothes seemed to personify them. The young man felt suddenly that he was back in the conclave of harshness in the dingy room of his home. Misunderstanding chilled their hearts. The room seemed no longer warm.

Teh-tsen rose and bowed. This, after all, had been a respected teacher. He must not forget his own breeding and politeness.

"I grieve that we disappoint you, sir, and I bid you good-bye, sir," he said proudly and went again into the street. He felt suddenly weak, and a sob came into his throat. He stared resolutely ahead to keep back tears, and he began to walk, wholly regardless now of the flowing filth against his shoes.

How it rained! The warmth of the few minutes was soon dissipated, and he felt tired and dispirited. Where could he go now? He could only go home—there was no other place for him. It meant giving up. But life was insupportable. He would have to sacrifice himself as others had done and as others would have to do in this old country—throw away his dreams—crush out his individual longings. He would have to marry. The law could compel him—the old, invincible law of the centuries not yet broken and cast away. He thought of the sullen face of his betrothed—of her unkempt hair. What was she but a servant, cheaply bought? His memory presented him cruelly with a hundred pretty faces, gay faces, the faces of the girls at that American university. They might marry whom they chose—even women there could marry as they chose. He thought of the young men who had been his classmates. They would choose, too, each would choose among the pretty girls who were their equals. But they could not help him. It was idle even to think of them.

He turned his head aside restlessly and looked from one side of the street to the other. The dark brick houses huddled together silently in the steady cold rain. How he wished he could get away! But he had no money of his own. If he could run away to Tientsin, to Shanghai, even, he could find work and be free. But then, he thought bitterly, he never could be free. Wherever he was they would reach him, force his return. And, after all, could he be free in himself? Could he bear to be an outcast from his clan? An eldest son could scarcely so forget himself. No, he had better keep his self-respect, at least.

The streets were now nearly empty of people. A few beggars crept about, whining and drenched. A woman hurried past him to buy hot water, her kettle in her hand and her patched apron thrown over her head, the two ends caught in her teeth, to protect her from the rain. A child walked sedately home from school under an enormous oiled paper umbrella. The short November day was darkening. It continued to rain. Soon it would be night. He must go somewhere, for he was wet and chilled to his very bones. Of course he must go home. But going home was to give himself up. Well, there was nothing else for him.

He turned his steps slowly toward his home. The future years passed before him—drab, full of work of some sort perhaps, but always with emptiness within. He seemed to see again that fantastic, sentimental picture of his own children, begging not to be born. And then it came to him in a flash of light the service he could render them at least. He stopped and stared through the rain, a smile breaking across his face. How stupid he had been all this long, rainy day! He stopped at the little apothecary's shop on the corner and gave a low order. The fussy little shopkeeper bent his head.

"Three pills of black opium?" he repeated softly. "Ah, yes—"

He wrapped them furtively in a bit of brown paper and gave them to the young man, and his yellow hand curled about the money dropped into it.

Then Teh-tsen walked home erect, his head up, regardless of the rain upon his face. Strange he had not thought of this before! He smiled a little. After all, it was not necessary that he should have gone abroad and spent all the money to learn. In this moment of crisis it had not been any of his American professors who had taught him what to do. Not one of them had told him how to live. True, they had helped him to write the brilliant essay. It was wrapped up carefully in oiled silk and put away into the bottom of his trunk together with his diploma and some other things he did not use every day. No, this was now the time-honored revenge his ancestors had used, the time-honored protest against a world awry, which was to be his solution, his self-sacrifice, now.

He entered again the courtyard of his home. The kitchen opened on the left of the gate. The door was wide open and the fire from the brick cooking stove shone upon the face of a stupid, sullen girl who was feeding grass into the stove.

He shivered a little and set his lips. Ah, he had decided wisely!

He went into the living-room. It was empty now. On the table was a pot of tea and two bowls. He felt of the pot. It was cold. Everything was cold, he thought with a touch of irritation—this miserable, cold rain! He poured a little of the cold tea into a bowl and rinsed it out and threw the rinsing on the floor. He placed the pills in the center of the bowl. Then he poured in a little tea very carefully. Three black pills in an ounce of tea. He swallowed them and drank another gulp of the cold tea.

Then he went into his room. It was dark and for once he had it to himself. His brother had not yet returned. He went to the bed and took off his ruined shoes and pulled his dripping coat from his shoulders. Then without troubling to remove his other clothing he lay down and turning his face to the wall, he dragged the quilt up around his shoulders and, shivering, he closed his eyes for sleep.

On the tile roof over his head the rain beat steadily down with a soft, soothing murmur. The day slipped gently into night.

REVOLUTION

WANG LUNG

WANG LUNG was the son of Wang the Farmer. All his life he had lived in the Wang village on the borders of the city of Nanking, and, since he daily carried green vegetables into the city to sell, he was no common, ignorant fellow. He knew, for instance, sooner than anyone else in the village, when the Emperor finally relinquished the throne. Indeed, the event could not have taken place more than a year before he heard of it. He at once informed his father, who told his uncle, and his uncle, who was the village letter-writer, told all the villagers who came to beg him to write to their relatives, and in a short time everyone knew of it.

For three days at least they all spoke in whispers, being much distressed and hourly expecting catastrophe. No one, of course, had ever seen the Emperor, but still each person had felt him to be a supporting, eternal power, the Son of Heaven, who arranged matters with the magistrates in the upper regions. In short, one could leave both the welfare of the nation and one's own little sins to the Emperor while one tended garden and took vegetables in the spring and ducks in the autumn to sell in the market-place. Now, with the Emperor gone, no one dared to leave the village. Indeed, Wang the Grandfather, who perfectly remembered the time of the Taipings, immediately expected looting and robbery. So he gathered together certain family valuables, such as the deed to the land, a coat of goatskin, dingy from generations of use and yet good for several more, and some bits of silver, and secreted them in the hollow mud wall of the house. Three days he sat stroking his sparse, yellow-white beard, his eyes fixed on the loosened earth, and at night he ordered his bed moved out and slept beneath it.

But, since nothing happened by the end of the fourth day, he took the treasure from its hiding-place, grumbling and a bit disappointed, and people began to go about their business again, although at first a little fearfully. At last, however, they no longer felt any need of the Emperor, and, as time passed, they even began to rejoice that he was gone, since their crops were as good every year as if he had intervened for them with Heaven.

Indeed, one day in the tea-shop in the city Wang Lung heard a young man cry in a loud voice over his tea-bowl that emperors were but idle fellows and cost the nation a great deal of money. Wang Lung was struck with cold horror at this speech and at such disdain of the honorable dead, and he watched for a long time to see whether a tile would not fall from the roof upon the young man or whether he would not choke over his tea and die. But, when nothing of the sort occurred, Wang Lung, after reflecting with some effort, because thinking was never easy, decided that the young man must have spoken the truth, so that the gods did not dare to rebuke him. He gazed respectfully at the young man.

The young man wore a long gown of dark blue cloth neither heavy nor light but perfectly suited to the season, which was the third month of spring. His hair was cut very close to his head and oiled as smoothly as a woman's. "This man must be from southern parts," Wang murmured to himself, "since I have not seen his like before."

The young man was talking rapidly and casting quick eyes over the crowd in the tea-shop. When he saw Wang Lung staring at him, he smoothed back his brow with his long, pale hands and raised his voice a little. "We Chinese have more people than any other country in the world, and all foreign countries should fear us. Nevertheless they despise us because we have no fire-wagons and fighting-ships. Yet these are simple things. In the ancient times did not our wise men ride upon clouds of fire and upon dragons breathing out smoke? What has been done, can be done again. Now we are a republic and the Emperor is dead. All things are possible."

Wang Lung had come nearer, and, stooping, he picked up the hem of the young man's gown and inquired politely, "May I ask how much this gown cost?" With the fine, soft cloth still between his thumb and forefinger he felt of it again and muttered: "Ah, what is this stuff? It feels like cloud material. Sir, is this foreign goods, and how much does it cost?"

But the young man became suddenly angry and snatched the garment away with a quick movement. "Do not soil it with your fingers, filthy one," he cried. "I paid two dollars a foot for it, and it is good English woolen cloth!"

Two dollars a foot! Wang's mouth gaped suddenly like a fish's mouth. He did not see two dollars in a month of labor. How many feet would it take for such a gown as this, swinging to the ankles and clinging about the throat, even to the very ears? While the young man continued to speak of republics, Wang Lung reflected carefully upon the amount of blue cotton cloth he had bought for his wedding garment six years before. Five feet for the front, five for the back, five for the sleeves—say, a ten-foot length and a half—say, a bit of extra thrown in, as was the custom when one bought ten feet of cloth at the shop. It would all come to not less than twenty-eight rounds of silver. He was aghast at such wealth. Twenty-eight dollars, a year's income, wrapped about the fragile body of this short-haired youth! "It is very dear," he murmured.

The young man turned to him complacently. "It is foreign goods grown upon the backs of English sheep and woven especially for the black-haired people by the hands of English slaves," he explained. Then, seeing Wang Lung's astonishment and admiration, he went on in a fluent, oracular manner: "As I was saying, we no longer need the Emperor. Our great nation may now be governed as our ancient sage has said, by the people, for the people and of the people. Even you, my poor fellow, may have a share in deciding who is to be our president."

"I?" said Wang, suddenly drawing back. "I have my father and old grandfather to support and my wife and three slaves, since she has given me only girls and no son yet. Their empty mouths are forever stretched wide around me. I have no time. Please, sir, attend to this matter for me."

The young man laughed loudly at this and struck the table with the flat of his hand, so that everyone in the tea-shop looked up and Wang, embarrassed to be so much seen, turned his face away.

"How ignorant you are, you fellow!" cried the young man. "You have only to write a name upon a bit of paper and drop it into a box."

"Sir, I cannot write," pleaded Wang anxiously.

"Get someone to write for you then. Oh, how ignorant you are!" said the young man, swallowing the last of his tea and throwing two pennies upon the table.

"Sir, I am a worm," replied Wang. "But what shall I write?"

"Write the name of the man you wish to be president," said the young man.

He spoke with such impatience that Wang Lung did not dare to ask, further, what "president" might mean.

By this time many people were listening to the conversation, and the young man, turning on the threshold and resuming his former manner, said with great emphasis: "Therefore, my countrymen, the time of prosperity is near. The rich will become poor and the poor will become rich."

Wang pricked up his ears. How was this—the poor become rich? He ventured timidly, fearing the young man's wrath. "Sir, how shall this be?"

"In all republics it is so," said the young man. "In America all men live in palaces, and only the rich are compelled to work. As soon as emperors are put away and the Revolution comes, these things happen. That is why my hair is cut off. It is to show that my spirit is free. I am a revolutionist. I and the other revolutionists will save the nation and uplift the poor and oppressed!"

He bowed and turned to go. Wang Lung still squatted upon his carrying-pole, whither he had withdrawn when the young man had been angry. He sat there now, in front of the door, staring as in a dream, and the young man could not pass because of him. "Out of my way, you!" the young man cried, and scornfully he pushed the pole with his foot.

Wang Lung rose hurriedly, removed his baskets into the street and then stood watching the young man as he walked away, his blue gown swaying from side to side.

Of everything said, Wang had really heard only this, that the poor would become rich. This hope he had cherished all his life, but of late years he had given it up as unrealizable. His ancestors had worked upon the bit of land he was cultivating, and none had ever become rich. But now it all seemed really true; now that the Emperor was dead, anything might happen.

He stared down the street, thinking, seeing the blue gown glow out of the gray distance. If he should become rich, he would have just such a gown as that, soft and bright and warm. He looked down his body upon his patched, yellowish trousers and upon his brown bare feet. He saw himself clothed with that warmth and brightness.

But, as he bent his head, his queue fell down, rusty from sun and wind and uncombed for many days. "How can I wear my new gown with a head like this?" he muttered.

It seemed to him that the gown was already buttoned about him with the very same kind of small gilt buttons that had been on the young man's. So, although he had sold only a little green stuff, he counted his coins carefully and, going down the street to a traveling barber's stand, he shouted, "Shave my head entirely, and I will pay you ten copper pieces."

Thus Wang Lung became a revolutionist.

But he himself was not aware of the fact. When he returned to the village at evening, the villagers, idling about on the threshing-floors before the houses, saw him shaven like a priest and began to laugh. No one knew what to say except Wang Liu's only son, who went daily to school in the city and therefore understood more than the others. He cried now: "He is a revolutionist! My teacher says only revolutionists cut off their hair."

Wang Lung was very much embarrassed to hear this. He knew nothing of revolutionists, and he was afraid because he had inadvertently become that which he knew not. So he put down his carrying-pole with a loud noise, that he might not appear disturbed or unlike himself, and shouted to his wife as he did every evening: "Now then, Mother of Slaves, where is the rice? I have spent my precious breath all day to buy you food and, coming home at night in exhaustion, find not even a bowl of tea ready."

The villagers at once saw that he was acting as usual

and dispersed from his door, merely marveling among themselves at his appearance. Nevertheless, the idle name clung to him. He was called "Wang the Revolutionist" from that day, and gradually the name ceased to have any meaning at all except as attached to him.

As for Wang, he thought for a long time of the blue gown he would have when he became rich. At first he daily expected this miracle to happen, and, as his hair grew, he kept it smooth with two fingers wet in bean-oil. But summer followed spring, and autumn died into winter, and the year gave birth to the new year, and his life was the same as ever. He still was compelled to work from morning until night, and he still had no sons. At last he became angry to the depths of his spirit, so that at night he could not sleep upon his bed.

It was not that any one thing overwhelmed him. Rather he was beset with many vexations, which augmented his rebellion at being destined, seemingly, to have no leisure in his old age. This idea made him so angry that he reviled his wife three times each day, saying, "Cursed is earth full of useless seed!"

Whenever he heard that other women had given birth to sons, he felt himself ill used and ground his teeth together. He was angry when the price of cloth and oil and fuel rose, while he could not wrest more produce from the land. He was angry every day in the city because he saw men idling along the streets in satin and velvet and sleeping over the tables in the tea-shop and gambling on the counters of shops, while he, on his way to the market, must bend his bare back under the load to feed them. In the end, the least thing angered him; a fly, settling on his sweaty face, made him shout and leap as if at a mad dog, so that, seeing him, people cried, "This is a madman who roars at a fly!" And the secret symbol of all his wrath was the blue gown he could never buy.

One day in the city he passed, as was his custom, through the Street of the Confucian Temple, and there upon a wooden box stood a young man, talking loudly. He was a mere white-faced lad, and he wore a long black cotton gown. He moved his thin, childish hands and looked restlessly over the heads of the people gathering around him. Wang Lung said to himself that he was tired and would therefore stop to hear this new thing. He sat down upon his pole and wiped his face with the towel that hung from his belt.

At first he could not understand what it was all about. He expected to hear something of emperors and republics, but instead this youth spoke of foreigners. He had a small voice, which cracked when he tried to speak loudly, and he cried: "They have killed us and trodden upon us. They are imperialists—robbers of all nations!"

Wang Lung listened, astonished. He knew nothing of foreigners. He had, it is true, always rather enjoyed seeing them; for they were strange to look upon and were a marvel to speak of in the village. But what manner of men they might really be, it had not entered his mind to inquire. He was not specially interested even now, and so he felt for his small bamboo pipe. At any rate he would blow a little tobacco before going on. And then he heard the lad scream in his high, wavering voice: "These riches are ours. Houses and lands and gold and silver they have taken from us. They live like kings while we are their slaves. Steamwagons and music-machines, clothes of blue and red and yellow satin—like kings! Down with the capitalists! A thousand thousand years to the Revolution, when the poor shall become rich and the rich become poor!"

Wang Lung started forward and dropped his pipe. The poor become rich? Again? He pressed to the lad's side and asked with a sort of surly timidity, "Sir, when shall these things be?"

The youth turned fiery, unseeing eyes on him and answered: "Now, now! When the revolutionists enter the city, everything is yours. Take what you like. Comrade, you are a revolutionist?"

"I am called 'Wang the Revolutionist,'" answered Wang Lung simply.

But the youth was not listening to him. He was screaming again, "Down with the capitalists, down with the foreigners, down with religion, down with imperialism! A thousand thousand years to the Revolution, when the poor shall become rich and the rich become poor!"

When Wang Lung heard these words, he knew suddenly what revolution meant. Capitalism, imperialism, religion, these words meant nothing, but he understood that the poor should become rich and the rich become poor. Ah, he was a revolutionist, then.

He stood staring at the young man and, even as he stared, a policeman suddenly appeared with a fixed bayonet and, before anyone knew what he was about, placed it at the young man's back. "Off to jail then, young revolutionist," he said in a loud, gruff voice, "and let us see how quickly you will become rich!" The young man, suddenly turned into a yellow-faced wraith, descended without a word and walked away, the policeman propelling him gently from behind with his bayonet. The crowd disappeared like a cloud before the sun, and Wang Lung in great terror and confusion of mind picked up his baskets and trotted rapidly toward the market.

He was very much frightened, and he said nothing all day to anyone. In the evening, instead of sleeping over a bowl of green tea as he usually did, he harnessed the water-buffalo to the plow and plowed the sweet-potato field until the moon sank behind the willow-trees and he could no longer see the furrows.

The next morning he rose at an early hour to go to the market. When he approached the city gates, he saw that upon them were pasted large fresh sheets of paper covered with characters. At these he stared for a long time, wondering what they meant, but, since he had never been able to read a character in his life, he could make nothing of them. At last he asked an aged man who was passing to read them for him, discerning by the great horn spectacles and slow walk that this was a man of learning. The scholar stopped and read every word with great care, and Wang Lung waited patiently, although the sun rose higher and higher until its rays crept into the deep arch of the gate itself. At last the old man turned to Wang and said: "These words concern others than you, my poor fellow. They announce that revolutionists have been found in the city and have been beheaded."

"Beheaded?" gasped Wang Lung.

"Yes, indeed," answered the scholar, looking very profound. "And furthermore it says that, if you go to the Bridge of the Three Sisters, you will see their heads in a row. Our Governor will have none of these Cantonese rebels." And the scholar walked on, his skirts swaying from side to side in excess of dignity.

Wang Lung stood gazing at the crooked letters, sick with fear. Was he not called "Wang the Revolutionist"? He cursed the blue gown that had brought him to this pass. His desire for riches was quite forgotten, and some terrible dread drew him toward the Bridge of the Three Sisters. He left his baskets at the hot-water shop of an eighth cousin on his mother's side and went to the bridge, which was a mile away, although he could ill spare the time with his vegetables drying up in the heat of noon.

He saw that what the old scholar had said was true. There at the bridge, upon seven bamboo poles, were seven bleeding heads, bent on ragged, severed necks; heads with fringes of black hair hanging over their dull, half-closed eyes. One head had its mouth open and its tongue thrust out, half bitten off between set white teeth. Looking more closely at this head, Wang Lung saw with a leap of fear at his heart that this was the head of the lad to whom he had listened the day before. But then they were all the heads of very young men.

About the place stood a jeering crowd. An old man with broken teeth spat upon the ground and cried, "See what happens to revolutionists!"

Wang started at the word. Revolutionists? Suppose some

212

who knew him should pass and call out, as his acquaintances so often did, "Ha, Wang the Revolutionist! Have you eaten?" It was an idle salutation, meaning nothing on other days but today meaning anything. He hurried off.

Thereafter he worked very hard indeed and spoke little. He did not even complain to his wife, so that finally she went in alarm to the blind soothsayer of the village and asked whether her husband was going to be ill. But the whole trouble was that Wang Lung continually beheld in his imagination an eighth head hanging beside the seven already there on the Bridge of the Three Sisters. In the evening, when he could no longer work, he saw very clearly his own dead face with half-shut eyes and drawn gray lips. When his third cousin passed the door and cried gaily, "What has Wang the Revolutionist heard today in the city?" Wang Lung strode to the door and cursed him a thousand years and would not listen to his words of astonishment. The hardest thing was the impossibility of telling anyone of his fear. To speak would have been to invite the knife to his neck.

From that day he hated everything. He hated the land that ate up his life and demanded increasing toil. He hated those neighbors of his, to whom he could not explain his fear; he despised the villagers, who were content to remain as their ancestors had been, clothed in coarse cotton and eating brown rice forever. He hated the city with its streets full of careless, idle people.

As his hatred grew, his fear lessened. He heard no more of revolutions and was all the angrier because he saw now no way for the poor to become rich. He thought about the rich and he hated them. He knew what these rich were like. Once a year he went to pay his respects to the gentry in the village, as the custom was, and there he saw satin curtains at the doors and satin cushions on the carved chairs. Even the servants were decked out in silk. As for him, he had never touched silk in all his life except furtively at a cloth-shop, that he might know its smoothness.

And the foreigners—the lad had said they were the richest of all. Sometimes he heard in the tea-shops about them now. They sat upon chairs of gold and at tables of silver. They walked upon lengths of velvet as carelessly as he walked upon the wild grass at the side of the country roads. On their beds were covers of brocade embroidered with jewels. Riches! He grew to hate the foreigners more than anything else, because it was wrong that foreigners should live like kings so long as there was one Chinese as poor as he. At first he had only longed for the poor to become rich, but, thinking of all the wrongs he endured, he longed equally for the rich to become poor.

Turning these matters over in his mind incessantly, he ceased to work so hard. Since he was not accustomed to so much puzzling, he found it impossible to hoe and to think at the same time. He was obliged therefore to stop when his thoughts became too much for him. Since he accomplished less than of old in one day, he became poorer and poorer until his wife cried at him: "I cannot say where the cotton wadding for our winter clothes is to come from. We shall not be able to feed our bodies within and clothe them without at the same time." This speech made him very angry, so angry that he ground his teeth together without knowing why.

One day in great heaviness of spirit he cast down his baskets carelessly at the tea-shop and determined not to work that day, come what might, since all his work brought him no nearer riches. He sat down at the table nearest the door and ordered a bowl of tea. There was another man at the table, a youngish man in a long black cotton gown, with short hair brushed straight up from his forehead. As he wiped his wet face on his towel, he looked at Wang Lung and said softly, "You work too hard, my comrade."

"I do indeed, sir," replied Wang Lung, sighing and pulling over his shoulders the patched gray coat he had taken off in the heat of the walk. "But how can it be helped? With rice what it is and a house full of idle women to feed, my flesh is torn from my bones in the day's toil."

"You are poor, bitterly poor," whispered the young man, bending toward him, "and you should be rich."

Wang Lung shook his head. He would not allow himself to be disturbed again by that word "rich" in the mouth of a young man. He poured himself a bowl of tea and sipped it loudly, thankful for its heat in his rapidly chilling body.

"You work and starve while others play and eat," continued the young man.

"That is true," said Wang Lung suddenly.

"Yet you are a good man and deserving of far more than they."

Wang Lung shook his head again, smiling a little.

"Yes, this is true," the young man insisted. "I can see it in your honest face. Allow me to pour you more tea."

215

Rising, he poured tea into Wang Lung's bowl as courteously as if Wang's coat were whole and new.

Wang Lung rose to thank him, and to himself he said: "How wise this young man is! He discerns my quality at once." Aloud he said, "Sir, where is your honorable palace?"

But the young man answered: "Oh, I am a poor man, too. But I am come to tell you and your friends that you will soon be rich. When the revolutionists come into the city—"

Wang rose hastily to his feet. "I am no revolutionist!" he declared.

"No, no," said the young man soothingly; "you are a good man. I can see it."

Wang Lung sat down again. By now the sharp air felt icy upon his sweat-dampened skin. He pulled his garment more closely about him.

"You are too poor," said the young man. "I pity you with all my heart."

Wang Lung felt very sorry for himself. No one had ever pitied him before. Indeed some had even considered him fortunate, since, though burdened with a family of women and compelled to work hard, he was his father's only son and would some day own the six acres of family land and the three-roomed, mud-plastered house. So now, at the thought that somebody realized how very poor and hardworked and pitiable he was, tears welled up into his eyes. "It is true," he said in a broken voice.

"And it is very wrong," the young man continued. "You are a clever man. I can see it. You deserve to be rich. I say

it again. But your chance is coming. When the revolutionists enter the city, the poor will become rich and the rich
will become poor."

"How?" asked Wang Lung, bending forward to catch
the answer, since they were speaking very softly indeed.

The young man cast a hasty glance about. "The foreigners are surfeited with riches beyond anyone," he replied in a whisper. "They throw away silver as of no account, caring only for gold. The very walls of their houses
are filled with gold—gold they have stolen from us Chinese.
Else why do they remain in this country? Why do they
not return to their own land? They take the gold from us
so that you and I have none. It belongs to us. When the
revolutionists come, be ready!" And immediately the young
man rose and left the tea-shop.

Wang Lung, remembering the heads he had seen, did
not like even to recall the young man's words. Only, when
he thought of the gold possessed by others, especially the
foreigners who had no right to it, he grew very bitter
within. He said to himself, "Doubtless they have whole
boxes of blue gowns like mine"; and suddenly he seemed
to see the blue gown again in all its first beauty, and he
was sick for its warmth and brightness.

Not more than a month later he heard that the revolutionists were approaching the city. He had not forgotten
what the young man said: it must be that all the years of
talk about the Revolution were coming true at last. In the
market one day, when he was haggling with a customer
over a pound of cabbage, someone whispered in his ear,
"In ten days be ready!"

Turning quickly, Wang Lung saw the young man who had pitied him. Though he would have spoken, the man did not stay and the customer cried impatiently, "Now then, son of a robber, two coppers!"

Wang Lung was compelled to answer as usual, "Never! May I starve if I let it go for less than four!"

To himself he said, "Ten days? Well, we shall see it when it comes."

Thus he waited, half skeptical, half afraid. But it became evident soon that something was about to happen. Into the city poured silently like dark water from the river thousands and thousands of soldiers. He marveled, staring at the endless procession as it went by the tea-shop. "Are these revolutionists?" he asked the waiter.

But the waiter cast him a fiery look and hissed at him: "Be silent, O double fool! Do you want us all to be beheaded? Can you not see the coarse bones of these men and hear the rattling of the words in their throats and the way in which they swallow bread and refuse rice? These are Northerners, anti-revolutionists, and the heads of many fools like you hang at the bridge." Then, bending over Wang Lung to take his cup, he whispered, "In seven days be ready!" and he went quickly away.

Those words again! Wang Lung started. Ready for what? He was by this time wholly bewildered and, not daring to speak to anyone all that day, he went doggedly about his business, avoiding the main streets where the great stream of gray-clad figures continued to pass.

Then, on the evening of the next day, a terrific noise began to descend out of the sky. Thunder roared back and forth, and the very earth shook. They were eating their supper around the table, he and his father and his grandfather, while his wife and daughters waited on them. Putting down his chopsticks to listen the better, he discerned two noises, one a loud, intermittent bellow and the other a frantic pup-pup-pup, which he disliked very much because he had never heard any noise like it before. He rose to go out and investigate and then was afraid and turned to his wife. "Go and see what this is," he commanded.

She crept slowly along the wall and peered out. Something struck the earth at her feet and made her fall back; a fan-shaped spray of earth flew into the room and was scattered into the food and over the table. They were all smitten with horror; Wang Lung rushed to the wooden door, flung it across the opening and barred it tight. They sat there then in the darkness, not daring to light even the bean-oil lamp, hearing the earth as it struck upon the roof and the incessant broken noises that came out of the night. To himself Wang Lung said in dismay: "Is this the Revolution? We shall all be dead of it, and my life will be gone for a blue gown."

But the next morning the noise had died into the distance. Wang Lung peered forth from his door and at once grew very angry. His plots of vegetables were ruined with holes and buried under earth. He ran out and cursed Heaven, forgetting his fears of the night before in the catastrophe that had now befallen him. He collected a few heads of the remaining cabbage. There were not enough to fill one of his baskets. He went slowly into the house.

"It is the end of my days," he said mournfully to his

wife. "The turnips do not mature for another month. What shall we eat?"

His wife sat down upon a wooden bench and rocked back and forth, wiping her eyes. "I am as good as dead," she sobbed. "Nothing but evil all my days! Nevertheless, sell the cabbage. It will bring something, and, that gone, we must starve until the turnips swell at the roots."

Wang Lung went therefore toward the city in great dejection. But, before he had gone a third of a mile, he stopped in horror. A corpse lay across the road! He stared, unbelieving. The man's blood spread over the dust, and the edges of the pool curled over. It was not well to be seen beside a dead body. Lifting his eyes to pass on, Wang Lung noted to his astonishment a dozen or more sprawling shapes and beyond these others. Had all the inhabitants of the city been killed by the wrath of Heaven on the preceding night? He ran breathless through the gates and found in the street a surging, singing, yelling mob.

"What is it, what is it?" he cried, speaking to the nearest men. But they were as people insane, struggling and pushing, and Wang Lung found himself swept on, unanswered, into the midst of the crowd. "What is it, what is it?" he continued to call loudly. But no one told him, and he could walk neither forward nor backward of his own will. He began to be afraid. "Why did I not send the Mother of Slaves this morning to the market?" he muttered to himself.

Then he heard a hoarse voice cry: "This way to the rich man's house! This way to the foreigners!" Instantly he knew what was happening. It was the Revolution. As his heart began to beat quickly, he gave himself to the multitude, only struggling to keep from being trampled. In the midst of the mob were soldiers, but not soldiers like the dead ones on the roadside. These were short, slender men, and they kept shouting in a sort of rhythm, "On—on—riches—riches!"

He grew dizzy. He did not know what it was all about, or what had happened. But he rushed on with the others until they came before a tall gate set in a brick wall. It was in a part of the city that he could not recognize. Ordinarily he would not have dreamed of entering such a gate as this. But today the wild daring of the crowd caught him, and he felt he had a right to anything.

Two soldiers struggled forward and pounded on the gate with the butts of their guns. He stared at them and saw that their faces were flushed as if with wine and their eyes terrible and glittering like glass. They beat against the gate again and again until at last a board gave way. Then they turned to the mob. "All is yours, now," they cried. "The poor shall become rich and the rich become poor. A thousand years to the Revolution!"

But the mob halted an instant, wavering. Then the boldest of those excited men and women crept through the hole and unbarred the gate, and afterward they all passed slowly in. Wang Lung was upon the outskirts, and, when he had crawled through the gate, he straightened himself and looked curiously about him for an instant at a square of smooth grass edged with trees and a row of many-colored flowers. It was very clean and quiet, and there was no one to be seen.

The crowd straggled toward the two-story house set at the end of a brick wall. No one seemed to know quite what to do. But the two soldiers sprang upon the steps and pounded against the door. Someone unlocked it instantly. Wang Lung had a glimpse of a tall, strangely clothed figure and a white, calm face.

Then the crowd suddenly gathered itself and surged into the house, with a loud, prolonged murmur like the howl an animal gives above its prey. Hearing it, Wang Lung was filled with a lust stronger than lust for food. He suddenly became fiercer than a wild dog and, snarling like the others, he rushed ahead, pushing and fighting through the narrow doorway. Once within, they halted; then they swept up a flight of stairs.

There the mob broke to pieces, becoming merely separate beasts that fought over a common booty. Wang Lung fought with the rest, although at no time did he see clearly for what he was fighting. Through his hands passed many things: cloth, glass, paper, wood. Once he caught the gleam of a bit of silver and laid hold on that, but, when it was snatched from him, forgot it to seize something else. He stopped to look at nothing, seeing always in other hands an object more desirable.

His eyes burned and blurred with his beating blood, and like the others he yelled incessantly without knowing that he made any noise. He was possessed of a greed so great that it left room for nothing else in his mind. Whenever a fresh closet or fresh drawer was opened, a score of struggling men fell upon it, fighting, pulling, tearing. Though his arms were full of things, he dropped them all and pressed to seize on what was newly discovered.

And then, swiftly, like a gale passing on a summer's day, the crowd swept out. Since he had been among the first to come into the house, he was now among the last to leave. He found himself alone at the end, and, like a man who wakes from a sleep, he looked around him. The room was bare of everything except two broken chairs, a small table and a chest of drawers with gaping holes where the drawers had been pulled out.

He came then to his right mind. What was he doing here? This was a foreigner's house. He looked at the chairs. They were of common wood. The table, too, was of cheap wood and not of gold, as they had told him. The walls were whitewashed and bare, and the floor was of rough, painted wood.

For the first time he looked curiously at the things in his hands. They were a child's garment of white cotton cloth, a large leather shoe, two stiff-backed books, full of strange characters, and a small, worn purse containing a dollar and some copper money. There was nothing even remotely like the blue gown.

He sighed and felt all at once very tired, and then he knelt and packed everything securely in the garment and turned to go downstairs. He had come up those stairs quickly and easily, but now he found them difficult and strange, since he had never been on stairs before that day. He shifted his bundle and clung to a railing and went stiffly down. He was quite exhausted.

Down-stairs there were still a few women, picking up

articles that others had dropped in their haste. Wang Lung stopped, thinking he might see something of value. But there were only many books scattered about and one or two wooden chairs, another wooden table, a picture torn and trampled—nothing of any value anywhere. He saw a bit of gray cloth and stooped and, as he did so, caught sight of a little group in the inner room.

They were people such as he had never seen before—a man, a woman, two children, standing close together. Their clothes were torn and soiled and their upper clothes were entirely gone. The woman had drawn a piece of cloth about her shoulders. On the man's forehead was a cut, and a rill of blood was trickling down the side of his white face. Wang Lung had never seen blood so red.

He stared at them, and they looked steadfastly back at him in silence, even the children uttering no sound. He found this gaze difficult to endure at last. He looked away and then back again, and the man said something in a strange tongue. The woman smiled a little bitterly, and they all continued to look at him with their shining, steady eyes. "These people are not afraid!" Wang Lung said aloud, and then, hearing his own voice, he was suddenly ashamed and ran quickly out of the gate.

The streets were deserted, but in the distance he could hear the howling noise of the mob. After a moment's hesitancy, he turned and walked steadily toward his home. Still the dead soldiers lay on the road, and flies were beginning to gather from the hot sunshine. Country people were hurrying along toward the city. They asked Wang Lung many times what was taking place there, but he only shook his head. He was very tired of everything. He cared for nothing in the world.

When he reached home, he put his bundle on the table and said to his wife, "There is my share of the Revolution."

Then he went into the inner room and threw himself on the bed. He remembered nothing definitely except the strange clear gaze of those foreign eyes. "They were really not afraid," he muttered to himself. And then, turning over, he said, "I do not believe they were even rich people."

In the other room he heard his wife exclaiming, "These books are fit for nothing but to make shoe soles, but at least this dollar will feed us until the turnips can be eaten."

THE COMMUNIST

⊱≈⊰

THE next morning at six o'clock she was to be killed. That was the only thing that stood out perfectly clear and perfectly certain in her mind after these dazed, wild months. Just as in the old days when she had sewed in the mission-school industrial class she had cut straight across a piece of new cloth, spoiling forever its newness, so tomorrow morning would someone cut across her life, severing this mind of hers from these astonishing, scorching memories that were still hot in her heart. She had liked to cut across cloth that way. Even after the white stuff was all folded into a roll ready for tomorrow's sewing, she liked to pick up the bits of cloth on the table and floor and cut them across again and again until there was only a heap of worthless scraps left. There was never more than a small pile; the sharp-eyed sewing teacher saw to that—a small, worthless pile such as she would be tomorrow after they had stood her up among the hundreds of others. Among them all she would scarcely be distinguished by anything—nothing to mark out her dead body from any other. No one would come to take it away—no one

227

knew she was herded like this into a prison. She had not once during these ten months since the revolutionists entered the city thought of her parents—not, at least, for more than a moment of impatience at their unreality. They were dull, stupid people living in the established respectability of a well-to-do village homestead. Established? Nothing was established except this—that tomorrow at six o'clock she would be shot.

This had been the glory of these months—that everything was to be changed, everything destroyed, everything marvelously rebuilt. What a child she had been ten months ago, as she sat sewing in her boarding-school with the dull teachers walking to and fro between the desks—stupid American women who, when they spoke, marred the syllables of their words with their clumsy tongues. That was quickly over. In a day the school had been overturned. Everything had been overturned. The revolutionists had come marching down the streets, singing, drunken with their singing but not with wine. Some spirit possessed them that had made the other girls, everybody, afraid of them. She was not afraid. She had bent from the window, looking at them, seeing the white sun upon the flags, the flags of the new world, and she had bent farther still and shouted, "A thousand thousand years to the Revolution!" All their passionate faces had turned up to her at the sound of her voice, as leaves upon a tree are turned by a wind. Hundreds of faces had suddenly looked at her, and they were all alike, bronze with black eyes. All except that one. Why did she think of him? She would not—not when only these few hours remained to her.

They had come swinging into the school yard, that stupid, dull yard where day after day she had moved her arms and marched unwillingly to the sharp command of a teacher's voice. "Hold your head up, please. Siu-mei, hold your head up! Now then, breathe deeply—one, two, one two." All that was quickly done with when the revolutionists came marching in, glorifying forever that barren bit of school yard. They had come in shouting, and the foreigners had had to flee swiftly. Some of the girls had wept and hidden them in the fuel-house. She would have nothing to do with that; she never saw them again. Let them go. She would not waste the few hours in remembering that long-nosed woman—what was the use of remembering her name even? All that was finished forever.

Some of the girls had been afraid when the solid gray ranks came singing through the gates. That fat Meiling— how she had run screaming and trying to hide and wedging her fat body into impossible corners! As if any man would desire her! But *she* had not been afraid. She had stood at the door and held it back, facing them gravely, and, when they swept in with their faces like hawks' faces and their eyes glittering, she had saluted and cried again, "A thousand thousand years to the Revolution!" All those faces were alike to her, none more shining than another. Then that one man had come forward, throwing his arm roughly about her shoulders, that one who was like none of the others, with his ruddy skin and blue eyes, taller by head and shoulders than anybody she had ever seen.

"This one for me, comrades!" She had not dreamed that any foreigner could speak Chinese like that—scarcely a burr. She looked at him as if the heavens had opened suddenly above her, and he clapped her upon the back and laughed a splendid, lusty laugh that shook in his strong white throat.

Why should she think of this one, when tomorrow she would be dead? She had thought only of him from that instant—never of anything else. Let her try to remember now why she was to die and where she could get a little strength to die with.

He had not let her go all day, hurrying her everywhere in the circle of his arm, saying a dozen times in his great voice: "Not afraid? Ah, that's a comrade for me! I hate them running and screaming and hiding. Someone not afraid to come with me!" She had not said one word; she could not say one word. When she looked at him, there was no possibility of words. There was no fear at all— what did it matter what he did to her? He covered her under his blanket that night in a shadow of a gutted building when the men were exhausted with burning and looting and their singing had mounted to a frenzy of shouting and screaming.

Dead people lay everywhere, men and women and children, their bodies flung about in any shape and order. At first they had killed only those who opposed them, but after that it became hard to distinguish and some of them began killing anyone they saw. They were all mad at last —but not that one in whose arm she was held that day! He laughed a little all the time, his eyes glittering. He killed scarcely anyone—once a fat, frightened merchant in a silk gown who ran trembling out of his house when the soldiers went in to loot. The old man had fallen just like a stuck pig, his jowls waxen and shaking after he had writhed an instant upon the cobblestones. She had not been at all frightened, and he had drawn out his bayonet and wiped it clean on the merchant's delicate fawn-colored gown. His blue eyes had smiled down on her, hard and clear as ice. "All who are fat and overfed ought to die because they are hideous," he said, laughing. "Capitalists!" He said the word with a sort of lazy, amused hatred. She did not know what it was, that word, beyond having heard it sometimes in fragments of political speeches caught at street corners when the students were marching along two by two on their way to church, their Bibles folded in white handkerchiefs under their arms. Did she once do that? She pondered. Think of walking to church to sing psalms! There were no churches any more. He had laughed at the churches that day, with the soldiers sprawling about the altars, gambling and disputing for loot, chopping up the pulpits for fuel to cook their food, and sleeping at night upon benches.

"Well, the churches are some use after all," he had cried gaily when they saw the poor, the people who swarm through the hidden streets and byways searching for food, tearing at the windows and the floors and the high holy seats where the preachers had once sat in their robes, tearing them up for fuel to cook their food. When she told him that she once had sat there decorously, he said, "And did you learn to be good, little thing?" She shook her head and said with that strange passion that ate at her always since

231

she had been with him, "I never learned anything until you came."

Why did she keep thinking about him? The sun was creeping high in the heavens and sending a scanty beam into the window. All over the wretched room shapes of human beings took on life, stirring out of sleep, yawning, exposing yellow teeth, hawking, spitting, groaning. All of them would be dead when the sun was as high as this tomorrow. Today she stood erect among them, clinging desperately to the bars of the window, catching a faint fragrance of new willow-leaves and peach-blossoms. Tomorrow morning she could not stand if she would. Her body would lie helpless—was it possible there could at last be no feeling in this body of hers? Every nerve in it had been alive since that night when he had covered her with his blanket and drawn her to him. "Do you like the Revolution?" he had said to her once in the night. "Do you like the Revolution? Think what I have saved you from, little one. I'll wager you were betrothed to some respectable country lad—those red cheeks of yours are from the country. He'd never love you as I have done." He shook her gently and then fiercely. "Answer me or I shall kiss you to death! We Communists have all sorts of ways of killing. Shall I kiss you to death? I could. I will, if you don't tell me you are glad I found you."

She held her head against the bars. Why was she thinking of him? It was perfectly true that she had been betrothed all her life to a neighbor's son. They had played together in those far-off days when she had lived in the little village. When they were older, her parents had sent

232

her away to school because it was not seemly for a maiden to be seen daily by her betrothed. She had not seen him for many years, but they told her, others—the old servant in her father's house told her, whispering and ogling—that he was a fine lad, filial and earnest in his study of the Confucian ethics. Ethics, Confucius—she knew nothing except that one time she had lain all night in a man's arms, her cheek against the bare white flesh of his shoulder.

"I do not even know your name. You do not know mine."

He had laughed in the darkness. He laughed easily, that lusty, careless laugh.

"What does it matter, little thing? I am called Piotr the Communist, and my address is the world! But tonight my home is here with you, like this."

"You will not leave me? Surely you will not!"

His laughter again. "You brown-skinned little thing—even that does not matter."

"It is all that matters to me, now," she whispered.

She waited, half expecting to hear through the darkness the laughter welling up from his throat. She wished that she could brush the darkness away and look at him again. It seemed to her that she had forgotten since darkness fell exactly how the lines of his ruddy face curved. There had been houses burning and flames leaping up in the distance, and she wished that there were a house burning here that the light might be a lamp to her. But there were only ashes around them.

He did not laugh. He said with a sort of hurried seriousness: "You might come with me. No, I do not stay anywhere—one can't take women along. You see, I have work to do in the world."

"What work?"

Now he was laughing. "What, all day with me and you haven't seen my work—that fat merchant, these burning houses, you little freed thing? All my work!"

She fell into silence, wondering with a dawning bitterness whether tomorrow he would free another girl and sleep with her all night. But his hands on her humbled her pride utterly. It did not matter. It was the Revolution. What came after the dawn broke was nothing, nothing. She pressed herself into his bosom; she took his hand and buried her face in it, a big, rough, hot hand; she was speechless because she had never known the words of love. She said she would not sleep—only lie like this. But before dawn she was exhausted and slept, and, when she woke, he was gone and the sun had come up as yellow as brass. She rose and looked about her at the ashes and broken bricks of what had yesterday been houses. A few people moved miserably about, searching for possessions. She held back her long black hair wildly with one hand and stared at them. They were none of them he. He was gone. She had never seen him again.

What did it matter that she was to die tomorrow? She had never seen him again.

She had searched for him everywhere among the ranks of the Communists, asking for him. "I, too, am a Communist, comrades. I was converted by Piotr the tall Russian. Have any of you seen him?"

But he was not to be found. They taught her the songs

and the slogans, and she learned them because they were his songs. Sometimes they talked, and they said: "We do not need these Russians. We Chinese, we must manage our own Revolution. That tall Russian now—even though he was a Communist, it was not seemly that he killed Chinese. We will do our own killing."

Then there was a change in sentiment. People whose houses had been burned and kinsfolk killed, people who were against Communism, came into power again through one of the twists of the Revolution, and her comrades were swept in hordes to the prisons and to execution.

It was very easy to seize her. She had been proud of being a Communist. When her parents had sent from the village for her to come home to safety, she had bade the servant return, saying that she was safe—she was serving the Revolution. Her father even came at last, creeping secretly through the city gates by night, desperately frightened, knocking at the gate of the little inn where she was quartered with the other women Communists. She went to the gate and saw him there, his scanty white locks blowing in the wind and his jaw quivering with fright. He had at last fallen to his knees, this old man, before his daughter.

"Oh, my daughter, we fear for your life."

"You need not. I am safe."

"We are your parents."

"I have no parents. The Revolution is my father and my mother."

"But your betrothed, he who waits for you!"

"I am married already."

235

"Married?" He was very old indeed, and the moonlight was amber-colored on his wrinkled face.

"I am married to—to the Revolution!"

She had shut the gate then. She could never go back. One place on earth where she knew she could never meet Piotr was in that quiet village, wedded and shut behind walls.

Dawn came breaking in a streak of silver. So had dawn broken for her once before. There were the guards coming now; they would get the killing over early before people began to stir. It did not matter about killing. The people had seen a great deal of it first and last—she herself—a dead body was nothing, part of the Revolution. A heavy-faced man rose, yawned and glanced over the crowd. "A hundred of us to be sent to the Yellow Springs this morning? Ah, well, I have taken care of as many in a good day!"

She, too, would be ready. But what should she do in memory of the hour before that other dawn? How celebrate on this her last day the moment in which she had lived?

They drove them all out and only she was left, standing against the wet brick wall. The guard pricked at her with his gun. "Get on."

She looked about her desperately. "I will not."

"What, you will not die?"

"I do not care for that. I will not be driven out like these sheep. I wish to—to go to my death singing."

"What—a Christian?" The guard smiled. He was enjoying her. He nudged his assistant. "Pretty, isn't she!—

236

Speak, then. What do you want? A bridal-chair? A car like the Governor's? Anything!"

She seized at the idea. Anything to be lifted out of that mass of stooping, frightened people. "I demand a car. Look, I am weak. Yesterday I could not eat."

"Well, I will see," said the guard indulgently.

But in the end it had only been the police wagon drawn by heavy black oxen. She refused at first to climb upon it, but the guard was impatient. "They will all be dead before we get there," he cried, and then she climbed over the wheel.

Up over the edge of a black cloud shone the light of the coming sun. People were beginning to stand in their doorways, and, seeing the procession, they called to one another. "They are killing the Communists! See, see, a killing! Ah, the killers killed at last!"

She stood swaying on the old ox-cart, clinging to the top. The oxen were sleek and stupid, and they made her think suddenly of her father's farm in the village and of the wet fields of black earth ready for the planting of the rice. Well, that was all ended. She heard someone say, "See that one—what a young, pretty girl to die!" and suddenly her breath came short and she knew that she was very pitiable indeed. She looked down at her slender body in its blue-cotton coat and trousers. He had called her over and over, "Little one, little thing."

She began moaning softly. Was she going to weep? No, there was nothing sad, nothing pitiable. She was dying free. Piotr had freed her. Out of all these hundreds of people she alone had had that night which was better than years in a courtyard. The sun showed a hard silver rim above the cloud, and she began to sing clearly a song of her own making, the words coming into her mouth as she spoke them. No one understood what she sang. If he himself had been there, he would not have understood. It was the song of one who has had an hour of life, an hour that has passed. The people listened. As she sang, she remembered, and her body straightened and her eyes grew luminous. But the people only murmured: "See what a stanch Communist this little one is! Ah, but she must be a bad one! She goes to death singing!"

FATHER ANDREA

FATHER ANDREA lived all day for the hours at night when he might study the stars. The days in his parish in the Chinese city were long and crowded, filled with people and voices crying and complaining and demanding, and the nights were short and radiant with the silent, peaceful stars, shining like torches out of the dark purple sky. He could never get enough of them. The hours with his telescope went so quickly that many times he remembered to sleep only when the dawn came up out of the east with such ruddy splendor that the stars faded. But he did not need sleep. He could return to the day refreshed and braced by those hours of study and observation of the golden stars, when the voices that clamored after him all day were asleep for a brief while. "Bless sleep!" he would say to himself, chuckling as he climbed the steps to the tiny observatory he had built on top of the schoolhouse.

He was a small, stout, smiling man, whose exterior revealed nothing of his soft, mystic soul. If one saw only his apple cheeks and dark beard and red, smiling mouth, one would say that he was a lover of visible life. One needed

to see his eyes to discover that he was a lover of things un-
seen. His lips went on smiling even when a leper came
twisting and beseeching about his feet, or a wretched slave-
girl ran in, cowering and crying, through the gates of the
mission. But his eyes, deep set and dark, were often full of
tears.

During the day he lifted up the lepers with his hands
and washed them and fed them and soothed them and
smeared oil upon their wounds. He stood between the
slave-girl and her angry, cursing mistress, smiling, waiting,
talking in that quiet, ceaseless, murmuring way he had.
The woman's angry voice rose above it like a storm above
a brook, but sooner or later his gentle, insistent speech
won, and she would sit sulking, in answer to his invitation, in the seat of honor at the right of the square table in
his little guest-hall, and sip the tea he had asked the servant to bring. And then, with his small, dark, tragic eyes
grave above his smiling mouth, he would talk on, praising,
suggesting, regretting, hinting gently of the necessity of
better things, until in the end the slave went away with
the mistress. He would never help people to break away
from what held them fast. His great concern always was to
help them bear more easily the inevitable yoke that life had
placed upon each of them. That was the one thing he was
sure of—that there was no getting away from the oppres-
sion that life itself brought.

Talking in the morning to the boys in his school, he said
one day more earnestly than he had ever before said anything:

"My sons, I will tell you a thing. You think, when you

are children, that you will break away from the bondage of your parents and that when you go to school you will be free of them. In school you dream of manhood, when there will be no more teachers for you to obey. But you can never be free! When your immortal souls took on flesh, they became even as the Son of Man was—bound. No man is free—we are not free of one another—we can never be free of God.

"The thing is, not to cry futilely after freedom, but to discover cheerfully how to bear the burden of bondage upon us. Even the stars in heaven are not free. They too must obey the paths of order in law, lest by their wantonness they wreck the universe. You have seen the shooting stars in the sky in summer. They seem beautiful in freedom, a burst of light and splendor against the clouds. But their end is destruction and darkness. It is the stars marching steadily on in their appointed ways which endure to the end."

The little blue-coated Chinese boys stared at him, wondering at the passion in his quiet voice and at the unwonted somberness of his round, smiling face. They did not understand him at all.

All day long he trotted hither and thither about his duty, beginning at dawn by saying mass for a few faithful old women who came decently garbed in their cotton coats and trousers, with black kerchiefs folded about their heads. It troubled him sometimes that they did not grasp much of what he said; his Chinese had never been perfect and it was spoken with a soft Italian elision that could never seize the gutturals firmly. But at last, seeing their patient faces as they fixed their eyes on the Virgin and her Son, he decided that it did not matter what he said so long as they looked at the sacred picture and struggled to think of its meaning.

Before noon he tried to teach a little in the boys' school, but it was a harried business, because at any moment he would be called without to settle some affair of the poor.

"Father, I sold this man tenpence of rice last night and trusted him until this morning for the money, and now, having eaten the rice, he tells me he has nothing."

Two men in coolie trousers, their backs bare and blackened with the sun, stood before him, one angry, one defiant.

"Now, then, was not my stomach empty? Am I to starve when you have food? The revolutionists are coming, and, when they come, all men like you who have rice must give to us who have not, and no talk of money, either!"

The two glared at each other as angry cocks will glare before attacking, and Father Andrea put a hand on each man's arm. His hands told the story begun by his eyes, small, brown, perfectly shaped hands that were broken and wrinkled with the washings and scrubbings he gave them. It was one of the agonies of his life that he could not subdue his flesh to the point of touching dark, unwashed bodies without some shrinking of his spirit. It was an obsession with him to wash his hands again and again, so that they were always scented faintly with carbolic soap. One of his private penances was to go without washing his hands, making himself endure the shuddering when he put them upon a child's head, crusted with the scald of disease. He had schooled himself to touch everything that made him recoil and, seeing his freely moving, kindly, expressive hands, no one dreamed of the inner withdrawal.

So now, one of his hands warm and persuasive upon the arm of each man, he said to the defiant one: "My friend, I know nothing of the revolutionists. But this I do know. My garden needs weeding today, and, if you will weed it, I will gladly pay you wages and, out of the wages, I who know your good heart am sure you will not withhold the tenpence to your neighbor. He is a poor man with children, and you have eaten his rice. It is written, 'If any would not work, neither should he eat.' It is one of the laws of life, which even the revolution cannot rightly change."

Instantly the tension on the two faces faded away, and the two men laughed and showed their white teeth, and Father Andrea laughed, wrinkling his round, rosy face, and went back to his boys. At the end of the day he paid the man double wages. "Take it," he said when the man made a feint of refusal. "Some day I will ask you to work for me again, and on that day I may not have the money by me."

In the afternoon, after his dish of rice and beans and macaroni, he put on his flat black hat and went out and visited the people and drank tea with them and ate the hard-boiled eggs the housewives would cook for him, although his soul loathed them, and listened, smiling, to all that was said. He knew no rich people. These scorned him as a Catholic priest and a foreigner, and he would not have forced his presence upon them even if he could. He went into the low, thatched houses of the poor and into the mat sheds of beggars, and he gave them his money as fast as it came into his hands. Of the great storm gathering without, the storm of the revolution, these people knew nothing, and no more did Father Andrea know. He had read no newspapers for years, and he had no idea of anything that was happening beyond this round of days and splendid nights.

Once a week he allowed himself to remember his own country. On the evening of the seventh day he washed himself and trimmed his dark beard and put a little scent upon his hands, and then he went up into the tiny observatory and sat in an old easy chair he had there. On the other nights he sat upon a stool by the table and took out his pens and papers and his measuring instruments and in his small, accurate handwriting he made notes which he sent to his Superior in Siccawei. Through all these years of evenings he had gradually become one of the chief of a group of astronomers in the Far East, although he did not know it. To him his study of the heavens was the relaxation and exhilaration of a brain formed for meticulous observation and keen, hard thinking.

But on this seventh day he took no paper and pens. He sat down and opened the windows and fixed his eyes upon the stars and allowed his thoughts to take him back to Italy, his country, to which he had not returned for twenty-seven years and which he would never behold again. He had been a young man when he left, scarcely thirty, but even after all these years he remembered with passionate sharpness the agony of that parting. Even yet he could see the bay, rounding into a circle smaller and smaller as the ship drew out from the land. Every week he thought gravely and with a sense of guilt that above his sense of mission still was the memory of that parting, and that sharper than the parting of his body from his motherland, from his home and parents and his sister and his brother, was the parting of his spirit from his beloved, his Vitellia, who had loved his brother more than him.

He had done penance all these years for this sin, that he had come into the Church, not for devotion to God and Mary, but because Vitellia did not love him. Not that she or anyone else knew it. His brother was tall and handsome and grave, with beautiful, languishing brown eyes, and Vitellia was tall and pale and exquisite as an olive-tree in new leafage, her colors all soft and subdued and mist-like. She was head and shoulders above the little rosy man he always was. No one thought of him seriously. He was always laughing and joking and merry, his small, deep-set, black eyes crackling with humor.

Even after his brother's marriage he did not stop his joking. But he waited to see whether or not his brother was good to Vitellia. There was nothing to complain of there. His brother was a good man, although a little dull inside his beauty of body, and, when he found himself married and soon with a child coming, he settled down into his father's wine business and they were very happy. No, there was nothing to complain of there.

Then it was that Andrea became frightened at the power of his passion. He saw that nothing would keep him from revealing himself except entire submission to his fate. That took a year of fever and agony, and it was not complete until he saw that for him there was no renunciation wholly efficacious except priesthood in some far country. Then he fled to the fathers in his village.

His family had laughed at him—everyone laughed at him—and Vitellia had nearly ruined him by clinging to his hand and saying in that voice of hers that was more to him than music, "But brother mine, my Andrea, who will play with my children and be always in my house?" He had shaken his head, smiling and speechless, and she had looked at him in surprise and seen that his eyes were full of tears. "Must you, if you mind so much, Andrea?" And he had nodded.

Ah, well, it was all done, long, long ago. For many years he had not allowed himself to think of her because she was another man's wife, and he had come to the stars night after night and prayed passionately for peace. It seemed to him that he could never do penance enough for loving Vitellia more than anyone else always to the very end. That made him deny himself fiercely and force himself to every distasteful touch and duty. Once, when his flesh had burned after her, he had gone wildly out into the streets and had brought in a beggar from the winter's night, a poor, shivering wretch, and had laid him in his bed and covered him with his blankets and had stretched himself out beside the creature all night long, his teeth clenched and his stomach sick. But in the morning he whispered triumphantly to his body, "Now will you be quiet and cease troubling me!" All this explained the smiling tragedy in his eyes and his constant preaching of bearing one's yoke.

When one day a black-bordered letter came, the first letter in many years, he opened it, and within was the news of Vitellia's death. Then it seemed that peace of a sort came upon him, and after a while he allowed himself this relaxation on the evening of seventh days and even at last permitted himself to think a little of her. Now that she was dead, he could imagine her up yonder, moving in that free, light way she had, among the stars. She was no one's wife now—she belonged to no one. She was a part of heaven, and he could think of her as of a star and be without sin.

He began to preach less vehemently and more patiently about bearing the yoke. When one of his schoolboys ran away to join the revolutionists, he went out with a sigh and sought him and talked with him gently, begging him to come back to his weeping mother.

"The good God puts us into life with a duty to perform," he said tenderly, smiling a little, with his arm about the boy's shoulders.

But the boy shook himself free and moved away. "In the revolution there is no God and there is no duty," he said imperiously. "We are all free, and we preach a gospel of freedom for everyone."

"Ah?" said Father Andrea softly.

For the first time a premonition fell upon him. He had up to this time paid no attention to the talk of revolution. His paths had not led him a mile from the congested quarter where he lived. It occurred to him that now he must look into such talk, especially if his boys were going off like this. He began to speak then of other things, but the boy was wary and obviously eager to have him gone. There were other lads about and an officer or two. The boy's answers grew shorter and shorter. He cast angry looks at his fellows. At last Father Andrea said kindly: "I see that you have other things on your mind. I will leave you now. Do not forget the prayers that you have been taught, my child."

He put his hand on the lad's head for an instant and turned away, but, before he left the barracks, a hoot of laughter arose, and he heard the lads shouting to their comrade, "Running-dog of a foreigner, are you?"

He had no idea what this meant, and he thought once of going back. He stopped to listen. Someone cried out, laughing like a whip's cut, "Ah, a Christian!" Then he heard the boy's voice raised angrily, half-sobbing: "I hate the priest—I know nothing of his religion. I am a revolutionist! Does anyone dare to question me?"

Father Andrea stood stricken. What words were these to come from his lad's mouth, his lad who had been in his school ever since he was five years old? He trembled a little, and a thought shot into his mind like a pang. "So did Peter deny his Lord!" And he went back into the little mission that was his home and shut himself up in his room and wept bitterly.

After that it seemed to him that he had been standing on the edge of a whirlpool and had not known it. He had said that he must investigate this revolution and see that his boys were not carried away. But there was no need of investigation. Knowledge and experience came pouring over him, and he was caught in a maze of difficulties.

There was so much he had not known. He had never heard of political differences between East and West. He had come only as one who wished to bury himself in his mission to a land where there was not his true Church. In this one spot in an immense crowded city he had lived day after day for twenty-seven years, and his small, black-robed figure had become as much a part of the street as an ancient temple or bridge. Children, as long as they could remember, were accustomed to the sight of him, trudging along in all weathers, his pockets bulging ridiculously with peanuts for them. No one thought of him. Women washing at the well looked up as he came by, knew that it must be an hour after noon and sighed to think of the hours before sunset. Men nodded at him carelessly from the counters of the little shops open to the streets and accepted with good humor his tracts and pictures of the Virgin.

Now this was changed. He was no longer Father Andrea, a harmless, aging priest. He became instead a foreigner.

One day a child refused to take the peanuts he held out to it. "My mother says they may be poisoned," the child said, looking up at Father Andrea with wide eyes.

"Poisoned?" said Father Andrea vaguely and in great surprise.

The next day he returned with his pockets as heavy as when he started, and after that he took no more peanuts. Once a woman spat after him as he passed the well. Then men shook their heads coldly when he smiled and proffered his tracts. He was completely bewildered.

At last one night his native assistant came to him. He was a good old man with a straggling, scanty white beard, honest and a little stupid, so that he never quite got his *Aves* right. Father Andrea had wondered sometimes if he should not find someone more able, but he could never bring himself to tell the old man that he was not perfect. Now he said to Father Andrea, "My Father, do not go out until this madness is past."

"What madness?" asked Father Andrea.

"This talk about foreigners and revolutions. The people are listening to these young men in long black gowns who come from the South, and they say that the foreigners are killing the people and stealing their hearts with new religions."

"New religions?" said Father Andrea mildly. "There is nothing new about mine. I have been here preaching and teaching for more than a quarter of a century."

"Even so, sir, you are a foreigner," replied the old man apologetically.

"Well," said Father Andrea at last, "this astonishes me very much!"

But he listened to the old man after the next day; for, when he stepped from the gate into the street, a great stone flung at him flew against his breast and broke into two pieces the ebony cross that hung there, and, when he put up his hand, aghast, another stone flew against him and cut his hand badly. He turned white and went into the mission house and shut the door and fell upon his knees and looked at the broken cross. For a long time he could say nothing, but at last words came to his lips and he prayed an old prayer. "Father, forgive them; for they know not what they do."

After that he stayed in the compound. Within a few days no one came any more, and he locked the door of the empty schoolroom sadly. It was as if he were in the quiet center of a storm. From outside the lonely compound where he and his old assistant pottered about the garden, strange sounds rose up in confusion from the streets. He locked the gate, opening it only once a day in the evening for the old man to creep out and buy a little food. At last one day the old man came back with his basket empty.

"They will not let me buy food for you," he said piteously. "To save your life I must pretend to leave you, and I must pretend to hate you. But every night I will throw food over the western corner of the garden. And every evening at the hour I will repeat the *Ave*. Our God must look after you beyond this."

Thereafter Father Andrea was quite alone. He spent a great deal of time in the observatory, and he allowed himself to think and remember every evening now. The days were long and solitary, and he missed even the lepers. There was no more need to wash his hands except of the clean garden earth that clung to them after he had been working among the vegetables. And, outside, the noise rose and mounted until he fancied that he was on some small island in the midst of a raging sea and that one day the waves would break over him even there.

He withdrew into his thoughts more and more, and he built little dreams of Italy and of the grape garden where he had played as a boy. He could smell the hot sun on the ripe grapes—incomparable fragrance! Sitting in the old easy chair night after night, he began to reconstruct from the beginning his life. It was May, and the stars were brilliant in a purple sky. But he no longer touched his note-books and pens. He had become indifferent to anything of the stars except their sheer unearthly beauty. Thank God for stars and sky everywhere! These Chinese skies in May were like the skies of Italy in summer, the stars hanging heavy and golden in the dark sky. Once on a night like this in Italy he had leaned from his window and gone suddenly mad with the beauty of the stars, and he had run blindly out of the house to Vitellia. His heart was beating like a great drum, shaking his body with every throb, and he had cried that he must tell her that he loved her. When he had got to his brother's house, his brother had opened the door and said kindly: "We were just about to sleep, Andrea. Is there anything we can do for you?"

Behind his brother he saw Vitellia, shadowy in the room, her face pale and indistinct as a flower in the twilight. She came forward and rested her hand lightly upon her husband's arm and leaned her head upon his shoulder. She was quite content. Passion went out of him.

"No, thank you," he stammered. "I thought—I did not know it was so late—I thought I might come in and talk a little while, perhaps."

"Yes, another day," said his brother gravely. And Vitellia had called, "Good night, brother Andrea!" And the door shut, and he was alone.

That was the night he had stayed in the garden the whole night through, and at dawn he had said at last that he would give himself to the poor, since Vitellia did not need him—the poor of a far country.

Ah, all that passion and pain and the youth he had had to wear down by sheer indomitable will to suffer! He would still never be free of it—never, so long as he lived, quite free. He wondered if there among the stars Vitellia knew—there where surely everything was known. He hoped so. That would mean that he need not tell her of all the pain. She would understand as she had never understood on earth, and they could start in at once on the new heavenly relationship.

He sighed and went down into the garden then, and there at the western end he found a small bundle of cold rice and meat wrapped in a lotus leaf and he ate it and then said his *Aves,* his fingers hovering over the broken cross on his breast.

From outside the wall, in the street, there came the sound of steady, marching feet, thousands upon thousands of feet. He listened awhile, wondering, and then, with a sigh, he went up again to his observatory and sat down, and, looking off into the clear spaces of heaven, he slept lightly.

In the morning he awoke with a start of premonition, as if he had been aroused suddenly by a noise. He could not for an instant collect himself. The stars were weak in the gray light of the dawn, and the roof of the church was dark and wet with dew. From without there came a sound of mad confusion, and shooting and shouts rent the air. He listened. There were several shots in quick succession. He sat up, trying to think what this could be. Was this what had waked him? There was no more marching. A huge blaze lighted up the distant eastern sky. Something was burning—that was the rich quarter of the city, where the streets were hung with the scarlet and yellow banners of the big grain-shops and silk-shops and sing-song houses. But it might be only the sun rising? No, there was no such splendor of sunrise out of this gray sky.

He dragged himself from the chair and went down-stairs heavily, with vague alarm. He had not slept rest-fully, and his mind felt fogged. As he reached the foot of the steps and stood upon the grass, there came a terrific pounding at the gate, and he moved quickly to open it, rubbing his head a little to collect his thoughts. This was the noise he had heard in his sleep! He fumbled at the great wooden bar and withdrew it at last and opened the gate and stared out in amazement. Hundreds of men stood there in a mass—soldiers in gray uniform. Their faces were ferocious as he had not dreamed human faces could be, and he shrank from them as he had never shrunk from his lepers. They leveled their guns at him then with a tigerish shout. He was not afraid, only completely amazed.

"But what do you want, my friends?" he asked in sur-prise.

A young man, scarcely older than his schoolboy who had run away, stepped forward and tore the rosary from about his neck. The fragment of broken cross, all that was left of the cross he had worn for so many years, fell to the ground.

"We have come to rid the world of imperialists and cap-italists!" the young man shouted.

"Imperialists and capitalists?" said Father Andrea, won-dering. They were words he had never heard. It had been many years since he had read anything except the ancient

Church fathers and his books of astronomy. He did not have the faintest idea what the lad meant.

But the boy cocked his gun and pointed it at Father Andrea. "We are the revolutionists!" he cried. His voice was rough and harsh as if he had been shouting for many hours, and his smooth, youthful face was blotched and red as if with drinking. "We come to set everyone free!"

"Set everyone free?" said Father Andrea slowly, smiling a little. He stooped to pick up his cross from the dust.

But before his hand could touch that cross, the boy's finger moved spasmodically upon the trigger and there was a sharp report, and Father Andrea fell upon the ground, dead.

THE NEW ROAD

LU CHEN kept a hot-water shop on the corner of the street of the North Gate, where the alley of the Hwang family intersects it. As everyone knows, that was one of the chief places in the whole length of that street. Not only did the silk-shops fling out their banners of orange silk, but down the alley of the Hwangs lived other great families. A score of times a day the clerks idling about the dim shops sent the tea-coolie for pots of scalding water to brew the tea that they sipped the whole day through. A score of times a day the ladies of the alley, gambling delicately as a pastime in one another's houses, sent their slaves to get water from Lu Chen. It was a thriving business and had been a thriving business even in his grandfather's time, when an emperor had lived but a few miles away and that very street had ended in a prince's pleasure-grounds.

From his father Lu Chen had received the shop, together with a rice-sack full of silver dollars. The rice-sack had been emptied to pay for his wedding, but gradually it had been filled again to pay for the schooling and then the wedding of his son. Now, after this last emptying, it was a fifth full again, and Lu Chen's grandchild ran about the shop, terrifying the old man with his venturesome spirit and his curiosity regarding the great copper caldrons built into the earthen ovens.

"When I was a child," Lu Chen proclaimed at least daily to his small grandson, "I never ran near the caldrons. I obeyed my grandfather and did not eternally run about like a small chicken."

Of this the grandson understood nothing. He was as yet too young to speak clearly, but he was able to understand that he was the center of his grandfather's heart, and he continued to stagger about near the ovens under the old man's agitated eye. He had become accustomed, of course, to being lifted suddenly by the collar of his small coat and to dangling in the air while his grandfather set him in the inner room.

"I cannot understand this child of yours," remarked Lu Chen to his tall young son. "When will you teach him obedience?"

Lu Chen's son, who had been inclined to idleness and discontent ever since finishing his fourth year at the government middle school, shrugged his shoulders in reply and said half petulantly, "We do not so worship obedience these days."

Lu Chen glanced at him sharply. He would never acknowledge that his son was at all idle. Even at night, when he lay within the curtains of his bamboo bed beside his wife, he would not acknowledge it.

Sometimes she said: "The boy has not enough to do. The shop is small, and there is really only one man's work. If you would only rest now—are you not fifty years old?—and allow our son to manage the business, it would be better. He is twenty years old, and he feels no responsibility for his rice or for the rice of his wife and the child. You do everything. Why did you send him to school if he is to be idle?"

Lu Chen threw back the thick blue cotton-stuffed quilt. This talk of giving up his work in the shop always stifled him. The real reason why he had allowed his son to continue in school year after year was that he might have the shop to himself.

"That bigger caldron," he muttered, "is never so bright as I could wish. I have said to him a dozen times, 'Take the ash from the oven and wet it a little and smear it upon the copper and, when it is dried—' but he never will do it."

"Because you are never satisfied when he does," said his wife. She was a large, stout-bodied woman; Lu Chen's small, dried figure scarcely lifted the quilt at all in comparison with the mound of her flesh beneath it.

"He will not do it as I command him," he said in a loud voice.

"You are never satisfied," she replied calmly.

This calmness of hers irritated him more than any anger. He sat upright and stared down at her placid face. Through the coarse linen curtains the light of the bean-oil lamp shone with a vague flicker; he could see her drowsy eyes and her full, expressionless lips.

"I do as my father taught me," he said shrilly.

"Ah, well," she murmured. "Let us sleep. What does it matter?"

259

He panted a moment and lay down.

"You care nothing for the shop," he said at last. It was the gravest accusation he could think of.

But she did not answer. She was asleep and her loud, tranquil breathing filled the recesses of the curtains.

The next morning he rose very early and himself scoured the inside of the two caldrons until they reflected his lean brown face. He would have liked to let them remain empty until his son awoke and so show him how they could be made to look. But he dared not, since the slaves and servants came early for hot water for their mistresses' baths. He filled the caldrons, therefore, with water from the earthen jars and lighted the fires beneath them. Soon the steam was bubbling up from under the water-soaked wooden covers. He had filled and refilled the caldrons three times before his son sauntered in, rubbing his eyes, his blue cotton gown half buttoned around him and his hair on end. Lu Chen gave him a sharp look.

"When I was young," he said, "I rose early and scoured the caldrons and lighted the fires beneath them, and my father slept."

"These are the days of the Revolution," said the young man, lightly. Lu Chen snorted and spat upon the ground. "These are the days of disobedient sons and of idle young men," he said. "What will your son be, seeing that you do not yet earn your rice?"

But the young man only smiled and, buttoning his coat slowly, went to the caldron nearest him and dipped into a basin water wherewith to wash.

Lu Chen watched him, his face quivering. "It is only for

you that I value the shop," he said at last. "It is that the business may go to you and the child after you. This hot-water shop has stood here sixty years. It is well known. All my father's life and my life and your life have come from it—and now the child's."

"There is talk of the new road now," said the young man, wringing a steaming cloth from the water and wiping his face.

That was the first time Lu Chen heard of the new road. It meant nothing to him then. His son was always away, always full of talk of new things, ever since the Revolution had come into the city. What the Revolution was Lu Chen did not clearly perceive. There had certainly been days when his business was very poor and when the great shops had been closed for fear of looting and when the families he regularly supplied had moved away to Shanghai. His business then had been reduced to the petty filling of tin teakettles for the poorer people, who haggled over a copper penny. People said it was the Revolution, and he had become anxious and cursed it in his heart. Then suddenly soldiers were everywhere, and they bought water most recklessly. That was when he began filling up the rice-sack again. That was the Revolution, too. He was mightily puzzled, but he no longer cursed it. Then the great shops opened and the old families came back and soldiers drifted away again and things were much as they had been except that prices were high, so that he could raise the price of water too, and was relieved.

"These revolutions," he said to his son one morning, "what are they about? You have been to school—do you know? It has been a great stir. I am glad it is over."

At that the son raised his eyebrows. "Over?" he repeated. "It is only begun. Wait. This city will be the capital of the country, and then everything will be greatly changed."

The old man shook his head. "Change? There is never great change. Emperors and kings and presidents or whatnot, people must drink tea and must bathe—these go on forever."

Well, but this new road? On the very day his son had mentioned it, that impudent young slave-girl from the third alley down had turned up the corner of her lip at him and said: "I hear talk from our master of a great new road sixty feet wide. What then of your caldrons, Lu Chen?"

Lu Chen's arm was bare to the elbow and wrinkled and reddened by the continued steam from the water. He scarcely felt the heat. But now, as the slave-girl spoke, he dipped his bamboo dipper more deeply into the water and grunted. His hand trembled and slopped a little water over the edge of the caldron into the hot coals of the fire. A hiss rose from them. He did not speak but made a pretense of stirring up the fire. He was not going to speak to that silly creature. Yet, after she had gone, he remembered that she was a slave in the house of Ling and that, since the eldest son of Ling was an official, there might indeed be talk of the road. He gazed about on the gray brick walls of his little shop in a sort of terror. They were darkened with smoke and dampness and had cracks that he could remember even from childhood. Sixty feet wide? Why, it would mean the whole shop ripped away!

"I will ask such a price that they cannot buy it," he

thought. "Such a price—" He cast about in himself for a sum enormous enough to stagger a government. "I will ask ten thousand dollars!"

He was happy then. Who would pay ten thousand dollars for this twelve square feet of space and the two caldrons? Where was so much money in the world? Why, when his father had been a young man, the Prince Ming-yuan had built a palace for that. He laughed a little and was more lenient with his son and forgot the new road and daily preserved the life of the child from the caldrons. Everything was as before.

One morning midway to noon he sat down to rest and drink a little tea. He always brewed his own tea after the fifth emptying of the caldrons, just before he began to fill them again for the noon call. In this interval, when people had bought for the morning tea and the hour had not yet approached for the midday meal, he could enjoy a little leisure. He took the grandchild on his knee and let him drink also and smiled to see him grasp the bowl in two hands and drink, staring gravely over the rim.

All at once there was a sharp rap like a sword-cut at the door. Lu Chen set the child down carefully and moved the teapot out of his reach. Then he went to the door and, fumbling a little, drew back the wooden bar. A man stood there in a gray cotton uniform. He was a young officer of some sort, with an arrogant eye, but he scarcely looked at Lu Chen.

"Sir," said Lu Chen a little timidly, since the young officer carried a gun and a belt stuffed with cartridges. But he was interrupted.

"The new road passes your shop. What is your name, old man?" The officer rapidly consulted a sheet of paper drawn from his pocket. "Ah, yes, Lu! Thirty feet off your house. Fifteen days from today your shop must be gone. Else we will tear it down for you." He folded the paper carelessly and put it back into his pocket. Then he turned to go away. At his heels were three common soldiers, and they turned also and fell into step. Lu Chen could not speak. He swallowed but his throat was dry. No sound came forth. One of the soldiers glanced back at him, a curious, pitying glance. That pity suddenly released the knot in Lu Chen's throat.

"Ten thousand dollars!" he called hoarsely after the young officer.

The officer halted instantly and wheeled about. "What is that?" he said sharply.

"The price of the shop is ten thousand dollars," faltered Lu Chen. The young officer grasped his gun, and Lu Chen shrank in alarm behind the door and closed it. But the young man would not have it. He walked back and thrust his gun so suddenly against the door that Lu Chen staggered and bumped into the child, who began to cry. Every time in the child's whole life that he had cried, Lu Chen had rushed to him. But now he did not even hear. He was gazing fixedly at the young officer, murmuring over and over, unconsciously, "Ten thousand dollars, ten thousand dollars."

The officer stared at him and then broke into a chilly laughter. "It is your contribution, then, to the new capital," he said, and, shouting a sharp command, he went away.

Contribution? What contribution? The child lay on the earthen floor, wailing. He was used to lying wherever he had fallen, since someone always picked him up, but now no one came. Lu Chen stood looking out through the door after the young man's figure. His heart lagged in his body so that he could scarcely draw his breath. Give up his shop, his life? What was all this talk of a new capital? It was none of his business. He turned and, seeing the child, dazedly picked him up and put him on his feet. Then, with the child in his arms, he sat down. Why, the shop was the child's! No one could take it away. Anger rose up in him and relieved him then, since it drove out his fear. He never would give up the shop—never! He would sit there in it until they tore the last tile from over his head. He set the child on the floor again and bustled mightily and filled the caldron and started roaring fires, so that within the hour the water bubbled and steamed and lifted the wooden covers. He was very sharp with his customers and, when the impudent slave-girl came with her cheeks pink and her black eyes saucy, he skimped her a little on water and would not fill the kettle for all her scolding.

"It will be a good thing for us all when the new road comes and takes away your shop, old robber," she flung at him when she saw that he would give her no more.

"Nothing can be taken from me," he shouted after her and, when her mocking laugh came back to him, he shouted again, "That for the new road!" And he spat.

After a while the door opened and his son came in.

"What of the new road?" he asked indolently, feeling of the teapot to see whether it was still hot.

265

"Now then," said Lu Chen. "You still return for your food, do you? Where have you been today?"

"But it is true of the new road," said the boy, sipping the half-cold tea from the spout of the pot. "Quite true. It comes straight past us. The shop—'thirty feet off'—will leave but half of the two bedrooms at the back."

Lu Chen stared unbelievingly. He was all at once so angry that his eyes grew dim. He raised his hand and knocked the teapot from his son's hand, and it fell upon the ground and broke into three pieces.

"You stand there," Lu Chen muttered thickly, "you stand there and drink tea—" and, seeing the young man's astonished face, he began to weep and walked as fast as he could into the room where he slept and crawled into the bed and drew the curtains.

In the morning, when he rose, he was still angry with his son. When the young man ate his rice, innocently, Lu Chen twitched his eyebrows and muttered: "Yes, you eat and your son eats, but you do not think where the money is to come from." But for all of this he did not believe that they would really take away his shop, and he went on about his work as before.

The eleventh day after he was warned by the officer, his wife came to him with unwonted consternation on her face. "It is true that the road is coming," she said. "If you look up the street, you will see a sight. What shall we do?" She began to weep softly, her large face scarcely disturbed.

Lu Chen, seeing her, felt himself quivering. He went to the door and gazed up the street. Always the street had been so narrow, so winding, so darkened with the overhanging shop-signs of varnished wood and colored silk, that one could see for only a few feet. But now there was the strange light of the sun shining upon the damp cobbles. A score of feet away all the signs were gone, and men were tearing down houses. Heaps of age-stained bricks and tiles lay on the street, and caravans of donkeys with baskets across their backs stood waiting to carry them away. The same officer that he had seen was walking about, and behind him followed four angry women, their hair streaming down their backs. They were cursing and wailing, and Lu could hear them say, "We have no life left, no life left— our homes are gone!"

Lu went into the shop then and shut the door and barred it. He sat down on the short wooden bench behind the caldron, his knees shaking, his mind in a maze. Inexorably the road was coming. The child ran out of the inner room and leaned against his knee, but Lu beheld him apathetically. The child, seeing his remote gaze, looked roguishly up and touched the great caldron with a tentative finger. But Lu, for the first time in his life, did not cry out at him. A dim thought went through his mind. "Burned? It is nothing. You will starve at last."

There was a thunderous knock at the door at that moment, and Lu's heart leaped. With his whole body taut, he went to remove the bar. It was the officer in a very clean new uniform, and behind him stood the three soldiers. No one could dream from their appearance that they had been bitterly cursed but a few moments ago, so sure and confident did they seem. Lu, looking at them, suddenly felt that he was a very old man and that it was best for him to die.

"Four days," said the officer, "and your shop must be gone. Tear it down yourself, and you will have the materials. Otherwise we will confiscate it."

"But the money?" faltered Lu Chen.

"Money?" repeated the officer sharply, tapping his shining leather boot with a small stick he carried.

"The price is ten thousand dollars," said Lu Chen a little more firmly, gathering himself together.

The officer gave a sharp, short laugh.

"There is no money," he replied, each word as clear and cold as steel. "You are presenting this to the Republic." Lu Chen looked wildly about. Surely there was some redress. Surely someone would help him.

He began to scream out in a broken, shrill voice to the passers on the street. "Do you see this, sirs? I am to be robbed—robbed by the Republic! Who is this Republic? Will it give me food and my wife and my child—"

He felt himself twitched slightly by the coat. The soldier who had looked back at him the other day whispered hurriedly, "Do not anger the officer—it will be worse." Aloud he said: "Do not complain, old man! In any case your shop would have to go. In the new day that is coming we shall not want hot-water shops. Hot water will come pouring forth from the self-going pipes."

Lu Chen would have answered him, but was at that moment pulled backward by his son, who stood there in front of him, facing the officer. The young man spoke anxiously, courteously: "Sir, forgive an old man who cannot understand that the Revolution has come and brought new light. I will answer for him. We will pull down the house, sir. It is an honor for us to sacrifice all we have to the country."

The red anger that had been rising over the officer's face faded: he gave a short nod and walked quickly away.

The young man barred the door against the curious, half-pitying crowd that had gathered to see the scene. Then he stood against the door and faced Lu Chen. Lu Chen had never seen him thus, firm and decided. "Shall we all be killed then?" he demanded. "Are we to die for the sake of a shop?"

"In any case we shall starve," said Lu Chen, seating himself on the other side of the table, opposite his wife. She had continued to weep the whole time, without noise or disturbance, merely wiping the large tears from her cheeks with the corner of her blue jacket.

"I have found work," said his son. "I am to be an overseer of workmen on the new road."

Lu Chen looked up at him, then, without any hope in his heart. "Even you, my son?" he whispered.

The young man pushed back his hair restlessly from his forehead. "Father, there is no use in fighting against it. It will come. Think of it, a great new road sweeping through our city! Automobiles, passing to and fro! Once at school I saw a picture of a street in a foreign city—big shops and automobiles rushing back and forth. Only *we* have wheelbarrows and rikshas and donkeys crowding against one another in the streets. Why, these streets were made a thousand years ago. Are we never to have new ones?"

"What is the use of automobiles?" muttered Lu Chen. He had seen them often in these past weeks, crowding, pushing, insistent, making people rush to doorways and side-alleys. He hated them. "Our ancestors," he began.

But the young man snapped his fingers. "That for them!" he cried. "I shall get fifty dollars a month from the new road."

Fifty dollars a month? Lu Chen was stunned. He had never seen such an amount of money. He was diverted a little, and his wife stopped crying.

"Where will so much come from?" he asked, half fearfully.

"The new government has promised it," replied his son in a complacent tone.

"I shall buy myself a new black sateen coat," the young man's mother said, a light beginning to break over her face. And then, after an interval during which she thought about the coat, she gave a rumbling, hoarse laugh.

But to Lu Chen, when he had pondered the matter, it seemed that there was no hope for his shop, now that it was no longer their only means of support. He sat all day without lighting the fire, and the great caldrons for the first time in threescore years were cold.

When people came to buy water, he said: "There is no more need. You are to have pipes. Until then heat your own water."

The saucy slave-girl stuck out her tongue at him, a small,

red tongue, as red as a cherry, but he shook his head at her without anger or interest.

The next day his son asked, "Shall we not call the masons to tear down the house, lest we lose everything?"

That roused him a little. "No," he cried. "Since they will rob me, let them rob me utterly." And for four days he sat in his house, refusing to eat, refusing even to open his door, although he heard approaching nearer and nearer the destruction—the crash of falling bricks, the groaning of timbers placed centuries ago and now lowered to the ground, the weeping of many people like himself, whose homes were thus demolished.

On the morning of the fifteenth day there was a great knock upon his door. He rose at once to open it. There stood a dozen men, armed with picks and axes. He faced them. "You come to destroy my shop? I am helpless. Here it is." And he sat down again upon his bench while they crowded in. There was not one touch of sympathy in their faces. In this fashion they had already destroyed hundreds of shops and homes; and to them, he saw very clearly, he was only an old man and one more troublesome than others.

His wife and his son and his son's wife and child had gone away that morning to a friend's house, and they had taken with them everything except the bench whereon Lu Chen sat and the two caldrons. His son had said: "Come with me, Father. I have prepared a place—I have rented a little house. They advanced me some money on the first month." But Lu Chen had shaken his head stubbornly and sat still as they went out.

There were the great copper caldrons, firmly embedded in the clay of the ovens. Two workmen hacked at them with pickaxes. "My grandfather put those in," he said suddenly. "There are no such workmen nowadays."

But he said nothing more while they took the tiles from the roof and the light began to seep down between the rafters. At last they took the rafters, and he sat there within four walls with the noonday sunshine beating on him. He was sick and faint, but he sat on through the long afternoon, and, when evening came, he still sat there, his shop a heap of bricks and tiles and broken rafters about him. The two caldrons stood up naked out of the ruins. People stared at him curiously but said nothing, and he sat on.

At last, when it was almost dark, his son came and took him by the hand. "The child will not eat because you have not come, Father," he said kindly, and then Lu Chen rose, like a very old man, and, holding his son's hand, went with him.

They made their dwelling, then, in a little thatched house just inside the North Gate, where there are fields and empty lands. Lu Chen, who all his life had lived in the bustle of the streets, could not endure the silence. He could not bear to look out across the blankness of the fields. He sat all day in the little bedroom that belonged to him and his wife, scarcely thinking. Since there was no need for him to work any more, he became very soon an old, old man. His son brought home at the end of the month fifty round silver dollars and showed them exultantly.

"It is more than the shop ever yielded," he cried. He was

no longer indolent and careless, and he wore a clean gray uniform buttoned neatly about him.

But Lu Chen only muttered, "Those two big caldrons used to hold at least twenty gallons of river water."

One day his wife, as placid again in this house as she had ever been, showed him her new sateen coat, smoothing it over her great bosom. But he only stared at her. "My mother," he said heavily, "once had a gray coat that was bound in silk." And he fell to musing again.

No one could make him go out of the door. He sat day after day, his hair getting quite white and his lined face loosening from its former busy tenseness. His eyes, which had always been narrow and watchful and snapping, grew dull and hidden behind the veil of dimness that belongs to old people. Only the child sometimes beguiled him for a brief moment.

It was the child at last who beguiled him beyond the door. He had sat all through the shortening days of early winter, gazing out of the small window of his room. His day was marked off into the three periods of his meals; and at night he slept fitfully, sometimes still in his chair with his head on the table.

There came then, after a week of rain, one of the mild, deceptive days that are an interlude of autumn before the intense cold sets in. He had been conscious all morning of the soft, damp heat. The sun, shining obliquely through gray clouds, lighted up the landscape. He was restless, and he pushed open the window. The fresh smell of earth and moisture rose up. "I could have caught a caldronful of the rain-water," he said, sniffing the dampness. Rain-water in the old days could be sold at a high price.

Just then the child came tugging at his hand. "Out, out!" he cried, laughing. "Come and play!"

Lu Chen felt a stirring in him. Well, he would go out just a little, perhaps. And, rising slowly, he took the child's hand and went out. It was very warm, and the sun felt heartening to him. He straightened himself with an effort and began to walk toward some houses near by. He would just go and learn what news there might be. Not for a long time had he heard any. His son was busy all day, and, as for the women, who would talk with a woman?

The child was chattering and a small cheeping of autumn insects filled the air. It was almost like spring. He looked about curiously. Where was he, exactly? There was the North Gate yonder. Ah, that would be the end of the street where his shop had been. He would just go and look at it. Could he bear it? He walked a little more quickly.

Then he turned a corner, and the street lay before him. The street? What was this? A great wide sweep of emptiness, straight through the heart of the city! On all sides the same narrow, winding, dark streets and alleys that he had always known, and straight through them, like the clean swath of a sword-blade, this—this new road!

He stared along it, suddenly smitten with fright. Why, it was enormous—what would they ever do with a road like this? The men working on it were like midges—like ants. All the people in the world could go up and down it and not jostle one another. There were people standing about, like himself, subdued and silent. Some poignancy in their

274

expression drew his interest. "You lived here?" he hinted to a thin-faced man who stood near him. The man nodded slowly. "The house was all I had," he said. "A good house, built in the time of the Mings. It had ten rooms. I live in a hut now. You see, the house was all I had—I rented the rooms."

Lu Chen nodded. "I had a shop—a hot-water shop," he said with difficulty. He would have liked to say more; it was on his tongue to say, "There were two huge copper caldrons." But the man was not listening. He stood staring down the vast new roadway.

Someone drew near, and Lu Chen saw it was his son. The young man broke into a smile and came running. "My father!" he cried. And then, "Father, what do you think of it?"

The old man's lips trembled. He felt that he might either laugh or weep. "It—looks as if a mighty storm had swept through the city," he answered.

But the young man only laughed and said eagerly: "See, Father, this is my bit of the work. Look, at the side there will be pavements, and, in the middle, room for the electric cars and on both sides great space for vehicles of all sorts— room for everything! People from the whole world walking and riding on this road—the road through the new capital!" Someone called him, and he walked away, bustling a little.

Lu Chen stood still, gazing up the road. Infinitely wide, it stretched on both sides of him, infinitely long it extended into the distance. How far did it go, he asked himself solemnly. He had never seen anything in his life like it for space and straightness. Far at the other end, as far as his eyes could pierce, it went on and on, astounding, magnificent, new! Well, here was a thing. Not even emperors had made a road like this! He looked down at the little child beside him. This child, he supposed, would take the road for granted. The young always took things for granted—the way his son had taken the destruction of the shop, for instance. For the first time he did not use the word "robbery" in his mind when he thought of his shop. Instead, this question occurred to him: Had it taken this new road to make his son a man? He perceived that, as he had cared for his shop, so his son cared for the road. He continued to stand with the child, looking up it soberly, absorbed, pondering its import. This Revolution—this new road! Where did it lead?

FLOOD

BARREN SPRING

———※———

LIU, the farmer, sat at the door of his one-room house. It was a warm evening in late February, and in his thin body he felt the coming of spring. How he knew that the time had now come when sap should stir in trees and life begin to move in the soil he could not have told himself. In other years it would have been easy enough. He could have pointed to the willow trees about the house and shown the swelling buds. But there were no more trees now. He had cut them off during the bitter winter when they were starving for food and he had sold them one by one. Or he might have pointed to the pink-tipped buds of his three peach trees and his six apricot trees that his father had planted in his day so that now, being at the height of their time, they bore a load of fruit every year. But these trees were also gone. Most of all, in any other year than this, he might have pointed to his wheat fields, where he planted wheat in the winter when the land was not needed for rice, and where, when spring was moving into summer, he planted the good rice, for rice was his chief crop. But the land told nothing this year. There was no wheat on it, for the flood had covered it long after wheat should have been planted, and it lay there cracked and like clay, but newly dried.

Well, on such a day as this, if he had his buffalo and his plow as he had always had in other years, he would have gone out and plowed up that cracked soil. He ached to plow it up and make it look like a field again, yes, even though he had not so much as one seed to put in it. But he had no buffalo. If anyone had told him that he would eat his own water buffalo that plowed the good land for him, and year after year pulled the stone roller over the grain and threshed it at harvest he would have called that man idiot. Yet it was what he had done. He had eaten his own water buffalo, he and his wife and his parents and his four children, they had all eaten the buffalo together.

But what else could they do on that dark winter's day when the last of their store of grain was gone, when the trees were cut and sold, when he had sold everything, even the little they had saved from the flood, and there was nothing left except the rafters of the house they had and the garments they wore? Was there sense in stripping the coat off one's back to feed one's belly? Besides, the beast was starving also, since the water had covered even the grass lands, and they had had to go far afield to gather even enough grass for fuel to cook its bones and flesh. On that day when he had seen the faces of his old parents set as though dead, on that day when he had heard the crying of his children and seen his little daughter dying, such a despair had seized him as made him like a man without his reason, so that he had gathered together his feeble strength and he had done what he had said he never would; he had taken the kitchen knife and gone out and killed his own beast. When he did it, even in his despair, he groaned, for it was as though he killed his own brother. To him it was the last sacrifice.

Yet it was not enough. No, they grew hungry again and there was nothing left to kill. Many of the villagers went south to other places, or they went down the river to beg in the great cities. But he, Liu the farmer, had never begged. Moreover, it seemed to him then that they must all die and the only comfort left was to die on their own land. His neighbor had come and begged him to set forth with them; yes, he had even said he would carry one of the old parents on his back so that Liu might carry the other, seeing that his own old father was already dead. But Liu had refused, and it was well, for in the next two days the old mother was dead, and if she had died on the way he could only have cast her by the roadside lest the others be delayed and more of them die. As it was he could put her safely into their own ground, although he had been so weak that it had taken him three days to dig a hole deep enough for her little old withered body. And then before he could get her buried he and his wife had quarrelled over the poor few clothes on the old body. His wife was a hard woman and she would have buried the old mother naked, if he had let her, so as to have the clothes for the children. But he made her leave on the inner coat and trousers, although they were only rags after all, and when he saw the cold earth against his old mother's flesh—well, that was sorrow for a man, but it could not be helped. Three more he had buried somehow, his old father and his baby daughter and the little boy who had never been strong.

That was what the winter's famine had taken from them. It would have taken them all except that in the great pools lying everywhere, which were left from the flood, there were shrimps, and these they had eaten raw and were still eating, although they were all sick with a dysentery that would not get well. In the last day or so his wife had crawled out and dug a few sprouting dandelions. But there was no fuel and so they also were eaten raw. But the bitterness was good after the tasteless flesh of the raw shrimps. Yes, spring was coming.

He sat on heavily, looking out over his land. If he had his buffalo back, if he had his plow that they had burned for fuel, he could plow the land. But when he thought of this as he did many times every day, he felt helpless as a leaf tossed upon the flood. The buffalo was gone; gone also his plow and every implement of wood and bamboo, and what other had he? Sometimes in the winter he had felt grateful that at least the flood had not taken all the house as it had so many other houses. But now suddenly it came to him that he could be grateful for nothing, no, not even that he had his life left him and the life of his wife and the two older children. He felt tears come into his eyes slowly as they had not come even when he buried his old mother and saw the earth fall against her flesh, bared by the rags which had comforted him that day. But now he was comforted by nothing. He muttered to himself.

"I have no seed to plant in the land. There the land lies!

I could go and claw it up with my hands if I had the seed and the land would bear. I know my good land. But I have no seed and the land is empty. Yes, even though spring comes, we must still starve!"

And he looked, hopeless, into the barren spring.

THE REFUGEES

〜〜〜

THEY walked through the new capital, alien and from a far country, yes, although their own lands were only a few hundred miles perhaps from this very street upon which they now walked. But to them it was very far. Their eyes were the eyes of those who have been taken suddenly and by some unaccountable force from the world they have always known and always thought safe until this time. They who had been accustomed only to country roads and fields, walked now along the proud street of the new capital, their feet treading upon the new concrete sidewalk, and although the street was full of things they had never seen before, so that there were even automobiles and such things of which they had never even heard, still they looked at nothing but passed as in a dream, seeing nothing.

There were several hundred of them passing at this moment. If they did not look at anything nor at anyone, neither did any look at them. The city was full of refugees, many thousands of them, fed after a fashion, clothed somehow, sheltered in mats in great camps outside the city wall.

At any hour of the day lines of ragged men and women and a few children could be seen making their way toward the camps and if any city dweller noticed them it was to think with increased bitterness,

"More refugees—will there never be an end to them? We will all starve trying to feed them even a little!"

This bitterness, which is the bitterness of fear, made small shopkeepers bawl out rudely to the many beggars who came hourly to beg at the doors, and it made men ruthless in paying small fares to the riksha pullers, of which there were ten times as many as could be used, because the refugees were trying to earn something thus. Even the usual pullers of rikshas who followed this as their profession cursed the refugees because, being starving, they would pull for anything given them, and so fares were low for all, and all suffered. With the city full of refugees, then, begging at every door, swarming into every unskilled trade and service, lying dead on the streets at every frozen dawn, why should one look at this fresh horde coming in now at twilight of a winter's day?

But these were no common men and women, no riffraff from some community always poor and easily starving in a flood time. No, these were men and women of which any nation might have been proud. It could be seen they were all from one region, for they wore garments woven out of the same dark blue cotton stuff, plain and cut in an old-fashioned way, the sleeves long and the coats long and full. The men wore smocked aprons, the smocking done in curious, intricate, beautiful designs. The women had bands of the same plain blue stuff wrapped like kerchiefs about their heads. Both men and women were tall and strong in frame, although the women's feet were bound. There were a few lads in the throng, a few children sitting in baskets slung upon a pole across the shoulders of their fathers, but there were no young girls, no young infants. Every man and every lad bore a burden on his shoulder. This burden was always bedding, quilts made of the blue cotton stuff and padded. Clothing and bedding were clean and strongly made. On top of every folded quilt with a bit of mat between was an iron caldron. These caldrons had doubtless been taken from the earthen ovens of the village when the people saw the time had come when they must move. But in no basket was there a vestige of food, nor was there a trace of food having been cooked in them recently.

This lack of food was confirmed when one looked closely into the faces of the people. In the first glance in the twilight they seemed well enough, but when one looked more closely one saw they were the faces of people starving and moving now in despair to a last hope. They saw nothing of the strange sights of a new city because they were too near death to see anything. No new sight could move their curiosity. They were men and women who had stayed by their land until starvation drove them forth. Thus they passed unseeing, silent, alien, as those who know themselves dying are alien to the living.

The last one of this long procession of silent men and women was a little weazened old man. Even he carried a load of two baskets, slung on a pole on his shoulder, the same load of a folded quilt, a caldron. But there was only one caldron. In the other basket it seemed there was but

287

a quilt, extremely ragged and patched, but clean still. Although the load was light it was too much for the old man. It was evident that in usual times he would be beyond the age of work, and was perhaps unaccustomed to such labor in recent years. His breath whistled as he staggered along, and he strained his eyes to watch those who were ahead of him lest he be left behind, and his old wrinkled face was set in a sort of gasping agony.

Suddenly he could go no more. He set his burden down with great gentleness and sank upon the ground, his head sunk between his knees, his eyes closed, panting desperately. Starved as he was, a little blood rose in dark patches on his cheeks. A ragged vendor selling hot noodles set his stand near, and shouted his trade cry, and the light from the stand fell on the old man's drooping figure. A man passing stopped and muttered, looking at him,

"I swear I can give no more this day if I am to feed my own even nothing but noodles—but here is this old man. Well, I will give him the bit of silver I earned today against tomorrow and trust to tomorrow again. If my own old father had been alive I would have given it to him."

He fumbled in himself and brought out of his ragged girdle a bit of a silver coin, and after a moment's hesitation and muttering, he added to it a copper penny.

"There, old father," he said with a sort of bitter heartiness, "let me see you eat noodles!"

The old man lifted his head slowly. When he saw the silver he would not put out his hand. He said,

"Sir, I did not beg of you. Sir, we have good land and we have never been starving like this before, having such good land. But this year the river rose and men starve even on good land at such times. Sir, we have no seed left, even. We have eaten our seed. I told them, we cannot eat the seed. But they were young and hungry and they ate it."

"Take it," said the man, and he dropped the money into the old man's smocked apron and went on his way, sighing.

The vendor prepared his bowl of noodles and called out, "How many will you eat, old man?"

Then was the old man stirred. He felt eagerly in his apron and when he saw the two coins there, the one copper and the other silver, he said,

"One small bowl is enough."

"Can you eat only one small bowl, then?" asked the vendor, astonished.

"It is not for me," the old man answered.

The vendor stared astonished but being a simple man he said no more but prepared the bowl and when it was finished he called out, "Here it is!" And he waited to see who would eat it.

Then the old man rose with a great effort and took the bowl between his shaking hands and he went to the other basket. There, while the vendor watched, the old man pulled aside the quilt until one could see the shrunken face of a small boy lying with his eyes fast closed. One would have said the child was dead except that when the old man lifted his head so his mouth could touch the edge of the little bowl he began to swallow feebly until the hot mixture was finished. The old man kept murmuring to him,

"There, my heart—there, my child—"

"Your grandson?" said the vendor.

"Yes," said the old man. "The son of my only son. Both my son and his wife were drowned as they worked on our land when the dykes broke."

He covered the child tenderly and then, squatting on his haunches, he ran his tongue carefully around the little bowl and removed the last trace of food. Then, as though he had been fed, he handed the bowl back to the vendor.

"But you have the silver bit!" cried the ragged vendor, yet more astonished when he saw the old man ordered no more.

The old man shook his head. "That is for seed," he replied. "As soon as I saw it, I knew I would buy seed with it. They ate up all the seed, and with what shall the land be sown again?"

"If I were not so poor myself," said the vendor, "I might even have given you a bowl. But to give something to a man who has a bit of silver—" He shook his head, puzzled.

"I do not ask you, brother," said the old man. "Well I know you cannot understand. But if you had land you would know it must be put to seed again or there will be starvation yet another year. The best I can do for this grandson of mine is to buy a little seed for the land—yes, even though I die, and others must plant it, the land must be put to seed."

He took up his load again, his old legs trembling, and straining his eyes down the long straight street he staggered on.

FATHERS AND MOTHERS

—⊷—

O N this edge of dry land, which rises out of the
flood stretching from horizon to horizon, there
are little heaps of what appear to be wreckage.
Each heap has a few wooden benches, a rude table, a little
cupboard, a small iron caldron set upon a hollowed clay
base which is blackened with smoke. But the caldrons are
cold and have been cold for weeks, for there is no fuel to
burn beneath them. The flood has taken everything.

Each of these heaps is all that is left of a home and a
farmhouse. The rest lies under the flood, where lie also
the harvests which were planted and never reaped. About
every such heap of salvage clusters a group of human
beings, a man, a woman, and children, and perhaps an old
man or woman, but of these there are not many. For the
most part, the groups are fathers and mothers and their
children. There is a sort of subdued quarrel going on between these fathers and mothers, or else there is a dreadful
silence. What is this quarrel?

Here is a father, a young farmer casting surly looks at
his young wife. They must have married very young be-

cause, although all these five children are theirs, the eldest child is not more than eight, and the father is not more than twenty-six or -seven, and the mother younger. The father is strong and brown, albeit very thin now. But he is such a man as one sees anywhere in a countryside, a man who loves his land and takes pride in his good plowed fields and in his heaps of yellow grain and in all his good produce. He takes pride in it all because it is the fruit of his labor and he is proud to be thrifty and able. He has a grave, somewhat hard face, but it is a good face, even now when it is surly; and the eyes are honest, though full of despair.

The mother does not look at him except secretly and then she turns quickly away. She has been a pretty, round-cheeked country maid, and her feet are unbound, and her whole body, if it were not so thin now, would be well-shaped and strong. But her eyes are sunken and her black hair is rusty and tousled by the wind, for she has not combed it for many days. Her lips are dry and gray, although she constantly passes her tongue over them to wet them.

She is very busy. She is watching the children continually. Two of them never leave her. One is at her breast, which is now but a poor, shriveled bit of skin. Yet the little pale creature she holds to her is comforted by it even though it is empty, and moans a little more softly for a time. The other child is a little girl, two years old, a small, shrunken creature who remains perfectly silent and motionless in the mother's arm. The other three children do not move much, but when one of them creeps away a little, or goes near the water's edge, the mother cries out and is not satisfied until she has every child within reach of her hands.

Especially is she restless thus at night. She sleeps almost none at all, and she has all of the children about her. A score of times she wakes out of her doze and passes her hands quickly over the children. Are they all there—the five of them? Where is the other girl? Yes—here she is—they are here. If the father so much as moves she calls out sharply,

"What are you doing—what is wrong?"

Sometimes the father breaks into a bitter curse on her. She knows why he curses her. She does not answer a word. She only keeps the children by her and counts them over and over in the darkness.

When morning comes she tries to make a bustle as though she had much food to prepare. She dips up some of the cold river water and mixes it in a gourd with a little of the flour they have left. She tries to say cheerfully,

"There is really more flour left than I thought. There is enough to last us for many days."

She manages so that the largest portion goes to the father, and she hushes the clamoring of the two older boys in a sort of terror, glancing again and again at the man, who stares at them all sombrely and says nothing. Her own share is least of all, although she makes a loud supping over it. If she can she takes nothing, pretending that she is not hungry, that she has an inward pain. If she can seize a moment when the man's back is turned, she feeds the two little ones hastily and secretly.

But the father is not deceived. He roars at her if he sees what she has done and he cries,

"I will not let you starve even that one of these shall live!"

He is not satisfied until he sees her hold her bowl to her lips. She takes the sups small and mincing, to make it seem more.

But in spite of all her contriving the man knows how small their store is, and how the children clamor for food. They will not always heed their mother's hushing, and the two boys sometimes break into wailing. They were stout and rosy once and had always all they needed to eat and they do not understand how it is that the water has come and covered over the land like this, and to them it seems their father must think of a way.

He goes and sits by the water's edge then, and holds his hands over his ears while his sons wail. It is at such times that the mother's face is fixed in its terror, and she beseeches her sons, whispering to them,

"Do not make your father hopeless—be still—be still!"

Seeing her face, they are frightened into silence, sensing danger, but not knowing what danger.

Thus the silent, dreadful quarrel goes on between the father and mother. Every day the flour is less in the basket, and the flood does not recede. Every night the mother counts her children in the darkness.

But she cannot go sleepless forever. There comes a night when her starved body sleeps and she does not know it. She has her arms outspread over the children. But she does not know it when the father stirs and whispers to the two little silent girls. They follow him trustingly to a little distance. He comes stumbling back after a while, alone, and lies down in the darkness. Once or twice he sighs heavily, and each sigh comes from him like a groan.

In the gray dawn the mother wakes suddenly. She is in terror, realizing even before she wakes that she has been asleep. Her hands fumble over the children—where are the other two? She screams and leaps to her feet, suddenly strong. She rushes to her husband, seizes him, shrieks at him,

"Where are the two children?"

He is sitting crouched on the ground, his knees drawn up, his head upon his knees. He does not answer.

The mother is beside herself. She is weeping wildly and she shakes the man by the shoulder and screams at him,

"I am their mother—I am their mother!"

Her screaming wakes everyone in that wretched encampment. But there is no sound of a voice. Everyone knows what this quarrel is. There has been this quarrel everywhere. The mother breaks into dreadful moans, and she gasps out,

"Could a mother ever have done such a thing—it is only fathers who do not love their children, who begrudge them a little food!"

Only then does the sullen man speak. He lifts his head from his knees and looks at the woman in the gray dawn and he mutters,

"Do you think I did not love them?" He turns his head away and after a while he says again, "They are finished their starving!" He weeps suddenly and noiselessly, and seeing his twisted face, even the mother falls silent.

THE GOOD RIVER

⟐

ALL her life Lan Ying had lived by the river with her father and her mother and her three younger brothers. The good river, they called it, because the river helped them in many ways although its name was Yangtse, or Son of the Sea. In the spring the river brought swelling tides down from the snow melting on a hundred mountains where was its source. Many an hour had Lan Ying wondered about that source as she sat watching the fish net for her father. The river ran so wide and deep and yellow here at her feet, below the great net spread out on bamboo poles, that it seemed impossible to believe that it was ever a small stream somewhere, tumbling down some rocky cliff, or running small and sluggish through some sandy desert. The only way she could realize it was to think of her baby brother, newly born three years ago, how small he was and how different from a man, and yet he, too, would grow out of that smallness, even as the river did, until it was so great it could be called truly a Son of the Sea.

Sitting by the fish net and waiting patiently until it was

time to pull the rope that lifted it again, Lan Ying stared across the river. She could see the opposite shore only as a line of clear green. On misty mornings she could not see it at all, and she might have been sitting beside a muddy ocean. Nearly all her days did Lan Ying sit here beside the great river, and it had come now to mean something like a person to her. Her father was not a fisherman, but a farmer, and he planted rice and wheat on his land that edged the river and ran back inland an acre or two to the hillock where the hamlet was where they lived with half a dozen or so other families. They were all families of farmers like Lan Ying's father, but they all had nets tended, too, by children or by old grandfathers who had grown too old to work any more in the fields. Fish brought them in the extra pennies they could spend for the various holidays and for incense to burn before the gods, and for new clothes sometimes, and besides all this fish was good meat to eat, as well.

Lan Ying rose suddenly from the low, little bamboo stool where she sat, and pulled with all her might at the rope. Up came the net slowly. Many a time there was nothing in it. Sometimes there were tiny fish that she had to scoop up with a long-handled dipper. Sometimes there was a big fish, once in several days or so. But there was none now, only a flash of tiny minnows. She stooped and dipped them up. Her mother would pin each one by a sliver of bamboo to a bit of matting on a board and dry them in the sun and then they were salted and very good to eat with morning rice. She let the net down slowly and sat down once more.

Sometimes the days were very long sitting here alone. She came just after her breakfast and sat until noon when she could go home again. But she liked it better than the other things the children must do on the river farms. She liked it better than herding the buffalo and sitting astride its hard and hairy back all day, as her second brother did. She liked it better than herding the ducks in the little inlets from the river as her eldest brother did. Yes, she liked it because there was something very companionable about the moving river, about the boats that passed by her there, and the coveys of wild duck that floated down sometimes, great flocks of them, carried askew by the currents, and bobbing up and down on the water. There was always something to see. As for the boats, there was every kind, from small fishing sculls to the sailed junks with their painted eyes staring out at her from their bows. Once in many days low-set foreign craft came by and sometimes smoking steamers. She hated these and the river hated them, too. It always swelled into angry waves and rocked back and forth as they passed. Sometimes waves grew so high that the little fishing boats almost capsized, and the fishermen shouted loud curses at these foreign ships. Seeing the river angry like this, Lan Ying was angry, too, and ran out to hold her net steady. Still, oftentimes after these steamers passed there would be fish in her net, frightened there into commotion, and Lan Ying, when she saw the big silver bodies flopping in the bottom of the net, gave thanks to the river in her heart for sending her the big fish. It was a good river. It brought them food from the land and meat from its waters, and to Lan Ying, whose life

299

was there beside it, it came to mean something like a god, and staring out over it day after day, she could read its face and catch its mood for the day.

It was, indeed, the only book she could read, for she did not dream of going to school. In their hamlet there was no school, but she knew very well what a school was, because in the market town to which she and her mother went once a year there was a school. There were no pupils there on that day, for it was fair day, and school was out for the day, but she used to look curiously into the empty room as she passed, and see the empty seats and the tables, and pictures hung on the wall. The first time she had asked her mother,

"And what is it they do there?"

To this her mother said, "They learn the books there."

Now Lan Ying had never seen a book and so she asked with great curiosity, "Did you so learn when you were a child?"

"No, indeed!" said her mother loudly. "When did I ever have time for such stuff? I have had to work! It is only idle people who go to school—city people and such like. It is true my father talked of sending my eldest brother to school for the looks of the thing. He was a proud man and he thought it would look well to have one of the family who could read and write. But when my brother had gone three days he grew weary of so much sitting and begged to be sent no more and wept and pouted so that my father did not make him."

Lan Ying pondered awhile longer on all this and she

asked again, "And do all city people learn books, even the girls?"

"I have heard it is the new fashion," said her mother, shifting her load of cotton thread she had spun and now brought to the fair to sell. "But what use it can be to a girl I do not know. She has but the same things to do, to cook and sew and spin and tend the net, and when she is wed she does the same things over again and bears her children, too. Books cannot help a woman." She went along more quickly, for the load on her back grew heavy, and Lan Ying hurried a little, and then saw the dust on her new shoes, and stooping to brush them, forgot about books.

Nor did she think about them any more when she went back to the river. No, books had nothing to do with her life here by the good river. To lift the net and lower it again, to go home at evening and burn the grass fuel in the earthen oven upon which two iron caldrons were set and in which the rice was heated for their supper, and when they had eaten it with a bit of fish, if the river had been kind that day, to run with the bowls to the river's edge and rinse them there, and back again before the night was too dark, to creep into bed and lie and listen to the soft rush of the river among its reeds—this was all her life of every day. Only on a feast day or a fair day did it differ and then but for that one day.

It was a quiet life thus spent, but a very safe one. Sometimes Lan Ying heard her father say that in the market town where he went often to sell his cabbages and grain, he had heard of famine to the north because there had been no rains, and he would always add:

"You see how fine it is to dwell beside a good river! Whether it rains or not is nothing to us, who have only to dip our buckets into the river and there is water for our fields. Why, this good river of ours brings us the water from a hundred valleys, and rains or none is nothing to us."

And when she heard this Lan Ying thought that theirs was surely the best life in the world, and life in the best place, where fields were always fruitful, and willows always green and the reeds ever lush and deep for fuel, and everything came from this river. No, she would never move away from this river so long as she lived.

Yet there came a spring when the river changed. Who could have foreseen that the river would change? Year after year it had been the same until this year. Lan Ying, sitting beside the fish net, saw it change. It is true that every year it swelled with spring flood as it did now. The water ran high against the clay banks, but so it ever did in the spring. The yellow water curled in great wheels and tore at the banks, so that often a great clod would shudder and tear itself away from the land and sink, and the river licked it up triumphantly. Lan Ying's father came and moved the net away to an inlet's mouth, lest the bit of land upon which she sat might so sink and bear her away. For the first time in her life Lan Ying felt a little afraid of the river.

The time came for the river to go down, but it did not subside. Surely by now those upper snows were melted, for it was summer and the winds were hot, and the river ought to lie quiet and smooth beneath the bright skies. But it did not lie quiet. No, it tore on as though fed by some secret and inexhaustible ocean. Boatmen who came down from the upper gorges, their craft buffeted by high rapids, told of torrents of rain, days and weeks of rain when the times for rain were past. The mountain streams and the lesser rivers thus fed, all poured into the great river and kept it high and furious.

Lan Ying's father moved the net still farther up the inlet, and Lan Ying, when she was left alone, did not look over the river any more. No, she turned her back on it and looked over the fields. She was actually afraid of the river now.

For it was a cruel river. All during the hot summer months it rose, each day a foot, two feet. It crept over the rice fields where the half-grown grain stood; it covered the grain and took away the hope of harvest. It swelled into the canals and streams and flooded their banks. Stories came everywhere of dykes falling, of great walls of water rushing over deep, rich valleys, of men and women and children engulfed and swept away.

Lan Ying's father moved the net far back now, for the inlet was flooding its banks, too. Again and again he moved it back, cursing the river and muttering, "This river of ours has gone mad!"

At last there came a day when he tied the handle that lifted the net to one of the many willow trees that grew at the edge of the threshing floor that was the dooryard to Lan Ying's home. Yes, the water had risen as high as this, and the little hamlet of half a dozen earthen houses, thatched with straw, was on an island now, surrounded by the yellow river water. They must all fish, for there could be no more farming.

Now it did not seem possible that the river could do more than this. At night Lan Ying could scarcely sleep, the water rushed so near the bed where she lay. At first she could not believe it would come nearer than this. But she saw the great fear in her father's eyes. It was true the water was rising nearer. Was it half way across the threshing floor the day before yesterday? Yes, it was rising. In three days it would come into the house.

"We must go to the innermost dyke," said Lan Ying's father. "Once before in my father's father's time I heard the river did this, and they had to go to the innermost dyke, where the water does not come once in five generations. It is our curse that the time has fallen in our lifetime."

The youngest little boy began to howl in a loud voice for he was suddenly afraid. So long as the roof of the house was over them and its walls about them it was only a strange thing to see the water everywhere, and be like a ship perched above it thus. But when he heard they must go and live on a dyke he could not bear it. Lan Ying's tears came in sympathy and she drew him to her and pressed his face against her breast.

"But may I take my black goat?" he sobbed.

He had a black goat that he had taken as a kid for his own from the two or three goats his father kept.

"We will take all the goats," answered his father loudly, and when his wife said, "But how can we get them across all the water?" he said simply, "We must, for we will have them as food."

On that very day, then, he took the door from its wooden hinge, and lashed it together with the wooden beds and with the table, and he tied the rude raft to a little scull he owned, and upon the raft climbed Lan Ying and her mother and the little boys. The buffalo they tied to a rope and let it swim, and the ducks and four geese also. But the goats were put upon the raft. Just as they left the house the yellow dog came swimming after them and Lan Ying cried, "Oh, my father, look! Lobo wants to come, too!"

But her father shook his head and rowed on. "No," he said, "Lobo must look after himself and seek his own food now, if he lives."

It seemed a cruel thing to Lan Ying and the eldest boy shouted, "I will give him half my bowl of rice!"

Then did the father shout as though he were angry, "Rice? What rice? Can a flood grow rice?"

The children were all silent then, not understanding but afraid. They had never been without rice. At least the river had given them rice every year. When at last Lobo grew weary and swam more and more slowly and was farther and farther behind, there came a time when they could not see his yellow head against the yellow water.

Across the miles of water they came at last to the inner dyke. It stood like a ridge against the sky, and it seemed a heaven of safety. Land, good dry land! Lan Ying's father lashed his raft against a tree and they climbed ashore.

But there were many there before them. Along that ridge stood huts of mats and heaps of saved furniture, benches and tables and beds, and everywhere were people. For even this inner dyke had not stood against the water. It had been a hundred years since it had been so attacked by the river, and in many places people had forgotten there could ever come such attack and they had not kept the dyke sound and whole. The river crashed its way through these weak places and swept behind even into the good lands behind the dyke. The dyke stood then still an island, and upon it clung these people from everywhere.

Not people only, but the wild beasts and the field rats and the snakes came to seek this bit of land, too. Where trees stood up out of the water, the snakes crawled up into them and hung there. At first the men battled with them and killed them and threw their dead bodies into the flood. But the snakes kept coming and at last they let them be, unless there was one more dangerous than the others.

Through the summer and the autumn did Lan Ying live here with her family. The basket of rice they had brought was long since eaten. The buffalo, too, they killed at last and ate, and Lan Ying saw her father go and sit alone by the water when he had killed the beast and when she went near him he shouted at her surlily, and her mother called her and said in a whisper, "Do not go near him now. He is thinking how will he ever plow the land again with the buffalo gone."

"And how will he?" said Lan Ying, wondering.

"How, indeed!" said her mother grimly, hacking at the meat.

It did not seem possible it was the good river that had done all this. They had eaten the goats before the buffalo, and the little boy had not dared even to complain when he saw his pet kid gone. No, there was the grim winter ahead of them.

There came the day they knew must come, when no food

was left. What then? Well, they had their fishing net left. But the river sent no large fish here into these stagnant flood waters. There were only shrimps here and crabs crawling slowly up the muddy banks. Among all the people no food was left. Each family kept closely to itself, hoarding its last bit, telling no one what was left. A few families had a little left and they ate secretly in the darkness of the night lest they be forced to share. But even these slender stores were soon gone. There was nothing left then but the shrimps and the crabs. Nor was there fuel to burn that they could be cooked. They must be eaten raw. At first Lan Ying thought she could not—that she would rather starve. Her father said nothing, but he watched her and smiled a little grimly when, having starved a day she picked from the heap of shrimps one that did not move.

"At least I will not eat them alive," she muttered.

Day passed after day. Winter drew near in chill winds, and sudden frosty nights. When it rained they were all drenched to the skin and huddled together like sheep. But it did not often rain, and the next day they could dry their garments in the sun. Lan Ying grew very thin, so thin she was always cold. But she looked at them all, and the boys were thin, too, and very silent. They never played. Only the eldest would move slowly to the water's edge when his father called to him to come and help to catch the day's shrimps. Lan Ying saw her mother's round face grow pale and hollow, and her hands that had been red and plump and dimpled at the knuckles were like a skeleton's hands. Still she was cheerful and she said often, "How fortunate are we to have even shrimps, and how fortunate that we are all strong enough to live!"

It was true that many had died among those who had come to the dyke, so there was no crowd as there had been. No, there was plenty of room now for those who were left.

No boats ever passed by in these days. Lan Ying, sitting by habit and looking over the water, used to think of all the boats that had been wont to pass by in a day's time of fishing. It seemed another life. Had there been a time once not like this? It seemed they were the only people left in the world, a little handful of people perched upon a bit of land in the midst of a flood.

Sometimes the men talked together in faint tones. Not one of them had his old strong voice now. Each man talked as though he had been ill a long time. They talked of when the flood would abate and of what they would do to find new beasts to pull their plows, and always Lan Ying's father would say somberly, "Well, I can harness myself to my plow, and my old woman will do it for once, I swear, but what is the good of plowing when there is no seed to put into the ground? Where shall we get our seed, having no grain?"

Lan Ying began to dream of boats coming. Surely somewhere there were people left in the world who had grain. Might not boats come? Every day she sat looking earnestly over the waters. If a boat would come, she thought, at least there would be a living man in it and they could call to him and say, "Save us who are here starving! We have eaten nothing but these raw shrimps for many days—"

Yes, even though he could do nothing he might go away

and tell someone. A boat was the only hope. She began to pray to the river to send a boat. Every day she prayed, but no boat came. It is true that one day she saw on the horizon, where the yellow water was dark against the blue sky, the form of a small boat, but it passed into the sky and came no nearer.

Yet the sight heartened her. If there was this boat, might there not be others? She said timidly to her father, "If a boat should come—"

But he did not let her finish. He said sadly, "Child, and who knows we are here? No, we are at the mercy of the river."

She said no more, but she still looked steadfastly over the water.

Suddenly one day she saw, sharp and black against the sky, the shape of a boat. She watched it, saying nothing. She would wait lest it fade away again as that other boat had faded. But this boat did not fade. It grew larger, clearer, more near. She waited. At last it came near enough so that she could see in it two men. She went to her father then. He lay sleeping as all the men slept when they could, so that they might forget their gnawing bellies. She shook him, panting a little, plucking at his hand to waken him. She was very faint, and too weak to cry aloud. He opened his eyes.

"There is a boat coming," she gasped.

Then he rose, fumbling and staggering in his feebleness, and peered out over the water. It was true there was a boat. It was true it came near. He pulled off his blue coat and waved it weakly, and his bare ribs stood forth like a skeleton's. The men in the boat shouted. But not one among those men on the land could answer, so feeble they were.

The boat came near. The men tied it to a tree and leaped up the bank. Lan Ying, staring at them, thought she had never seen such men as these, so fat, so fed. They were talking boisterously—what were they saying?

"Yes, we have food—yes, food for all! We have been searching for such as you! How long have you been here? Four months—heaven have pity! Here, eat this rice we brought cooked! Yes, yes, there is more! Here is wheat flour, too—no, not too fast—remember to eat a little at first and then a little more!"

Lan Ying stared as they dashed into the boat and brought back rice gruel and loaves of wheaten bread. She stretched out her hand without knowing what she did, and her breath came as fast as a spent animal's does. She did not know what she did except that she might have food at last —she must have food. One of the men gave her a piece of the loaf he tore off and she sank her teeth into it, sitting down suddenly on the ground, forgetting everything except this bit of bread she held. So did they all and so did they eat, and when all had something the two men stood and looked away as if they could not bear to see this famished eating. No one spoke.

No, not one voice spoke, until suddenly one man said, having eaten awhile and as much as he dared, "Look at this bread, how white it is! I have never seen this wheat to make such white bread!"

310

Then they all looked, and it was true; the bread was white as snow. One of the men from the boat spoke, then, and he said, "It is bread made from wheat grown in a foreign country. They have heard what the river did and have sent us this flour."

Then they all looked at the bits of bread that were left and men murmured over it how white and good it was, and it seemed the very best bread they had ever eaten. Lan Ying's father looked up and he said suddenly, "I should like a bit of this wheat to plant in my land again when the flood goes down. I have no seed."

The other man answered heartily, "You shall have it— you shall all have it!"

He said it as easily as though he spoke to a child, for he did not know what it meant to these men who were farmers to be told they had seed to plant again. But Lan Ying was a farmer's daughter and she knew. She looked at her father secretly and saw he had turned his head away and was smiling fixedly, but his eyes were full of tears. She felt the tears knot together in her throat, too, and she rose and went to one of the men and plucked at his sleeve. He looked down at her and asked, "What is it, child?"

"The name—" she whispered, "what is the name of the country that has sent us this fair wheat?"

"America," he answered.

She crept away then, and unable to eat more, sat and held the precious bit of bread she had left and looked out over the water. She held it fast, although the men had promised them more. She felt suddenly faint and her head was

311

swimming. She would eat more bread when she could—only a little at a time, though, this good bread! She looked out over the river, and feared it no more. Good or bad, they had bread again. She murmured to herself, "I must not forget the name—America!"

*TODAY AND
FOREVER*

CONTENTS

I
THE LESSON

THE LESSON

"I HATE to let Ru-lan go like this," said little Mrs. Stanley to her husband. "I don't believe she knows anything at all—she's not fit to be married."

She had just come in from the garden and her arms were full of roses, the swift-blooming, vivid roses of a Chinese May. Wyn Stanley looked at her, smiling, his heart caught in his throat at her loveliness. He and Mollie had been married five years but he never grew used to her. He saw her every day—how lucky it was that his work at the mission was to run the schools and not to be an itinerant evangelist! If he had had to go off on long preaching tours as Dr. Martin did, and be weeks away from Mollie, he could not have borne it. Sometimes in the night he woke to trouble and shivering, fearful lest God call him to such work, lest something happen that he and Mollie might have to be separated—suppose one of the children were to fall ill and have to be taken home across the sea to America like the Burgess child, and Mrs. Burgess away for nearly two years, or—he would put out his hand to touch Mollie's round little body lying deeply and healthfully asleep beside him. He would not wake her—but somehow she always woke and somehow he always told her his fears, and then waited to hear her laugh her sweet contented laughter. "Oh Wyn, as if— Anyway, God hasn't called you to evangelistic work, has he? And if I had to go home you'd come too. We'd find another job. You suppose I'd *let* you stay here by yourself?" He was asleep before he knew it then.

3

Now he looked up at her from his desk, adoring her. She dimpled and put her hand on his cheek and pretended to pout. "You haven't heard a thing I've been saying. You never listen to me."

He caught her hand and held it to his lips, a little firm hand, scratched with rose thorns. "It's because I can't keep from looking at you. What's going to happen to me if I keep loving you more all the time?" He drew her to him and leaned his face against her breast. Under his cheek he could feel the steady pounding of her heart. "True heart—true heart—" he murmured to the rhythm of her heart. She bent over his dark head, pressing it against her. They both forgot the girl Ru-lan. They were swept back into the summer morning five years ago in the little old churchyard behind the red brick church where her father had preached so many years, and where Wyn had come as substitute for a month of vacation. She and her mother had sent her father off for the trip to Palestine he had planned for a lifetime. What destiny it had been, that on the summer when the family did not all go away together Wyn had been the supply— just before he was to sail as a missionary to China!

They had fallen in love at once. The first moment she saw his tall young figure mounting the steps of the pulpit she knew him and loved him. And he, when he looked over the congregation, saw her and thereafter her only. And then in just a few weeks, that July morning after church, when she was running home to the manse by the short cut through the churchyard, he came striding after her, still with his surplice on. He had, he said, meant only to ask her to—to walk with him, perhaps, in the evening. But when she turned and looked at him, under the deep shadows of the old elms and hidden by the lilacs along the path, he had taken her into his arms and enfolded her. There

4

was no question asked and no answer given, simply meeting. Whenever they came together it was the same thing, the same deep union again—like this.

There was a small sound, and they jumped apart. The older missionaries always said, "The Chinese are not used to demonstration between the sexes." Mrs. Burgess had taken her aside very soon and said, "Try not to take your—Mr. Stanley's—hand in front of the Chinese, dear. It is—they would consider it indelicate." So she and Wyn had tried very hard to learn to wait until they were alone. But hand went so instinctively to hand, his arm was around her so naturally. Now they looked guiltily toward the door.

There she stood, Ru-lan, the girl she had come in to see Wyn about, the poor stupid girl. She was standing there in the doorway, dressed in a clean blue cotton coat and trousers, with a blue and white print handkerchief tied full of the books she never could learn. Her father had come for her to take her home to be married, and she was ready to go.

"Come in, Ru-lan," Mollie said. She smiled, her heart full of compassion. The girl's round placid face responded at once with a childlike pleasure. Above the large full cheeks her black eyes shone faintly. Mollie Stanley put down the roses and went over and took the girl's plump hand.

"I'm sorry you must go," she said in Chinese. "But your father will not consent to your staying longer. Sit down, child, and let me talk with you a little."

The girl sat down obediently, in silence. The smile had gone from her face now and she sat staring quietly at these two, observing all they did.

Mollie looked at her and was discouraged. She had so often in the school room faced that dense placidity.

5

"Wyn, what shall we do?" she asked, turning to him. "She's seventeen and she's been here ever since we came, and I don't believe she will ever learn much. She's been through all the classes—Bible and arithmetic and hygiene—she reads a few hundred characters and that's all you can say. She just isn't fit for marriage—such a good, faithful, kind, *stupid* girl! You know she came up for baptism twice, and she just can't remember enough to answer Dr. Martin's questions, however hard I coach her. I'm sometimes afraid she's still heathen."

"No, I know," answered Wyn. "It's no good her staying here. If she had any promise at all I'd try to persuade her father to let her finish at least the grades. But I haven't the heart to let him think she ever could finish. Maybe she'd better go on and be married."

"Wyn Stanley!" his wife cried out at him, "as if it weren't serious that a girl like that is to be married and have a lot of children! Of course she will have a lot of children!"

They both looked, troubled, at Ru-lan, who, meeting their eyes instantly broke into her great beaming smile, not understanding a word of their English. They were baffled by her smile.

"Do you know whom you are going to marry, Ru-lan?" asked Mollie gently in Chinese. The girl shook her head. "It is a landowner's son," she answered simply. "My father is a landowner, too. The son of another village landlord, it is."

She seemed to put the matter aside and continued to watch them intently. Mollie Stanley sighed. She put down the roses on the desk and went over to the girl and sat down on a chair next to her and took her hand again. "Try to remember," she said, "some of the things you have been taught. Remember about keeping things clean and remember how dangerous the flies and mosquitoes are, especially to little children—and how little chil-

6

dren should not be given cucumbers and green melons to eat,
and—remember about your prayers, and about the kind Christ,
who came to save our souls—remember all the things we have
tried to teach about being clean and good."

"Yes, teacher," the girl replied. She was looking closely at
Mollie Stanley's wedding ring. Now she asked suddenly, "Did
the other teacher give you the ring?"

Mollie dropped the hand she was holding and turned to her
husband. "Oh dear—" she said.

"Don't worry, dear," said Wyn instantly. "I can't bear that look
in your eyes. You mustn't, mustn't try to bear on your dear self
all the troubles of everyone else. We've done the best we can for
this child. Now she must go home. Come—" he stood and took
up the roses. "Here are your roses, darling. Run along now. I'll
see that Ru-lan gets away. Where *is* her father? In the school
hall? I'll go, then."

"No, but, Wyn, I can't go so lightly. Tell her—tell him we'll
come to see her sometime, anyway—Ru-lan"—she turned to the
girl and changed her tongue quickly—"we shall come to see you
some time—I'm coming to see if you remember everything—
you must try—do not let yourself be like all the others who have
never come to mission school."

"No, teacher," the girl said. She was staring at Wyn's hand
resting unconsciously upon Mollie's shoulder, and he took it
abruptly away.

Crossing the school lawn ahead of her, he thought to himself
that Ru-lan was really a very tiresome girl. It was not only that
she was so stupid, it was also that one could not be sure of what
she was thinking. He would have said, for instance, that she was
stolid and unfeeling; yet just now when she was about to follow
him out of his study she had made one of her great broad smiles

that seemed to enwrap him and Mollie, and she had taken Mollie's hand and held it, and had said with simple utter gratitude, "You have both taught me. Together you have taught me."

He remembered now how often they would find her staring at them in her silent persevering way, that time at supper, for instance, when he had sat holding Mollie's hand as he ate—they always sat side by side—and Ru-lan had come in with a note from one of the teachers. She always contrived, he did believe, now that he thought of it, to be the one to carry notes. He'd supposed it was because she was such a faithful sort of person that they had sent her. But perhaps it was because she wanted to come. There she had stood, staring at them with that silent beaming look—slightly feebleminded, undoubtedly. He sighed. Well, it was sad when years went into teaching someone like that, someone who could never learn, when there were so many who could, and had no chance. But she had been there when he and Mollie came, and her father had come twice a year with her fees, and so she had stayed. There were not many fathers who paid full fees for a daughter.

He entered the hall, and there the father was, a plain brown-faced countryman in a blue cotton gown cut a little too long and too broad for him, but of good stout homewoven stuff. He was not a poor man, it was evident, from his bearing. He rose politely as the white man entered.

"Sit down, please, Mr. Yang. Do not be polite," said Wyn, seating himself also. The girl stood a little to one side, waiting.

"This girl," said the father nodding his head toward her, "I might have left her with you to become a teacher for you out of gratitude for all your efforts, but unfortunately she was early betrothed to the son of a friend whom I do not care to offend, and now the family demand the marriage. Otherwise I would give her to you to help you in your school."

"I thank you certainly," said Wyn. He wondered uncomfortably if in honesty he should tell the father that they could never have used Ru-lan as a teacher because she was too stupid. He thrust an apologetic thought toward God—it was difficult to be honest if it hurt someone else. Mr. Yang was obviously so proud of his daughter. He turned toward Wyn now saying, "She has had, you will remember, sir, eight years of schooling. It is not every man's son who has such a wife. But I have treated her as though she were to be my own daughter-in-law and to remain in my family. I value my friend as myself."

"It is very honorable of you," murmured Wyn. At least he would not tell lies and say he was sorry that Ru-lan must go. He waited in courteous silence until the father rose, briskly dusting cake crumbs from his lap. "There—it is pleasant to sit drinking your tea and eating your cakes, but I have miles of country road to put beneath my beast's feet before night comes. Say good-by and give your gratitude to your teacher, Ru-lan."

"I thank you, teacher," murmured the girl. "I thank you for all I have learned."

They bowed to him together, father and daughter, and Wyn bowed, waiting at the door while they turned and bowed again.

He watched them while they went out of the compound gate. "I suppose," he thought a little sadly, "that measured by any standard it must be said that we have wasted the church's substance upon that girl. Mollie's hours and mine, too! I wonder why they do not seem so important as dollars in the mission budget? Anyway, all waste! She's not even a church member."

He walked back, a little discouraged. It was so difficult to know what was worth while in the work. One was conscientious, did

9

each day what it seemed should be done, should be taught, and then realized suddenly, as he and Mollie had today, that no fruit was possible. He sighed a little grimly. Well, Ru-lan was gone.

In the village of Long Peace the people were all very well content. They had just finished three days of great feasting entirely at the elder Liu's expense, since he was marrying his eldest son to Ru-lan, the daughter of his brother-friend Yang in the village of The Fighting Cocks. Everybody had eaten. First the tables were set for Mr. Liu's friends among the gentry, and the common people had waited their time, patiently and decently. Then the tables were set again and again, with pork and with fish, broiled with sugar and wine and vinegar, with beef and pork ground and stewed with cabbage and greens, with noodles and with sweet rice. In fact, nothing had been left undone, and everyone had drunk all the wine he could and had eaten far more than he could, and mothers had prudently tied into large blue and white handkerchiefs such tidbits as they could not eat or force their children to eat at table. Servants had been tipped, gifts had been given, and firecrackers exploded in immense volleys. The bride, moreover, had been exhibited and commented upon, and though after all she seemed to be nothing extraordinary, no one liked Elder Liu and Mr. Yang any the less for it.

There had been a great deal of curiosity to see her, because everybody knew Mr. Yang had sent his eldest daughter to a foreign school for eight years, and anything might have happened. She might even have changed the color of her eyes and hair, or the white women might have taught her how to bleach her skin, since it is well known the white people have magic. But she was nothing at all out of the ordinary. She was, in fact, a little more common than otherwise, a large lumpish girl with very plump round cheeks and small mild eyes. In addition her feet were large. Country wives nudged each other and whispered, "Look at her feet—big feet!" "Yes, but the foreigners do not allow their pupils to bind their feet!" "Ah, indeed! How lucky that the Elder Yang betrothed her in babyhood and to his best friend's son!" Young men glanced at the bride and made jokes concerning the width of her nose and the size of her mouth, and went home in high good humor because they need not be envious of the Elder Liu's son. Indeed, everybody was happy because for once the Elder Liu did not seem to be so very lucky, and one or two fathers whose daughters had been teasing to be allowed to go to a foreign school went home resolute for refusal. What— to waste eight years of fees and then have a daughter at the end who looked exactly as though she had never left the village! So everyone was happy. They went home by moonlight the night of the third day, full of cheerful vilifying talk.

In the house of the Elder Liu, in the court belonging to his eldest son, Ru-lan sat upon the edge of the large nuptial bed, hung with pictures of babies and pomegranates and mandarin ducks and every lucky sign for marriage, and waited for her husband. She had enjoyed everything very much, so much that she often forgot to keep her eyes downcast as she should. But this did not greatly trouble her. She had remembered enough, she thought comfortably, and tonight they had given her a good dinner. The more tedious part of the wedding was over. She had now come to the part which was her own affair.

This was the time, she knew, when maidens should feel shy and uncomfortable and even afraid. She knew because as a very small girl in the women's courts of her father's house she had squatted on her heels listening as all the little girls did to the women's talk. They listened while the women whispered loudly

to each other, "I tell you, he was like a tiger—his great eyes—"
"I tell you, nothing told is so terrible as—" "I tell you, I was like
a chicken before a wolf—"

They all enjoyed telling each other of this hour when their
unknown bridegrooms first appeared. She thought now, staring
reflectively through the old-fashioned veil of beads that hung
over her face, that it was natural they should be afraid of marriage. What they had seen of the thing between men and women
was not comfortable. But she had been to school for eight years
with the foreigners. There was the difference. Not that the first
years she had been there were of any use to her at all. She could
not see much use, for instance, in reading books. In the first place
books told nothing interesting. If they were about God, there was
no understanding them—how could humans understand gods?
She had listened politely to Mrs. Burgess and been glad when
Mrs. Burgess had been compelled to go to America. For then
the dear little Stanley teacher had come, that little pretty round-
faced teacher, whose eyes were also brown so that one liked to
look at her. The Stanley teacher had worked so hard to teach
her that sometimes she almost felt she should try to learn something, to listen perhaps to what the Stanley teacher was saying,
but when she did it had seemed not valuable.

No, she had learned nothing until that day when she had observed the man Stanley place his arms about the woman Stanley.
At first she thought with consternation that these were two
wicked and unmannered people. But they were not punished if
they were. In rapid succession they had two small sons, both
healthy, both dark-eyed. Evidently their God was pleased with
them. After that she had watched them many times. When they
did not know it she had stolen in the night across the school
campus, and had gazed steadily between the curtains of the room

where they sat after the children were put to bed, and, watching them, had come to learn something from them. To this learning she applied her mind. So now she was not at all afraid. She waited peacefully for Yung-en, sitting at ease upon the bed, her hands folded in her red satin lap.

Everywhere through the courts quiet was descending after the noisy days of feasting. Children who had eaten too well ceased their crying and fell asleep, and servants yawned and barred the doors of courtyards and went to their own beds. Her own serving woman was only waiting until the master came in to spread her pallet down across the door to sleep. When everyone was still, when the young men had all gone home, wearied at last with their baiting and teasing of the bridegroom, then through the silent empty courts he would come. She had stolen her glances at him and she was pleased with his looks. He was an honest sturdy young man, with a square dark face, not too smiling. He was shy, she could see, not quick to speak. A woman could live with such a man. She was not afraid, having learned so much about a man and a woman.

Then suddenly the door creaked upon its wooden hinges and there he was, still in his bright blue wedding robes. He did not speak, nor did he look at her at once. He came in and sat down beside the table and began to crack watermelon seeds. She rose and poured out a cup of tea for him and he nodded and she sat down again. She was not impatient. He could not go on cracking watermelon seeds all night. Outside the door she heard a loud yawn and soon a muffled snore. Her serving woman was asleep. Now everyone slept except these two.

She waited, smiling a little, watching him through the beads of her veil, but he did not look at her. She waited and at last she caught his eyes, stealing toward her. She answered instantly,

13

frankly, smiling her beam of a smile. He stared at her and coughed and after a second of surprise he grew very red and made haste to return to his watermelon seeds. She suddenly perceived that he was afraid of her.

"And why are you afraid of me?" she asked, making her voice soft as she had heard the little Stanley teacher's voice soft.

He turned his head from her's. "I am so ignorant," he said at last in a low voice. "You have been away to a foreign school and I have always lived in this village. You will laugh at me."

She watched him. How now would the Stanley teacher speak if the man Stanley had spoken like this? Once the man Stanley had put his head down upon the woman's shoulder and for some trouble had wept as a little boy weeps, and the woman had not laughed. She had taken him into her arms and pressed his head down and murmured to him as a mother murmurs to a suffering child, and soon he was quieted. Ru-lan had not understood the woman Stanley's words, but the sounds she understood, and the way she understood. It had made the man Stanley feel strong again and cease his weeping.

She looked demurely down at her hands and spoke in a small plaintive voice. "I have to confess to you," she said, "although I was so long in that school I have remained ignorant. You cannot be as ignorant as I am. I do believe there are a thousand things you know I do not know. There I remained for eight years shut behind walls, but my brain is too stupid to learn from books. So I am very ignorant. I have everything to learn from you."

He gazed at her now, forgetting that she was his bride and that he was afraid of her. "Did you not learn to read?" he demanded.

"Only a very little," she replied.

"Did you read to the end of the Four Books?" he asked again.

"Alas, I never read any of the Four Books," she answered.

"Then what did you do in all that time?" he inquired, astonished.

"I sat on benches in school rooms," she replied humbly, "and there were those who talked to me, but I could not understand them, being stupid from birth. They told me of gods and of magic, and of small insects that cause disease if eaten, but then who eats insects? At least we do not. So I learned nothing."

"Nothing at all?" he asked severely.

"Nothing at all," she answered sadly.

He was silent, but now he looked at her quite easily and he had stopped cracking watermelon seeds. She could see the shyness leaving him as he thought over what she had told him.

"I only learned one thing," she said after a long time. Now she leaned forward and looked at him and he looked at her.

"What is that one thing?" he asked.

"There was a white woman who was my teacher," she said, "and she was married to a white man, and they were very lucky, for one after the other they had two strong dark-eyed sons, and this when the other children of white people all have blue or green eyes. I learned from them something."

"What was the thing you learned?" he asked. "Certainly two dark-eyed sons are very lucky."

"I learned," she said considering, choosing some one thing among all she had learned, "that it is lucky when a man and his wife speak together freely and always with kind voices, as though they were friends speaking easily together and not as they do in our houses, where it seems shameful so to speak."

"Do you mean speak together anywhere?"

"Yes, I mean that."

He gazed at her steadily. "What then?"

"And then it is lucky if the husband helps the wife if there is a thing to be done, such as to carry a basket or a bundle, if there is not a servant near."

"What does the wife do?" he asked, astonished.

"She also wishes to carry the things, and so they try mutually to help each other."

"And who wins?" he asked.

"They share the thing," she replied simply.

She waited a little, thinking, remembering. . . . Once she had seen the man Stanley lift his wife over a pool of mud in the road, and carry her through and set her down on the other side, one afternoon, when they thought none saw them. But before he set her down he had held her hard and placed his cheek against hers, and then they had gone on hand in hand until they saw her. But she had seen them long since. She had wanted to say, "Do not drop your hands apart. I know it is your pleasure to walk thus." But she had not spoken. . . .

"What else have you learned?" he asked.

"It is lucky," she said slowly, "for a man and his wife to clasp their hands together sometimes—it is not shameful."

He coughed and looked away and she went on quickly. "There are many things not shameful that we have thought shameful— they are lucky between man and wife. But I cannot speak them —they are things to be done rather than to be spoken."

He looked down and did not answer. He did not answer for quite a long time. Then he said a little gruffly, "Then do them— do what you have learned."

She rose slowly and went over to him. She knelt down on the floor before him as often she had seen the woman Stanley do. But she could not go on, although she knew quite well what

16

came next. Next was to put her head down upon his knees and clasp her arms about his waist. But she could not do it. Now it was she who was shy. It had looked so easy when the woman Stanley did it.

"I cannot do it all at once," she faltered. "A little every day. But perhaps—at least take my hands."

He sat quite still and then he lifted her hands in his own. Something rushed between them through their hands, and suddenly her heart began to pound. Did the woman Stanley's heart pound like this also? What was the matter with her?

"What next did you learn?" he asked.

She could not answer. She drew their hands together and laid her head down upon their knotted hands. She should have asked the woman Stanley about this pounding heart.

"Lift up your head," he said. How gentle his voice was, as gentle as the man Stanley's voice was! "Lift up your head and let me take away your veil that I may see you."

She lifted up her head, and he drew his hands away and took off the headdress and the veil and set them on the table and then he looked at her. And then he went on speaking in that same gentle voice, "And did you learn it was lucky for a man to like very well the woman chosen for him?" He had taken her hands again. He was gazing at her, smiling, happy, as the man Stanley gazed at that woman who knelt to him. The man Stanley had also asked something of the woman in that strange tongue of theirs and she had answered. Oh, what was the answer to the gentle question? There must be an answer—she should have learned the answer—Then suddenly it came to her. It came to her, not out of her brain which was so slow and stupid and never quick to speak. It came from her pounding heart. "Yes, it is a lucky thing, I know, and the luck is perfect if the woman likes also very well the man to whom she is given."

She felt his cheek against hers, even as she had learned.

If Ru-lan had been able to write she would long ago have written to her teacher Stanley to ask her why, when she had said she would come to see her, she had not yet come, although it had been now nearly five years since Ru-lan had left the school. In the five years she had grown heavier, as what woman would not who had given birth to three large strong sons and now a small pretty daughter, so pretty that the child's father went against all nature and loved her twice as well, apparently, as even he loved his sons.

But then there was of course no man on the earth's surface like Yung-en. The man Stanley was never better to his wife than Yung-en was to Ru-lan. Bit by bit, through the five years, she had told him what she had seen those two white ones do, how they looked at each other, how they spoke, and with the telling new comprehension had come to them of what those looks and words meant. She was now sure that when those two spoke to each other in that strong soft fashion they said in their own tongue what came welling up from her own heart and Yung-en's. It was wonderful to think how alike were hearts. She knew this because it was so soon instinct to move freely with Yung-en, walking beside him freely, moving toward him freely and fully when they were alone. She knew that the women in the courts were often disapproving. She knew they said, "It is the boldness she learned in the foreign school—it is the freedom of the modern ways." She smiled, knowing there was a truth in what they said.

She pondered a good deal on her own ease. It did not occur to her, for instance, to share the anxiety of the other women lest their husbands take concubines. Did she not know Yung-en's heart? That was what she had learned, how to know his heart. They talked together sometimes about it, and how their life was different from those about them, and Yung-en said gratefully always, "If the man and woman Stanley should ever come to see us, there would not be enough I could do for them to thank them for what you learned from them. If you had not seen and learned, my life would not have been above any other man's. As it is, you have contented me so that all other women in the world might die and I should not know it." She smiled, knowing she had never been beautiful and now was less so than ever, if one should measure her by a beautiful woman. But she feared none of them.

So when suddenly one August morning a letter came from the school she could hardly wait for Yung-en to come home to read it. She had long given up any pretense at reading. The characters she had once known had quite slipped out of her memory. If some woman asked her in curiosity sometimes what a character was on a bit of paper found, she laughed comfortably and said, "If once I knew, that once is long gone. I have so little use for letters these days." Or if her elder son, now beginning to learn, ran to ask her the meaning of a word she would say, always laughing, "You must go ignorant if you ask learning of me, my son!"

She put the letter by until she heard Yung-en come and then she went to him and waited while he opened it, her hand upon his arm. After these five years it was more than ever necessary to her to put her hand upon his arm, and he moved toward her when he felt her touch, understanding.

"It is a letter from the man Stanley," he said after murmuring the letters aloud awhile. "They wish to open a chapel here in our village and preach their religion, and there will be also a school, and he is coming and with him the woman Stanley."

"Of course they would not be separated," she said gently.

"No," he said, folding the letter. He was planning rapidly. "We shall have them here in our own house. There is the south room upon the old peony terrace where I have my few books and where I never go. Prepare it with the best bed and with the blackwood furniture my father gave us from the south. And I shall invite guests—all my friends. I do not care to invite guests for the religion, but it is a way to repay these two if I show myself a friend. Now I can thank them for all they taught you."

"Yes," she said. "And we can show them our sons—"

"And we can send our daughter to their school," he cried, smiling. They sat down together in simple pleasure, holding each other's hands, laughing a little. "Everything is lucky in our life," he said.

"Everything," she echoed fervently.

So it was that on a certain morning in August, nearly at the end of summer, she welcomed those two. There they were at the door, standing together, a little thinner than she remembered them, a little gray in their hair. "You are tired," she cried, her heart rushing out to them. "Come in—rest and eat. Oh, how welcome you are!"

Yung-en gave up his work when they came and stayed at home, running hither and thither, himself carrying trays of sweetmeats and keeping plates full and pouring tea and going to see what quilts were rolled upon the bed and if the mosquito net was properly drawn. "I can never do enough for them," he said to her in passing.

Well, there it was. The two Stanleys stayed three days and into the days Yung-en and Ru-lan heaped all that they had, all the years of their happy life together, all their luck in the three sons and the little girl. Ru-lan had meant to dress the children in their best, but then it was so hot that she let it go. It was better that they be comfortable. Besides, they were so beautiful and so healthy it must be a pleasure for anyone to see their little brown bodies bare to the waist. She had meant, too, to clean the house a little more, to wipe the dust from the table legs and from the gilt crevices of the family gods. But the summer days passed so quickly until the guests came, and once they were come there was no time for anything except urging them to eat, to talk, to rest themselves, to enjoy the huge feast and the lanterns hung to welcome them, to see the fireworks Yung-en bought and bade the servants fire for their amusement.

She had planned to try to tell the dear teachers Stanley a little about her own life and how much she owed them. She had planned to say at least that she had been very happy. But there was no time for anything. They were busy about the new school, planning, working hard as they always did.

But they were still happy. She knew that. They still paused as they used to pause, to look at each other deeply. When they went away, so soon, so far too soon, she loved them more than ever. She stood beside Yung-en at the gate waving to them, crying to them to go slowly, to return quickly. And then when Yung-en shouted after them, "Our daughter shall be your first girl pupil!" her heart overflowed toward them and she cried after them, "Yes —teach her, for you taught me so much!" That was all she had the time to say. But she did not worry—they would understand. She went back into her house with Yung-en. His hand sought hers comfortably, and they sauntered across their courtyard, well content.

Rocking down the road in their rickety mission Ford, Mollie leaned back against Wyn, grateful to be alone again with him. Now, as always, when she sat beside Wyn she began to feel warm deep peace welling up in her. They were going home, they were together. They were going back to the children. She crept more closely to him, and he put his arm about her. He drove very expertly one-armed.

"Sweetheart!" he said gently. "It was wonderful of you to leave the children and make this trip with me. I shouldn't have blamed you, you know, if you hadn't."

"I can't be away from you, Wyn."

"No, I know." They fell into intimate, peaceful silence.

Over the Chinese landscape twilight was beginning to fall, creeping up in small mists from the ponds and the canals, darkening over the hills from the sky. From the thatched roofs the blue lines of smoke of fires kindled for the evening meal rose straightly into the still air. How strange, how different the scene was from the rough hills of her own home country, from the sharp angular American towns! And yet how little strange, how little different! These were homes, too, and these were people, living together in their families. And here was her home. Wherever Wyn was, was her home. She was instantly deeply content, content with everything, with everybody.

Then suddenly she thought of Ru-lan.

"Wyn!" she said.

"Yes?" he answered.

"What did you really think of Ru-lan?"

"Well?" asked Wyn, twinkling at her a little. "What did you really think?"

"It was just exactly as I was afraid it would be," she answered dolefully. "She's lost even the little she had. Wyn, you wouldn't

22

have known, now would you honestly, that Ru-lan had ever been outside that village? Did you see the slightest difference between her house and any other ignorant village woman's house?"

"No," said Wyn thoughtfully. He guided the car skillfully between two deep wheelbarrow ruts.

Mollie stared mournfully over the landscape, the valleys tawny with ripening rice, the hills browning with ending summer, the willow-encircled villages. "No," she continued, "the house was dusty and not very clean, and the children were eating just anything. I saw that little girl chewing on a cucumber, skin and all."

"So did I," he said briefly.

"And Ru-lan is just like an amiable cow. She just sits and smiles and smiles. She doesn't read, she doesn't seem to do anything in the village, she's just an ordinary woman—after all those years away. I don't believe she does one thing different in her home for all the hours I tried to teach her."

"Mollie, did you see those idols?" Wyn said gravely.

"Yes," said Mollie reluctantly.

They rolled along in silence for a moment, remembering the row of gilt figures with the guttered candles before them. They had taught Ru-lan so patiently to say over and over again, "Thou shall have no other gods before Me. . . ." "Ru-lan, what are gods?" she used to ask. Ru-lan had smiled apologetically. "Teacher, tell me, for I do not know."

"They are idols, Ru-lan."

"Yes, Teacher, it is what I thought."

"You must not worship them, Ru-lan."

"No, Teacher."

And then when Dr. Martin had once asked her in the catechism class what God was, she had said, "Sir, God is an idol." Poor stupid Ru-lan! There was no telling how she would learn a thing. . . .

She thought over the two crowded days, days full of too much food and too much noise and many children and curious neighbors coming in and out to see the newcomers. But Ru-lan had not seemed to mind anything. She had sat tranquil in the midst of the confusion, smiling and smiling. And everybody had seemed fond of her—her children ran to her often, and the neighbors called to her cheerfully, and Yung-en . . . She was struck now, remembering Yung-en.

"Wyn!" she said suddenly, looking up at him.

"Yes, darling?"

He turned and smiled down at her. There she was snuggled down by him like a kitten, looking not a day older . . .

"There was one thing about Ru-lan—her husband really seemed to like her."

"I believe he does," he said slowly. "Yes—I don't know why exactly—she certainly doesn't remember anything we ever taught her!"

II
THE ANGEL

THE ANGEL

THE old Chinese night watchman, standing at dawn by the gate of the mission compound in the midst of the crowd about him, said he had seen an angel in the starry night. He had not, he said gravely, been able to sleep for a long time afterwards. True, it was his business to stay awake all night and walk slowly about the brick walks of the school and about Miss Barry's little house, clacking his bamboo sticks together to warn away thieves who might be loitering there. This he had done very faithfully when he was young, but as he grew old he slept once or twice in the night, waking to clack the more assiduously, and then more and more often he slept. Now since last summer he frequently curled in a dark corner of Miss Barry's garden in her fern bed, and slept very hard, only waking at dawn to clack tremendously and dutifully.

As for Miss Barry, she had wondered often what dog lay in her ferns and was regularly irritated that her ferns were being spoiled, so often irritated, in fact, that the old man, fearing her discovery of him, slept sometimes under a tree or elsewhere. But always he liked the soft ferns best, and he could not forbear creeping back there sometimes in the night when his bones ached, although always the next morning, when he heard Miss Barry's clear quick voice cry, once more discouraged, "Oh, who has let that dog in again?" he shook his head, smitten with secret guilt, but pretended ignorance lest he be discharged.

27

For Miss Barry was not to be counted upon. She might be endlessly patient, as she was, for instance, when cholera got into the compound and sixteen girls died in the school, and he nearly died as well and would have except that she came herself and injected the foreign medicine into his blood and saved him. Then as suddenly, quite without reason, she would lose all her patience over some small thing, a flower dried up for want of water, or dust upon her veranda steps. At these times he had even seen her lips tremble and tears come into her eyes, to his astonishment, and it seemed as though she suffered somehow a loss to herself.

Now on this day, he was wakened out of the fern bed by the cry everywhere that Miss Barry had suddenly disappeared; and, rising dazedly, his spiky hair full of fern leaves, he was questioned as to whether or not he had seen her. But he had not, he said earnestly. He had only seen an angel. He had, he repeated over and over, seen it just before dawn on this moonless night just passed. But, as he told them all as they stood about him in the early sunlight, the men and women teachers of the school and the girl students, and even the two foreigners, Mr. and Mrs. Jones, the stars had been very bright, since it was autumn and beyond the time of the rains. Therefore he had been able to see the angel clearly. It had approached him noiselessly over the grass, its long hair floating and white, and it wore long loose robes and on its shoulders were misty tips of wings, almost hidden by the hair—fluffy tips like the woolly white shawl Miss Barry sometimes wore. . . .

How did he know it was an angel? When Mr. Jones, the missionary, asked this, the old night watchman stared at him indignantly. Had he not been an immersed Baptist for many years? He had gone clear under the water in the pool beneath the pulpit in the compound church on a very cold day fifteen years ago, when the water was supposed to be warmed and was not because the pastor preached too long a sermon and let the water get cold, and afterwards two out of the three of them who were immersed had caught cold and Miss Barry had said "they couldn't even baptize right." Naturally, the night watchman now said, "I know an angel when I see one, being so good a Christian as I am." Besides, he added in argument to Mr. Jones, had he not seen photographs of angels on the cards the Americans sent when they did not want them any more, and was there not an image of an angel set on top of the school Christmas tree every year? Of course he knew an angel when he saw it.

"And then," Mr. Jones asked abruptly, "what became of the angel?"

The old watchman rubbed his rough head thoughtfully and tried to remember. He had been waked out of a sound sleep, he remembered, by a cry.

"The angel screamed," he said.

"What did it scream?" asked Mr. Jones.

The old watchman tried to remember again. He was somewhat nervous under this direct questioning and afraid of making a mistake, which might be very disastrous, since Mr. Jones paid him his monthly salary of six dollars. He considered awhile and then decided that an angel would not only scream. It would scream something—some words. He decided to guess, piecing together his memories of mission Christmases.

"The angel said, 'Hallelujah, peace on earth,'" he replied bravely, his brown and wrinkled face apprehensive.

Mr. and Mrs. Jones looked at each other.

"How strange!" breathed Mrs. Jones. It was early in the morning and she had not combed her hair, and now in the sunshine she felt uneasy and touseled, the more because she was a large woman of fifty and her hair was scanty and wiry gray, and was always a trial to her, and because Mr. Jones noticed it so often and was critical of her about it. Now she endeavored to look at him as though she were not conscious of her appearance in the present exigency. She had come as she was because the alarm had been given to Mrs. Jones first when Miss Barry's amah went to her room with early tea according to her habit, and found Miss Barry gone and the bed tossed in utter confusion. This in itself was strange, because Miss Barry was by nature the neatest of creatures; she rose every morning and laid her covers so exactly back that the bed looked scarcely slept in at all and was never any trouble to make, although even so the amah had to be careful, since Miss Barry was very particular. But this morning the amah had run straight to rouse Mrs. Jones, and two hours had passed and Miss Barry had not been found, nor had Mrs. Jones combed her hair.

Now Mrs. Jones turned to her husband. "I really think, my dear," she suggested, for hers was a nature which never did more, "that we had better go home and get things together and think over what we have heard and what the night watchman says, and I will just tidy myself a bit." These last words she added since she caught Mr. Jones's eye even now fixed in distaste upon her hair and there was no use in pretending.

But Mr. Jones would not at first take her suggestion. He never did, preferring to ignore it until it seemed to be the thing he would have done in any case.

"What did the angel do then?" he demanded of the watchman sternly. He was a small, precise man, a little younger than his wife, but seeming older because of his dictatorial look and manner. Now he fixed his dead gray eyes upon the old Chinese, profoundly distrusting this declaration of what the angel had said, distrusting, indeed, all this tale of an angel. After all, one believed in them, of course, as an orthodox Christian, but still . . .

The old man's face now cleared in relief. He knew quite well what had become of the angel. He had sat up in his ferny bed and stared after the white figure which had moved with great swiftness over the lawn to the gate. He considered an instant. He would like, for the sake of his dramatic soul, to have said it spread white wings and flew over the gate into the eastern sky above. But he regarded with terror Mr. Jones's eyes, impenetrably disbelieving and gray as a fish's eyes. He decided hastily upon the truth.

"The angel went across the grass as though without walking, and then opened the gate, but without noise, and then went away," he said. And, suddenly realizing he was hungry and that the sun was high, he added firmly, "That is all I saw and all I know of the affair."

Mr. Jones, seeing this was true, was ready now to take his wife's suggestion. Together they went out of Miss Barry's exquisite little garden, blooming in this early autumn with chrysanthemums and late roses, into the bare schoolyard and then into their own rather barren court. Mrs. Jones found flowers a trial to care for, what with the long drought and equally long rains of the China climate, and Mr. Jones did not think of flowers or notice them. Occasionally Miss Barry had brought over a handful of tea roses or a stalk of lilies. Especially when she was invited to supper, she came bringing flowers in her hand, and watched a little anxiously while Mrs. Jones arranged them tightly in a glass.

"Oh, let me," she often cried out, and under Mrs. Jones's surprised eyes she pulled and loosened and arranged the flowers. "There!" she would say at last. "They hate being crowded."

"Well, I never," Mrs. Jones had said helplessly the other day. "Really, Miss Barry, one would think they were creatures!"

"So they are," Miss Barry had replied sharply—her temper grew on her, poor thing, as she got older. Then she added fearlessly in her somewhat downright way, "Besides, I like seeing a thing done *right*."

Mrs. Jones now thought of this remark as in a large, vague melancholy she followed her little husband up their steps. It was what Miss Barry said more and more often as she grew older— she was always wanting things done right. She would tidy a school girl's black hair, loosing the braid to plait it again swiftly and strongly and tie it firmly at the end with a bit of cord.

"Learn to do your hair right," she admonished. Or she would summon a servant sharply and point out dust in a corner. "If you sweep the room at all, do it *right*," she said sternly.

Scarcely a day passed, Mrs. Jones reflected, when she had not heard the phrase upon Miss Barry's lips. It had come to be almost an unconscious thing with her, a constant hovering upon the lips of her inner determined spirit. And last summer, when she was having the masons and carpenters repair the school, the phrase became really a mania with her. Mrs. Jones remembered meeting her one hot August morning, very damp heat it was, so that one felt quite dead and inert with it, and yet Miss Barry had looked as carefully dressed as ever in her white linen; and although her thin oval face was flushed a dark red, her white heavy hair was smooth and coiled neatly on top of her head. She was hurrying down the brick path from the school and talking to herself strangely and loudly when she met Mrs. Jones. Indeed she had not seemed to see Mrs. Jones at all, looking full at her but with completely blank eyes, while she cried out passionately,

"I simply will not have it slipshod—it's got to be done right—done *right*—done *right*—"

Then suddenly perceiving Mrs. Jones she controlled herself, forcing a smile to her rather thin, delicate lips, "Oh, it's you, Mrs. Jones. I—I—do forgive me! I am afraid I have lost patience. These Chinese workmen—still, I try not to be unjust—Mrs. Jones, will you be so kind as to come and see what they have done even in the little while I was eating my breakfast? I can't leave them an instant without something going wrong."

And although Mrs. Jones had not wanted to go at all, she was unable to refuse the passionate demand of Miss Barry's dark and tragic eyes, and so she had lumbered after Miss Barry's thin quick figure, sighing a little because what she had to see was on the third floor of the school dormitory. They had picked their way among the bits of fallen plaster, and the gaping masons had stopped to stare and comment upon the white women and guffaw after they had passed. Miss Barry, hearing the coarse laughter, held her white head higher, and pressed her lips together more firmly, ignoring them. But her eyes glittered.

"Look at that, if you please," she said at last, pointing at a wall. She had a delicate hand, fleshless, and always trembling a little now, but with beautiful shapely bones. Mrs. Jones followed its direction. At first she could perceive nothing but a lathed, plasterless wall.

"Look at these laths, Mrs. Jones," said Miss Barry. Why, actually there were tears in the woman's eyes! "Year after year the plaster falls from these laths because they are so closely and carelessly placed that the plaster can't get between. Have I not begged and besought and showed these masons what to do, and offered to pay double—anything, anything, to get it done *right*? This year I paid a carpenter to tear it all down. Look at them—he has torn the laths off and nailed them back just as they were! It's impossible for anybody in this whole race to do anything *right* —Until they learn, all the Christianity in the world won't save them!"

Mrs. Jones had been genuinely shocked at this. She suggested gently, "My *dear* Miss Barry! Really, such talk is very near to blasphemy."

"It is true," replied Miss Barry, her spare face setting into its habitual lines of tragic, repressed impatience.

That day, Mrs. Jones now remembered, Miss Barry had first mentioned the dog in the fern bed, although afterwards she spoke of it often, always with increasing agitation. They had walked back to Miss Barry's home together, and on the way Miss Barry's darting glance had sprung about her garden. She spied a faded rose or two on the bushes and twisted them off swiftly and dexterously and tucked them into the loose earth underneath.

Then irritation had lit her face again. She was looking at the fern bed, and quickly she walked to it. "I declare, that dog has been in here again," she said. "Look at these little new fronds all broken!" The irritation was gone. A tender sorrow had its place. Kneeling on the grass, she slipped her daintily pointed old fingers under the silvery curls of the broken fronds. "The poor little struggling things," she whispered, under her breath, forgetting Mrs. Jones. "As soon as they have courage and come up again, so lovely and so fragile, that beast gets in—" She rose to her feet energetically. "I *must* get hold of that watchman," she said. "He sleeps at night and doesn't remember to look for the dog—I know he sleeps—he's like them all—lazy and careless. You have to be after every one of them to get anything done *right*. . . ."

This morning in her own somewhat untidy sitting room Mrs.

34

Jones sank into an old wicker chair and breathed awhile and remembered these things about Miss Barry. She must go upstairs and do her hair, but just a minute's rest. . . . Well, of course Miss Barry had never known that it was the old watchman himself who slept in her ferns. Poor soul, it would probably have finished her if she had known *that!*

Later, at breakfast, seeing her slipshod Chinese manservant as he shuffled about the table, his bare feet thrust into the toes of his shoes, she was reminded again of Miss Barry. Only three nights ago she and Mr. Jones had been over there to supper. Miss Barry always had everything so nice. There were lace mats on the dark shining table and a bowl of pink roses in the middle of it. The servant was neat and white-robed and well trained. Miss Barry had expended endless effort on him. And now, although he knew perfectly what he was to do, her glance followed him as he served the cream soup, the chicken jelly, the lettuce, the smooth cylinder of vanilla ice cream.

"She always wanted things too perfect," Mrs. Jones said suddenly, aware comfortably of the value of her own carelessness.

"Who?" said Mr. Jones.

"Miss Barry," replied Mrs. Jones.

"I wish I knew what to do next," said Mr. Jones, perturbed. He had been eating rapidly and in silence, thinking hard. "It's perfectly evident she got up out of her bed and wandered about in the garden and out of the gate. But she was such a rational creature—and had she anything to disturb her recently that you know about, Nellie?"

"No, nothing especially," said Mrs. Jones, reflecting. "You saw her at supper the other day—I haven't seen her since."

"I've sent runners out on the streets to inquire if anybody saw a foreign lady," said Mr. Jones. "And I've sent word to the magistrate's office. It's very embarrassing, I'm sure. I've never heard of such a thing happening before in the mission. If you are finished, let's go to her room. We may find a family letter or something which will explain. You are sure she has confided nothing of a personal nature to you recently or at any time?"

Mrs. Jones looked surprisedly at her husband. "Why, no, Elmer," she answered mildly. "You know she was the sort who never tells anybody anything. We've lived here next to her all these years and still I don't even know what family she has. I didn't talk with her easily. If we did talk, she was always full of something she was trying to do. She never rested. I think there is an older sister somewhere in Vermont, but I don't know. You know how she was—just putting her life into the school, and her garden the only pleasure she took. Why, she hasn't been away even in the summers for years. Last time I asked her if she didn't think she ought to go, she answered that if she did, she knew her garden would be ruined while she was away because the Chinese were so slack they'd never do a thing all summer, and she wasn't going to have all the time and energy she had put into her flowers thrown away as it was that one summer she wasn't here seven years ago. She's never been away from the mission since. She always acted about the flowers as though they were real creatures."

Mr. Jones said no more. He waited with obvious impatience while Mrs. Jones placidly finished her last slice of toast, her large face tranquilly mournful. Then he rose briskly. "Now," he said, "let's go to work. If we can't find her, I'll have to notify the American Consul at the port."

But when they had arrived in Miss Barry's sparsely furnished, neat room, they found nothing. There was the tossed bed, the linen sheets strangely crumpled. "She always had to have linen sheets," said Mrs. Jones sadly. "And such a time as she had getting them washed right! She used to talk about it."

Mr. Jones opened the closet gingerly. It seemed improper to do so, for Miss Barry's garments, hung up neatly and straightly within, were startlingly like herself, and she was the last person into whose room one could consider a man's venturing. . . . Yet, Mr. Jones had thought sometimes, once she must have been beautiful. The shape of her face, the very slightly arched, delicate nose, the fine lines of the head, the dark, keen eyes, the white fine skin, and the masses of straight, smooth hair, white as long as he could remember—surely once she had been beautiful. But no one really knew her. She had lived alone here so long in the square mission house, vigilant, unsparing of them all, but most of herself, somehow always an exquisite New England spinster even in the midst of this sprawling, dirty, slipshod city, summoning all the dauntlessness of her forefathers to maintain herself against its overwhelming amorphous, careless life. Yes, staring at these garments, Mr. Jones saw her, always shiningly neat and clean, always embattled.

Then suddenly they found out everything about her. While Mr. Jones was staring at the gauntly hanging dresses, silver gray poplin, white linen, a lavender silk for best, all with the neatest little collars and cuffs, his wife cried out, "Elmer, I believe there's a letter to her sister here—I found it under the blotting pad on the desk—"

She held four carefully written sheets toward her husband. He took them and glanced at them, and then looked at his wife. "I suppose," he said nervously, "that under the circumstances we would be justified in reading it?" He could not somehow imagine reading casually Miss Barry's private letters.

"Well, how else are we going to know anything?" said Mrs. Jones, wondering at him.

So they sat down on the gray wicker couch and silently began to read the letter, Mr. Jones holding the pages, Mrs. Jones looking over his shoulder.

"Dear Sister Elizabeth," it began, "I hope you are fully recovered from your rheumatism. The climate in Vermont is conducive to this trouble. I trust you are taking every care of yourself. I sent you the usual amount by the last mail. Do not worry that I cannot spare this. I need very little for myself, and you are now all that is left me of my dear ones. I regularly give a little in charity, but find much given or given openly only works harm, as these people are naturally lazy and ready to receive indefinitely and so be spared effort, although I truly wish to be helpful to them."

Here the fine handwriting changed. It was as though Miss Barry had paused awhile and then taken up her pen again in agitation. "My dear sister Elizabeth, pray for me that I may have love in my heart toward these people for whom I have spent my life. For I am distressed to find, as I grow older, that I like them less and less. Indeed, I fear they are incorrigibly set in their idle ways. It may be, as my neighbor Mrs. Jones says, that their souls can be saved even though their bodies are unwashed and their minds and their hands idle. But to me God must be served aright, and He is better served, surely, in cleanliness and order—"

Here again there was a break, and the hue of the ink was fresh. The date was changed also.

"She wrote this last night," murmured Mrs. Jones. . . .

"I have not been able yet to finish this letter, my dear sister. The repairs on the school have been interminably slow due to slipshod careless work. I have not been able to endure it with patience, I fear. I have exhausted myself in repeated demands that paint be repainted because dirty fingermarks were left on it, bricks reset that were carelessly placed, and a thousand like things, which, seeming small, yet render life intolerable to a cultivated and sensitive person. I think tonight with an agony of loneliness of our dear childhood home in New England. I think there never was paint so white as on our house and fence. How did it keep so white? I remember the garden. Here in my tiny poor garden my life is a struggle against weeds, against dirty footsteps, even against incessant spittle upon my walks, for this is the distressing habit of casual persons here. Indeed, my life, which once I planned so nobly, has, now that I look back upon it, resolved itself into nothing but a battle against filth and laziness—and I have lost. I might as well have tried to stop the dirty muddy Yangtze River as it flows past this heathen city. Yet I have only a few more years left me and am too old at the battle now to give up. I shall go on trying—trying to get even a few small things done *right*."

Here there was the last break, here were the last few lines: "I must pause now, while it occurs to me, although I am undressed and ready for bed, to go and see if a stray dog is sleeping in my ferns. It has done so spasmodically all summer, to my great annoyance, each time crushing a dozen or more of the delicate fronds—oh, Elizabeth, I think I am not well! Something is wrong with me. I feel so often as though I would scream aloud like a child if I have once again to make one of these Chinese do a thing over *right*. I suppose I have begged the watchman hundreds of times to keep this dog out of my garden. I have struggled so long and he will not learn. Elizabeth, I will confess to you that secretly I have come to hate this people. May God forgive me—I cannot help it. They have killed me."

Here Mr. and Mrs. Jones were interrupted by the old night watchman. His face was quite distorted with weeping and he cried out, beside himself, "O sir, O mistress, Miss Barry is found! The men you sent out have returned—they say a few night vendors saw a white woman with long streaming white hair running down the street to the river, crying out as she went some foreign words. And we all went down to the river then, where the bank rises to a cliff, and we were afraid to look down except that a servant at the gate of the temple told us that near dawn he had seen a spirit pass, screaming as it went, and it ran straightway and leaped over the cliff, and he turned his face away and dared not follow. So we went. Sir, she essayed to leap into the river, but she failed. She only fell upon the rocks. There she lies, all white! Oh, she was good—we all knew she was good, though she had a temper not to be loved. It was she I saw, sir—she appeared before me as an angel—I said I saw an angel —now I have seen an angel—" He turned and ran from the room, babbling and weeping.

Mr. and Mrs. Jones looked at each other silently. Then Mr. Jones coughed and spoke, "I must notify the consul—and I had better keep this letter and send it to the relative," he said solemnly, and, taking out a little notebook, he slipped the letter into its pages. Then he and Mrs. Jones tiptoed from the empty room. Upon the shining, dark, immaculate floor there were now their unconscious dusty footprints and the dustiest of them all were the prints of the old night watchman's bare feet.

III

MR. BINNEY'S AFTERNOON

MR. BINNEY'S AFTERNOON

IT was next to the last day of Mr. Binney's visit to Shanghai and he had left the most important thing until this afternoon to buy. This was a new cookstove. The cookstove he and Mary had brought to China with them twenty years before, and in which Mary had baked bread and pie and cake and sugar cookies for all the years they had lived in the dusty little Chinese town just south of the Great Wall, had suddenly refused to bake any longer and had collapsed. He should not perhaps have left so important a thing until nearly the last day, but he and Mary had decided they must not spend more than ten dollars on the stove, and when Mr. Binney had asked timorously at a large English shop about cookstoves the answer haughtily given had been of such an overwhelming amount that he could only leave in complete silence after murmuring, "Thank you, sir," to the tall thin floor walker dressed meticulously in formal morning clothes.

Mr. Binney had gone back to the Missionary Home where he was stopping, since he was a missionary, and there in his dingy small room he had made the subject a matter of prayer. The result was that the very first thing he saw this morning was a second-hand shop filled with every sort of goods, and in the midst of much else was a cookstove not too badly worn. He hastened in, and, after a little polite argument with the apathetic Chinese proprietor, he bought the stove for ten dollars.

He had known he would, but the sense of exhilaration he always felt after answered prayers sent him happily down the street. One never could be sure if what one asked was in accord with God's will. When, as in this case, it proved to be so, it was very pleasant. He arranged with a riksha man to deliver the stove and then turned delightedly to thinking of how pleased Mary would be.

For the cookstove was something he had planned especially for his wife Mary, his dear Mary, as a sort of present for their twentieth anniversary. This day fortnight he would be home with her again in their little four-roomed Chinese house under the Wall, and she would be unpacking the box he had brought —first the cookstove, with which she would be so pleased, then a few spices, some tracts and a little hand printing press to print more, some cotton stockings for her and warm underwear for them both, and the lengths of strong plain woolen stuff she would make into a suit for him and a dress for herself. It was not pretty material. Even as he bought it at a Chinese cloth shop he realized it would not be pretty; plain dark gray cloth it was, but strong and cheap, and so he took it. They had so little money that one must think of strength and cheapness first.

Left to himself he might never have thought of anything else, except that he had learned by now that Mary loved pretty things. She was, for instance, always coaxing along little stunted flowers in pots and boxes. He remembered once her joy over a bit of red geranium someone passing through had brought her from Peking. But it had died. The bitter sandy winds out of the desert had killed it, as they killed everything. Those same winds had made Mary's rosy face pale and lined, and her curly dark hair gray and dry. Sometimes she looked almost as dust-colored as the Chinese women. His heart ached suddenly as he thought of her. She had been very pink and white as a girl, he remembered.

He thought of this especially at this moment, for he had been wandering as his feet led him among the streets, and suddenly he came upon a beautiful gay street. "It is so pretty, Mary would like it," he thought to himself, looking about him. It was a street of hospitable houses whose doors were open, and from one door and then another he saw ladies come out, prettily dressed, and step into carriages which seemed waiting for them, and then drive smartly off, their Chinese coachmen brilliant in uniforms of red and blue, and tasseled hats. He stopped and stared as one of the carriages passed him. Two ladies in it threw him the gayest of smiles. He smiled back, surprised, and tipped his hat. It was very friendly of them, he thought. Perhaps they took him for someone else. But when he looked and saw another carriage pass and caught another smile as brilliant, he said to himself, "It is only that they are charming and kindly ladies," and he was grateful to them, for no one else in the city had smiled at him.

Somehow when they had passed him and he had trudged away, the other streets seemed less cheerful than they had been. In fact, he thought, that one street was the only really cheerful one he had seen. He began to walk slowly to the Missionary Home. When he opened the door, the place seemed suddenly unutterably dreary. Yet it was quite as it had been when he left it after his tiffin. The unframed texts in the hall, the strips of matting upon the worn floors, the unpainted wicker furniture, were all as they had been. He went slowly upstairs, stepping aside once to allow Mrs. Browntree, the housekeeper, to pass by. He looked at her as she passed. She was not changed, he knew. He had sat next her at meals for nearly a week, and he knew very well by now her mouse-brown hair and her faded hazel eyes and her protruding front teeth which were stopped with silver fillings.

Seeing him she paused and said in her usual worried manner, "Oh, Brother Binney, *will* you take prayers tomorrow morning? Everybody seems so busy—"

Quite to his own surprise Mr. Binney heard himself saying, "I'm sorry, Mrs. Browntree, I am leaving early."

This, he realized when she sighed and went on, was practically a lie. His boat did not leave until noon. He went upstairs very gravely indeed. To lead prayers he had always regarded as a duty and an opportunity. One never knew what listening soul— why did he suddenly dislike Mrs. Browntree so very much that he had lied to her? She was a worthy woman, widow to a fellow missionary whom he had thoroughly respected. He should think of this instead of remembering that her black dress hung on her in slack rusty folds, and that there were spots on its front, and that her teeth were stopped with silver fillings.

He did not know what was the matter with him. He entered his room. He was, he thought, tired. He lay down upon the narrow iron bed and drew a cotton blanket over his knees. He would rest a little while and then spend a time in prayer, asking God to forgive him and keep him steadfast. But instead he let the moments pass and he remembered again and again the beautiful ladies. They were, he thought, like angels. Their dresses were bright. He could not remember the colors, but they had all been so bright, such happy colors. And their faces were rosy, and their smiles so free and kind. He began to think suddenly of Mary's smile. It was kind, too, very kind, but not radiant. No one could call Mary radiant, although he now remembered, she had in her youth been merry at times, too. But this had passed.

46

Hers had been, he now perceived for the first time, rather too hard a life for merriment, although he felt he had done the best he could. And, of course, when he had felt his "call," after he was graduated from the seminary in the little Ohio town where had lived until then, Mary had been perfectly willing to come to the foreign field with him. Certainly he had not compelled her, although if she had not been willing, as he told her, he would have felt he must proceed without her, since it did not occur to him to go against his "call."

But he was sincerely glad Mary had felt as earnestly as he did about the Work. In the twenty years they had lived together she had been a comfort to him, although she had borne him no children. This in itself was of not such great importance, since he was aware that children would have brought problems. There was, for instance, no doctor nearer than three days away by camel. The chief inconvenience he had felt, in fact, in regard to her childlessness, was when skeptical heathen had asked too cleverly, "And if this foreign God of yours is all you say, why do you not ask him for a son, seeing you have none?"

To this one could hardly answer that such prayer had been made and refused. Indeed he knew, when Mary had at times abstained from food and had stayed in her bedroom, that she made this prayer with fasting and weeping, for once he had stood outside her door and before he could enter he had heard her voice cry out in an agony he had not heard before, nor dreamed possible in her, "Oh, God, if you would just give me a little baby—dear God, just one!—I am sure I could be happier— and I would be a better woman—I promise, I promise!"

He had not gone in, after all. He crept away astonished and miserable. He had not known her unhappy; indeed, she was even-tempered and cheerful by nature. And how could she be better? When she came down to supper, rather pale, he said nothing, since they had never been emotional with each other. . . . Now, remembering the cry, he felt a slight sense of hostility against God, who had not answered. Every dusty slatternly Chinese woman in the town had many babies, and only his Mary had none.

He longed passionately for the first time to make it up to her. Ah, how good she had been all these years! She had kept his home as comfortable and as clean as any home in Ohio, and somehow she managed to make the things he liked to eat, cinnamon rolls and sugar cookies and pies. . . .

But, now he decided, her life had been too dull. A woman needed romance. He thought again, very gravely, of the beautiful ladies he had seen, and of their lovely bright smiles. They had, doubtless, romantic lives of ease and pleasure. Mary's life had, of course, been very different. In the Chinese town they had lived quite as much without romance as they might have lived in a little Ohio town. They had soon grown accustomed to seeing yellow faces instead of white, and camels and donkey caravans and sedan chairs became as everyday to them as horses and buggies once had been. He preached daily in the little white-washed chapel, and taught the scanty, curious listeners a hymn tune or two, bearing patiently their loud laughter at the strange foreign music. And since he was not very good at carrying tunes, Mary played the little folding organ and after the service went to see mothers and told them what to do for their sick babies and grieved when they did nothing, and wept more than the mothers did when the babies died.

Certainly neither of them dreamed of romance, not even when Mr. Binney was nearly captured by bandits and only escaped by pretending he was insane, nor even when a mob threatened to kill them because it had not rained for nearly a year, and the town gods must be angry because of the two foreigners. In this case Mr. Binney, after prayer and a long look at the clouds, had averted death by promising the rain that fortunately fell the next day, although one could not be sure of God's will, and they had been ready to die if rain did not come, and had sat waiting hand in hand.

Now, remembering these and other things in their life, he cried out in his heart again, "She has had it too hard. I must make it up to her."

And then it occurred to him to buy her a real present, something lovely and for herself, not a common gift such as the egg beater of which she had spoken, nor a package of safety pins, nor a box of pencils. As for the cookstove, he would not count it at all, he suddenly determined recklessly. No, he thought in excitement, the next morning before he started he would buy Mary a pretty dress, a really bright, pretty dress. He saw her clothed as the lovely ladies had been, fashionably, with a little hat the color of the dress—perhaps pink. One of those ladies had been dressed entirely in pink. Pink was pretty on a lady.

The supper bell rang shrilly. He rose, relieved, excited. He would buy the dress. He could see Mary unfolding it, her eyes suddenly soft above the color, as they always softened before beauty. He was not quick to see things, and sometimes the softening of her eyes first made him know there was something to be seen, or he would not have known it—a flower, perhaps, or new green leaves or something which seemed special to her. His heart melted in him, and flew to her defense. In the new dress she would look as lovely as any lady. How he loved her!

He went downstairs almost gaily and took his place beside Mrs. Browntree, and bowed his head for grace. But he could not keep still. It occurred to him now that he knew nothing of where to buy ladies' garments and he must ask where he could find the dress he wanted for Mary, one exactly like the pink one. He would ask Mrs. Browntree tentatively about ladies' dresses.

"I want to take my dear wife a present, Mrs. Browntree," he began eagerly. "Next month we will have been married twenty years. I thought of a dress—" His rather ordinary hazel eyes began suddenly to shine. "I know just what I want. This afternoon I saw some very nice-looking ladies, Mrs. Browntree. In fact, the street I happened to be in seemed full of them. They were really very pretty, and they were evidently going for a drive, a number of them together. One of them had a very pretty pink dress. I thought of my wife—"

Mrs. Browntree, who was ordinarily abstracted in the service of the table, now stopped her ladling of the pale soup, and stared at him suspiciously. "What street was it?" she asked in a whisper, glancing at the other guests.

"I forget," said Mr. Binney surprised. "Now I think of it, I believe it was Yinching Road."

Mrs. Browntree set her lips against her protruding teeth. She stared at him hard and, holding the ladle suspended, she leaned across the soup tureen to whisper to him, shocked to the soul, as he could see by her perturbed face, "*Pretty* women, Mr. Binney?" she said. "In the street of—of—*prostitutes?*"

Mr. Binney stared back, and Mrs. Browntree decently averted her eyes, for after all, he was a man. But Mr. Binney answered nothing at all. He bent his head over his soup and ate it spoonful by spoonful methodically. For a moment he also was overwhelmed at what Mrs. Browntree had said. Those—those creatures of whom one had heard—against whom the Bible warned all men—he had stood gazing at them, taking pleasure in their smiles! For a moment he felt a little faintness within him. . . .

But suddenly, to his own astonishment, he recovered. He glanced at Mrs. Browntree's set lips, from which her two front teeth protruded and he disliked her intensely. He disliked her drab hair and her faded black cotton dress and the gray pebble brooch she wore at her throat. Above all he disliked the righteousness of her whole bearing, although he knew he ought to be glad she was a righteous woman, and all this dislike drove him to a boldness he had not known was in him. It was still true, he thought, in spite of—of everything, that the ladies—those women —had been beautiful and their smiles kind, and he did not believe that necessarily every smile meant—meant . . . Anyway, Mary should have as pretty a dress as any of them! She, as good as gold, should at least have as pretty a dress as—as a prostitute!

He wished he could tell Mrs. Browntree that merely to be pretty was not sinful—not at all sinful. When Mary was young she was very pretty. But how could he tell her, and how make her understand? He lifted his head and looked about him belligerently, searching for speech. But he felt quite helpless. Mrs. Browntree's righteousness was as vast as Gibraltar.

Then God helped him. At his movement someone asked conversationally, "Did you have a pleasant afternoon, Brother Binney?"

"I did," he replied distinctly and slowly. He stared solemnly at Mrs. Browntree. "I had a perfectly lovely afternoon!"

IV
THE DANCE

THE DANCE

OLD Mrs. Ling sat with her back against the wall in the
brilliantly lit dance hall of the French Concession in
Shanghai. She sat immobile, dignified in her long robe
of silvery satin, beautiful hands folded quietly in her lap. She
was the figure of serenity and tranquillity. Nothing about her
moved or was agitated. In the course of three hours no one had
come to speak to her, but she had smiled occasionally with complete correctness and then resumed her tranquillity. Nothing of
her seemed to move. Yet, if anyone had observed her closely, he
would have seen that her eyes were moving. They were moving
constantly, back and forth, up and down the dance floor, her following gaze threading in and out among the dancers. People of
every race and nationality were about her, but she saw only one
of them. Her eyes were fastened faithfully and anxiously upon
an elderly rather stout man in a long dull blue silk robe. He
was short and most of his partners were taller than he. But it
seemed to make no difference to him who these partners were.
He grasped them to him with equal fervor, impeded only by the
rotundity of his own figure. Upon his round smooth face had
sat now for three hours the same happy, slightly silly smile.

When certain of her women friends had come to Mrs. Ling
in the quietude of her own courts in the native quarter of
Shanghai, and had told her that her husband was making a fool
of himself, she had not at first thought it serious. Her husband

was middle-aged, and she knew from hours of languid talk among the women of the household that at middle age women must expect their husbands to behave with an unseemly skittishness for a short time. If a wife could be patient he would recover without consequences, especially if she ignored a temporary outside establishment. It would only be a short while, because respectable men, men like her husband, always came to their senses very soon and realized that their years were their years and that they had sons and grandsons watching them and snickering up their long sleeves, and this brought health to their souls. There is nothing so restraining upon age as the ridicule of the young. Dignity is all that the old have left, and if they lose it they have no weapon at all against the young. The worst that could happen would be a young concubine, too young for the rest of the household and therefore inconvenient. When her husband prolonged his night absences she sighed and resigned herself to the thought of a concubine, hoping only that it would be a nice simple ignorant girl and not one of these modern educated hussies.

It was at this time that her friends called upon her, five of them. When they had drunk tea and eaten small cakes and played mahjong five or six hours, she perceived they had come with a purpose, and that they had something upon their minds. So she invited them to dinner, and when all the maidens and unmarried daughters of the household were gone to bed, and there remained only her three sisters-in-law and an aunt and a few elderly cousins and some of the old women servants, they sat in privacy, and she discovered what was wrong. Her husband was not behaving in the usual proper and permissible way of middle-aged men. He was not going to the good old-fashioned sing-song houses, nor was he paying court to some respectable established courtesan nor setting up a temporary apartment for some hired lady until his fever was over. No, the worst had happened. He had fallen a prey to the lowest possible form of vice. He was going to the dancing halls in the foreign concession, where went only modern women, white women, Chinese women, Russian and French women, all dangerous because they were modern and had as their aim the breaking up of stable and old-fashioned homes.

When Mrs. Ling heard this, she looked from one to the other of the faces about her. They were all pitying and sympathetic, and none blamed her. They all knew that she had been the best of wives. She had been a very general in her management of the immense household; the slaves and servants were all contented; her daughters-in-law were devoted to her; and her husband respected her and never reproached her, since she had had five sons and none of them dead. By some stroke of extraordinary fortune the three children she had lost were all girls. She had nothing for which to blame herself. Yet this had fallen upon her!

At first she would not believe it. She said stoutly, sucking at her brass water pipe, "I do not believe it. He would have said something. He is as talkative as a child, and if he had been wandering about in strange places and seeing strange things it would have leaked out of him. A woman he might have kept silent about, but not strange foreign sights."

Then of course there had been nothing to do except to tell her the truth. Old Mrs. Wu got out her large handkerchief and touched the corners of her eyes carefully and said, "The third son of my second son is a wild youth, and we are in misery about him. On the thirteenth day of this month he went to a place kept by a Russian for this dancing. He could not believe his eyes, but he saw the form of Mr. Ling there, walking about in this way they call dancing, and with a woman in his arms."

57

"What color of a woman?" asked Mrs. Ling.

"I dared not ask," said Mrs. Wu gravely, "but in these times it might have been any color."

Then Mrs. Li took her turn and said, "Two days ago in the evening, about midnight, at the foreign pleasure hall on the largest street in the French Concession, a place kept by a Frenchman for public dancing, the husband of a friend of mine, who is also ill with Mr. Ling's present sickness, saw Mr. Ling with a lady, undoubtedly foreign—since her hair was as red as a barbarian's beard—clasped against his own person, and he was also walking about with her. My friend's husband laughed a great deal about it and he made remarks of great disrespect to his wife about Mr. Ling, since he said the foreign lady was tall and Mr. Ling's face reached only to her bosom. It was a very peculiar thing to see."

At this the ladies all fell silent and looked delicately away from Mrs. Ling, and there were a great many sighs about the room. Mrs. Ling thanked them all and remarked that she thought the next day there would be rain. Very soon thereafter her friends took their leave, having accomplished the thing for which they had come.

But of course, although her relatives pressed their attentions upon her and although at their insistence she smoked a small pill of opium to make her sleep, she did not sleep. She lay awake for many hours, and when Mr. Ling came in very late and somewhat drunk she did not reproach him. She waited until he was asleep and then she leaned over him and smelled of him keenly. He did smell foreign. There was a foreign odor about him, an odor of a scent she did not know. So she knew it was all true.

This was how it came about that she herself now sat in this garish noisy enormous room. She had lain awake until dawn

58

planning what she must do. When the next night came and Mr. Ling put on his best robes and oiled the ring of hair about his baldness and smoothed down his few whiskers and said, "I go to play with a few friends," she answered calmly, "I hear you have been enjoying the foreign city. I have been wanting to go for a long time and see it. Take me with you."

He was horrified, so horrified that his eyebrows flew upright and his mouth drew down and his eyes goggled at her. "My dear," he said, "you would not like it."

"Why?" she asked. "Are there no women there? If there are no women I beg your pardon."

He stared at her, reflecting, and she knew him well enough to know that he was trying to decide if it were safe to lie to her. So she said innocently, "I hear in the foreign city that the men and women play together like little children." Then he knew that he had better not lie, so he coughed and pretended to laugh and said, "By all means, come with me. I am delighted."

So she climbed into their big motor car beside him, and they sat immobile and intensely respectable behind their liveried chauffeur. When they reached the dance hall she followed him through the door, and sat down in the seat he called to have placed for her. She looked about her. There were no other women there of her own age. All the other women, and there seemed to be hundreds, were young, young and pretty, and looking strangely alike, in spite of the fact that they were of every race and their garb was very different. But they all contrived to have the same look, a look too painted, too eager, too pretty, too petulant, too greedy. She instantly disliked them all. But she only said to her husband, smiling pleasantly, "Go and find your friends. I shall sit here and drink tea and watch you. It will be a pleasure to me."

So he had departed, a naïve and dubious look on his moony face.

At first when he danced he had done so very decorously, stepping about slowly, his partner held at the length of his short arms. He had glanced frequently at his wife, and once he had come to her and said, "You understand this is a beneficial form of exercise. It is recommended for those who grow too fat as I have."

She concealed her horror behind her smile and said sweetly, "I can see it is very good exercise. Pray continue. It amuses me."

Plainly he did not know what to make of her, so he went away and drank heavily alone during a dance or two. Then he forgot her. Thereafter Mrs. Ling had the hideous spectacle of her beloved husband, an honorable man, one of the richest silk merchants in the native city of Shanghai, trundling about with the most absurd-looking women. It even added to her anger when she perceived that he danced very badly, and while she pitied him for his ridiculousness, she hated the women who danced with him, because she knew they could not know how good he was. They only thought he was a silly rich old man and they danced with him for money.

But soon her anger passed and she fell into great despair. Sitting beautifully erect and motionless against the wall, the hard white electric light falling upon her exquisite and delicately lined face, the tears began to shine in her eyes. She opened her eyes proudly and did not wipe them away. They gathered slowly and rolled down upon her stiff brocaded satin robe, which would not absorb them. Then they fell into small wet balls upon the dusty floor.

For what she saw now was her utter destruction. These women were not honorable and decent courtesans. They were not those women who humbly keep their place in the scheme of life and earn their living in quiet ways serving men. These were the women of whom she had heard, the bold modern women, the women who clutch at a man and demand to be the only woman in his house and hold back their bodies and clamor and refuse until he has lost everything for their sakes, until he has divorced his own real wife and sent her in shame away and put in her place this—this painted image of a woman. She stared at her husband, her face smooth, the tears gathering in her eyes. In his arms now he held such a woman, a small young girl with a bold rosy face and bright black eyes. She was wrapped in a tight scarlet satin robe split to the thigh and showing her bare flesh. In her wifely place would this one be set. She was sure of it. She knew her poor old silly man. She knew that weak trembling fatuous look that was now upon his face. When he looked like that it was all over with him. Why, when she was young, she had even used it herself, once to get a pair of rubies she wanted, and once or twice to—several times, in fact. He always gave in to her when he looked like that. And even at her best she had never been seductive as this girl was seductive. They were dancing nearer and nearer. She did not move. She sat very proudly.

But she had not counted on what it would do to her to have her husband come so near. Out among the others she could follow his figure, mourning, but still he was one among others. But when he came near she saw him closely. She saw his well-known face and his fat old figure, and the garments she knew so well. She had even ordered them for him, choosing the satin in the shade of old blue suitable to elderly men. It matched very ill with this raw young scarlet pressed against it.

Now they were just opposite her. She looked piteously into her husband's face. He did not even see her. He was looking, his eyes shining and his mouth loose in a smile, at the small lovely careless face not six inches from his. The girl was looking at him, too, smiling, inscrutable, scornful, promising. Mrs. Ling forgot herself. She rose hurriedly and stared at them both and began to weep aloud, her hand clenched and pressed against her mouth. But still her husband did not see her.

Then the girl saw her. She stared straight into Mrs. Ling's eyes, and her slender arms dropped from about the fat old man. She came the two steps toward Mrs. Ling, and Mrs. Ling heard a soft hurried voice purring into her ear, "Sit down—you are not well—what is the matter? What can I do for you? Why are you here?"

Mrs. Ling felt two firm little hands pressing her back into the seat and the voice hurried on, "Sit here. I will shield you so no one can see you. Tell me what is wrong."

Mrs. Ling looked up imploringly into the young face above her. It was unbelievably pretty and imperious and petulant. It was all she dreaded. But it was kind. To her astonishment it was kind!

"He is my husband," she faltered. "I beg you to spare him. He is my husband."

The girl turned, astonished, and looked at Mr. Ling, who had come up and was mopping his brow. "Go away," she said, "I want to talk to your wife."

Then in the midst of the dance hall Mrs. Ling heard herself pouring out all her fears to this girl whom she hated—how her husband had been coming here night after night and how she saw herself deposed and sent into the country away from her home, to die. So many old women were having to do that now, now that the young women came and took away their old husbands because they were rich. At this thought she leaned her head against the slight young body and wept afresh.

"Come here," she heard the imperious young voice above her call. She looked up. There her husband stood. It smote her afresh that here was her husband at this woman's beck and call. But it was all over anyway. She was only an old woman. She ought never to have come here. She had no place here, no place anywhere nowadays. Men wanted women young and pretty, and able to read and write and above all to dance. She could never dance, not with her little feet that had been bound in childhood. . . . She wiped her eyes with her silk handkerchief, and then caught her hands together because they trembled. She heard her husband give a laugh, a meaningless embarrassed laugh. He began to speak.

"Eh, this is—"

But the girl cut ruthlessly into his speech, her voice a silver dagger to stab him. "I know who she is. She is your wife. You are a silly old fat man. Go home with her and stay there. Do you think I love you? Who could love you? Your stomach is like a rice bucket. No one could love you except this wife of yours. She loves you because she remembers what you once were. But I have no memories of you. To me you must always be what you are—only a fat old man, a funny fat old man—very rich—but fat—fat—fat—and old—"

Then she changed her voice and bent caressingly over Mrs. Ling. "No one has seen you. Anyway, they will only think I am your daughter. I don't want him. I wanted his money. I tell you that quite plainly. I have to earn my living. But I don't want to earn it from another woman—not from an old woman like you—a good old woman—"

Someone called to her, a gay hard loud voice. It was a man,

63

tall and young. Her face lit up suddenly. She forgot these old two—

"Where have you been—oh, where have you been?" she cried, running to him. "I've been waiting hours for you."

He swept her away into the dancing brilliant crowd.

So the two were left there, the old two. Mrs. Ling sat silent a moment, looking down. She was suddenly afraid of her husband. He might blame her bitterly for taking his pleasure away from him. But he did not say a word. She stole a look at him. He was staring at the moving tripping weaving figures. He suddenly appeared very tired. He swallowed once or twice, and then, looking closer, she saw he was hurt. Instantly she longed to do something for him, to fetch him some tea, to push him down gently into a comfortable chair and make him easy and happy, to restore his spirit and make him know he was honored and respected and the head of a house. She rose, instantly herself.

"I am tired and want to go home," she said.

"Of course," he answered. "I will take you."

Together they went out of the hall. She turned once and looked about. Far away she saw a gleam of scarlet pressed ardently against a tall black robe. She went on.

They climbed into their motor car and drew the rug over their old knees.

After a while she glanced out of the corner of her eye at her husband. He sat timidly and in silence, his round face hanging, the smile quite gone from it. She yearned over him. Somehow she must make him know she would never speak to him of what had happened, never reproach him. She coughed a little.

"These modern women," she said, her voice carefully light, "are amusing. I am glad to have seen them just the once. It has been an interesting evening for me." Then after a moment she said tenderly, "Your legs are weary, I know. I will rub your ankles with oil when we get home. It was so good of you to dance with that rude young girl! I was quite angry because she was so rude to you."

She waited. He cleared his throat loudly.

"Yes," he said at last. "But really, I am too old to dance. Besides I am a man of affairs and I have no time for this sort of thing."

"Indeed you have not," she said warmly. "You are a very important man."

"Yes," he said. "I really am very busy. Tomorrow I must—"

She did not listen. She leaned back smiling, weary, at peace That young girl, that dear young girl—these modern women were wonderful—wonderful—

still tougher, aye, for personal... I know, I will buy your order until all other work is bright. Is sure as good. If you go back... with it is her very... but I was quite right... because the pays to follow.

She went on thoughtfully... she is still...

"Yes," she said slow, "I'm sorry I am not old to do... I'm old... I am a ... in state... old... force me time for this sort of thing."

"Indeed... if you are not. She said with a... You are... securing perhaps man...

"O yes," he said heartily and wearily. "I am grave... She then went... I would... and wait... in it... peace. That where... and the... is... going... old—them my dear woman were... to win in... of relief—

V

SHANGHAI SCENE

SHANGHAI SCENE

Yuan had, of course, been looking for work many months, or he would not have accepted so small a position at the Shanghai railway station. On the day he was handed his college diploma on imitation sheepskin he had seen himself an official in the national government in the new capital, or at least a secretary to such an official, since his English was excellent. He had written many weekly themes in English on subjects of the highest nature, arguing such a point, for instance, as whether or not the ancient walls of Peking should be torn down in the interests of the modern age, or whether they should be allowed to stand as historic monuments. He always proved triumphantly that they should be torn down, for he believed passionately in what he and his fellows called "the new day."

But after his graduation he found he could not, in spite of his ability to write English themes, secure a position in the government, not even a position of fourth secretary. There were, it seemed, many hundreds of young men like himself, equally gifted in writing English themes, and differing only in the sort of titles they chose, some preferring to write on such subjects as "Moonlight on West Lake," or "Dying Love," or even on "Our Hero Sun Yat-sen." Yet Yuan could not be convinced that the reason for his failure was that there were these other young men. When he had considered everything many times, he decided that the real trouble was his old father, who was mediocre and without influence.

His father was nothing more than a general shopkeeper on a small street. It was true that he sold some foreign wares, such as second-hand bicycles, but still he was only a shopkeeper. He could do nothing even for his only son, although he loved Yuan and spent much time he could ill spare, going to offices and places of government to ask for appointments with various officials whose names he had seen in the papers. He even had special cards printed on square bits of cardboard announcing himself as a dealer in Western machinery of all kinds. But this was no use, especially after one day through ignorance he asked to see an official who had already been removed in some disgrace.

When Yuan heard this he groaned in shame for his father's ignorance and rushed to his room and there cried out to himself in despair, "No wonder I can find no position worthy of me, when my father is such a fool!" And he passionately hated all common and stupid people like his father.

Nevertheless, even he could understand that his father had done all he could, and so when one day the old man came home rubbing his hands and laughing aloud and crying out, "Oh, Yuan, at last I have a government position for you," Yuan smiled although he did not expect much. But even so it was less than he had expected. His father had had a customer a few days before who wore a uniform, and, seeing this, the old man had had an idea. He inquired of the man:

"And which is your honored government department?"

"Railways," the man replied carelessly.

So the old man, when this official had chosen a bicycle, and it was the newest in the shop, told him of his wonderful son who longed to serve his country in the government, and at last he offered the bicycle as a gift if the official would give Yuan a job in railways. And the official, who liked the bright red color of the bicycle, agreed. Telling of this, the father ended by saying joyfully:

"And, Yuan, his uniform was incomparable! It is blue, a bright blue, with a star here, and here, and a foreign cap. You shall have one exactly like it."

But in his ignorance this old man did not know that naturally Yuan could not be allowed to wear such a uniform in so lowly a position. It is true he had a sort of foreign cap, but his uniform was of plain black cotton cloth, for his sole duty was to hold back the stupid country folk who crowded into third- and fourth-class cars of the trains.

This was his life, then. Instead of sitting in the quiet, orderly class room, filled with students, studying literature and English, now all day long, except for the brief intervals between trains, Yuan held the gate against these people. They understood nothing. They came at dawn to buy tickets for a train that did not leave before noon, and they would not go away. There they sat, huddled upon the ground, their cloth-wrapped bundles tied upon their backs, their worn hands idle, waiting for the gate to open. Whenever the gate opened they leaped up and rushed to it, crowding and pushing, their faces instantly strained, anxious, bewildered, yet determined. Now it was Yuan's duty to shout at them, asking, "What is your train? Where do you go? Have you a ticket?" And then he must shout over and over, after hearing their replies given in all imaginable country dialects, "This is not the train you want—you may not pass!" or to a few he said, "Show your ticket!"

These things he said every day, day after day, to people who seemed not to vary at all from each other. Every day there were

these same brown, anxious, weathered faces, the same dull bewildered eyes, the same patched blue cotton clothes, the same
awkward bundles tied with bits of rope, the same stupid rushing
to any open gate.

He grew to hate these people with a passionate, mighty hatred.
And he hated them the more because he could think of no way
in which he could improve or enlighten them and so remove
from himself the weight of their daily stupidity. He spent two
evenings writing out large placards of the simplest instructions;
but these people could read not one word, he discovered, and
they regarded the placards as having nothing to do with themselves. When Yuan pointed furiously at them the first morning,
the man in front of the crowd, a young farmer with a wide
mouth, grinned and said in apology:

"Sir, I have not one character in my belly, for I never went to
school, being so bitter poor all my days."

There remained nothing, therefore, but to remove the placards
and go on as he had before, shouting and screaming and threatening the crowd of peasants until the mass were thrust back
and the few separated from it who were to go on the train next
to depart. All day Yuan struggled there, every day from dawn
until dark.

At last it came to be that even at night he felt himself struggling against these stupid people. In his sleep he dreamed of
them, dreamed of their dark, frightened faces, of their bewildered eyes. For they never learned. Day after day they were the
same. It could not be possible that they were daily and forever
new people. Men and women who left their homes must return
again. It must be that at least some of them time and time again
rushed to the gate and tried to push through, struggling against
him.

And he was only one against so many. There was only he to stem this dull tide, to clarify their endless confusion. It began at last to be too much for him. He saw himself as he was, young and ineffectual, his learning and education worthless since all he could find to do was this one same thing which taught no one anything. Against this mountain of the stupidity and ignorance of these his own people he might fling his body daily and daily bruise his spirit, and they were not even aware of him.

The result of this was that he began to grow morose and was always filled with threatening tensity. Daily he still flung himself more madly and more bitterly against the crowds, pitting himself against them, his one brain against the mountain of their ignorance. He became a shrieking, shouting machine, cursing the people while he struggled to hold the gates.

And then one morning for a few moments quite suddenly he went insane. There was not even a crowd at the time. It was between trains, and he leaned against the gate, his teeth set, girding himself for what must come within the half hour. And just at that moment an old farmer came hurrying to the gate, his bare feet dusty and gray with long walking on country roads, his bundle on his back, his blue coat patched, his staff in his hand, his face brown and strained with anxiety lest he miss his train. Without a word this solitary old man ran a little and tried to push open the gate.

But Yuan, looking at him, did not see him solitary. In this one face he saw millions of others everywhere in the country, everywhere these bewildered eyes, this patched coat, these dusty bare feet, this ignorance—this hopeless ignorance! And seeing, he went mad. Grinding his teeth, he fell upon the old man without mercy, beating his head, his face, his shoulders, and weeping aloud as he did this. One or two men who stood near tried to pull him away,

73

but no one could restrain him. Upon the person of this old man Yuan wreaked an unutterable vengeance for all his disappointment and for all his dreary days.

But his English did him some good after all. For he heard an English voice cry out:

"Oh, look at that wicked young man beating the poor old farmer!"

What the others had not been able to do this English voice now did. Yuan came suddenly to himself. One could not behave thus before a foreigner. He glanced up quickly, his breath coming in great gusts. There stood a foreign woman, her face moved with compassion, and compassion not for him but for the stupid old man. Seeing the look, Yuan turned his eyes also upon the old man. It was evident he had understood nothing. He had only cringed and tried to shield himself as best he could, accustomed to blows he did not understand. Now, seeing they were stopped, he stared humbly at Yuan, and then approached the gate once more, timidly but again with dull determination, not knowing that the beating had anything to do with it.

Yuan choked and wiped his lips with his hand. He sighed heavily. And after a moment's rest again he said as he had said so many, many times:

"Where do you go? Have you your ticket? It is too early!"

VI
HEARTS COME HOME

HEARTS COME HOME

Young David Lin stood moodily in the corner of the large parlor and watched the eight or ten couples of his friends gravely dancing. The music of an industrious brass band blared forth from behind a clump of palms planted in pots. He knew, of course, it was a very rich and expensive room, since it belonged to Mr. Fang, who was one of the leading bankers in the city of Shanghai. Mr. Fang would not tolerate anything that was not rich and expensive. The walls therefore were hung in modern oil paintings and also in very delicate and exquisite old scrolls, for, Mr. Fang always said, his fat and shining face expanding into great thick wrinkles of laughter, "I have the best of everything, new and old. There is room for it all in my house."

Mr. Fang sat now watching the young people dance, and beside him sat two pretty girls. One of these was his daughter, Phyllis, and the other was his latest concubine, a young actress. They were about the same age, but they were very different. Phyllis, David had decided earlier in the evening, was the prettiest girl in the room. He did not understand how anyone so fat and ugly as Mr. Fang could have this slender bamboo of a girl for a daughter. For she did look like a bamboo. She was pale and a little tall, almost as tall as himself, and she wore a soft green long robe, and her face was not painted, so that it was the color of new ivory. And her hair was not like these other women's hair. It was not clipped or frizzed or curled or any of

77

those things. It was long and straight and very black and drawn back from her face into a firm knot on her neck. She sat placidly watching her guests, an expression of tranquil pleasure about her pretty lips. As for the concubine, she looked like an actress. She made great eyes and moved her body about and her hair flared out from her too pink and rounded face. David, staring briefly at her, hated her instantly. She would chatter—she would chatter in some barbarous mixture of English and Chinese.

He had for some ten minutes been planning to go and ask Phyllis to dance with him, but he had been held back by this actress. Suppose, he said to himself, that this actress put out her hand—she was forever putting out her hand to the young men who approached her—and before he knew it he would have to dance with her; he would not, he said to himself, dance with any more frizzy-haired women, no, nor women with painted, powdered faces. Their hair tickled his neck and their faces ruined his foreign coat. He glanced down at his shoulder and brushed it off with the palm of his hand. There was a patch of powder upon it. That was because Doris Li's face had lain there earlier in the evening. He hated Doris Li—a silly creature who pretended she had forgotten how to speak her own tongue because she had been in Paris so long.

With Phyllis he had never danced, because this was the first time he had seen her. She worked somewhere in a school, not in this city, and now she was home for the spring holiday. Mr. Fang had said, introducing her, "This is my one industrious child. The others are content to do nothing."

"You must be proud of her," David had murmured, not looking at her face. He was very tired of girls' faces.

But Mr. Fang only laughed loudly. "She doesn't make enough

money for me to be proud of her," he said cheerfully. "She does it to amuse herself."

Then he did look at her—a girl who worked to amuse herself! He had never seen such a thing. For the first time in months he was interested even for a moment in a girl. With something more than his usual fixed smile he said, "May I have a dance?" But she had already promised every dance. For a moment he was sorry. Then he said to himself it did not matter. After all, she was only old Fang's daughter and another girl. He danced desultorily through the afternoon with several girls. He could scarcely remember them now. They all left powder on his coat, though, he remembered gloomily.

Then old Fang had decided they would not stop at the end of the program. He loved dancing, bounding about the room like a huge balloon in his floating silk robes, his round face glittering with smiles, and his laughter roaring out when he stepped on someone's foot as he passed. Now he shouted at the musicians, peering at them through the palms, "Play three more numbers and you shall have a double tip!" So saying, he seized his concubine and they were off. Against his protruding bulges she leaned herself gaily, her eyes roving away from him and about the room.

It was David's chance. Hastily, for he saw converging upon Phyllis three dapper, beautifully dressed young men, he hastened himself and appeared before her. "May I—"

But the young men also hastened themselves— "May I—" "May I—" "May I—" Their voices were like the rounds he used to have to sing in the American school where he was educated. He stood back stiffly—let her choose. She chose very easily, rising and moving toward him. "You were first?" she said in a pleasant little voice. "Yes," he said, and they moved out into the room.

79

In the noise of the music it was impossible to talk. That was like old Fang, too, to go and hire a double brass band for a tea. The room shook in the noise. He held her to him in the approved modern fashion, breast to breast, thigh to thigh. Her cheek was against his shoulder. He danced well and he knew it, but then, he found, so did she. She gave and swayed so easily to his body that he grew suspicious and looked down at her. Was she being perhaps a little too easily yielding? He was tired of girls who yielded too easily. But her small pale face was quite cold, and her eyes, when she turned them up to his prettily were passionless. She smiled and said something, but he could not hear her voice. He raised his eyebrows and she laughed, and they did not try again. At the end of the dance the young men were waiting for her solidly, so he let her go with no more than his usual carefully effusive thanks. "You dance swell, Miss Fang. Gee, it's good to get a good partner!"

"Thank you, Mr. Lin. You dance swell, too," she answered easily.

He did not dance again, although there were girls without partners. Doris Li was one of these, and she came languishing and laughing past him. But he bent ostentatiously to tie his shoe-string. He wasn't going to dance again. He pondered on Phyllis a moment, although he had now for a long time not thought about any girls at all. He thought in fact about nothing except his work, which he liked very much. It was that of a manager in his father's printing house. He thought all the time about how to improve the printing of their books. He used to think about girls a great deal, but that was before he tired of them. They were so much alike. Every girl in Shanghai, he had long ago decided, was like every other. He listened cynically when his friends grew excited over a new beauty. There was not such a thing.

The tea ended and people began to go away, gay couples hand in hand going off together to some other amusement. The band was silent, and instead the air was filled with a clatter of thanks and farewells, Chinese and English mingled in word and sentence. It was very smart to speak so, just as it was smart to take foreign first names. He could speak the jargon, too, when he must. He had, in fact, many ways of speaking. He could speak American college boy or Oxford English or the precise old Chinese his father still demanded of him, or this jargon of English and Chinese his friends now practiced. It all depended on where he was.

But he secretly liked the Chinese best, although he made fun of it to his own friends. They all said over and over "There are so many modern things we cannot say in Chinese. How, for instance, do you say—" He always agreed, and they had fun trying to twist the old staid words to say even such things as "Hot mamma," "You're my baby," "I'm nuts about you." But afterwards he felt uncomfortable, as though he had taught a child to say innocently an obscene thing. For the old words would not say these things. Twisted thus, they made no sense, saying nothing at all, remaining serenely themselves and refusing to be perverted.

He joined the ebbing crowd at the door. Phyllis stood there, smiling, answering gaily, putting out her hand freely to her guests. He looked at her and said to himself gloomily that he was probably wrong in thinking she was different from any of the others. Just now she seemed like any of the others—like any girl. Probably she powdered too. He looked down at his shoulder involuntarily. But no, it was quite clean. He made up his mind instantly.

"May I stay a little while and talk?" he asked.

She hesitated. "I am going to the Casino with friends," she said.

"May I come with you?" he asked at once.

"I suppose you may," she answered.

A servant was there with her coat, and he took it and put it about her shoulders. Suddenly he saw the small fine hairs upon her nape, black against the ivory pale smooth skin. He felt a strange shock of pleasure in him.

That was the beginning, but the end was almost instantly there. For before the night was over he was wildly in love with her, though the accumulated hatred he had for all girls was worse than ever. He loathed every girl he saw at the Casino that night. They were the worst of their kind, he thought, his heart scornful behind his smiling face. He danced with them when he could not get Phyllis, practicing all the little attentions of smart behavior while he hated them. When he took a hand, he hated it for its prettiness and its scarlet nails. It made him curious to know what Phyllis's hands were. He must look the first moment he could. In the little alcove where he sat out a dance with another girl he kissed her coldly, when she leaned toward him for his kiss. It was nothing to kiss a girl, nothing to him. He rubbed his lips secretly while he was pretending to wipe his face with his handkerchief. He hated rouge—Phyllis's lips—he began wondering about her lips.

There it was. Once he began this sort of wonder he could not stop it, and day after day of spring sunshine hurried him. Besides, she would be going away again. He had to hurry. He begged a holiday from his father and beset her daily, using all his technique. After all, he told himself, she was a modern girl, and probably she liked all this stuff. He sent her flowers and candy, and found copies of freshly printed books and had them under his arm when he appeared before her, so that he never went without gifts.

But of course all these gifts—they must have meaning. He watched her to see if they meant anything. "Like candy, kid?" he inquired of her carelessly, presenting her with a five-pound box of foreign chocolates. Did her face fall a little? But her voice came with careful enthusiasm. "Oh, swell, Dave," she replied. They spoke English almost entirely, and since they had both gone to an American university they spoke what they had learned there. "Sure you like it?" he pressed her. "Crazy about it," she replied. He stared at her. She talked as they all did, but somehow it never seemed her language. She opened the box and exclaimed cheerfully, "Oh, aren't they lovely—oh, how nice." Then she put it down on the table.

Yes, he used his technique, all the modern technique they used on each other. He took her everywhere, to dance, to the theater, and she went willingly. In the taxicab he reached for her hand and held it, and once he seized her by the shoulders and would have kissed her, but unexpectedly she bent her head quickly and his lips touched her cheek and not her lips. He had planned the kiss with some enthusiasm, too—more enthusiasm than he had felt in such things for a long time. But, foiled, he had no enthusiasm at all. Her cheek was quite cold. She did not take her hand away from his, but it lay there passively, and he wished it would not be rude to put it down.

Yet he loved her more all the time. Because he could not seem to get at her he loved her. She did not repulse him, she never repulsed him. She took her part in all his plans, she refused him nothing. If he took her arm, she leaned against him a little—she had no old-fashioned ways. But so she was. She did all these things as though it were a pattern she had been taught to do. It was a technique with her. It was a technique of love for them both. He wanted her to know he loved her, and he had no way to tell her except this modern way. "I'm crazy about you, kid," he said. "Sure, I'm crazy about you, too," she answered politely, and his heart chilled in him.

And all the time the days were passing, the days of the short month he had, and he could not break away this barrier of modern technique. Once at the door after a late dance he leaned to her, "Kiss me good night, Phyllis?"

"Yes," she answered readily, and touched his cheek easily with her calm lips.

It was all nothing. They were growing not nearer but further apart. Words and touch only were pushing them apart. He did not know what to do, so he kept on doing what they were doing.

Then suddenly the day before she went away they discovered each other. They were dancing together at the Casino again, close, welded together, when suddenly she stopped and pulled away from him and looked at him.

"Do you truly like this?" she asked him. He was startled. Her voice was changed, softer, deeper. She was speaking in Chinese, in their own tongue! Why had they never spoken in Chinese? There had been some nonsense of different dialects. She was not native to Shanghai—her family had come from the north—English was smarter, and so they pretended it was easier. But it was not. He understood her perfectly in Chinese. He looked back at her intensely. The tawdry dancing hall faded from around them.

84

"I do not like it," he replied. "I cannot tell you how greatly I do not like it."

"Then let us go away," she said simply.

She was quite different from anything he had known of her before. In the car she sat with such reserve and dignity that he did not want to take her hand. At this moment he was nearer to her when he did not take her hand. At her door he hesitated. But she said, "Will you come in? I think there is speech we wish to have together."

"I have many things to say," he answered.

It seemed indeed that they had never talked at all. All the foolish foreign words they had interchanged had said nothing. Now crowding to his tongue were other words, their own words. Everything remained yet to be said. She sat down on the satin-covered couch, and he sat on a chair near her. She looked at him, and then she looked around the room. "I dislike all of this," she said, sweeping her hand through the air. "You do not know me at all. You do not even know my true name. I am not what I have seemed to you. Now that I am about to go away I want you to know that I am very old-fashioned. I have been all this month doing things with you which I hate. It is better for you to know. I do not like to dance. I dislike foreign sweets. I do not like to kiss people. It makes me feel ill to kiss anyone or to feel anyone's lips upon my face or hand—even yours I do not like."

"Wait," he interrupted. "I see now I have felt what you were all along. I see why we were never near to each other. Why did you come with me to dances, and why did you let me kiss you? If you had said you did not like it I would not have done so."

She dropped her head and looked at her hands tightly clasped in her lap. She answered, shyly, "I thought you liked these foreign ways and I wanted to be what you liked. I thought if I refused you might not—come again." Her voice was very small indeed when she finished.

"What is your true name?" he demanded of her.

"It is Ming Sing—Shining Heart," she replied.

"Mine is Yung An—Brave Peace," he said.

They were silent a moment.

Then he went on. He leaned forward in his chair. "You mean —you do mean truly that you like our own ways best?"

"Much, much best," she faltered.

"You would not like a house like this?" he questioned her sternly.

"No," she faltered.

"Nor dancing nor motoring nor any of these things the women do all day?"

"No."

"We need never waste our time so any more," he said, after a moment.

"Never any more," she answered.

He waited another moment. "I also do not like to kiss," he announced.

"Then let us not kiss each other any more," she said.

"We will speak our own language and I will take off these foreign garments and put on my robes again and we will live in old comfortable ways and I will smoke a water pipe."

"I will never wear leather shoes again," she said. "And I will never eat butter again, which I hate, nor any foreign foods, and our table will always be set with bowls and chopsticks, and I shall have a house with courts and no stairs, and I want many children."

He saw it all as she spoke, their house, their home, everything

86

their own, and themselves as they really wanted to be. He began to pour out his words, "Will you then marry me? Shall we—" Then he stopped. He rose to his feet and stood resolutely before her. "No," he said. "Miss Fang, my father will write your father a letter. It will come soon—at once—" he was already halfway to the door. Now he was at the door, and he looked back at her. She rose and bowed, and stood looking at him, too, waked, and warm as a rose. He saw her for the first time. This was how she truly was, this lovely, natural creature of his own kind. They would raise lotus flowers in the pool in the court, and they would have a little bamboo grove and read poetry there in the summer—old four-lined verses. He had always wanted to have time for it.

"Are you going, Mr. Lin?" she asked in the old formula of farewell.

The words came so sweetly from her tongue that his feet had carried him back a step before he knew it. Then he caught himself. No. "No more foreign ways," he said firmly. He went out into the hall, and then he put his head in to look at her once more. She was sitting quietly upon the couch, her little hands folded, her little feet placed neatly together, exactly as his own old mother might have sat as a girl. She was looking ahead of her, seeing, he knew, the house, the court, the many children, the safe old ways of living. She was there waiting, so pretty, so pretty— "At least not yet," he amended, hurrying.

VII
HIS OWN COUNTRY

HIS OWN COUNTRY

JOHN DEWEY CHANG had always known that Mott Street, New York, was not his own country. People said Chinatown, but it was not the same as his own country. He was perfectly familiar with all these noisy, narrowing streets, he knew the shops whose windows were filled with a mixture of things from across the sea and things American, he knew the men and women and the many children whose skin was yellow like his own, and whose eyes were all black. Many of them, like himself, had been born in these crowded lively streets, and had never seen anything else. But still he knew this was not his country.

Not that he was at all strange or that, at least as a child, he had disliked Chinatown. For a long time, indeed, he had not thought about any other country. He had grown from placid babyhood, eternally carried on his mother's arm when he was awake and staring with her into the moving variety of the street outside his father's curio shop. Asleep he was carried into a little dark inner room smelling of dried herbs and ginger and tea, and these two places were his world, and, so far as he knew, his country.

The first time, indeed, that he knew he did not belong here, that none of them belonged here, was when he went to school. His parents, discussing the matter loudly over their rice bowls, had decided against kindergarten, and he had not minded. It was more fun to dart about the streets with many other small boys, more white than yellow, to crouch on the backs of automobiles, and tease the kindly policemen. But the day came when he was six years old and this sort of thing had to cease. It was time his education began. His mother, her old black cotton Chinese coat unfastened at the throat and her hair yet uncombed, early in the morning dressed him immaculately in a blue striped sailor suit, admonishing him in their own language the while as to how small boys behaved their first day at school. She never had learned English, not in all these years. He spoke her own language to her, but when he was in the streets he forgot that he spoke anything except the jargon of the white boys. He listened to her gravely, aware of some decorum settling upon him that was not of New York. "So small Chinese boys behave," his mother said very gravely, and his father said, "Do not forget you are a son of Han, and that you do not belong to these wild white tribes among whom we must live until I can grow rich. Be polite to your teacher, obey what your elders command, and keep your mind on your books."

All during breakfast, his father and his mother paused, holding their chopsticks above their bowls of rice gruel, to give him further excellent advice. After his breakfast his father had given him his school name, John Dewey Chang. To this time he had been called at home Little Dog, and on the street Chink. But his father had written this name down upon a bit of paper, so that he might give it to the teacher, that it might be written correctly in the records, John Dewey Chang. John Dewey, his father explained, was the name of an American who had helped to start good new schools in China. He had read about it in the papers from his home town there.

Almost immediately after his father had taken him to school and introduced him to the teacher, his education began. For it happened that the pupils were told to form in line and march from this small schoolroom into a larger one. Two by two they must march. John Chang took his place with alacrity, his face beaming with interest. Two by two they went ahead of him and behind him, but no one came to stand beside him. Two by two they stood, with himself alone in the middle, until finally there was only a small fat white girl left, a round little girl with tight light braids tied with bits of red ribbon. She stood alone also.

"Mary," said Miss Pinckney, "you may come and stand by John."

But Mary would not come. To his astonishment John saw the little girl shake her head violently. "I won't," she said unpleasantly. "I won't walk beside a Chinaman."

Miss Pinckney stared severely for a moment at her and then took John's hand herself. "Very well," she said, "you may walk alone, and I will walk with John."

There was intense silence along the double row, and John Dewey Chang knew that it was not the silence of sympathy. He grasped Miss Pinckney's hand gingerly, but without pleasure. He would, he knew, much rather have been walking with Mary. This was the beginning of his education.

His education, thus began, continued through many years. He became accustomed after a while to other things. Quietly he learned to wait until everyone else found partners, and then, if he were lucky enough to be the odd one, he stood alone at the end. If the number were even, particularly if the other were a girl, he learned to stand a little aloof, delicately, waiting. He grew to feel, as though he had antennae, the atmosphere, whether it was welcome or rebuff. He never complained, never told his parents. He withdrew into himself instead and became a silent, studious youth, very quiet and neat and dark. He made it a point to be first in his classes and to carry off prizes. His parents were very proud of him. They talked together of what they would do when he was old enough to take the shop. But though he spent his evenings over his father's ledgers when his lessons were done, he knew he would never take the shop. For by now he knew this was not his country, and he had one deep secret purpose, one aching ambition. He must find his own country.

The curios, the beads, the idols, the misty paintings on the scrolls, the hundreds of odd bits of strange beauty his father had for sale, only made him more eager to go to their source. He unpacked them tenderly from their straw-stuffed boxes, great wooden boxes, stamped with red and black hieroglyphics, wondering, dreaming, of another land where beauty like theirs was shaped—his own country.

Of this country he had, of course, heard from many. He had learned to read not only Shakespeare and American history and Whittier and Longfellow, but he had learned also the long straight lines of the letters of his own language. At night an old man came to tutor him, and to teach him the sing-song rhythms of old poetry. His neighbors, George Liu and Ruth Kin, rebelled bitterly and never learned enough to understand the inner meaning of those curves and squares. Ruth tossed her pretty curled black head, and, chewing her gum quickly, she said loudly, "Gee, what's it all about! Say, I gotta 'nough without that stuff!" She had a dark slanting eye upon Harry Sills, the young grocery man next door. Not that she would marry a white man, of course, but white men were fun. Of course she'd settle down and marry a Chink one of these days, but not one of the old-fashioned kind. She'd marry a smart fella, maybe George Liu, if he turned out smart enough, and they'd have a little flat with an electric range. When anyone asked her if she ever wanted to go home to China, she screamed with laughter and said, "To what? Not for mine!

Say, they tell me they ain't even got electric lights in the ole home town in China! And say, they're still keepin' the girls at home over there!" She screamed again with her high light laughter, a little loudly, for Harry Sills was at the door of his store. He grinned at her lazily. "Say, I'll bet they couldn't keep you at home, if you was there!" he called to her.

"That's no bet—that's sure!" she retorted, narrowing her eyes at him. She'd seen Anna May Wong do that in the movies, and she liked it, liked that Oriental lure.

John Dewey Chang watched her gravely. It was just after sunset and he was home from high school. It was his last year. Next year he'd go to college, and after that he'd go to his own country. His country—that word was now beginning to mean something beautiful and secret. He gazed thoughtfully up and down the street. Noise was everywhere, the noise of cars and of children. On the next street a trolley shrieked around the corner. At his feet his last brother picked industriously at John Dewey's shoe-strings. He was not quite two, and with his coming the small flat above the shop was crowded to its last limit. But it had not occurred to them to have more room. They slept more thickly in the two bedrooms, but always decorously, his sisters in the other room, his parents' bed curtained and partitioned away with wall board. But he would be glad to be gone. Staring into the noise and confusion of a late spring evening in that crowded street he thought with longing of his own country. There, there were quiet streets and singing country folk and richly tilled fields and courtesy and stillness and certainty. He would be among his own there, his own kind. He had heard his mother tell such tales of the small country town where she grew up, a town in south China where everybody, she said, was happy. All the girls were pretty and good, not like these girls with yellow hair and painted

95

lips and especially not like silly Ruth Kin. He was suddenly very homesick for that which he had never seen.

All during his four years at the state college he held steadfastly to his plan. He grew very Chinese indeed, and he allowed his fellows to think that he had come, not from that crowded rowdy street in New York, but from the sedate and dignified little Chinese town in south China. It was during these years that his country fell into revolution, and he organized a band of patriots among the seven Chinese boys in the college. He denied himself his luncheon each day and saved the money, and he bullied the other members of the club into paying more than they were able, and when after three months the fund amounted to more than ninety dollars, they debated fiercely as to what it should be given for in China. Studying the newspapers and the bulletins from their country, they perceived there were many things for which this sum could be given; it might be given for the starving, for there was a famine again, or it might be given for the airplanes the new government needed, or it might be given for roads. After weeks of indecision, they decided on new roads. So the money was changed into a note, and sent to the government in Nanking, with a long letter explaining the wishes of the donors. After nearly six months a courteous letter came in reply, to which was affixed the seal of the Republic, saying that the money had been received and would be assuredly spent for roads, and then after words of commendation for such patriotism the letter closed, and was signed by the Third Secretary to the President.

It was the first touch with his country. John, holding the letter in his hand, felt his heart thicken with emotion. When he read the letter aloud to the others, he could scarcely keep from weeping. When Art Lok said with cynicism, "Yeah, it's fine talk—my dad says the same chaps used up all the money they sent over last year to buy an airplane, only there wasn't any airplane!" John Chang flew at him, "Will you revile your own country? Will you say your own President's secretary lies?" he cried.

Art twisted his thin handsome mouth and sneered and fell silent. After all, it was no business of his. He began thinking of an engagement he had to keep that night at a certain small café with a very yellow-haired girl. He began to whistle softly.

But there it was. All during college when the others were playing football or going to movies or making dates, John Chang worked on his plans for his country. Here was the question: Should he delay his return further by taking some sort of special course—say, be an aviator or an architect or a doctor—or should he go straight home as soon as he was through? He argued it with himself, longing to go straightway, waiting for nothing. After all, a college education was something. He could get a job teaching or in the government—there were jobs everywhere these days, in these new and glorious days in his own country. It was not as it was here in the United States, where people were pushing and jostling each other for work. Over there roads were growing, airplanes were flying, new buildings going up, business developing—the whole nation was moving, running ahead—better to join his youth to it now, without waiting. Anyway, better to go on and see what was wanted and if necessary he would come back. Only he knew he would never come back. He graduated from college and then hurried back to Mott Street, to bid his parents good-by, to buy a third-class ticket to China.

Then he was delayed after all. He was delayed by his own most surprising reluctance to go. When he had endured the noise and the heat of the flat for two weeks, when he had bought his ticket and had talked with his parents about everything, when his mother had said to him over and over again, "Now when you see my honored mother-in-law, you must say it is my grief I am not there to serve her, and when you see my honored father-in-law and my brothers and their ladies—" and when his father had talked with enthusiasm of the new times, "In my youth there was nothing a lad could do if he were the eighth son on a little land, and so I had to seize the chance of my father's eldest cousin to come abroad with him in his business, and here I have remained and they sent your mother to me, and here you have been born. I return you proudly to my own country—" when everything was said and everything was ready, suddenly John Chang found he did not want to go.

At first he could not understand his reluctance. Certainly it was not this noisy city which held him. He stood looking at the traffic one night in a melancholy fashion. He did not love these dashing lights, approaching, glaring for an instant into his face, disappearing again. There was no music in the roar and the grind of trolley cars to have made him homesick. Except the faces of his family there were no faces which he cared if he saw again or not—no faces—and then with fury he realized there was a face, a little round merry face under frizzy black hair. It was that face which was making all the trouble. He wanted to see it again and again and again, and it was Ruth Kin's face!

When he realized this he went quickly into the house and into a dark corner of the dark little curio shop and there, among the Buddhas and the pottery Han horses and the hanging mandarin coats, he sat down and held his head in his hands. He did not at all wish to love Ruth Kin. He did not want to marry. If he thought about marrying, it was not to someone like Ruth Kin. His mother had spoken of the women across the sea, their stillness, their gentleness, their mild sweet eyes, their obedience to their lords. Some day, perhaps, he had thought, some day, in a little house with a court and a bamboo grove and an oleander tree he might live with a sweet obedient woman. But not with slangy, lively, noisy Ruth Kin! Yet there it was. He did not want to leave her.

He had seen her, of course, many times—how, he asked himself bitterly, could one avoid seeing her? She still lived next door, and she came and went loudly and cheerfully to the business school where she was learning stenography so that she might be her father's assistant. Her father, a tea and oil merchant, had never learned the intricacies of customs and accounting, and Ruth long ago had made up her mind that she would take the business in hand as soon as she could. She was always wanting to take things in hand—to manage things. So year by year she had managed a little more and a little more of the stout peaceful old man's affairs, until now, when American retail men came into the wholesale tea shop, it was a smart young American who greeted them, an American with coal black hair with a strong tendency to straightness, in spite of sedulous care to curling, and black pointed eyes and a rich smooth olive skin. But the voice was American, clear and a little hard, and the words that came from the vivid red lips were pure New York. The men looked at her with laughter and occasionally with longing, longing at least for a little fun. But she never promised them anything, never quite promised them anything. Everyone knew Ruth Kin could take care of herself.

And of course everyone had thought that she would marry George Liu. Even the two families had thought so. Then suddenly, only six months ago, Ruth Kin changed her mind. "No," she told her father firmly. "I don't want to marry George." Everyone knew how she said it, for he told all his friends and they told their wives and so John Chang had heard his mother tell it at the family supper table.

"That Ruth Kin," she said mournfully, "she is like the Americans. All these years she has been as though betrothed to the son of the Lius, the parents have arranged it, and now she will not marry him."

"Why not?" said the father absently. He was not interested in Ruth Kin or in George Liu, but it was a bit of gossip on Mott Street.

"Who knows?" said his mother, sighing. "She says he is not smart enough. She says she will have only a very smart man."

John Chang, sitting in the curio shop alone, thought of this bitterly. "She will not think me smart," he thought. "She has always made fun of me because I want to go home to my own country. I have heard her say often that I am a fool—that I would do better to take my father's business."

Then remembering Ruth Kin's shining black eyes and her little full red mouth he knew it was no good—he loved her hopelessly.

So he put off his trip a little, not much. He had allowed himself a few more days than necessary in order to see the sights on the west coast. He would see no sights. He said a little sullenly to his parents the next day, "I do not feel well. I will wait a day."

He waited a day, thinking furiously and staying away from Ruth Kin. Ever since he had returned he had made it a habit without knowing it to go and stand at the door and watch for her coming home. Now he would not go, not for a whole day. But the second day was a Saturday, and suddenly he was compelled to see her. He felt if he did not see her just once he could not start next day, and he must start or he would miss his boat. He was angry with himself, he threw himself on his bed and muttered and tossed. Then suddenly he leaped up and ran down-stairs and into the shop next door. Because it was a Saturday he knew exactly where he would find Ruth. He would find her in the inner room balancing her father's weekly accounts, her red lips a little pursed, her small brown hands nimble with the pencil.

There she was exactly. He did not waste an instant. He stood before her, his hair still rumpled, his shirt without any tie. He began hostilely, because she had delayed him in his dear plan: "Will you come to China with me or won't you?"

She looked at him, astonished, her eyes open very wide. She never used any lure with John Chang, never at all. They quar-reled too often, and there was too much to say to him. They had quarreled, for instance, over this very going back home to China. She thrust her pencil into her curly mop, and there it stood up-right like a feather of defiance.

"Why should I go to China?" she answered instantly. "I don't want to go to China! I'm an American—anybody that's born in New York is an American."

"Because your country has use for you!" he shouted at her. She was so very pretty that he was furious with her. Need she have put on a rose-pink linen dress this morning and need her skin look as smooth as golden cream? "You stay here when your country can use you!"

"Thank you," she said coolly, "I'll think about it when there are a few electric lights and a bath tub in the ole home town."

"You think of nothing but comforts," he said. He wanted to shake her, to slap her, to tell her she must come because—because —"You must come!" he said loudly.

Then she stood up. She put her two little hands on her narrow hips and looked at him from the crown of his stiff rumpled black hair to his rather too yellow oxfords. "Will you please tell me who you think you are, Mr. John Dewey Chang?" she demanded. "You can't talk to an American woman like that and get away with it! And why must I come?"

"Because——because I love you!" he said unexpectedly. He had not really meant to say it.

They stared at each other, and Ruth sat down suddenly and drew the pencil out of her hair and began to figure briskly. "Go away, John Dewey Chang," she said coldly. "Don't be funny."

"It is not funny," he said desperately.

"It is only funny to me," she said. "I go back to China? And with you? It's a joke." She pursed her very red lips merrily and looked at him, for a second, this time with her sidewise look. But when he started toward her, she cried out, "No, I mean it. Go away."

"You mean—to China?" asked John Chang in a small voice.

"Yes, to China," said Ruth Kin, with determination, and shut her mouth hard and turned a page of figures.

He watched her for a second, but she did not change, she did not look up, and he turned. Well, then, he would go. But just at the door she called him again, and he glanced back. She was looking at him thoughtfully and now she said in another voice, a coaxing small voice, and she drooped her lashes a little and looked up at him, "Would you," she said, "would you if I said I would—care about you—stay?"

He stared at her aghast. What—give up his own country, after all these years of dreams, his beloved and beautiful country?

"No!" he shouted. He would not give himself time to think.

She shrugged her shoulders, laughed, and said airily, "Then go—go away to your China!"

So he had gone, in haste and hurry to be gone. Before he could stop to think he was on the train whirling across green country, through great roaring cities, through little towns and vast prairies to the sea coast. Before he could stop to think he was on a great ship, crowded among third-class passengers, and outside there was only the roar of the sea, and inside among all these strangers there was infinite time to think—to think and to dream.

But now his dreams would not come right. They would not take the shapes of old, the shapes of his own people, his coming home to his own race, his life, a leader in the revolution, a governor, a diplomat, a great man of some sort in his own country. No, those dreams came stealing into his mind in the shape of a small round willful face, of black eyes, Chinese under a crop of American-curled hair, of a slim yellow Chinese body in a rose pink American dress. He leaped out of his berth again and again and paced the few feet of deck, for he had not ceased to love her and he had not ceased to be angry with her. He told himself many times that she was full of faults—that she was all those things which a Chinese girl should not be—she talked before men and she laughed too loudly and she was disobedient to her parents. Why, she even made fun of her father's lisp when he tried to speak English! It was true that her father had spoiled her and that he laughed at her, but then she was not respectful. How many times had he not heard his own mother say she came home late at night, every time with a different man! He cast up all her faults and tried to see how well off he was to be alone—and groaned because he loved her and wished he were not alone.

He began to look forward to his country with renewed eagerness. For now his country was the only thing which could make him forget Ruth. There among all that new life, working, serving, achieving, he would forget about her. He would even—of course he would find the woman whom he really sought—not Ruth, but another. There he would live and found his home and have his children, their mother not Ruth, but a dreamy-eyed, quiet, obedient woman in his house. But first he must work and he must achieve. And first of all he must find his country.

But where was his country? Upon the sea it had seemed so near, there where the sea ended, there where the river began. This was his country, this first line upon the horizon. He had passed indifferently in the Inland Sea one lovely isle after another; coldly he had gazed at the rocky exquisitely outlined mountains of Japan, waiting for this first dark edge between sea and sky. He rose early to see it, and soon after dawn, staring into a gray and misty sky he saw it, that silent line of dark land. Soon the ship was embraced as though by two arms of that land. There were no hills, no houses, nothing to speak to him—only those two dark arms reached out into the sea to embrace him, to draw him home. He hung over the rail of the deck, staring, his heart beating in his throat.

Then upon the land appeared tiny low houses, isolated, the color of earth, and then the brown of the earth changed to brilliant green. The sun did not shine and the sky was gray. Against the gray the green was deeply vivid. But houses and fields were small and solitary upon the immensity of these ever broadening arms of land. Here, here was his country. He yearned to it, he gazed upon it, he longed to leap across the yellow waters of the river and feel it beneath his feet, old, sure, unchanged, silent, welcoming him in silence.

Then suddenly he lost it all. Suddenly the ship passed between tall buildings, edged ponderously to a dock, and all silence was gone, all peace was lost. A horde of small brown blue-coated men leaped across the rails, chattering, shrieking a language he did not even understand. He used upon them the tongue he had from his mother, but they stared at him wild-eyed, searching. He pointed out his few bags, neatly strapped and ready to be taken ashore, but they passed him by as though he had not spoken. They were looking, he realized suddenly, not for him. It was nothing to them that he was come home at last. They were looking for richer folk than he, for tourists, for white men. He set his teeth a moment, staring after their tumbling, crowding figures, and then one by one he picked up his own bags and staggered across the narrow gangway to the dock.

It was at that moment that he lost his country completely. For standing among the crowd pouring from the ship, pouring from the streets, he might have been in any country again. He might even have been again in New York. He heard no tongue he understood except the English he had left behind him. About him were tall Western buildings; he heard the din of street cars in his ears. Suddenly the rain poured in a drum of noise upon the tin roof of the dock, and he was walled in by it, and he could do no more than wait, walled in with the crowd of alien motley people, not one of whom he knew, and not one of whom were coming to welcome him home. He stood forlornly staring through the rain across the yellow water. A small junk struggled through the mists, its sails lowered, and an oarsman standing at the oar, his brown body naked except for the loin cloth about his hips. From his unfamiliar form John Chang looked at the ship, the ship from which he had longed so desperately to escape. But now somehow it looked like home to him, a home of a sort, whose ways he knew. At least there he had been safe and sheltered.

Then suddenly he shook himself. This would not do. He must be strong. There was no going back now. In his pocket he had the name of a good inn his father had given him and the name of the cousin who was his partner, upon whom he was to call for aid. He must be bold and remember that somewhere his country lay behind this dock, these crowds, these streets. He laid a hand upon a coolie standing near and pointed to his bags. "Ricksha!" he said with authority, "ricksha!" The man halted, stared, hesitated, took up the bags with a grunt. In a moment John Chang was rolling along, buttoned behind an oil-cloth curtain. He could see nothing, except the brown bare legs of the puller, streaming with the rain, and above his head upon the thin roof of the ricksha the rain beat steadily down.

Where, where was his country? After three days in the small bare room of the inn he sat and stared across a narrow street into a tenement house. Except that the clothes hung upon bamboo poles were shaped differently, it might have been a tenement in New York. In and out of the cheap houses dirty children ran, naked in the stifling midsummer heat. Women shouted after them; slouching men and furtive-eyed young girls came and went. He had seen them all before and they were not his. They were not his, and yet their eyes were black and pointed like his own and their hair black and their skin his skin. But he would not have them for his own.

Already he loathed the inn and determined he must leave it. Yet, when he asked, his cousin shrugged his fat shoulders. "It is good enough, that inn," he said. "A better one would be very dear."

"It is dirty," said John Chang briefly.

"You are like a foreigner," remarked his cousin. "You will become accustomed."

He had been twice to see that cousin, and twice he had come away angry.

It did not seem possible to him that such a man was his cousin. He lived in half-a-dozen different courts, his many children ran about unwashed, and the noise of quarreling women was everywhere. And with all these women, these wives and these servants, there was no one to brush away the flies from the tea bowls upon the table; and when the cousin invited John Chang to eat with him at his house, the flies sat upon the food. Yet the cousin was not a poor man. He had money, since he was the partner in the curio business, and he it was who shipped the Buddhas and the little ivory boxes and the silver trinkets and the embroidered robes and the incense sticks and all those things which John Chang had known all his life in the shop on Mott Street, all things which had set him dreaming of his own country. Now when he saw the fat brown hand of his cousin and saw the grease upon his silken gown and the rolls of fat about his neck and about his belly, when in the heat of the day he put his gown from him and sat with his upper body uncovered, he wondered that he had ever dreamed.

His cousin's daughters, too, came and went, and the cousin snapped his fingers to them when he wanted tea or his pipe or his old shoes to ease his feet. The man boasted of these girls. He said, "As for my girls, I have kept them where they should be kept, in the home. They have fretted now and again to go to some school or other, but I have seen these bold modern girls on the streets, and I know they are nothing but trouble with all their learning and their boldness—trouble for their father who must feed them, and trouble for the men they must marry. I have married ignorant women and they have done me very well." He puffed at his pipe and shouted at his daughter who stood before him to hear any further commands. "Go to your mother and do not hang about to hear men talk!" When the girl was gone he said with complacence, "You see how obedient she is. She will be as obedient as that one day to her husband. It has been my care to prepare my daughters for marriage, for there is nothing else a woman can do."

And, indeed, John Chang, watching, saw the girl go docilely away; as silently as though no one stepped she went in her little satin shoes. But although her face was very pretty and she was well-mannered and said not one word, and was the sort of maid he had dreamed about once, he did not feel his heart move at all when he looked at her. He said to himself, "It is because she is the daughter of my second cousin," but when he went back to his room in the inn and sat down alone he found in surprise that it was not because she was the daughter of his cousin, but because she seemed stupid to him, and her pretty silent face was only like a doll's face; and, thinking further, he was not sure it would be such pleasure to have a doll for a wife, who put up her arm when she was bade and kissed him when she was bade and came when she was bade and went away when she was bade to do it. Suddenly there flew into his mind the thought of Ruth Kin and how no one could make her do what she would not do, and there she was before him, laughing and willful and mischievous. He was glad she was not here.

But after a while, thinking and staring through the rain, he came to the thought that this was not his country, not this dirty city of Shanghai, noisy with vehicles and crowded with every sort of people. Somewhere beyond these flat horizons was more, miles upon miles of his vast country, for him to discover.

So again he went to his cousin and said, "I want to go further away, into the inlands; I want to see and I want to discover."

At this his cousin fanned himself quickly and said, "I hope you are not one of those young revolutionists who have been the pest

of our country in these last years! But if you are, do not tell me
—I do not want to hear any of it. But if you want to go inland,
then I have an errand for your father on which you may go. You
are to go to the regions at the end of the great river, into the
province of Szechuan. I hear there have been new graves discovered there of ancient princes, and if it is true, you can find curios
cheaply and buy what you can and bring them back. But do not
buy this and this—" and then the cousin detailed what he should
not buy and what was true and what was false, because at such
times among the true there are many false things, made by men
who think it possible to sell them mingled together.

Thus John Chang went in search of his own country, following the sweep of the great river.

Everywhere he searched for his country and everywhere he
found only the same thing. He found cities crowded and noisy
and filthy with generations of filth. He grew afraid to drink anything except the hottest tea, although the summer sun scorched
his flesh, and he ate only a little rice and cabbage, because there
was no ice and nothing to keep from putridness the slabs of pigs
hung in the sun and the fish dying in their tubs of stale water
and the crabs upon which the flies sat unceasingly. At night the
mosquitoes fed upon him, and if he stopped in inns the insects
swarmed to him. He could not see the beauty of the distant hills,
nor could he see the rich green banks flourishing in rice and the
great nets let down to catch the large river fish, because upon
the little river steamer with him were two hundred pilgrims going to an ancient temple on a mountain top to worship there,
and holy men have the vilest bodies to be found, and these
reeked with all their filth and holiness. Yet they were his countrymen. Yes, they were all his countrymen—the blind he met so
often on the streets of any town where the steamer stopped; the

children running as they would, unclothed; the brawling women washing by the river's edge and beating out their rags upon the rocks, and quarreling as they worked; and the shrewd petty shopkeepers; and the beggars whining everywhere, full of leprosy and holding out their maimed limbs. One day he stopped among them and cried to his own heart, staring at them, "Is this the country I dreamed of all these years, and can any lifetime save them?"

And for a moment he was conscious of an aching in him for some other place, a homesickness. But he was at home. And then it seemed to him he would give all his years to be back in his father's shop again, in that small clean quiet shop. The street in New York seemed the cleanest best street in the world, and he thought with utter longing of the white clean tub in the bath-room above the shop. He turned and walked back swiftly to his cabin and he sat down and wrote a letter. But it was not to his father and his mother. It was to Ruth Kin, and he said, "You were right and I am but a fool. Stay by your home there. You were very right." And grimly he went on day by day up that great river until it wound small and deep and narrow among the gorges, and so at last he came to where he had been sent.

Time and time again he wrote to Ruth Kin, and why he did not know, since she did not care for him. But it seemed to him that now forever his country was lost. It was not what he dreamed, and not being that, it was nothing. He learned to bicker with the dealers to whom his cousin sent him, to suspect falseness in every bit of pottery or bronze they brought him, to know a poor man who pretended to be a farmer bringing in a bit of something he had unearthed from his field might be as great a liar as another. He learned to twist his tongue to speak their languages, to hold to his money, to haggle, and to postpone and do all the paltry business he must do. At night, lying in his bed, he sneered at himself that he had come to this, he who would not work for his father, but must follow dreams for thousands of miles and come to this, this sorry quarreling search. And so he wrote to Ruth, not because he asked anything of her, so he said, but because he must write somewhere and he could not write his father and he would not write his friends and let them know he was so shamed.

"For filth and flies and beggary," he wrote to Ruth Kin, "I have not seen the like of this country. Yes, I suppose this is my country. And here in my country I must watch daily or I am robbed, and here in my country men are kidnaped and nothing is said. And—"

And so he poured out all his bitter disappointment and his shames, and eased himself a little, although he never ate a meal without a fuss about the dust upon the table or flies upon the meats, so that in that whole city he got a name for himself, and the inn dreaded to see him coming, and he was nicknamed the Foreign Devil, since he was so full of fuss about a little dust and dirt or about a fly or two.

Then like a sharp cold wind across the sea one day he had a letter, sent to his cousin and his cousin sent it on, and it was from Ruth Kin. He had come back to his inn at night after a long day of searching in a newly opened ruin, and there upon his table the letter lay. He opened it and found the inner envelope and opened that and read, like Ruth's voice, her laughing pitiless truthful words. "You sap," she wrote, and whereas once he hated such speech, he only laughed now aloud—it seemed so good to have a word come hard and direct against his cheek—oh, how he was weary of the false polite palavering of the dealers! "You sap, what did you expect? For a penny I'd come—not to marry you, you understand, but just to see if it's what you say. And I'd like to sort of clean things up if it is as bad as you say."

Looking out of his window, down the narrow, crowded street, he knew that he did not want Ruth Kin to come. It was evening in August, and the end of a hot day, and the people were quarrelsome. Their voices rose sharply and angrily into his window. Two women were cursing each other, and there was a crowd about them, listening, to hear and to be amused. Suddenly one snatched at the other's hair, and they rolled in the dust, their curses shrieking. But it was a common sight after all, and the people moved and scattered and brought out their bamboo beds and spread their pallets for the night. Men and women and children lay down to sleep, the men stripped near to nakedness, the children naked, and the women in their thin grass-cloth coats. Above them rose the hum of mosquitoes. He stood looking down on them. A child wailed through the dusk and a dog howled. These, these were his people. He did not want Ruth Kin to come.

He went back into the room and lit the small kerosene oil lamp and sat down to answer her letter. The night insects fluttered about him, and twice he got up and stepped upon the body of a centipede and felt its crusty body crack beneath his American leather shoe. He wrote and wrote, and, pausing at last, he added one more line, "Even the kerosene lamp," he wrote, "is American. You had better stay in America." He went to bed exhausted and silent to the heart. There, he thought, having told her everything, there was the end of Ruth Kin.

There was no going back, of course. He was far too proud to go back. After all these years, after he had organized the Chinese boys' patriotic club in his high school and after he had collected money in college to send to the revolutionary government, after everything he had dreamed, there was no going back. He settled himself grimly to his own country. Once he went to the new capital and walked silently and unknown about the streets. He had, he realized, expected to see something like New York, like Washington, like the postcards he had seen of Paris. Instead he saw a few carelessly made wide streets, fringed by new cheap one-story shops. There were two or three large buildings, new and half empty. When he walked up the steps, a guard stopped him sternly, and he turned and went away. Perhaps if he had had influence he might have gone in, but he had no influence at all. He walked a long way outside the city and came to the grave of the hero of the revolution and stood staring at it. The grave was there, enormous, hideous, new, a treeless scar upon the mountain side, and inside it the hero lay dead. He went away again.

Once he begged a holiday from his cousin and went south to the village of his mother's girlhood, traveling by small rat-ridden steamers and at last by wheelbarrow across the flat fertile fields. It was the last stronghold of his dreams. But when he slipped off the vehicle a dog rushed at him savagely, and though he beat the beast off, he had to watch, and so sidling and wary he came to the village. Yet what was it but a village, after all? It was a small cluster of houses made from brick of the field earth, and the people were like all the country people he had seen. They were quite the same, the men suspicious of his foreignness and the women silent and shrinking away. A narrow filthy street, a dirty teashop or two, the smell of human waste upon the fields for fertilizer, the silent staring girls—he did not even wait to search out his kin. If these were his kin, then let him not know it. He turned and shouted to the wheelbarrow pusher, "Let us go away!" he shouted. "I want to go away at once!"

Shaking along over the cobbled country roads, he said to himself he was very glad he had written so to Ruth Kin. He was very glad he had told her she must stay there where she was and marry George Liu and live in a little clean flat and have an electric stove and ice and cleanness—and cleanness—and cleanness—everywhere.

Then how could he have been prepared for Ruth Kin's letter in Shanghai? It came after three months across the thousands of miles. He almost felt its briskness through the envelope. The paper was crisp beneath his fingers, used now to the soft thin paper of his cousin's ledgers. The letter crackled when he opened it, the words leaped out, incredible, lively, determined words. He could see her snapping eyes, hear her laugh, see her slight straight saucy figure, see her tossing hair. "Well, I'm coming, John Dewey Chang," the letter began straightly. "I've changed my mind. You've got me—I guess the old home town needs me—and you do, too—"

This was her letter. A little news, a joke or two—"George Liu has gone and married the girl at the soda fountain—I always knew he wasn't smart! Anyway, my folks have stopped ragging me," and at the end, "I've got my ticket and I'll be along in a week after you get this. My dad's coming on business. You're my business." At the end, in a small squeezed note he read with difficulty, "You can have the ring ready—if you want to—"

He folded the letter in a daze. All these days she had been coming toward him, and he had not known! Straight as wind and ship and day and night could bring her she was coming. And for the moment his first thought was he did not know what to do with her. He had a frantic feeling that he must clean everything up before she came. He was suddenly ashamed of everything, ashamed of dirt and poverty and silent ignorant women and of his fat cousin and of the inn and of this room. He ran to the mirror and looked into it. Yes, he was ashamed of himself, too. He had let his hair grow long and unkempt and he wore a soiled shirt. He looked as he would not have dreamed of letting himself look in New York. It did not seem worth while to be different—until now. But now—now—what could he possibly do in a week?

But after all, he did everything in a week—that is, nearly everything. In this country of his, he determined, there should be one spot, a little single spot, clean and homelike for Ruth Kin and him. He rushed to his cousin and borrowed money of him extravagantly. "An American girl?" said the cousin, suspiciously, breaking into the words pouring out of John Dewey Chang's lips.

"Certainly not," John Chang said. And then suddenly he paused and thought, "A sort of an American girl," and did not say it, knowing his cousin. His cousin would not lend money on an American girl, and so he shook his head. After all, Ruth Kin was not an American.

With the money he rented a little house, not in the Chinese city where the inn was and where his cousin lived and where the shop was, but a little bungalow on the edge of the foreign concession where the Americans lived. He must spare his Ruth what he had had—the sudden death of dreams. There was a little banksia rose growing over the porch and even in this autumn it put forth a few blossoms. In spring it would be a bouquet of fragrance for them. In the court there was even an oleander tree. The little house had been long empty, and he hired a stout serving woman from his cousin to come and scrub and clean, and then among the foreign shops he searched for things for Ruth, a rug, two chairs, a bed, a table, some dishes, curtains at the window, and some pictures. At the last moment he remembered pictures and he ran to a shop on Avenue Edward VII and bought three pictures of mountains and lakes, brightly colored.

Then almost at once he had to hurry, for Ruth's ship would be at the dock in an hour.

It was, he felt, waiting, impossible that Ruth was coming to this dock. He could not imagine it. He felt newly sensitive when he looked about, as though he were responsible for the ragged coolies, for the vendors outside the palings, with their small baskets of dirty sweetmeats. A few well-dressed white people were standing there also, and he hated them for their cleanliness and their smartness. He saw gratefully two pretty Chinese girls with their mother and a maidservant, dressed in long satin robes. At least there were these. Somewhere, perhaps, hidden behind high walls there were many such people. Sometimes one saw them on the street. Among the great mass of noisy hungry common folk they were as though there were none, being so few. But at least today there were these, and Ruth would see them. She would feel strange—of course she would feel strange. He must let her see it all gradually and not be discouraged. He was glad that there was electricity in the little house.

Then almost before he knew it the ship had bumped the dock and the gangway was thrown and there was Ruth! He ran forward and she took his hand and held it and he stared down at her unbelieving.

"Here's Dad," she reminded him, laughing, and he bowed to the stout old figure behind her. "I have letters from your father and mother," she said, but it did not matter to him. He took

116

the letters she held out to him from her hand bag, and stared on at her. She was prettier than ever, but how foreign! In her little trim blue suit she looked wholly American until he saw her face.

She gazed with interest about her. "Queer," she said, "this doesn't seem funny to me—none of it. I've never seen any of it, but it's just as though I had!"

Beyond the customs and the dock he called to a taxicab, but she laid a swift hand on his arm. "Let's ride in those funny little things," she cried, pointing to a ricksha. "Taxis are so common!"

So in a moment they were gliding along the Bund behind panting coolies. She turned and waved her hand at him, smiling in delight, "It's more fun than a picnic," she cried.

Well, there it was. A week later, settled in the small house with the banksia rose, he was more astonished at her than ever. For some change had crept over her, already, some indefinable, softening change. In New York she had been as slangy and sharp as a little gamin. But here in this house on the edge of the Chinese city the sharpness was leaving her. She was more silent, and the slang in which she used to take such pride because it was American was day by day becoming more rare. He was dismayed. To himself he thought, "She's growing to hate it. She's feeling as I did—disappointed. It's all worse than she thought."

"Where's all the dirt and the poor you used to write about?" she asked once.

He was frightened. "I was too particular, I guess," he said, evading her, and hurried on. "Ruth, the oleander's going to bloom."

For once he had said to her that he chose his own country always, whether she were there or not. Now, knowing what it was to have her by him in the day, across the table from him

117

when he ate, and when the deep of night came, knowing her warmly in his arms, he knew that if she did not choose this country it was no longer his own. No country could be his where she was not. Suppose she was wanting to go back to New York, just now when this little house began to seem home to him, just now when he could look about him on the streets and not have his heart full, because at the end of the day there was this home!

For having this center now, this place to which he might come when his work was done, this clean bright spot, changed his whole country. He could come and go in narrow streets whose gutters ran with filth, he could bear blind and maimed beggars, he could bear ignorance and haggling dishonesty, knowing that he had a home. At night he could come back to Ruth and read and talk and listen to the phonograph and maybe go to a picture show, although he liked better just to hear her talk and laugh.

But here she was, growing daily less merry. "I've got to get her out into the foreign concession more," he thought desperately one night. "It's more like New York there." Aloud he said, "Like to go to a cabaret, honey?" They still talked in English together, since her Chinese was so little yet. They made a joke of their Chinese at first, she asking what this was and this. But now she had been picking up words from her servant woman, and then she asked him by the end of the second week to buy a primer—"the kind that the kids use in school," she explained—and then she wanted a tutor and he had to hire an old scholar to come and teach her how to hold the brush for writing. So they had gone to the cabaret and danced a little, but not much. And she had not seemed to enjoy it especially, after all, although it had cost him a great deal of money, nearly five dollars. It was not a thing to be done often.

By the end of the second month she looked at him sidewise one morning at breakfast and asked him, "What would you say if I quit wearing these New York clothes and put on things like the rest of the women here?" He stared at her. He could not imagine her in a narrow smooth-fitting robe. Her face seemed made for these little ruffly dresses she had brought with her. "Well," he began, when she broke in— "Wait—don't say until you've seen me!"

That very night when he came home there she was. She had gone out and bought herself a long green robe of a close-woven silk. The collar was high. She had smoothed down her short hair, and above the straightness of the robe her little round face stood like a grave, pretty flower. She moved gravely, gracefully. Her very smile was changed. It was not saucy and teasing. He could not imagine this demure creature making eyes at a groceryman on the street. He gazed at her entranced. "Like it?" she said, softly.

"Yes," he answered, and could say no more for watching her. Later, after their dinner, he asked with difficulty, fearing her answer. "Does that—dress—feel strange?" She looked up from some sewing she was doing. "No," she said. "The queer thing is I feel as if I'd never had my own clothes on until now."

But still, he told himself, coming and going every day to his cousin's shop, still the house shielded her. Her life was not hard. In the clean little house upon a macadam street, she need not see the other streets. He came and went everyday in the native city, but she could go the other way into the foreign concession and see great shops and motor cars. He talked a little, guardedly, about famines and bandits and wars in the interior, but she was not much interested. Such things were as remote from this place, seemingly, as they had been from Mott Street. She never read English newspapers and could not read the Chinese ones yet, and the little house bounded her life. He breathed the relief that this thought brought to him. He was keeping her safe and happy, secure from the knowledge of the dark native city. Really, he thought, she lived almost as she might have in an American city, as safe from sorrowful truth. He came home to her and rested in that haven, shut away from the real world. When sometimes she spoke of some chance sight—one morning there was a little dead girl baby thrown out even upon the macadam street—he coaxed her thoughts away. So in the end she was only gay when he came home, gay and demurely seductive. It came to him, as a miracle, that somehow Ruth Kin was often like that girl of whom he had dreamed, that sweet obedient woman in his house.

Then the knowledge he would have spared her came flooding down on her, flooding at the very time when he would most have kept it away. For she was going to have a baby, "a son," she said confidently. Now it appeared why she had wanted to wear a robe instead of the tight little American dresses. "As soon as I knew," she said, "I thought I'd like to wear them." Under the pretty, straightly clinging robe her figure rounded softly and with continued grace. And now he knew he must keep her safe in the world he had made for her, this safe, clean little modern world set in the midst of the huge dark old medieval country which was his. He hurried home from his work, hurried through the packing of cases and the shipping of goods to his father in Mott Street. More than ever now he must work to keep that little spot safe and sheltered.

And then, one morning, one spring morning, when their son was seven months known to them and they were planning his birth and he had chosen the very best foreign hospital in the British concession, they heard the crack of cannon. The deep roar burst, reverberated and ceased, roared and reverberated and ceased. He stared at Ruth and she stared back, astonished, questioning. He knew instantly what it was. He had not taken time to read the papers much of late, but the air had been thunderous with it—the Japanese were at the coast. The cannon burst out again and there was the sound of a falling wall, and they leaped from their seats. But he thought of Ruth, only of Ruth. "Never mind," he cried, and forgetting he spoke in his own tongue—it was natural to him now to speak in his own tongue. "You are not be frightened—I will take care of you somehow—" Oh, that he had never brought her here—oh, that they were back in Mott Street, where she might be safe and their child born in peace!

For soon, in a day, in two days, there was nothing left to hide from Ruth. The streets were full of terrified, wretched people, begging for a bit of shelter. Fire leaped everywhere, to the west of them. He had to spend his days and nights moving the stores of curios into the cellars of friendly houses of business in the foreign concessions. For a day and a night he had to work, not knowing what was become of Ruth, except that the little low house was safer, still, he felt, than any other spot. He watched the fire as he came and went. No, those flames were still safely away. He rushed home at dawn dreading to find Ruth terrified, ill, perhaps even in premature birth.

But when he opened the door she was not there. Instead it seemed as though all the folk in the city from whom he had been guarding her had taken the little house. Upon the rugs he had bought sat packed a crew of men and women and children, little precious bundles upon their knees, their faces haggard with bewilderment and fear and weariness. The house reeked with the odor of their unwashedness. They looked up at him mutely, timidly, silent in the din of the unceasing cannon in the west. Three days and three nights the roar had gone on, punctuated by the crash of the falling buildings a half mile away. But the small low house had still stood sturdily, full of these homeless folk, squeezing into every corner, clutching their poor saved possessions. The room was full of them. He rushed to the kitchen to find the maidservant to demand where Ruth was.

And there she was, standing over the little electric range he had bought with such pride, pots on every spot of its surface. She was desperately weary as he could see, her hair uncombed. But her eyes were not tired. They were elated and exalted. Over her robe was a big American apron, and she and the woman stood stirring the pots of food.

"What—?" he began.

"They are all hungry," she said, "they're starved. The poor things have run away because their houses are burned down."

"We can't feed them all," he began.

She stirred vigorously. "We can, too!" she said. "I've got enough here for everybody."

He stood uncertainly. "There's an awful smell in the house," he said suddenly. The smell of the unwashed crowd was coming even here, overcoming the fragrance of the rice. It was so vile he was ashamed for them before Ruth. He had never told her how the reek of the garlic-eating common folk sickened him, and now he must speak of it first.

She turned on him indignantly. "You ought to be ashamed of yourself," she cried, and then in pure New York, "You great big stiff, what does it matter how they smell if they're your own people?" She removed a pot rapidly and began filling bowls set out on the table. "Gee, if I'd known all I've learned since you've been away—" She dipped, competently, carefully, all the languor about her gone. She was electric with vigor. But he only saw her face, weary but perfectly happy.

"I didn't want you to know," he said. "If they do anything to hurt you now when the baby is about to come I shan't forgive them."

She paused in her dipping to stare at him. "Do you mean to tell me, John Dewey Chang," she demanded, "that you've been deliberately hiding things from me? I've wondered why every time we went anywhere you always took me into the foreign concession. That's just like New York—why, I've been bored to death!"

She dipped again, bowl after bowl, filling them to the brim, running to the stove for another pot.

"Bored?" he repeated.

"Yes," she answered. "There's nothing to do— And all the time there were all these people I didn't know about,—"

"Millions of them," he muttered, "millions upon millions upon millions of them!" He could not understand her.

"Well, that settles it," she said contentedly.

"Settles what?" he asked stupidly.

"Settles whether I like it here or in New York."

He stared at her, still stupidly, and she laughed at him, her old shout of loud laughter. He had not heard it just like that since that morning when she was working on her father's ledgers in Mott Street. "Silly!" she said, beginning on the fresh pot, "don't you see? I like to do things, and here's plenty!"

He began to comprehend. She did not mind these people. She was not in the least disappointed in them. They were only hungry people and she wanted to feed them. If they were dirty—

Almost as though she answered his thought she began, "And when they're all fed, I'm going to begin giving the babies baths —and maybe the grown people can take turns—" She turned around to demand, "How long do you think the war will keep up?"

Why, she was a child, nothing but a child, talking about baths! The sound of cannon was thundering steadily across the city. This morning the forts were down, he had heard. What would be the end of it?

"I don't know," he groaned.

"We might get everybody bathed if it only lasts long enough," she planned.

But he interrupted her, "Oh, Ruth, you should—you should go away for the baby's sake—out of the country—there's no telling about this war—"

But at this she turned and put her hands on her hips.

"My baby?" she said, firmly. "My baby is going to be born in his own country where he belongs." Then her voice changed again. "Now," she commanded him, "you take this trayful in and begin to feed them—the kids first. And hurry!" she added, "there's a lot to do around here!"

VIII
TIGER! TIGER!

TIGER! TIGER!

WITHOUT opening her eyes, Molly Chu knew it was time for her to get up. It was nearly midday. Upon the old square-tiled floor of her room she heard the soft tiptap of her little maid's footsteps bringing in tea and sweetmeats for her to eat before she got up. She lay a moment longer. She was suddenly very hungry for a good American breakfast, the sort she had eaten every morning at college. The American air was sharp and cold, and she had always been hungry. She let herself think about it, dish by dish, the orange juice, oatmeal and cream, bacon and eggs, toast and coffee—ah, the good coffee! She could smell it, fragrant and hot in her nostrils.

"Shall I pour the tea?" Orchid's voice was a soft whisper. Here in this house where Molly was the only child no one ever waked her sharply. There were soft small sounds subdued to her gradual rousing. And then came Orchid's whisper. Her father had bought Orchid to be her bondmaid years ago, long before she could remember. Orchid was only two years older than she was, and she had waited four years for Molly to come back from America, and while she waited she embroidered the delicate silk undergarments that had made the American girls exclaim so loudly.

"Oh, Molly, how wonderful—all those tiny stitches—that lovely design—oh, you lucky girl!"

She had only smiled, taking for granted Orchid's little stitches set so perfectly into flowers and birds and butterflies. When she was in America she could sometimes make herself grow a little homesick, seeing Orchid in a sunny corner of a courtyard at home, stitching. But she was never really homesick—there was so much to do in America. Oh, this idleness, now that college was over, now that she was home and there was nothing to do!

That was what her mother and father could never understand, what her friends could not understand, the girls she knew who had never gone away—how difficult to bear was the idleness.

She did not open her eyes. Why should she? It made no difference whether she got up or not. There was nothing to do in this quiet old seaport town in South China—nothing that mattered.

She felt Orchid's touch upon the silk-stuffed quilt.

"Your mother, little mistress—she wants you to go to the temple today with her. She said you were not to be waked, but when you woke yourself, I was to tell you she is ready. Besides, I have brought you something. When you open your eyes you will see—" Orchid paused, waiting.

Orchid could make her feel a little spoiled girl again. She who had been honor student at Wellesley, president of the senior class—"you have a gift for executive work," the dean had told her—Orchid, coaxing her, made her feel willful and pouting and naughty. She opened her eyes, and saw a great spray of small waxen yellow flowers.

"Spring!" Orchid cried joyously. She laid the leafless flower-laden branches upon the bed, and the canopy of silk bed curtains was full of their fragrance.

"Lamay flowers!" Molly cried, sitting up. "Oh, is the old bush in the bamboo court blooming?"

"Full!" said Orchid, smiling.

"I'd forgotten," Molly answered.

"I didn't tell you," Orchid said. "I waited until this morning, and I went out early. I knew yesterday that today the flowers would burst. This morning it stands a tree of gold!"

Spring! She leaped out of bed. When the lamay flowers bloomed the winter was over. Even though snow fell again, it was spring, and snow could not linger. The room was very cold. She warmed her hands over the bed of coals in the brazier. She had told her father again and again about the heat in American houses, how it was warm all winter and no one was ever cold, however high the snow was piled. These great old rooms with their tiled floors and plastered brick walls were like icehouses. She had been cold all winter.

"Ha!" her father said, swaddled in silk quilted robes, "those American houses! I should die. Put on more clothes, Ma-li." But she had said petulantly, "I won't go around looking like a bedding roll." It didn't matter—spring was here.

She washed herself quickly in the hot scented water in the brass ewer, shivering a little as the steam rose from her bare flesh, and while she dressed she drank the hot tea. Orchid had put the spray of golden flowers into a green glazed jar and she kept looking at it as she ate and drank.

It must be those flowers, she thought, which made her so restless and impatient today. She was ashamed of herself. Something in her hurried her feet, her speech, everything she did. She even wanted to hurry her mother.

"Now then, Ma-li," her mother was saying, "have we everything? The incense, the silver shoes to burn, the gift to the temple, the fowls, my water pipe, my kerchief—Orchid, does the wind blow? If it blows, I must have my little toilet case to mend myself before I pray—perhaps I had better have it anyway. The tea basket, Orchid, is it in the sedan? And some little cakes, lest we should be hungry—the ones made with vegetable oil, not lard, out of deference to the gods—the gods smell lard so quickly, you know, daughter, and it is so offensive to them. I always say the reason I lost your brother as soon as he was born was because I had eaten porkballs that day I went to worship—the day before his birth it was, and the gods smelled my breath—"

It was silly to be impatient with her chattering pretty little mother, swaying about on her small bound feet. She loved her mother and everybody loved her. But she thought, suddenly rebellious, "I'm tired—tired—tired of going to temples and hearing her talk all this nonsense!" She helped her mother into the sedan and said sharply, "Now, Mother, I've told you there is no truth in those silly old gods!"

"Hush!" her mother cried, "Don't! You don't know what spirits there are in the air!" Her mother's small round face grew piteous.

"Now Mother!" she said practically, "In America—"

"They have their own gods, haven't they?" her mother asked. "Each country has the gods that come out of its own winds and waters and earth."

"I'm not afraid of any of them," said Molly, and fastened down the screen in front of her mother's face, which was to hide her from staring crowds. No lady in Changchow would think of riding exposed through the streets—no lady whose husband was the son of the richest and oldest family, that is. But little Madame Chu pushed the curtain aside an inch to say emphatically to her tall strong daughter, "When you are in America you need not fear our gods. But when you come home again, you come back to their power." Then she closed the curtain and called to the bearers, "Go!" and they swung the poles to their shoulders.

In her own closed sedan Molly sat upright. What if those

American college mates of hers saw her now? At commencement last June they had clung to her in their affectionate way to which she tried to respond, though she had been taught not to touch flesh to flesh, and they had shouted to her in their fresh loud young voices, "Write to me, Molly!" "Say, Molly, if I take a world tour I'll stop in China and see you. I'm crazy to see your house."

"Do let me know," she had said, "do please come to see me."

Well, she was not in the least ashamed of her house. Not even the college halls were more stately than the old house where generations of her family had lived. Of course if any of them really came to see her she would simply tell her father plainly that Americans would not understand his spitting where he liked. And if they did not come in winter they would not know how bitterly cold it was. Quaint, that is what they would call it, the spreading roofs, the tiled courtyards with their little pools and dwarfed trees. And she would not tell them what they did not see—the kitchen with its old earthen stoves and servants' children running about with dirty faces, the flies—she did not go there herself. The servants took care of things. And she loved the house, though its peace irked her. The house had stood three hundred years, and it would stand forever.

Sometimes her father would say mournfully, "Nothing lasts any more—a man cannot build his house forever as the ancients did. Some day the Japanese will come."

When he said this she was always afraid, just for a moment, even though he had said it again and again as long as she could remember. "The little black dwarfs," the children shrieked on the streets in their quarrels, "the little black dwarfs will get you." Or they shrieked, "The Tiger will come down out of the hills and eat you!" The Japanese and the Tiger—the Japanese had

131

been the gnomes in her childhood fairy tales, the pixies, the wicked elves, and the Tiger had been the wicked giant. When she outgrew the fairy tales, they all ceased to be real. Besides, there had been a nice Japanese girl in college—Chiyo her name was. They had not been friends exactly. She was short and dark and rather ugly, like a gnome. But they had not been enemies. Many girls liked Chiyo. And as for the Tiger, he was only an old bandit chieftain whom people talked about and nobody ever saw. Besides, there weren't supposed to be bandits any more. The government had made a law against them.

She stared severely out of the small pane of glass sewed into the cloth curtain. If her father would only go to Shanghai to live they could rent a foreign house and have foreign furniture and central heating. Shanghai was fun. Shanghai was exactly like America. But when she said she wanted to live there, her father only rumbled up his big fat laugh out of himself. "I have always lived here," he said amiably, as if that was enough, and then he said peaceably, "Don't worry yourself, child. You'll be marrying soon, and you can make your husband take you to Shanghai. I'm too old, and much too fat. What would I do in Shanghai?" He was always talking of her marrying, and she would not listen to it. She had cried, "But what can I do here?"

He opened his eyes at her.

"Why should you do anything?" he said and smiled. When she opened her mouth to argue he heaved himself up by his hands on his fat knees and waddled away.

"It's disgraceful of Father to be so fat," she thought angrily. Through the few square inches of glass she saw a rectangle of the crowded cobbled street, a segment of coolies pushing wheelbarrows, of trotting donkeys loaded with rice bags, of children gambling with pennies, scuffling in the windy dust. There were not even rickshas in Changchow and not a single automobile. There wasn't a street wide enough for an automobile. Besides there was so many humped bridges over the canals. She was tilted sharply backward now as the bearer trotted up the steps of a bridge, and for a moment the square of glass held only blank sky. Then she was thrown forward, and the square was full of wet cobbles for another moment before she was righted and swinging along the street again.

"Father!" she thought bitterly. "The only thing he thinks of is getting me married. Why did he send me to America?"

Once she had asked her father why, but he only drew on his pipe and shook his head.

"For no special reason," he said. "I thought it would be interesting to know some of the things they do and I had no son to send. Now," he said with immense enthusiasm, "tell me again about those airplanes. You say they rise up like kites, only—"

She spent hours telling him about America. "Not," she thought, "that it does any good. He only wants to be entertained. I am an honor graduate of a fine Western college for modern women, so that I can entertain a fat old man in a little idle seaport on the coast of China!"

She felt herself being lowered with a bump to the ground, and then Orchid was drawing aside the curtain.

"We are here, little mistress," she said and put out her hand to help her rise. But Molly leaped briskly to her feet.

"I don't need your help," she said brusquely.

Her mother was already out, "fussing," she thought, "over the stuff."

"Now then, Orchid!" her mother was crying. "Where is the— oh, there it is? Where is my handkerchief? What—oh yes, I put it in my sleeve. And—oh, here is the good abbot!"

133

The abbot was hurrying down the steps, smiling and rubbing his plump hands, his gray robes flying in the wind. She hated him. Her mother could never see how greedy his eyes were and how cruel his mouth, and how repulsive his hands, so soft and fat. They were bowing and bowing—of course the abbot was glad to see a rich, foolish old lady.

"This morning when I rose from my prayers," the abbot was smirking, "I saw the lamay tree in full bloom and I knew the day held luck. And luck is come."

He led the way into the temple, and she followed behind her mother, sturdy and contemptuous, her American shoes clacking on the dirty marble steps. Behind her came Orchid and the bearers with the gifts, and all around them were eager curious faces, disheveled hair, staring eyes. They were the crowd of the poor, pressing forward. She never looked at them and she did not look at them now. She had never in all her childhood, sheltered behind the high walls of her father's house, even spoken to them. She followed her mother into the high shadowy temple halls, and the too sweet smell of burning incense fell about her like swathes of tissued silk. She could scarcely breathe.

"Go away," her mother said to her. "I want to pray for a private thing." She had stood waiting while her mother prayed her long usual prayers, for health and good crops for the ancestral farm and that the Japanese would never come and that the Tiger would leave them alone. For years her mother had prayed for these things.

"Go away," her mother repeated.

So she had gone away to a little distance. There was no question of her own praying. They had had that out when she first came home.

"I'll go to the temple with you, Mother, but I will never get down on my knees again to those old images," she had declared. That was the day when her mother had come to give thanks for her safe return.

"Oh, you wicked, wicked girl!" her mother had wailed, and then she had turned to her husband. "The gods will be angry at us all!" she wailed.

"Not if you don't tell them about it," he said jokingly. "I haven't been to the temple for years, and they don't know it." He leaned forward and patted her shoulder. "Besides, they wouldn't hurt anybody belonging to you after all these years."

"I suppose not," she said.

And afterwards Molly had said to her father, "Don't you believe in the old gods, father?"

He shook his head and whispered, "Don't tell on me!" And then he had waddled to one of his bookshelves and pulled out a small paper-bound book and said, "I read this many years ago." To her wonder it was a translation of Darwin's *Origin of Species*. She had never thought of him as reading anything except old novels and odes. "Your mother has to have gods," he said. "You and I don't."

A flicker of understanding passed between them. She lost it again when he coughed loudly and spat, she lost it over and over when he sat sleepy from too much food and drink, when he stretched himself on a couch and slept away his time uselessly. "How can he waste himself so?" she thought, half sad, half angry. And then when she told him about something she had seen in America, he would be suddenly alert and know what she meant, and for a little while there would be the flicker between them.

"There is nothing to make anybody do anything in this sleepy old city," she thought irritably. From a wing of the temple came the drone of chanting priests, slow and somnolent, the chant of centuries. She could not bear it. She went and stood by the great open temple door, where she could look out. The huge courtyard was full of vendors, selling vegetarian cakes, incense, paper money, and cooked foods for sacrifice. It was dirty and crowded and noisy. And then, suddenly, the spring wind caught her. It blew fresh and sweet from the hills beyond the city wall, chill but not cold. The sky over the dark tiled city roofs was bright blue with small white clouds racing across it. "I can't— I can't—" she thought passionately, "I can't stay here all my life and grow like all of the rest of them!"

It was at this moment that she heard Orchid cough behind her and she turned quickly. Orchid was smiling a little foolishly.

"What is it?" Molly asked her sharply, "Why are you laughing?"

"Do you know what your mother is praying for, little mistress?" Orchid asked mischievously.

"No," said Molly shortly, "it is not my business."

"I think it is your business," said Orchid laughing. "She is praying for a husband for you!"

Molly stared at her. A husband—for her—

"Be quiet!" she said. "Be quiet, you silly girl!"

"Yes, mistress," said Orchid docilely. But in her eyes was the contented look of one who has said what she came to say.

She did not ask her mother anything. Her mother came to her when she still stood by the temple door and her eyes were calm and her voice was refreshed.

"It is a good day for prayer," she said. "I felt today that the god leaned down to hear me and when I had asked I knew it was given. Let us go home."

She saw in her mother's eyes a gleam that she recognized. It meant her mother was planning something.

"If Mother thinks I'll marry someone she chooses," she thought, "she's wrong. She'll tell me the gods chose, probably."

They entered their waiting sedans again, and she looked away from the greasy abbot, bowing and bowing as they went away.

She would not ask her mother anything. No, when she reached home she would go straight to her father. "Father," she would demand of him—all the people in the street were only shadows moving across the square of glass—"Father, I won't— I won't marry anybody. I won't marry any man unless—" Over and over she thought what she would say to him. They were home almost instantly, it seemed to her.

"Where is my father?" she demanded of the manservant who had come to meet them at the gate.

"He is asleep in the library," he answered, and she flew through the courtyards.

But when she reached the library he was not at all asleep. She heard his heavy voice rumbling in talk, and she opened the door impetuously. Three old men sat there, tea bowls before them. She knew them. They were the city elders. But they were not drinking tea. They were leaning forward, their heads close together, whispering. When she came in they looked at her, and then her father rose to his feet.

"Ma-li, I was about to send for you," he said. "Where is your mother? You are both to leave at once for Shanghai—quickly— as quickly as you can."

"Why—why—?" she stammered. But he was pushing her by the shoulders through the door.

"The Tiger!" he whispered. "The Tiger is going to attack the city!"

He stared at her with terror in his eyes. "As though it were not enough," he said swallowing hard, "as though it were not enough that there is Japan glowering off our coasts, we must have the Tiger tearing at us from within!"

Then he closed the door.

She stood a moment, shut out, commanded like a child. The Tiger! Her father was really afraid. It was ridiculous. She had heard about the Tiger all her life. There was always the Tiger whom the people had feared. He lived off in the mountains to the east, a chief over twenty thousand bandits. The city paid him yearly sums to leave them alone, she knew that. She had heard her father talk about "Tiger Tax." Everybody paid Tiger Tax and was glad to do it if they were left in peace. The little towns too poor to pay had stories to tell of boisterous furies of bandits pouring through their gates and swarming into houses and shops. When he had gone they put placards on their city gates. "Pass— we have already been robbed," they wrote. "We have nothing left." That was in case other robber bands came by, such as the Blue Wolf band, for instance, though the Blue Wolf was supposed to stay on the lee side of the mountain. But nobody was so afraid of the Blue Wolf as they were of the Tiger. Everybody had hoped for the old Tiger to die until the Tiger's son grew up, and then there was no use in hope for he was twice as strong as his father had been and twice as clever, everybody said, though nobody had seen him.

She stood, remembering all this talk she heard from servants and from Orchid. She thought of America suddenly with envy and longing. And then she was very angry. "It's perfectly outrageous!" she thought, "in this day and time, that we still have to suffer from these warlords, at least. I'd be ashamed to have the girls in college even dream of it." She had laughed once in answer to a question Mary Lane, reading a newspaper, had asked her. "Warlords? Oh no, we don't have warlords any more in China!" She had not even thought of the Tiger in America.

She stamped her foot and opened the door of the library. All the old men looked at her. Her father was writing on a sheet of paper. She knew what it was. He was counting up how much money they could gather to bribe the Tiger to leave them alone.

"Forty-seven thousand, I make it," he said without looking. "I'll add three thousand more and make it fifty. Fifty thousand —will he let us alone for that?"

"Father," she said loudly, "why do you give anything to a robber?"

He looked up at her, surprised.

"Why, we always have had to give to the Tiger," he said mildly. "The old one wasn't so bad—it's this young one. He has big ideas."

"And you're going to help him!" she cried.

The old men looked at her patiently. A woman, she could see them thinking, a woman understands nothing.

Her father rose to his feet.

"I tell you to go to your mother," he said. "I want you out of this. You've been begging to go to Shanghai. Well, go, and visit your cousins there and do that dancing they all love, and enjoy yourself."

"And leave you here?" she asked.

"I'm not a young girl," he said pointedly. And once more he took her shoulders and pushed her through the door. "Go away," he whispered loudly. "Don't you see you're making me ashamed before the city elders? Pretend at least to obey me!"

She went to her room and sat down, hot with anger. What a country was hers! Those gods in the temple this morning—silly old images of clay pasted over with colored paper and gilt, silly ferocious faces to frighten the ignorant people—the abbot's fat open palm——sedan chairs instead of automobiles, and now a warlord about to attack the city!

"I don't belong here," she cried passionately to herself. "It's a hideous country—it ought to be dead and buried with all the other medieval countries!" And then she thought, "What if Mary Lane should really come to visit me? Lots of people come to China now. I wish they wouldn't." And then she remembered her mother kneeling, too, before the silly gods. "My own mother," she thought, and her father, paying tribute to a warlord—what were warlords anyway but bandits? "They ought to be put in jail," she said aloud, and then she thought bitterly, "There probably isn't even a jail in the city." . . . "And I," she thought, "I have a degree from Wellesley! It's about as appropriate to me as an automobile would be to these streets." She clenched her fists. "I won't stand it," she decided, "I simply won't stand it." What, she asked herself, would Mary Lane have done? What would any girl do—any girl, that is, who lived today?

She sat, plotting deeply. Across the swiftness of her thought she was barely aware of the sweet heavy fragrance of the lamay flowers upon their brown and leafless branches. The door opened and Orchid burst into the room.

"We must go to Shanghai, little mistress!" she cried. "We are all to go at once to Shanghai. It's the Tiger again! Your mother says I am to pack your robes at once."

Molly looked up at her mildly. "Very well, Orchid," she said gently, so gently that Orchid cried again in amazement, "Did you know? Aren't you afraid of the Tiger?"

Molly put out a finger and touched a waxen yellow flower. "I've been wanting to go to Shanghai," she murmured. "Besides, I'm not afraid of anybody."

"Oh!" Orchid breathed, "Then you are the only one who isn't!"

"Now!" she thought to herself, "Now is the moment!" The rickety little coastal steamer had blown its last feeble tremolo of a whistle. A bustle of coolies was beginning to die away. Her father had already gone. "Good-by—good-by," he had called from the dock. They had bowed and waved, and he had turned away and entered his sedan and her mother said, "I am going straight to bed, Molly, and prepare myself. I shall be sick."

"Yes, Mother," she had replied. And then she had said exactly as she planned, "Orchid, you must go with her."

"Bring my small bag, Orchid," her mother called over her shoulder. And Orchid had taken up the little pigskin case of toilet things. All the bags were heaped on the deck. She had counted on that, too, because when the last moment came she would take Orchid's bundle of clothes, plain blue cotton clothes, tied up in a big flowered kerchief. This was the moment. A few last visitors were leaving by the gangplank that two sailors were waiting to draw. The ship was creaking a little, easing away from the dock a few inches.

"Hurry—hurry!" the sailors shouted.

She stooped, picked up the bundle, and made herself one of the group. She followed them down the gangplank and into the street. Even if Orchid should be looking, she wouldn't think of this—she was glad she had put on her plainest robe this morning,

141

a dark blue thing. She melted into the crowded street, into the current, and turned. She was safe. No one could see her now. She stopped at a stand where sedans were for hire.

"How much for a day's ride?" she asked.

"A silver dollar, and what tea money your good heart says," a stout fellow answered.

"I'll take it," she said. "And let the bearers be strong, because we go to the mountains."

"A temple, lady?" the stout fellow asked.

"No," she replied calmly, "to the Tiger's mountain."

There, she had said it aloud! The men looked at each other. They muttered, "The Tiger's mountain—that's not—no—nobody —we won't—"

"What is it?" she asked.

"No bearers can climb that mountain, lady," the stout fellow said solemnly. "We'd never get home again to our wives and children."

"You will get home again, I promise," she said.

They were staring at her. "Who are you, lady?" the stout fellow asked in a whisper. It was better not to speak of the Tiger aloud in a street.

"You had better take me without asking," she said coldly. "The Tiger—" she paused.

"Only to the foothills of the mountain," the man begged. "There are horses there, lady, used to the narrow paths, as you must know if you know the Tiger."

"The foot of the mountain, then," she said. Horses! She had ridden horses in America. They had hired horses sometimes at college on a holiday and ridden through the New England countryside, she and Mary Lane. Mary had taught her how to ride.

She seated herself in a sedan and drew the curtain.

"Go!" she commanded.

There was a moment of silence. Then she felt herself lifted into the air and into the long familiar swing of steps. She waited an hour and then behind the curtain she began to change her clothes, taking care not to move more than she could help. She drew on Orchid's loose blue cotton trousers, and slipped into her blue cotton coat. She had put on her stoutest American leather walking shoes this morning.

"Sit still, lady!" a bearer shouted. "When you move, the pole grinds our shoulders."

"I am only putting on more clothes," she called back. "The air is growing colder already."

It was true. The foothills were rising before them. She tied her own clothes firmly into Orchid's bundle. A moment later she felt the chair bump to the ground and she stepped out. Around her was strange country, sharp low hills rising like waves around the base of the great mountain. She was standing on a threshing floor, a square of level yellow earth beaten out of the hillside. An earthen farmhouse stood at its edge, its back against the hill, and near it, tethered to a willow tree, were half a dozen horses. A sullen-looking farmer came to the door.

"What is the hire of a horse?" she asked quietly. She felt the bottom of her heart begin to quake a little with fear. She had never seen faces like those which now began to crowd about the door. She had lived in sunny walled courtyards.

"She is a friend of the Tiger's," the stout bearer whispered and jerked his thumb toward the crest of the mountain high above them.

"Why didn't you say so?" the sullen farmer asked. "You can't go alone, lady. The passes are narrow and there are wild beasts. I will go with you."

"Very well," she replied. She had ready in her hand the money for the bearers. She had taken it out of her purse while she was hidden behind the curtain so that they would not be tempted by the roll of bills which her father had given her. "Buy some new dresses in Shanghai," he had said. "Go to the theater and have a good time." But they scarcely looked at the money. They seized it and swung the empty sedan to their shoulders and made off.

"Good-by, lady," they called, thankful to be gone. She stood a moment, watching them run nimbly down the path. Her heart shook again in her breast. She was perhaps a fool.

"Lady, will you eat something before we go up the mountain?" a voice was asking. She turned and looked into a woman's face, thin and leathery brown. She had a bowl of hot rice gruel in her two hands. It was coarse brown rice with nothing to flavor it, but it smelled delicious. She was very hungry.

"Thank you," she said and drank it, and dropping a coin into the empty bowl she set it down on the ground. The sullen man untied two squat strong ponies and led them forward. The saddles were soldier's saddles, high and tasseled with bright silk. But when she had climbed up the seat was comfortable. The man had leaped up with one spring. He turned and looked at her.

"Ready," she said. By now her mother and Orchid would be frantic with fear because she was not to be found. But they could do nothing. The ship would be in open sea, and there was no turning back. There was no radio on that old tub, and so they could not wire her father until they reached Shanghai, two days from now. And in two days she would be home again—unless, that is . . .

The man said suddenly, "How long since you have been here, lady?"

"A long time," she said.

"Ah," he said, "I thought I hadn't seen you. But I've only been here a year. The old farmer died last spring."

She did not answer.

"You'll find the lair very different," he went on, "at least everybody says things are different now with the young Tiger. I don't know—is it the young one or the old one you know?"

"Both," she replied.

"Ah," he said curiously, "kin?"

"Yes," she said. She was lying beautifully. "But I do—I have known them, in a way, all my life," she thought, excusing herself.

They were crossing a narrow bridge, a slab of rough mountain rock thrown across a rushing green torrent, and she held her breath. The man was saying something, but his voice was lost in the roar. Then she was upon the open path again and his voice came loudly.

"—could be worse. The young Tiger is always just to those who are just to him."

"Just," she thought with contempt! She saw her father and the city elders, painfully counting up the Tiger Tax. But she did not answer. She went on planning quickly—she would say to him quite plainly, "I came to say to you—"

"Here is the gate," the man cried. He leaped from his horse and beat upon an iron-studded gate set in a high rocky wall. A little postern gate opened and a rough uncombed head was thrust through.

"Who is it?"

"A relative of the Tiger's," the man said.

"Relative!" the uncombed man cried. "Nobody told me—"

"I have come a long way," Molly said. She slipped from her horse and put a piece of money into her guide's hand. "Thank you," she said. "I will tell my cousin how courteous you have been to me." And before they knew what she was doing, she had pushed into the little gate.

"Tell my cousin I am here," she said. There was a bench by the wall, and she sat down.

"Who is your cousin, in the name of my mother?" the uncombed man demanded, astonished.

"Why, the Tiger," she said and looked at him and made her eyes bright above her quaking heart.

The man stared down at her. "Nobody told me you were coming," he said.

"Nobody knew it," she replied. "But here I am."

He stared at her again, scratched his head, and shambled away. She was left alone. The afternoon sun shone cloudlessly down into a great stone-floored court. At one side was the inner gate through which the man had gone. There was no other sign of life. She waited a long time. The man did not come back. Well, what she had planned she had done. She was alone on this mountain top, the Tiger's mountain. The horses were gone. It was mad—mad. She felt in her bosom. Yes, there it was, the little blue steel pistol. Her father had bought it once from a wandering American who was stranded and needed money. She had crept into the library last night and taken it out of the drawer of her father's desk. Was it only last night? Everything was a dream except this moment. She was sitting on a hard bench in a courtyard of the fortress the old Tiger had built for himself before she was born. "Out of the people's money," she thought, and tried to be angry. But she was beginning to be only afraid. Then suddenly the inner gate creaked and the man was back.

"The Tiger says, by his mother's name, he has no cousin." The man stopped to grin. "But, he asked, were you good-looking." She looked up at him. "I said you were so-so," he said, "and he said you were to come in."

She put her hand in her bosom against the steel and followed him.

"I have to remember," she told herself, "that this is the year 1937, and that I am a graduate of Wellesley, and that—and that—"

She was crossing one courtyard after another. It was not so strange now. There were women and children staring at her, roughly clad, peasant-looking women, and rough staring men— but people. She was glad she had on Orchid's cotton clothes. She was following him now into a hall, a great empty hall. They crossed it, and he opened a door.

"Here she is," he said loudly, and she was in the room.

At a desk a tall man sat writing at a typewriter. He looked up and she saw a bold handsome young face.

"Sit down," he said, and to the serving man he said, "Go away."

She sat down and put her bundle on the floor beside her. When the door was shut, the young man sat staring at her.

"Now tell me why you say you are my cousin when I have no cousin," he said.

He was the Tiger, and she knew it. But her heart was slowing now to its usual beating. She wet her dry lips and smiled. It had been as easy as that.

"I didn't expect to see a typewriter here," she said.

"There's something wrong with it," he said, frowning. "I have worked and worked on it—I very nearly gave it up and threw it over the precipice it has made me so angry. But it's hard to get them, so I wanted to try once more."

"I used to do my papers on one in college," she said. "I'll look at it."

He did not speak while she rose and came over to him. He was dressed in a sort of plain dark uniform of woolen cloth, and his hands upon the keys were big and finely shaped.

"Let me see," she said. "If you will get up—"

He leaped to his feet, and she sat down and studied the machine. Out of the corner of her eye she could see his feet in leather foreign shoes.

"Here is the trouble," she said. "The ribbon must go through this—" She adjusted it quickly and quickly typed off an English sentence— "Now is the time for all good men to come to the aid of the party."

"Do you know English?" he asked astonished.

"I went to college in America," she replied, "and I used a typewriter all the time." She looked up and met his eyes gazing down delightedly into hers.

"I have an English book I have been trying to read," he cried, "I can't understand it—can you—"

"Of course I can," she said, smiling.

He reached into a drawer and pulled out a book.

"Explain it," he commanded her. It was by Karl Marx.

"Tigers," she thought, laughing to herself, "why should anybody be afraid of Tigers?"

"I understand the separate English words," he was saying plaintively, "but I can't understand what he means."

"It will take a long time to explain that," she said. "I'm afraid I can't stay long enough."

"Who are you?" he exclaimed. "Why are you here?"

"I came to see you," she said.

"Weren't you afraid?" he asked.

She wanted to say, "I wasn't in the least afraid." But he had a nice face, an honest face. He was standing beside her, looking down at her, and his dark eyes were steady and good. So she said, "Yes, I was afraid." She put her hand into her bosom, about to take out the pistol and say, "I brought this along." But she did not. After all, he was still the son of the old Tiger. She said instead, "But I had to come for a special purpose."

"What purpose?" he asked. "You needn't be afraid any more."

"I am so hungry," she said. She was not sure now how to say what she had come to say. "I haven't eaten anything since I left the ship—except a bowl of rice."

"A ship?" he repeated. "Who are you? Tell me."

"It doesn't matter," she answered, "a daughter of the people in a city by the sea."

"I've never seen anybody like you," he said slowly. "Your clothes are rough like a bondmaid's, but—you are not a bond-maid. No, I won't let you go until you tell me."

She rose, but he put out his hand imperiously. "Everyone obeys me," he said.

She was fearfully aware of his firm hand on her dress. She drew away from it. After all, she did not know him. It was as well she had kept the pistol hidden. But she was not afraid of him. "He's only a man," she thought.

"I want to wash myself," she said, "and I am hungry."

"Will you promise to come back inside the hour?" he demanded.

She nodded.

"How am I to know if you will do it?" he asked.

"I haven't told you why I came," she replied. "I shan't go away without doing that."

He smiled. "Quick wits," he said and clapped his hands. A manservant came to the door.

"Eh?" he shouted, putting in his head.

"Tell your woman to come here," the Tiger commanded. In a moment an old gray-haired woman was there.

"Take this lady to the rooms where my mother used to sleep," he told her. And he said to Molly, "My mother died last year, and my father has moved into another courtyard. You will be safe and at peace. She was a good woman and her spirit is still there. And I shall wait here until you come back."

He sat down again before the typewriter, and she picked up her bundle and followed the old woman. She did not feel in the least strange, she thought, amazed that it was so. The old woman pushed open a door and she stepped into a large quiet room that opened into another.

"Here," the old woman said, "here are the rooms. It's all clean. I clean them every day. I'll go and fetch hot water and food."

She closed the door, and Molly stood alone in the middle of a big square raftered room. The walls were of rough plastered mud, but the furniture was polished and fine, and the bed curtains were of soft blue silk held back by clasps of gold. It was the private room of a lady. There were books in a case against the wall. She went to look at them. They were all old—old poetry, old philosophy, history. But it was strange that the woman who had lived here could even read. Her own mother could not read such books as these. "Who was she?" she thought. And then she thought, "And what sort of man would her son be?"

She was suddenly eager to be back with him. She wanted to

know him, to find out. She began unbuttoning the coarse garments she wore. "I'm going to wear my own clothes," she thought quickly. She wanted him to see her as she really was. "I must be myself," she thought.

"You see," he was saying earnestly, "why I have to have money."

It was nearly noon of the next day, but she had lost all count of the hours. They had talked last night until he himself said, "You must go now to your rooms, lest these rude people gossip. I have told that old woman to sleep near you and serve you. She was my mother's bondmaid, and my mother, wanting her to be happy, married her to a farmer from the valley. But she was not happy living there and so she came back, bringing her husband with her to serve my father."

But she had not slept until nearly dawn, because the old woman began talking and telling her everything.

"You should have seen how it was in the old days," she began, sitting on the footstool by the bed when she had drawn the silken quilt over Molly's shoulders. "Those were the days of greatness. Every day the old Tiger's men went down into the cities by the sea and they brought back loads of all the things they could carry—silks and jewels and garments of all kinds and fine furniture and bedding and anything we wanted. Everyone was afraid of the Tiger then, and we lived like kings and emperors."

"Isn't it the same now?" Molly asked quietly. For the first time all evening she remembered her father and the old city elders, gathering together the Tiger Tax. The old woman shook her head.

"The young Tiger reads books," she whispered. "That's no

way for a warlord. Swords and weapons, plots and sallies into the towns—that's what he ought to be doing." She leaned forward to whisper more softly. "It's his mother's fault. She taught him how to read. The old Tiger can't read."

"Who was she?" Molly whispered back.

"We don't know," the old woman replied. "A lady from some city—a lady the old Tiger saw and loved. She was a young girl when he brought her here and she did nothing but weep until her son was born, though the old Tiger gave her everything. I can't count on two hands the raids he made for all those fine things. He used to tell the men, 'Look for jade and pearls set in hair ornaments,' and he'd say, 'Bring back books for her.' You see all those books, and there are roomsful beside. But she never stopped weeping until the child was born. She was still then, but she never put her foot beyond that door. She never asked anybody anything. If I began to tell her of some great raid and of all that was brought back, she put her hands over her ears. So I learned to tell her nothing. But you see, she is in the young Tiger. He's not his father." She sighed. "Why, in the old days," she began, leaning her elbows on the bed—and Molly, listening, saw the old days unrolled and heard things she had never dreamed. She saw great roaring dawns and huge breakfasts before battle, she saw hundreds of men running down the mountainside, past flaring torches held at the pass, swarming down into the valley, gathering in attack, bursting into city gates, laughing, drunk, laden with loot.

"Did the young Tiger ever go with them?" she interrupted the old woman.

"Once," said the old woman, "only once—and his mother wept so bitterly that the old Tiger would not let him go again."

"Does he never go now?"

152

"Now!" said the old woman scornfully. "There have been no real raids these ten years. The old Tiger took to opium to ease a pain in his liver, and he lies asleep all the time. We live these days on taxes taken from the people, like magistrates instead of honest robbers, who only take from the rich and spare the poor."

She lay staring at the old woman. This, this, too, was her country. America was very far away. Had she ever been there? Was it not all a dream? Everything seemed a dream except this place where she now was. She fell asleep to the old woman's talking and dreamed she was a prisoner in this room, and still nothing bound her. She was free to walk out of the door, the door was open, but when she went toward it, she could not move. She woke in a sweat of fear. It was morning, and the bed was as warm and soft as her own. But the mountain sunshine that streamed in the window was brighter than any she had ever seen. The door opened, and the old woman came in with a brass basin of hot water and a pot of tea.

"The young master says if you will breakfast with him—" the old woman began.

She sprang out of bed. She was safe, and the evil was only a dream.

They had talked about everything. They wanted to talk about everything at once and it was like leaping together across mountain tops. Someday they would go back over it all, exploring every valley. But now because each must know everything about the other they asked great wide questions, swallowing the answers quickly, gazing at each other.

"I've never seen a girl like you," he said.

They had finished breakfast and in a courtyard in the sun they had gone on talking.

"Tell me why you know English as though it were your own language, and tell me—"

And she asked him, "Why are you what you are? Who was your mother and why do you stay here? Do you know—?"

They told each other everything, and they ate their noon meal and talked and when the sun went down and the mountain air grew cold they ate their night meal and went into the library and sat talking and talking. To him she told how she hated the temple, and how she was weary with idleness and longed to do something, only what? And how she had not wanted Mary Lane to visit her because she was ashamed of a good many things —even of her mother, a little, and her father who did nothing but eat and sleep.

"I have often thought I would like to do something, too!" he said. "I grow very tired of this old fortress, and my father lies half asleep—he's old."

The night grew late and they parted, and the second day passed like the first. She had forgotten that she was in the fortress—or that he was the Tiger.

That second night she thought, startled, "I must go home." Two days! Her mother would be telegraphing her father. She must go in the morning.

But it was hard to go. He took her hand and begged her not to go. He had been so imperious with her at first, he was imperious with everyone, but not with her now. His bold eyes were kind, and she saw only the goodness of his face and not the haughtiness.

"Don't go," he begged her. "There's is so much we have not told each other—and I haven't shown you the mountain."

"I must, I must go," she said. "My father will upset the city to find me."

They looked at each other, aching, longing. They were at the gate now. His own horse stood there to take her, and a man to guide her to the foothills where a sedan was waiting. She stood filled with reluctance. The feeling of the dream returned to her. She was free to go, and somehow she could not.

"When—how—shall we meet?" he whispered.

The guide was looking at them secretly, smiling under his dropped lids. She pulled her hand away.

"You could—" she suggested, "you could raid the city!"

She laughed as she spoke, but he was not laughing. He stood looking at her earnestly. When she was on her horse she turned. He was still looking at her.

All the way down the hills, all the way across the plains, she lived over again the astounding days. Only two mornings ago she had left the ship and her mother and Orchid. But in these hours the whole world was changed. She had never seen anyone like him. Her cousins, the young men in Shanghai—they were weaklings beside that strong straight figure she had left on the top of the mountains. All their clever talk, all their nimble clever brains — "There is no one like him," she thought, the son of a common warlord, but she could never forget him.

The sun was pouring over the rich landscape, over villages and shining canals and green and fertile fields. For the first time she felt the beauty about her as her own. These lands belonged to the Tiger. For years they had paid him tribute. She, too—her own father—paid him tribute. "We all belong to him," she thought, half shyly. "He is like a king over us."

Only when she was at the gate of her own home did she remember suddenly that she had forgotten the little pistol. It was still lying on the table in the room on the top of the mountain where she had slept last night. And then she laughed. She had even forgotten something else. She had forgotten to tell him why she had come.

In the courtyard of her own home the old gateman rubbed his eyes with his knuckles.

"It's not the young mistress!" he cried.

"Yes, it is," she said composedly.

"But you are on the ship, in the midst of the sea!" he cried.

"I am here," she replied. "Where is my father?"

"He is distracted," the old man said. "He is in his library, gnawing his fingers. We gave him food, but he can't eat. We don't know what's the matter."

Ah, he had heard she was gone.

"I will go to him," she said.

She crossed the inner court quickly and opened the library door softly. Her father was at the table, counting a heap of silver dollars. His fat face looked haggard, and the pale flesh hung in folds.

"Father?" she said gently, not to startle him. But he was startled. He looked up, his face like tallow in the hard sunshine.

"Ma-li!" he cried. "You—where is your mother?"

No, he had not heard she was gone. It was some other trouble.

"On the ship," she replied. She came in and shut the door and stood against it. "I didn't go," she said.

"Where have you been?" he asked.

At that moment she saw for the first time that what she had done was impossible, incredible. He would never believe her. For now for the first time it occurred to her that she had gone to a young man's house, a stranger's house. That alone was not to be explained. If she said she had been to the Tiger's Mountain, it would be insane. She shook her head.

"Where have you been?" he repeated.

"I can't tell you, father," she said simply.

He stared at her heavily. "As if I hadn't trouble enough—" he said slowly, "as if I hadn't trouble enough—the Japanese—your mother—how can I betroth you to a respectable young man? Your mother told me before she went to arrange your marriage. 'Arrange her marriage,' she said. 'Girls had better be married in war times.' Just like that, as though I were not having to collect all I possess for that robber! But who will have you at any price? How can I pay a man enough to make you his wife? *Where have you been these two nights?*" he roared at her. He pounded the table, and the heaps of silver dollars shook and fell, glittering in the sunshine. No, she could explain nothing to him.

"You needn't choose a husband for me," she said.

"Don't be silly," he replied peevishly. "It is my duty. Besides, if I don't, how will you ever marry?"

"I will marry," she said breathlessly.

"One of these new love marriages!" he snorted. "No, you will not marry in that fashion! I will choose your husband myself, decently, as my parents chose for me."

She went over to the table and looked down into his angry face.

"But I *have* chosen!" she whispered, and in that moment chose. Before he could speak, she had turned and run out of the room, out of the house, across the courtyards to the gate.

"Where is the sedan?" she cried to the old gateman.

"They went that way." He pointed with his chin up the street toward the mountain, away from the sea. "I never saw such surly fellows. Never one word of what village they came from or what their clan name was—"

But she was not listening. She was hurrying up the street.

There was a teashop near the edge of the town. They might be there, drinking tea, eating food before they went back.

They were there. She saw them, each with a bowl of noodles to his mouth. Everybody was staring at her, but she did not care. She went to them.

"I am ready to go back now," she said in a low voice.

They rose and followed her instantly, without surprise, as though they were waiting for her, and in a moment she was swinging on their shoulders over the country road, back to the mountain.

"I am joining the bandits," she thought in a daze.

No, she wasn't. She was going back to him.

She was going back to him. It was nearly night when she reached the fortress gates. They were open, as though she were expected. Torches were flaring in sockets of bamboo poles thrust into the earth, and the courts were blazing with light. Upon the air there was the odor of spiced roasting meats. She was hungry —hungry and tired. She went through the gates, asking nothing of anyone. She went straight to the room where she knew he was. But he had heard her footsteps. He opened the door and came toward her.

"You are here," he said. "I told them not to leave the city without you."

"You told them—" she faltered.

"They were to wait until nightfall," he said. "If you did not come of your own will, you were to be found and brought back to me."

"Kidnaped!" she whispered. "You were going to kidnap me!"

"Look!" he said. He drew her to a window. Far down below

them lay the darkening country. But in a certain spot there was a great cluster of tiny lights, moving toward the mountain.

"My army," he said. "If you had not come by night, the beacon fire would have been lit on the crest of the mountain, and they would have gone to your house and brought you back to me."

"I've kidnaped myself for you!" she cried, stupefied at what she had done.

He smiled down at her, not speaking.

"I think I am glad I came by myself," she said, slowly.

"In any case you would have come," he answered. "I had planned that before you went away."

He had planned everything, she found next day. She slept so deeply in her room that she felt she could never wake. But in the morning the old woman was shaking her awake.

"Your lord commands you," she was saying. "Your lord—"

Her lord! They were taking everything for granted. But she woke to the words and meekly she rose and bathed and dressed herself.

"You are to wait in the great hall," the old woman said. And in the great hall she waited, a little cold because the sun was not warm yet, and the hall was so big and flagged with stone. A servant brought food, and she ate it hungrily, and then he came, very formal and handsome in long robes of brocaded blue satin. She had not seen him dressed like that, and for a moment she was afraid. What was she doing, Molly Chu, graduate of Wellesley, American trained—a robber's son—a medieval man—

"Since we are to be formally betrothed today—" he began stiffly.

"I don't—I think I don't want to marry you," she cried wildly. "I think I—I want to go home."

159

He looked at her.

"You cannot," he said firmly. "It is I who choose." In his voice there was the sound of gates clanging, closing. If she ran away now there would be no waiting horse, no ready sedan. She was really kidnaped!

"Yesterday you came to me of your own will," he was saying. "But I know how women are. Today I am prepared to keep you, whether you will or not." He clapped his hands and the old manservant came in. "Tell my father," he commanded, "that we will present ourselves to him at once. At noon let the feast of betrothal be ready." He bowed to Molly. "Today we are betrothed, and tomorrow we will be married."

"No," she whispered, "no—it's too quick—I'm not sure—"

Her home rushed into her mind—her father, her mother—the rooms where she had played and slept—college, the American girls, Mary Lane—Mary would never believe all this—it couldn't happen except in China. "No—no!" she cried.

"You have your commands," he said to the manservant, and the manservant bowed and went away.

"Come with me," he ordered her in exactly the same tone of voice, and she obeyed him, not knowing what else to do. In a few moments she was standing beside him, in front of an old feeble man, sitting in a huge carved chair, wrapped in tiger skins. He had a great fleshless head. Every bone of the skull started from the skin. Over a beautiful sullen old mouth drooped wide long gray mustaches, and above the mouth sullen eyes burned through a gray film. It was the old Tiger.

"Bow to our father," the old Tiger's son was commanding her. And she bowed.

So she was married to him. They were over, the incredible two

days of betrothal, of marriage. They were over in a daze of noise
and wild feasting, of firecrackers and flaring torches and bonfires.
The old woman, setting the head veil of a bride on her head, had
chuckled.

"What the valley people will think!" she cried. "They will see
the fire and hear the noise and shake in their beds. The men are
beseeching The Tiger to let them raid some town for their
pleasure. They have eaten and drunk so much that they are half
mad."

The valley people! Her father was in the valley. She had come
here to plead for her father, to tell the Tiger angrily what she
thought of bandit warlords in this day and time, and instead . . .

"Now you are beautiful!" the old woman had said briskly.
"Ah, we are happy!" she had gone on volubly. "We have been
wanting him to marry for years. But he is so willful—he would
have his own choosing. A hundred women have wanted him—
why, half the women we capture will not leave the mountain
until he makes them go—"

She had wanted to tear the veil off her head.

"But when he sent the men after you," the old woman's voice
was laughing, "we all rejoiced. We never knew him to care before whether a woman lived or died."

Yes, he had sent after her. If she had not come of her own will,
he would have forced her to come back to him. She set the bead-
veiled crown more firmly on her head.

"A man like the young Tiger needs a young wife," the old
woman was saying as she knelt to adjust the folds of the embroidered skirt which once the Tiger's mother had worn at her
own wedding. The brocade waistband was tight for her now, and
they had had to move the buttons before she could wear it. "Now
that you are come, perhaps he will want to fight again as he

should and gain back what he has lost to the north of the mountain. The Blue Wolf seized it."

"I never heard of it," Molly said.

"You wouldn't," the old woman said carelessly. "Everybody
says as a warlord the Blue Wolf is nothing—nothing at all. It's
his woman that is the real one—a wonderful woman, everybody
says. It's she, really—There, you are ready."

She had forgotten the old woman's chatter. She was ready. She
went out and in the presence of the assembled army she drank
the wine mingled with his, and beside him knelt to his family
gods.

"Ma-li Chu," she had heard an American college president's
voice saying not a year ago, as she stood to receive her degree,
"it is with peculiar pleasure that I bestow upon you the degree of
Bachelor of Arts, knowing that yours is an opportunity un-
parelleled in your country to forward the light of civilization and
modern culture and science. Few women in our times are so
fortunate."

Ten thousand miles away, upon a wild mountain top, in the
presence of a robber band, she now knelt before these ancient
gods of clay. It was all over, irrevocably over. She had drunk the
wine mingled with his and eaten of the rice from his bowl.

"Who," she asked him teasingly, because she knew very well,
"is the Blue Wolf?"

They had been married four days, four beautiful, long, sunny
days. The fortress had stood in complete peace, wrapped about in
a haze of sunshine clear above the misted valleys. The hordes of
men were gone. She did not ask where because she did not want
to know—not yet. She put everything away from her, except the
moments of these days alone with him. Beneath the mists in the

valley there were her father and mother of whom she must think. Her mother would turn and come home again, weeping, mourning. And her father would be dazed, not knowing whether he had really seen her or whether she was a ghost. They would be in such grief—she must tell them everything. But not yet. This man whom she had married was a wonder and a dream—a medieval baron, and a boy of her own age. She would change him, she thought. She would take that self-confident lordly power of his and shape it to the times. But first she must find out all that he was, listen to him, watch him, let him pour himself out in talk of his great plans. It was as though there were no government, no rulers in the land. He was planning a simple enlargement of the realm over which he ruled, whose people paid him tax.

"I am going to make a big army," he said, "an army of young men trained in all the things I have heard about. Airplanes— guns—" From among his books he had pulled out a book about the construction of bombing planes and another on modern cannon.

"I hate wars," she had said violently.

He had opened his eyes. "What then?" he asked.

"You ought to do something for the people," she said. "Make schools, for instance."

But he had thought of schools.

"People's schools," he said.

He pressed her to know about American schools, Russian schools. She might have been talking to a young American man, a rich man's son turned communist, his father's conscience. Then someone had called him, and when in an hour he came back he was a savage.

"I shall fight that Blue Wolf," he cried. "He has robbed an-

163

other village on the south of the mountain. I've tried peace—it's no good. I'll fight and cut off his head with my own sword."

They were in his own room, a big square room, full of his books, his enormous bed, his carved chair, the carved chest. He was rummaging in a big camphor-wood chest. From its depths he brought out a great old curved sword and drew it out of its scabbard. He was so changed, his face was so furious, that she felt she had never seen him before.

"Only a few minutes ago you were talking about schools for the people," she said.

"I shall teach them more than books in these schools," he said grimly. "They shall be taught to fight."

He was gone. He shut the heavy wooden door behind him so loudly that dust flew from its cracks. She sat, motionless, struck by his fierce looks, by his rough words. What was this man she had married so madly and so soon?

The fortress was a bedlam of noise and shouting. It swarmed with men, coarse, rough, wild, their eyes bold, their hair long and uncombed. Where had they come from? They poured up the mountain. When she looked out she could see them climbing the narrow rocky paths like goats, leaping nimbly up and up. There was the clanging of blacksmiths' hammers upon anvils, the smell of fresh leather, and the whinnying of horses.

"Stay in your rooms," the Tiger ordered her, and at first she obeyed him. From her windows she looked into the busy court-yards. The old Tiger came out of his sleep and stood, holding his long dragon-headed staff, his white beard flying in the wind. He kept shouting out advice in his weak old voice.

"You must use retreat as a woman uses her fan!" he cried.

"Woo your enemy with retreat until he has advanced to the point you have set for battle!"

A roar went up from the men. "Yes, yes, old Tiger!" they roared amiably.

Thus encouraged he shouted again, "The aggressors are not the victorious at last!" He waited and gathered his breath again. "Retreat and stand and bide your time—and strike!"

"Yes, yes, old Tiger!" they cried, admiring him.

But the young Tiger wasted no time in shouting. He was in his library, planning. Upon the desk was a huge map of the mountain and all the country about it. She stole in and found him poring over it, drawing black firm lines along roads and circles about towns. When he heard her he looked up.

"A month from today I shall be there." He pointed his finger at a spot. "It is the Blue Wolf's camp."

She looked into his eyes. He did not know she was there. He had not thought of her for hours. Something bitter and angry rushed into her heart.

"What of me?" she asked.

"What do you mean, what of you?" he answered.

"Where shall I be?"

"Where you are now," he replied, astonished, "at home, waiting for me."

"No," she said quickly, "no, I won't be. You are wrong. I won't be here when you come back."

She ran out of the room and away and into her own room, and throwing herself on her bed began to weep with her whole heart, not knowing why she did, except that he was leaving her.

And after a moment he came in. She felt his hand on her shoulder.

"Tell me what you meant when you said you would not be here when I came back," he demanded.

She did not answer. She lay still, feeling herself grow sullen and contrary as a child because she loved him and because he was willing to leave her. He turned her over strongly, and held her down by the shoulders and stared into her face.

"Do you hear me?" he asked.

She struggled free, sat up, and smoothed back her hair. "I meant simply what I said," she replied coldly. After all, she was not a child. "All this fighting," she went on, "it's absurd."

That was the beginning of the great quarrel.

The war waited while they quarreled. She would not leave her room. He came in and they quarreled and he flung himself away from her again. Outside the men muttered and shouted and horses stamped and shook their heads. The old Tiger forgot all his advice and went back to his opium while they waited. She was alone in her room for hours while he sat in his library, his head sunk in his hands over the map he no longer studied. She did not read, she did not write the letter she had planned to her parents. Why should she write when at any moment she would be leaving to return to them? He had not yielded, except that he had not yet gone. But at any moment he might go. He had ordered that the horses be kept saddled and waiting and no man was to go down the mountain. So it had been for nearly three days, for so long they had quarreled.

It had all begun out of that moment of her jealousy, and it had grown and grown into a monstrous thing from which neither could retreat. For she had said if he went out to this silly war she would go home and never come back. And he had said he would order the gates locked so that she would be a prisoner.

And she said, "I'll hate you forever, then. My body may be here, but you will have lost me forever."

"Why?" he demanded.

"Because you would be too stupid, too crude, for any woman to love, except a woman as ignorant as yourself," she replied recklessly.

"I am not ignorant!" he had roared at her.

"You are, you are!" she cried. "Why, what other country has men like you? Why, I would be ashamed—ashamed before my American friends."

"You can go to America and I would not care," he muttered and flung himself out of the room.

And then he was back again and he shouted, "I don't know why I don't kill you and go on about my business!"

"Kill me!" she demanded. "It's all you know how to do!"

"No woman's worth all this!" he said, beside himself, and flung himself out again. But he did not kill her. And she waited, loving him and so angry she could have bitten her own hands.

Once he came in, deceptive and gentle, and sat down, his sword hanging at his side, and though she hated him, she told herself, she could not help seeing how handsome he was and loving him.

"Ma-li," he began, "what is this feeling you have against my way of life? I am a chieftain, and the son of a chieftain."

"You are a rebel against the government," she retorted. "There is a price on your head."

"Government!" he said scornfully. "Governments come and go. In the last twenty years there have been three. But I—"

"Do you know how the people hate you?" she cried passionately. "Do you know how the Tiger Tax oppresses them?"

"It's a lie," he said slowly. "I take from the rich, but never from the poor. It is against the tradition of all righteous robbers."

"My father—" she began.

"He is a rich man," he broke in, "and you are his daughter!"

She looked at him and began to laugh wildly.

"As if there could be such a silly thing as a righteous robber!" she cried. "Certainly there is no such person anywhere else in the world. A robber! I've married a common robber! I don't know any righteous robbers!"

He was gone again. The wall shook to the bang of the door. She leaned her arms on the table and bent her head down on them.

Then after a long time the door opened gently, and she listened without looking up. He had come back. If he had come back, she would beg him—but it was not he. It was the old woman. She tiptoed in.

"The men are growing angry over the delay," she whispered. "They are plotting something."

She lifted her head to look at the old woman.

"I heard talk. 'Get the woman—it is the woman,' they said. That's you, lady!"

And suddenly, staring into the rough, wrinkled old face and shrewd eyes, Molly was terrified. She leaped to her feet.

"I want to go home," she panted. "I wish I weren't here. I wish I had never come—they're beasts and savages. I don't know what I ever thought I could do."

She ran out of the room, across the hall, into the library. She would tell him to go on to his wars. She gave up. She wanted to go home because she wished she had never seen him. They were two who should never have been mated, a woman like her and a man like him. It was finished. She cared no more.

But when she reached the doorway he was standing by his

desk. He had taken off his sword, and he looked at her out of dark and troubled eyes, holding his sword in his hands.

"You are right," he said before she could speak, and his voice was so humble it was not his. "I know I am ignorant and a coarse crude man. If I lost you, I'd have no light ahead. You came to me like light that day. I will do anything you say. I love you."

They looked at each other and she forgot the old woman and the plotting men. She ran to him, holding out her arms.

"Why did we quarrel?" she whispered, and strained herself against him.

And she heard his sword clatter upon the stone floor.

It was hard to believe that they could ever have quarreled. They loved each other desperately. In the morning he went out and brusquely he told his men to go home to their farms and villages. There would be no war against the Blue Wolf.

"Never?" they asked, dismayed.

"No," he said abruptly.

He ordered money to be given them, and they went away in dazed silence, looking at each other. It was as though a king had stepped from his throne for a woman, only there was no heir, and they were left without a ruler. They went home, not knowing what to do, since so long as they could remember they had obeyed the Tiger, old and young.

"We have nothing left but the government now," they said mournfully as they went slowly away.

"What's the government?" another answered.

And in the quiet fortress alone with her the Tiger looked at Molly.

"What shall I do now?" he asked her, like a child.

She was overwhelmed with him and for a moment she was afraid. The fortress was strange about her.

"Let's go home," she said breathlessly. "I want to go to my home."

"I will do whatever you tell me to do," he said.

Before the day was at noon they were down the mountain and crossing the plains. And she, behind the curtains of her sedan, was planning what she would do. Her mother would be there by now, and she would walk quietly in with him. "Father, Mother," she would say, "this is my husband." Then she would wait a moment and then she would say, "He is the son of the Tiger."

After that—it was impossible to tell what would happen after that.

"Father," she was saying, "Mother, this is my husband."

In the library the two old people sat staring at her. Her mother was dressed in mourning. She wore white shoes and a white cord was bound into her hair. But her father was as usual.

"I thought you were dead," her mother whispered. "Young people kill themselves so easily nowadays. I thought you were angry with us for something."

"I told you it wasn't her ghost I saw," her father said.

Their old minds could not grasp it quickly enough. She was here—this tall young man—

"Your husband!" her mother repeated. "I don't know him."

"I've never seen him," her father muttered, looking away from them.

"I told you I had chosen," she reminded him.

"It's never been done like this," he answered, and still he would not look at her.

Then she said exactly as she had planned, "He is the son of the Tiger."

She was not sure they heard her at all. But her father looked up suddenly, his mouth open.

"There's something the matter with you," he said. "You—you're beside yourself—"

"She shouldn't have gone to America," her mother cried.

Molly turned to the Tiger. "Speak to them," she told him.

"What shall I say?" he asked.

"Anything," she said, "so they can hear your voice, and know you are real."

So he said, very pleasantly and simply, "She—your daughter—came to my house to—" He looked at Molly, taken aback. "You never told me why you came," he interrupted himself.

"It was like this, Father," she said quickly. "I saw you so worried that day with the city elders, and I made up my mind I'd go alone and see what the Tiger was and tell him how wicked he was to go on oppressing the people the way he had for years and years. I thought, 'He is only an ignorant old man. If someone told him he might change—if someone told him that he was a disgrace to our people'—and I really went to save you, Father."

Her father gasped, and then he coughed behind his hand. "I see," he said, "and so you brought the Tiger home with you."

"Oh, how I prayed the gods, too!" her mother wailed suddenly. "I prayed that you would be wed before the month was out—but they played a trick on me."

"I told you it wasn't safe to tell the gods things you want," her father said grimly. "They have such a sense of mischief—they grant prayers so wryly."

They sat in stricken silence. Suddenly the Tiger cleared his throat.

"I am not so bad," he said. "You might try me."

"If the gods sent him, Mother," said Molly, laughing, "you ought to accept him."

They clasped hands and looked steadily into the two old dubious bewildered faces.

But they could think of him only as the Tiger.

"He is very large," her mother said faintly one morning. "The house seems small for him."

Do what she would Molly could not get her parents to forget he was the Tiger. She gave him a name of her own—"Brave Peace" she called him. "Because of his own will he gave up being a warlord," she explained.

"What are you going to do with him?" her father asked one night. "He's not used to cities. He paces up and down like a beast in a cage. It can't go on."

And indeed she was beginning to see herself that something must be done. The soft peace of the old house was stifling to the Tiger.

"I can't breathe in this air," he complained. "The warm sea winds choke me—I'm used to the mountains."

He was full of remorse, too, that he had left the old Tiger.

"I shouldn't have left my father like that, so suddenly," he said to her again and again. "It's against what Confucius told us."

"He was asleep," she argued. "You know you said yourself he would sleep all day. And for days you didn't go near him."

"It's against Confucius," he repeated.

"Oh, people don't take Confucius for a god these days," she said half petulantly.

"Confucius was good," he argued.

"Go back if you want to," she cried at him. "No, no," she said quickly, "I don't mean it."

He did not go back. Sometimes she was sure he would never go back, sometimes after the long hours they were alone together. For there were those hours when they fell again into long intimate talk, and she saw his mind, untrained but powerful, and full of energy. She put aside all jealousy and angers then and wished with humility that she knew how to direct this energy. He was a man who could be made into anything if she knew how to do it.

"Would you like to study?" she asked him one day.

"What?" he asked.

"Many things," she replied, "books, science—"

"Yes," he said eagerly.

She fetched her old college books, and for hours they were happy together. Then suddenly he would stretch himself, leap to his feet, and go out into the courtyard and begin his quick pacing. It was that sturdy restless tread that made her father shake his head and say, "It's a beast caged."

"I never thought I'd be afraid of my son-in-law," her mother said faintly, "but I'll always be afraid of him."

"I'm afraid of him, too," Orchid whispered. "Everybody is afraid of him."

And suddenly Molly was afraid of him, not any more as the Tiger, but now as a man, a restless able domineering man, born and trained as a king is to command and to do, and now there was nothing to do. He was there, constantly with her, demanding everything of her. He was stretching her very brain with his demands upon her. She was studying as she had never studied in college that she might answer his ruthless questions into every book they read. And she saw that this learning would never be enough for him. She began to wake in the night afraid. Suppose she, too, one day were not enough for him?

She grew thin with her worry over him. He was too much for her—too strong, too willful, too restless.

"We must go out," she thought. She planned in the darkness. "If we go to Shanghai, it will amuse him."

When morning came she asked him, "Would you like to go to Shanghai?"

"Why should I go to Shanghai?" he said.

"To—to see all the new things," she told him. "You've never seen moving pictures and automobiles—you might like to dance, even. I do."

"Ha!" he said shortly. "Stuff for children."

She coaxed him. "Shall we have some feasts to celebrate our coming home?"

He grinned a little at this. "Do you think your friends would relish feasting with the Tiger?" he asked.

She did not answer. No, they wouldn't. Her father had been worrying over it. "I ought to give a wedding feast," he said, "in decency, that is. But my friends would be afraid to come. I know how they feel. I wouldn't come near the Tiger if I didn't know what he really is—just a young man—very restless, though, Ma-li, very restless!"

"What shall I do with him?" she asked herself desperately.

And then, one day, suddenly, he was gone. He had leaped to his feet in one of his restless fits and, striding into the courtyard, he had begun to walk up and down in the way she was learning to dread. She had looked after him, not knowing whether to go to him or not. Across the court she saw her father's grave face in a window. He was watching the young man, too, his eyes full of pity. It was that pity which she could not endure. She turned and ran into her room and shut the door. What could she do with this man she had married? There was no place for him in this house. If they went to Shanghai—but what would he do in Shanghai? She thought of her cousins, debonair dapper young men, working in offices by day, dancing at some club at night—they would shrink from this big, abrupt, uncultivated man. If she tried to teach him to dance, he would say, "What is this nonsense? I am no child." She could not imagine him following her into a theater meekly, or sitting beside her in an automobile. No, he would never do in Shanghai.

She crept to her bed and behind its curtains she began to weep, because whatever he was she loved him, and because she knew she could not make him happy. She rose at last, and, sighing, she wiped her face and smoothed back her hair. She would try again. She went to find him, and he was gone. The courtyard where he had been was empty. A cat sat crouched beneath a bird cage someone had hung on a bamboo tree, that was all. It was after noon of the summer's day, and the air was still. She listened and could hear no sound, except the soft murmur of the city from beyond the wall.

At first she thought, "He has gone into one of the other courts." She walked quietly from one court to another. But he was in none of them. Then she walked through the house. He was not there. In the library her father was asleep, his fan over his face. Her mother was in her rooms. Even Orchid was not to be seen. It was the hour when even the servants were sleeping. She went to the gate, and the old gateman sat sleeping on his wooden bench, his head thrown back against the wall and his mouth open.

She called to him sharply. "Has anyone—has my lord gone through the gate?"

175

He mumbled himself awake. "No—no—" he muttered, smacking his dry mouth, "no—no—no—"

"You wouldn't have known it if an army had come in," she cried. And then she looked at the gate. The bar was drawn back. She looked in the dust of the threshold. It was full of footprints —the footprints of big wide-soled shoes, the shoes that the bandits wore, the padded soles that clung to rocks and rough paths. Had they come for him, and had he gone back to them? And instantly this house was empty for her.

"I shall follow him," she cried to her heart. She ran back to the room and changed her garments and put on her strong American shoes and took her purse. She would go straight to the mountain after him.

And slipping through the quiet house, she drew the front gate softly open. The old gateman was asleep again. Outside on the street she bargained swiftly with the bearers.

"It is midsummer, and the sun is hot. There must be extra tea money," they said.

"Yes," she promised, "double tea money—anything."

And when she was safely hidden behind the curtains she began to plan wildly. They would live on the mountain—she would let him be what he liked—anything, anything if he could be happy.

At the foothills, where she paused for an hour, she asked the sullen farmer, "When did my lord pass?"

He shook his head. "No one has passed here today." He might never have seen her before. There was no recognition in his eyes.

"He did—he did!" she cried.

He thrust his chin at the tethered horses. "There his horse is," he said calmly. It was true. His horse was there, a black Mongolian that he always rode. He had not passed. She wavered. Far above her was the fortress. As the light lay now from the sun she could barely see its gray walls. Beneath her was the blue sea and the town and her home.

"Saddle me a horse," she commanded him.

"He is not—" the man began, without moving.

"Obey me," she said. "I am his wife, and you know it."

It was night when she reached the fortress gates. They were locked, but she beat upon them. She had come alone, knowing her way, not wanting the sullen-faced man to be with her. The gate opened. It was the old manservant. He peered out at her.

"Is your master here?" she demanded.

"Only the old one," he said, "—sleeping."

He was not there. What had happened to him? Where could she find him now? Her head drooped with weariness.

"I will come in and sleep," she said.

He opened the gate and let her in, and she slipped from her horse and walked through the courts. There was no one to be seen, until she came to the inmost court. There was the old woman, eating a bowl of rice gruel. She looked up, swallowed, and rose.

"You, lady!" she mumbled and looked away.

"Yes," said Molly. Across her mind sprang a flash. These people —the old man, this hag—they knew where he was, and she would pry it from them. If she did not find him her life would be nothing but this passing from one emptiness to another. Around her the fortress stood, empty of everything except the night wind. She went into her old room and opened the drawer of the table. There it was—her little pistol she had forgotten. The old woman followed her in, champing her jaws a little, chewing the fragments of salted vegetable in her rice.

"Do you want—?" she began.

But Molly went quickly to the door and stood against it.

177

"Now! she said steadily, "tell me where he is."

She pointed the pistol into the old woman's face and waited.

"I was going to tell you," the old woman mumbled. Sweat broke out on her forehead.

"Tell me now," Molly said.

"He has been taken," she whispered, "by mistake."

"What mistake?"

"It was you they wanted."

"Who?"

"The men."

"Why?"

"Because they said you held them back from their rights of war. So they sold you."

"Sold me?"

"To the Blue Wolf. You were to be taken—from your home."

"When?"

"Today—at the time for sleeping. Two men were to come in saying they—"

"Who were they?"

"They were to lead the Blue Wolf's men."

"Then what?"

"There were others waiting to rush in, if needful."

"I heard no one."

The old woman's whisper sank. "No, they enticed the Tiger to the gate of your house, so that they might enter more easily. They said his father—"

"But he is gone."

"The Blue Wolf's men took him."

"And his own men?"

"They were so afraid when they saw the Tiger taken instead of you that they ran."

"Did they say nothing?"

"They said, 'It was the woman we sold to you—not he.'"

"And then?"

"The Blue Wolf's men said, 'But we have been told to bring the man.' So they ran."

"It is not like my husband to let himself be bound," Molly said slowly. It was hard to believe.

"Ah, lady, there were five men to hold him—strong men."

"And no one saw?"

"It was the sleeping hour. They had a cart waiting, and three men were behind the curtains to bind him."

"Who plotted this?"

"His own men—two of them—"

"Send for them—no—wait—I am going home."

"Lady! Not by night!"

"Yes—now—I have his horse. It is sure-footed."

She put the pistol in her bosom and without waiting for food she mounted the horse again. She must believe the old woman.

It was nearly dawn when she reached home. She had ridden all the way. The gateman let her in, his eyes staring. She did not speak. She went straight to her father's room. He cried out when he saw her, "Ma-li! What?"

"Father," she interrupted him, "Father, give me the Tiger Tax. I need it. I must have it."

She felt her head begin to swim. It had been so long since she had eaten or slept. She swayed and fell.

How long she slept she did not know. But when she woke, everything she had planned leaped into her mind. She sat up. She needed a great deal of money, enough for an army. She would gather an army and go against the Blue Wolf—the Tiger's

179

own army. She would collect them all somehow, buy them guns. Once there had been a Chinese girl in history who had taken her father's armies because he was old and had led them to successful battle. The door opened suddenly, and her father came in, a telegram in his hand. His face was gray.

"We are lost," he said haggardly.

"What is it?" she cried. "Oh, something has happened to him."

"I don't know what you mean," he said. "The country's lost—the Japanese have come to Shanghai. Your uncle says—"

Her mind ran ahead of the words. The Japanese—then the last bogey of her childhood was real—everything was absurd—anything could happen—the Japanese—

"They will sweep the coast with their bombs," her father cried. "We'll all be killed. Oh!" he wailed, "we aren't ready—no one is ready—no armies trained—no generals—"

"If he were here," she said, "he would do something—Why, he has an army—it's all ready—"

They were staring at each other.

"Where is he?" her father asked.

"I know where he is," she said breathlessly. "The Blue Wolf—they kidnaped him—I wanted the money—to—"

"You shall have it," he declared. "It was to have been given them days ago, but no one came for it."

"An airplane," she said recklessly, "a little airplane that can land in a small space on a mountain—in a courtyard, even—and a pilot."

"I will telegraph your uncle in Shanghai for one to come here," he said.

"It must be big enough to bring him back," she said.

He nodded and went out. She sat a moment, her mind whirl-

ing madly. "It's a mad country," she thought, "it's all mixed together—the Blue Wolf and the Japanese—he and I—"

She had flown once in America, just to know what it was like.
She and Mary Lane had flown to Washington on a holiday to
see the Japanese cherry blossoms. And standing under the delicate flowers, shattering in the breeze, falling in fragrant drifts,
she had forgotten that her father had taught her always to hate
Japan. People who could give cherry blossoms could not be enemies. But bombs were dropping over Shanghai, like flower petals
out of the sky.

This being braced into the cockpit of a little plane was not in
the least like the great luxurious passenger plane. Even the earth
did not look the same. Here it looked too close, too clear. The
pilot was a young Chinese from Shantung. They had had to
speak in English because their dialects were different.

"Tell him to be careful," her father had said, his old face a
knot of anxiety.

"My father has never seen an airplane," she said to the pilot
instead. "He is anxious."

"He need not be," the young man said. "I spend half my time
in the air."

"Training?" she asked.

"For Japanese," he explained. "We get as many as we can."

The engine began to roar and they were mounting. The city
dropped away from them and the sea lay like a huge blue bubble.
She wanted to say proudly, "My husband will bring his army
against them," but when she opened her mouth the words were
torn out of it by the wind. They were going straight up, and she
clutched the sides of her seat. Three days it took to reach the

Blue Wolf's mountain, everybody said, three days by horse and foot.

"A little over three hours," the young man had said when they started. "I want to get back to Shanghai tonight. The money you give me will buy a load of bombs."

"I will double it," her father had said.

They began to drive into the eastern sky. The dawn was turning to day and they were rushing to meet the sun. The clouds flew by. Below them the land became a green blur, the shining spots were ponds, and a streak of light was a canal. This was to-day; she was going to her love on the wings of today. In the villages below them men and women were beginning their age-old life, the women to cook on age-old earthen stoves, the men to harness water buffaloes to age-old wooden ploughs. And in a little while she would drop into an ancient fortress. What she would find there she did not know, except that he would be there. He must be there. They could not kill him. She had not thought of it, that they might kill him. And yet they were his enemies—she had forgotten that. If he were dead, she would gather up his armies and sweep them from the earth. She would buy a bombing plane and drop bombs down upon them like falling petals.

"Faster!" she cried, but again the wind tore the word from her.

The pilot was circling slowly, close above the mountains now, searching them. They were barren mountains, covered only with a scanty green. He nodded and she looked down. There, between the two crests of a mountain was a shallow valley, and in the valley were low houses built of mountain rock. A wall encircled them. It must be the Blue Wolf's camp. There was nothing else anywhere near. Besides, he had gone to the magistrate's office and asked exactly the location of the mountain. They had given him a map. Everybody knew where the robbers lived, because merchants had to be warned if they went over the mountain pass. He began to slide rapidly down. The wind stopped roaring and now she could shout to him.

"You are to wait with your engine ready. The instant we come, be ready! We may come running for our lives."

He nodded. Below them tiny figures were gathering out of the stone huts. She could see their faces upturned, their arms upraised. The plane dropped suddenly and they scattered.

"They are afraid," she said to him. "They've never seen a plane. Keep your engine ready, I say!"

He nodded, and she felt the plane strike the earth once, twice, and then stand quivering. Men were looking out of doors and coming toward them, half fearfully. She leaped to the ground lightly, and facing them, she made her voice bold.

"Where is your lord?" she demanded. "I have come to see him." She had determined that she would say nothing of the Tiger, lest she be taken prisoner. No, let them wonder who she was.

No one answered. They looked at each other. If she had never seen their like before she might have been afraid of them. But she knew them—they were the same rude, wild malcontents that followed any warlord.

"You had better speak," she said quietly. "I come with important news for him." She turned to the plane. "You can see I have come in haste, by a ship through the air."

"Is that what it is?" a man asked curiously. "When I saw it I thought it was an eagle."

"We have heard of them but we haven't seen them," another said. They were like big children, wanting to touch the strange thing and afraid to do it. They had forgotten what she had asked.

"Take me to your master, and while I am gone you may look at it," she said.

They looked at each other and one of them laughed sheepishly.

"The truth is, lady," he said, "we haven't a master. The Blue Wolf is a woman."

"A woman?" She stared, unbelieving, from one face to the other.

"The Blue Wolf died last spring," the man said. "But no one knew."

"His woman told us not to tell," another man said. "She told us that she could lead us as well as any man."

They nodded. "Yes, she has done it, too."

"Take me to her!" Molly demanded.

A woman! She longed to ask where he was, what they had done with him. Perhaps he was already dead. At least he was bound and in one of these huts, a prisoner. It was going to be harder to free him if a woman . . .

"Well, I will lead you," one of the men said at last. And she followed him. Her hand was in her pocket and her pistol lay in her palm.

What sort of woman could this one be, she wondered, so bold as to take a warlord's place? There had been a few such—stories were told of them among the people. Orchid used to tell her the stories. But they were fairy tales, and this woman was a real woman.

"Here," said the man, "that's her door. Go in if you like. I will not tell her. She has such a temper that she would kill me if she knew it was I who led you here."

He was gone, and she was left standing before a closed door. She stood a moment and then softly she laid her ear against the wood. Listening, she could hear a murmur of voices, no, two voices. One was the woman's. She could hear it, clear and rather loud. The other voice—it was a man's, and she knew it. It was his. She pushed the door suddenly with both hands, and it flew open. There was the Tiger. A woman was sitting in a great carved chair, and he was standing beside her, looking down at her. When the door opened the woman's voice broke clearly into her ears.

"Together," the woman was saying, "together we could do anything."

Then the woman saw her and, seeing the look on her face, the Tiger turned and his hand dropped.

"You!" he said.

"Yes," she said quietly. He came a step toward her, but she did not move. "I thought I should find you bound," she said. She gazed straight into his eyes, accusing him.

"I was brought here bound," he answered.

"You are free now," she said. She heard her own voice.

"This woman had me freed," he said. "My ankles are still sore from those thongs," he said. He laughed. "It was partly my own fault. I fought against them."

"Who is she?" Molly moved her chin toward the woman a very little.

He laughed again. "Here is a strange thing—there is no Blue Wolf. It's she who has led his armies all these months. I've been fighting a woman!"

But Molly did not laugh. "What was she saying when I came in?" she demanded of him.

He turned to the woman. "What was it you were saying?"

Now she could look at the woman. She was a dark wild-looking peasant woman, young and big as a man, dressed in an old-

185

fashioned embroidered coat of plum color. Her skin was brown and red, and her mouth was full-lipped and yet hard. She looked at the Tiger as if Molly were not there and she said in the same voice in which she had been speaking when Molly came in, "If you and I join one to the other, our armies, our lands, our very selves, who could conquer us? We could overthrow the government as others have done before us, and we could bring back the empire. You would be emperor and our sons would be princes."

"I never heard such stuff!" Molly cried. She ran to the Tiger and took his arm in both her hands and clung to him. "You wouldn't believe her!"

But he did not move. He was looking into the woman's handsome dark face. Molly dropped his arm suddenly, and took a step toward the woman.

"Are you declaring war against me?" she demanded of her.

"Go back to Shanghai," the woman said. "That is where women like you belong. What do you know of war?"

The Tiger did not speak. He stood looking at the woman, and Molly could not endure the hesitation in his look. He did not move toward her, he did not smile. There was only that steady pondering in his eyes. He was deciding what it was he wanted to do.

"Have you forgotten me?" she cried.

"I was born to fight," he said, "not to sit around in cities."

His voice was sullen, and then he turned away from them both and went and stood by a window.

"Do you choose her instead of me?" she asked him, and was angry that her voice sounded so faint.

"I don't choose a woman," he said. "I choose a life."

"But she's asking you to go back into the past!" Molly cried.

186

"My men have guns, too," the woman said proudly, "and swords and spears."

Molly laughed with fury. "What use are they? Why, war now comes out of the sky! In a few hours a city is destroyed—by a few men!"

"It's your evil magic," the woman cried. "But I can kill you before you—"

"It's not mine, stupid," Molly said scornfully. "It's the magic of the new world. No one can stop it. It wouldn't matter whom you killed here on top of this mountain." She turned to the Tiger. "She doesn't know anything, locked up in these mountains!"

"Why should I believe you?" the woman asked.

But Molly gave her no heed. She had gone to her husband and taken his hand in both her own and she stood holding it against her breast. It was like holding a stone to her heart, but she pressed it there.

"Come with me," she said.

He did not answer, and the woman leaned forward in her chair.

"Your army and mine—" she said to him.

Molly dropped his hand. The real war was between her and this woman.

"Do you choose her?" she demanded. "A peasant, who can't write her name? Is this the one you want to be the mother of your son?"

She had begun quietly and bravely, but suddenly her blood broke its restraint and pounded through her body. She flew at the Tiger and seized him by the shoulders to shake him. He was twice as heavy as she, but she shook him. "I hate you!" she cried at him. "You know no woman but me shall bear your sons!"

He was looking into her eyes. A slow smile was creeping up from the depths of him.

"Will you come back to the fortress if I let you bear my sons?" he inquired.

She shook her head. "I won't promise," she said. The woman was looking at them painfully, eagerly. "I won't promise anything," she repeated stubbornly, "nothing—except a son!"

A smile was breaking to the surface of his dark eyes. She saw it coming like light into his face and she loved him and hated him together.

"I won't let you go—not you or him—" the woman said suddenly.

"You can't stop us," Molly replied. "I came by magic."

"What magic?" the woman demanded.

"By wings," Molly replied mischievously. She would use the woman's ignorance.

"I believe nothing you say," the woman shouted.

"This morning I was at the sea coast," Molly cried, "and it is not yet noon. By midafternoon I shall be at the sea again. Look out of the door!" She went quickly to the door and threw it open to the court. There was the plane in the midst of crowding curious men. When he saw her, the young pilot started his engine suddenly with a roar and the woman leaped in her seat, her eyes terrified.

"Come on!" Molly cried to the Tiger. He hesitated. Then she shouted with all her strength, "Come, I say! The Japanese are attacking Shanghai!"

He stared at her for one second. Then he leaped for the door. He pushed the men right and left, dividing them like a strong wind, and she was in his wake. He clawed at the plane.

"How do I get into it?" he was shouting.

But now the woman was shrieking after them. "Hold them—catch them!" The men saw what was about to happen and they rushed to hold him. He struggled with them, but a dozen hands were holding his legs as he scrambled into the seat. She felt them catch at her, too, and in that instant she put her hand into her bosom for her pistol. "Here!" she cried. He seized it from her and lifted it over their heads and the shots crackled in the still mountain air. They shrank back for a second, and in that second he leaned over and took her under the arms and lifted her into the seat with him. The plane was moving, was running across the wide court; it lifted itself above the amazed upturned faces and grasping outstretched hands. It cleared the wall and began climbing the sky. He cupped his hands.

"We must strengthen the fortress!" he shouted in her ear.

"They're only at Shanghai!" she screamed back at him.

"They'll get Shanghai!" he roared. "City people! Easy! The real war will be inland—at the mountains! We'll be there! Ready! Never give up! I've been waiting for this all my life!"

They were sweeping over the mountains now, which stood like a great wall to the inner country. She looked down over them, over the valleys, toward the sea. His voice was roaring in her ear again.

"I'll hire some fellows like this—buy bombing planes—"

He had never been in a plane in his life, but he sat at ease, as though he had done it every day. He was planning. She could see his puckered forehead. "I'll even offer myself to the government!" he shouted, his voice like a trumpet. "We must unite now—"

She laughed and moved her fingers in the air on an imaginary typewriter.

"What?" he bellowed.

"Now is the time for all good men—" she screamed, but he shook his head. He could not hear her. Her voice was too light.

She did not try to answer. She had him. They were miles in the air. The mountains lay like a knotted chain across the earth.

Drumming against her ear she heard his roar. "Why didn't you tell me at once that the Japanese were here? It would have saved time!"

She picked up his hand and with her finger she wrote in Chinese letters in his palm. "I wanted you to choose me—without the help—of the Japanese."

He threw up his head and laughed. She could hear the echoes of his great laugh through the wind. He cried:

"I chose you at my own door the first moment I saw you!"

She folded his hand and held it against her breast again. It was warm now, and full of power. It pressed against her. The young pilot turned his head to say something to them, then he looked away again quickly. But the Tiger did not care.

"A war!" he was roaring. "It is all I need!"

He was incredible. Nobody would believe in him. If she tried to tell Mary Lane about him, she couldn't explain him. The whole story of him was mad and impossible. It couldn't have happened in America, or anywhere else except here. They were driving across the sky. Ahead in time and space were their enemies. But beneath them were the mountains, filled with fierce wild men, the Tiger's men, guarding the old inner gates. She was not afraid.

IX
GOLDEN FLOWER

GOLDEN FLOWER

How it had happened that the Japanese had captured her she could not understand. She sat in a corner of the prison, a little away from her men, her back turned toward them, her knees drawn up to her body, and locked by her arms. None of them had said a word to her since hours ago they had been thrust into this windowless room and the iron bars drawn. She knew what the room was—the great granary and storehouse of the temple. The monks used to keep their supplies here. Once in a bad year she and Big Stupid Chen, the bandit chieftain to whom she then belonged, had talked about robbing it to feed the men. But Big Stupid had been afraid of the gods in the temple. She remembered this now because she had said to him angrily:

"I am not afraid of gods more than of men, and men I do not fear at all!"

It had occurred to her at this moment for the first time that if ever anything happened to Big Stupid, she would take over the band. Why not? Was there anything he did which she did not think of and plan and put into his head to do? When he had died—not of an honorable wound, but of eating too many crabs on a hot summer's day five years ago—she had been ready. She had called the men together and said:

"I am a woman, but other women in our history have led men to battle. Mu-lan, when her father's strength failed, took his

193

horse and his sword and led his army to victory." She pointed to a dividing line of light and darkness where the shadow of an old tree fell across a grassy hillside. "Let those who follow the banner of Golden Flower step out of the shadow and stand in the sunshine."

Of all of Big Stupid's men at that moment not one failed to move into the sunlight. She had watched them gravely. Had any not stepped to the light, she would have cried out a sharp command to those already prepared and in a moment they would have been dead. But this was not needed. They all knew who had been their true leader even before Big Stupid died. . . .

She hugged her knees more closely. Behind her in the dimness lit only by the cracks of light around the barred gate, she knew they were looking at her—these men who had chosen to follow her. She thought:

"They are saying to themselves that it is because I am a woman that we have been captured by the Japanese. I urged them too far. A man would have been satisfied to have retaken the city. But no, I must rush on and try to capture the whole Japanese army in retreat!"

She groveled in self-blame. Then her pride rose. She leaped to her feet and turned toward them. She flung her head backward to toss her short hair out of her eyes.

"Do not forget how often I have led you to victory!" she cried. "Remember that for five years you have had food to eat and shelter when it rained and warm clothing when you were cold!"

The men grunted. One of them spat on the ground. "Have we ever complained?" he inquired.

But Golden Flower pressed further.

"When the Japanese came, I offered myself and my men to Chiang Kai-shek before any others. He accepted us. In this province none have had as many victories as we have. No day has passed that in one way or another we have not killed Japanese. One lonely sentry is not too small to be called a victory. A hundred men in a scouting party does not satisfy us. We kill them all. And yesterday we took back the city we lost last month and killed as traitor the puppet magistrate the Japanese set up and his wife with him!"

She paused again and looked about.

"Do we complain?" the same voice asked.

She whirled nearer them in one of the swift acrobatic movements her father had taught her when she was a child, in those days when with her father and mother she had traveled from village to village in their little family circus. She never remembered a home or a settled house. That was why now she could move from place to place with such swiftness that the Japanese never knew where she would next attack them. Certainly they had not expected her yesterday at the city gates. No capture had ever been easier. She and her men had slipped inside the walls, disguised as farmers and laborers, until she had a thousand men there. When the last man was in, he came and told her, and exactly as she had planned, he had already cut the single telephone wire that connected the small Japanese garrison holding the city with General Seki's headquarters in the larger city, which was the capital of the province. They locked the city gates. Then quietly, in the absolute silence in which she had taught her men to work, they gathered about the Japanese garrison and mingled with the crowd. Big Stupid always wanted his men to shout and terrify the enemy by noise. Hearing their shouts his own courage grew greater. But she worked best in silence.

"Let them fear us by what we do," she had always taught her men.

So they had fallen upon the Japanese garrison and killed half of them before the rest escaped by a small gate they had made through the city wall for just such a purpose. When she saw this trick she had been so angry that she had followed them, shouting to the men around her. Fifty-odd men had heard and followed, and then the Japanese had suddenly surrounded them and taken them captive and carried them along to an old temple just outside the capital.

Now in this prison she shouted suddenly, "I shall not rest until I have recaptured the capital city itself! I swear to the god of this temple where we are now held that I shall restore the temple to him as I shall restore this province to the people!"

Time after time she had sworn to do a thing and it was done. But never had she sworn so large a thing as this. Her men now looked at her, whether with doubt or belief she could not tell in the darkness, except that no one spoke.

"Do not forget," she went on, "that there are only fifty and a few more of us here behind this gate. Left behind us are two thousand men free, a thousand in the city we retook, where they will have the enemy's stores of ammunition. A thousand remain in the hills. When I do not return, they will not stand idle."

She thanked her own wisdom silently that she had yielded to none of the men who had besought her, the young men of her band, to Ling the Tiger-Clawed, to Kao the Killer, to Wang the Buffalo, to Pan the Lion-Tamer. There were too many of them for jealousy. Each had come to her secretly and begged her to live with him in a double tent. But she had refused them all, using her loyalty as a widow as her excuse. In her heart she knew that Big Stupid, dead or alive, had been nothing to her. In her heart she knew that what she really wanted was not one of these men of her own bandit clan, these men whom she knew

as a mother knows her children. She wanted a man to whom
she could give life-long love. What sort of a man this must be
she did not know, because she had never known such a man.
But that was the way she put it to herself— "I must be able to
love a man with a life-long love." So she had not yielded to
anything less. Her tent remained a single tent, where she slept
with only an old farm wife for companion, an ancient woman
whose husband had been killed by Big Stupid in one of his village raids. The next day the wife had come toiling into the hills
and she had stood up sturdily before Big Stupid and said:

"Since you have killed the man who was my rice bowl, I am
come to you to be fed."

And Golden Flower, then a young and tender girl, in the
beginning of her years with Big Stupid, had liked her and
begged for her, and so she had remained ever since. She alone
dared to talk with Golden Flower about the young men.

"Yield to no man," she told Golden Flower. "When a woman
yields, she loses herself. That which is she is gone when a man
takes it in his hands. . . ."

Now in this prison Golden Flower thought how well it was
that she had not yielded. For had she done so, that one would
have set himself up in her absence to be chieftain of her bandit
clan. Only these days they called themselves guerrillas and no
longer bandits. Now since none would allow the place of chieftain
to another in her absence, they would devote their thought and
planning to her.

"There will come a way of escape," she told her imprisoned
men confidently. "All we must do is to be quick to see it. When
our comrades put forth a hand in the dark, we must have our
own ready to meet it. Meanwhile, we wait."

She could tell by her intuition that the men were beginning to believe her again. So often she had to bully them, persuade them, coax, and command them, that she could feel like an atmosphere the state of their minds. Upon the chill of apathy she had learned to pour the warmth of her own determination until from great mutinous silent beasts they turned, half unwillingly, to obedience again.

"Trust me," she said in her soft deep voice, "trust me—trust me! When I speak, agree, though you do not understand. I will lead you out of this prison. I promise it!"

One man after another stirred, rose, and stood as though she had called his name. And she held herself in that trance of compelling power over them. She could feel magnetism pouring out of herself over them. She knew what she was doing. By this same magnetism her father and her mother had compelled crowds of dazed people to believe that doves flew from their mouths, and bowls of water came from their sleeves, and fire went down their throats. But Golden Flower used it to make them believe in her, as she believed in herself. That was her secret—that she also believed.

It was at this moment that the prison gate was thrown open. For a second none of them knew what to expect. The sunlight poured in like a river and none of them could see.

"Are we to be killed already?" Golden Flower thought, startled. If so, then she must plan instantly a way to escape, and, failing that, a way to die, scorning death before those who brought it.

The Japanese soldiers were hustling them out, prodding them with their guns and pricking them with bayonets. What they said was unintelligible.

When her time came to go out she drew a little farther over her eyes the broken visor of her cap. She was not afraid of being recognized as a woman. She looked, she knew, simply one of her own men. Her uniform was like theirs, her hair unkempt, her skin brown and dry. Miles of constant marching had kept her body as flat as a boy's, and under her uniform her small breasts were bound tightly to her body by a strip of strong cotton. Her feet were bare. Long ago she had learned not to look like a woman. Someday, perhaps, when she found her life-long love—but certainly not here could she dare to look like a woman. She took care to keep in the midst of her men. She knew the brutality of the Japanese toward captive Chinese women. If she died she would die as a man. And her men, seeming to understand this, kept about her closely, their faces made stupid and impassive.

But they were not to die. Instead they were herded and driven into the central courtyard of the temple. She remembered it perfectly because here she and her parents had often come in the New Year holidays to perform their tricks. Around this great space she had leaped on and off her barebacked pony, now swinging by her legs under its belly, now standing on its back, now clinging by one hand to its mane. She had never dreamed, with all her knowledge of fortune telling, that this would be her future now, to walk here a prisoner of the Japanese.

And for what end? Suddenly they were pushed forward. What was it? Then, to her bewilderment, she saw a dozen of her own men from the hills standing there in the middle of the court, her free men. How had they come here? They made no sign of recognition, and she made none, and the men with her made none. The Japanese soldiers hurried their prisoners forward. She saw a fat old Japanese general sitting on a campstool. Beside him was a young and slender Japanese man holding not a gun but a camera. She knew what a camera was, because the band had once captured a white man who had one, and he took pictures of them all to amuse them and to ingratiate himself with them. But Big Stupid had killed him, nevertheless, because his feet were tender and he could not keep up with the marching. She had always felt sorry for him and had kept as a curiosity the picture he had taken of her.

Then she saw what they had been brought to see. On the tiles in the middle of the court lay a pretty woman, dead. She was the wife of the puppet magistrate in the city they had retaken. Golden Flower recognized her at once, because yesterday she had killed her. It had been easy because the woman was lying asleep on her bed. There Golden Flower had come upon her as in triumph she had pressed on through the puppet magistrate's palace, ahead of her men who delayed in the outer rooms for loot. She had crept close to the sleeping one and had admired her prettiness. It was sad so pretty a woman was a traitor. Even so, it would be a pity to spoil her, she had thought. So she had taken her little needle-fine dagger and simply pressed it into the woman's left temple. When she drew it out, she wiped away the few drops of blood and went on.

But her quick brain left yesterday's deeds. Why was this woman here? Her own men must have brought her. They had known who she was when they had found her dead, after Golden Flower herself had been captured. It had happened all within a few moments yesterday. But there was no reason why these Japanese should know the dead woman. They were all men, and they could not have seen a lady, hidden properly in her own apartments in her husband's house. The hand, she thought swiftly—the hand stretched out in the dark—

Tani, the young Japanese standing with his camera beside General Seki, knew he ought to be glad that Golden Flower was dead. They had been trying to kill her for the last eleven months. Of all guerrilla troops that harassed the Japanese army of occupation in this region, the men who followed Golden Flower were the worst. Hundreds of good Japanese soldiers were dead because of this woman upon whose body he was now gazing. They had not been killed in hundreds. Golden Flower was too clever for that. Everybody knew her men were nothing but ordinary peasant bandits whom she had collected about her after her bandit lover had died. But Japanese sentries here and there had dropped at their posts, and no one could find out how bullets had reached them. Japanese scouting parties were met by a handful of wild-looking dark-faced men and killed; garrisons in captured towns were attacked by night, and when they tried to call reinforcements, all wires were cut and there was nothing to do but die. It went on thus, today ten men, tomorrow twenty, until General Seki had grown infuriated with the drain, dribbling but constant, upon his army of occupation, the more especially as after each foray he found somewhere, against a wall, or upon a dead man's heart, the small gold-washed metal flower which was the sign of the Golden Flower.

So when yesterday the small city of Tunghsing had been recaptured by the guerrillas of Golden Flower and the newly set-up puppet magistrate killed, General Seki fairly swelled with rage.

"Dead or alive!" he roared. "Ten thousand yen to anyone who will bring me Golden Flower!"

Now only a day after he ordered this written down and had it pasted on city walls and gates and upon the earth walls of farmhouses, Golden Flower's body had been brought into the gate of the temple.

Here it now lay. The noon sunlight poured upon the slender

body. She had died, it could be seen, of a tiny wound in the left temple. It seemed scarcely to have bled, or if it had bled, someone had wiped the blood away. Certainly it had not marred her beauty. Tani, moving forward among his comrades as they gathered about the body of the woman who had been such a menace to them all, could scarcely believe this was she. She was rather tall for a woman, but otherwise delicate and feminine. There were gold rings in her ears, and on her first finger a jade ring. Her feet had been bound in her youth, in the strange Chinese fashion, but later unbound, so that they were almost natural, but she wore old-fashioned satin shoes. The face, so youthful in peace, was exquisite. The eyes were closed, the long black hair had come loose from its binding of silk net, and though the flesh had now grown waxen, upon the full lower lip was still a bold touch of red. It gave a living emphasis to a face otherwise porcelain.

The General spoke suddenly.

"What proof is there that this is she?" he demanded of Tani, who was the official interpreter because he could speak Chinese.

Tani turned to the handful of ragged and hungry-faced men who had brought her in.

"What is your proof?" he demanded.

The men looked at each other as though they did not understand. Then one of them said roughly:

"Have we not eaten with her and fought under her banner day after day? We know her as we know our mothers."

"Why have you killed her?" Tani asked.

These were brutish men, he thought, despising them because for the sake of money they had betrayed this woman who had led them. He felt contempt for them, even though they were only doing what the General had hoped they would. But then he had not expected Golden Flower to be so young and so beautiful and so much a woman. He would have said that she would have been like other Chinese girl soldiers whom he had seen taken captive, brown lean creatures scarcely to be distinguished from men in their uniforms.

"We are hungry," one of the men said.

"We are tired of this war," another said.

Tani translated this to General Seki, who looked pleased and stroked his stiff black mustache.

"Ask the prisoners also if they recognize their leader," he commanded.

Tani glanced at the prisoners whom they had taken yesterday. They stood close together, as though they were bewildered.

"You will recognize this woman," he said hurriedly. "Your own comrades have surrendered her to us. They will be given the reward and can go away free for what they have done."

They did not understand what he said, he perceived. They stood looking stupidly at the dead woman, as though they had never seen her before.

"She is Golden Flower," he added.

"Where is the mole that she had on her temple?" one of the men said to another suddenly in a low voice.

Tani was close enough to catch these words, muttered from one man to another. . . .

"Fools!" she thought passionately at this moment, and ground her teeth together. She pulled her broken visor down over the mole on her left temple and pushed her way from out of their midst. She must risk everything because they were such fools. She answered the man in her quick fresh voice:

"The wound has destroyed it, elder brother."

Tani looked toward this voice at once. It was an unusual voice, low and firm, and yet the youth who possessed it was young.

"It is Golden Flower!" this boy insisted. "I saw her every day, and it is she!"

He was not speaking to Tani, but to his fellow captives. Tani saw only the glimpse of his profile as he turned his head. Among the captives eye caught eye, face turned to face. No expression changed. They looked stupid and uncomprehending enough. And yet when the young man declared, "It is Golden Flower!" each agreed. "Golden Flower—it is she—" "Golden Flower— Golden Flower."

"What are the demons saying!" General Seki demanded of Tani.

"Sir, only that this is indeed Golden Flower," he replied.

"Of course it is," the General said in his harshest and most complacent manner. "Haven't I just told them?"

"Yes, sir," Tani said obediently.

Yet although obedience was a habit to him, it did not now keep him from an astounding discovery. The young man had turned around now, and Tani saw for the first time his full face. It was a young fresh face, full of life and vivacity in spite of the torn guerrilla uniform of blue cotton and the bare feet. Under a ragged blue cap with a broken visor this face looked out at Tani. He felt himself grow dizzy with unreality. For the face was the face of the dead woman, a chance likeness, yet the same face, though alive with spirit and daring.

"Take the prisoners back," General Seki said suddenly. "I am hungry."

He rose from the campstool, yawned, and patted his belly. Instantly the soldiers began to hurry the prisoners together.

"Give to the men who have surrendered their reward and

food," General Seki added. "But let them be put for the night with the prisoners, until tomorrow, when we will have investigated everything. If all they say is true, quarters can be arranged."

The prisoners marched away. The boy with the broken cap was the last. Tani, still staring at him, caught his eye.

"Poor Golden Flower!" the boy said, and smiled an impudent smile. While Tani still stared, the boy managed to walk away as though he were not chained.

"Take that body out to be burned," the General shouted harshly from halfway across the court.

Tani ran to him and spoke, saluting.

"Should we not take photographs," he asked, breathlessly, "lest we be asked from above for proof when we make the report?"

The General paused to consider.

"You are right," he said, "though I was about to think of it myself. Make the photographs clear and large to accompany my report."

He stood a moment, considering further. He was not pleased that Tani as a subordinate had suggested something so necessary as photographs. But he could think of nothing more to order. Besides, he was tired as well as hungry. He was heavy, and the hot Chinese summer was hard to bear, especially when he had the vexation of these guerrillas who were like vicious gnats, striking in the least expected places, knowing by some evil magic of their own where for a moment a place was undefended. It would be better now this woman chieftain was dead. It had been infuriating that a woman could so evade capture as this one.

"Dead or alive, though," he said to himself with a chuckle. "Men or women, I get them in the end!"

Tani heard the chuckle and looked up, startled. But the general only waved his hand imperiously.

"Go on—go on—" he commanded without explanation.

So Tani went back and dropped to one knee that he might turn his lens full upon the face, and then he focused carefully, so that he would have the picture he wanted.

In his little dark room that same afternoon Tani could not work quickly enough in the developing of his pictures. He dipped each film into the fluid, rinsed it, and hung it up to dry. In the darkness he sat down and remembered the young man's face, turned to him for that moment of impudent smiling. In his whole somewhat unimaginative life it seemed to him this was his most exciting moment. Even the night when he received his orders to sail for China had not been so exciting. He had been to war before in Manchuria, and he knew that if war was prosaic in its beginning, it was even more so in its carrying on. A man followed petty orders day after day without knowing what they meant. If he were killed, death in obedience was prosaic, too.

But such imagination as he had was already stirred weeks ago by Golden Flower, by her daring, her wild history, her success in every raid. She had been so invincible through all these months that he was startled and then ashamed when he felt a certain sorrow in himself today on seeing her body brought into the temple court by the ragged dusty rascals who were her followers. Remembering this, he excused himself somewhat now. Assassins, that was what such men were, he thought. Outlaw and enemy that she was, that she should have been killed by her own men violated his deepest decency. He felt relieved when he recognized this familiar decency. It was not that he was disloyal in wishing an enemy alive again, but simply that even to an enemy he wished a decent death.

And then he thought with a vague tenderness of her helplessness as she had lain there dead before them all. Doubtless they had fallen upon her unawares, the men whom she trusted. And those others, the captives, they, too, had agreed it was she. But they had not mourned. They had simply stared at her stolidly and agreed when the young man made his declaration.

Then he remembered that smile the young man gave him. Tani rose. The thing he did not like about the Chinese was that they laughed so much and so easily, not polite laughter, but hearty simple laughter, such as children love to make. And yet they were not simple. There was nothing simple, for instance, about that young man. The look in his face had been knowing and wise in spite of its merriment.

Well, photographs would be proof. There might have been something tricky in his mind at the moment, an illusion of likeness because of his concentration upon the dead face. But photographs had no illusions. He rose from the bench where he was sitting and lit a candle and then with nervous fingers lifted the first developed picture. There was the dead woman's face, brilliantly clear in the sunlight, perfect in its detail. He studied it carefully, the light falling across the smooth surface. There was no trickery here.

Allowing for the difference between life and death, the two faces were the same, the dead woman's and the young man's. On every picture, as he picked up one after the other, they were the same. He felt gathering upon him the shadow of a tremendous obligation. He must go and report to General Seki the resemblance he had discovered. What it meant he did not know.

But then it was perhaps not his business to know, merely to report. Solemnly he prepared to do his duty.

The whole thing might have turned out differently for Tani had his soul not been meticulously Japanese. For as he combed his hair and put on a fresh uniform that afternoon preparatory to visiting the General after he awoke from his usual nap, it occurred to him before he went that perhaps he was still mistaken in his memory, not this time of the dead face, but of the living one. Since he now had the dead face successfully held in a photograph, it would perhaps be well to compare it with the living face before he went to the General's headquarters. For this reason Tani went not directly to headquarters, but instead to the granary of the temple, which was the jail. The place had been chosen by General Seki as a prison because it had no windows. The thick high walls went sheer to the curved tile roof, and only the entrance doors needed to be reinforced with iron bars and guards. Guards with drawn bayonets stood now before the door as Tani drew near. But they knew him well enough as the General's interpreter and photographer and secretary, so they saluted and listened to his request.

"Sir, shall we bring the young man here, or will you go in?" the sergeant inquired.

"I will go in," Tani said.

He had brought with him the small pocket flashlight with which every Japanese soldier is provided, and he intended to throw this intense pale light full upon the young man's face and in that clarity scrutinize its every feature.

He followed the sergeant therefore as he went to the gate. Behind him the bayonets of the guard closed into a shining metallic semicircle against the possible escape of a prisoner.

"The Chinese are like snakes," the sergeant explained. "They escape where one would say no living creature could escape."

Certainly no creature could escape such a barricade, Tani thought. And yet the sergeant did not open the gate more than the chain allowed, and it allowed only Tani's own person.

"I will follow, lest they treat you treacherously when they see you are alone," the sergeant said, squeezing through after him.

"I'm not afraid," Tani replied.

"I will stand here," the sergeant said stubbornly, and took up his place just inside the door.

At first Tani could see nothing. Then in a moment he began to see shapes in the darkness. With his coming, all talk, if there had been any, ceased, and the silence was absolute. The air of the closed building felt cool and damp after the dry hot sunshine outside, and the packed earth floor was slippery. There was a fetid odor of human waste.

He turned on his flashlight cautiously and with it picked out one face after the other. They were all wild faces, he thought with distaste. They met the light like animals, their eyes startled and opalescent, and then moved to escape it. None was the face he sought. He shifted the light back and forth, but the face was not there. Then he heard a secret repressed movement and felt that somehow the young man was being hidden from him, and instantly he grew angry.

"Throw the gates wide!" he ordered the sergeant in a whisper.

The sergeant hesitated. Then he shouted, "On guard!" and unhooking the heavy chain, he threw open the gate.

The afternoon sunlight streamed like a river into the dark room. It caught the huddled prisoners unaware, and they had no time to avoid it. The young man was on the outer edge of the two or three score of prisoners. He threw his arms about his head as though to protect himself. But it was too late. Tani had seen him.

He went over to him cautiously, while all the prisoners watched him, and took the young man's chin in his hand. It was a soft chin, the shape of it round and the skin upon it smooth. The young man, feeling his face thus upturned, closed his eyes. It was the one thing he could have done to make the likeness to Tani's photograph perfect. Tani's heart beat hard twice and then missed its beat. All uncertainty was gone. He released the young man's chin and went back to the gate and out into the air again.

"Is that all?" said the sergeant.

"That is all," Tani replied.

But it was not quite all. He thought of one more thing to inquire of the sergeant.

"When are these prisoners to be executed?" he asked.

"Sir, tomorrow morning," the sergeant replied.

When she felt her chin taken into her enemy's hand, she felt the blood in her veins stand still. She had no protection except not to let him see her eyes, lest he know the truth. She was scarcely less easy after a moment when he loosed her chin and went away. She sat waiting, as they were all waiting, for the other men to come in. If only she had not yielded to that foolish impulse of mischief when she turned in the courtyard! She had been frightened and ashamed ever since. Had any of the men seen her laugh? None of the prisoners, certainly, since she was behind them, but what of the others who had come to save her? Clever—clever—she could not herself have thought of a better trick to save herself! But then she had not seen the chance resemblance between herself and the woman she had killed yesterday.

The long afternoon wore on after the Japanese went away. Soldiers brought them thin rice soup and beans. But still no one spoke. She dared ask nothing of what had happened to the men who had pretended to surrender. If they did not come, then her smile had betrayed them. Would the young man have come to find her if she had not smiled' and so made him uneasy? She put her own palm to her chin. Soft and round—a woman's chin, she thought in terror, and cursed herself. She could still feel his hand under her chin—a sensitive gentle hand, trembling a little. He was not like any of the men she had ever known. No, she told herself bitterly, he was the enemy, and she must not think of him. She must think of her men. Had she lost everything by her laughter?

He must, of course, go at once and tell the General that he strongly suspected—but if his suspicion was proved correct, they must strip the young man— And what would be his fate then, supposing—

Tani rose abruptly from the campstool in his own room. He had come here instead of going to the General, and here he had been sitting for nearly two hours. It was not yet sunset. He would go for a little walk to clarify his brain so that he might see his duty clear again. Outside the temple he turned to the fields which the monks had once tilled to grow rice and cabbages on which to make their vegetarian fare. These fields were full of weeds now, but the pebbled paths still wound among them to a quiet spot where a brook flowed beneath willows. Tani had often gone there alone on his hours off duty instead of into the village with the soldiers. He went there now.

But this time it was different from any other, for now he had scarcely stepped into the shadow of the willows before hands reached out from nowhere and seized him. He was taken and tossed and held by some dark fellows, who said not one word as they worked. They took him as though he had been a child and stripped him of his uniform and tied him to a willow tree, and wove the branches about him so cleverly that one would have said he was part of the branchy trunk. Then they bound him under the chin around the tree with a sweaty girdle one of them took from his waist.

He had never been so alive, intensely alive, as he was now. He was terrified. Every nerve was bright with a life made sharp by terror, and his wits were livelier than he had ever felt them. He could feel them moving and aware of his predicament. There was so much surplus energy in him that as his wits worked he heard more vividly than he ever had heard in his life before the call of a distant harvest bird, the scraping of insects' wings in the leaves above his head. He said in Chinese, "You are the followers of Golden Flower."

In himself he was measuring the distance to the temple. If he shouted with all his strength—but long before his voice could reach the wall, that heavy hand-wrought dagger would have been in his breast.

"She is dead," a man said roughly.

"Then why do you want my uniform?" Tani asked. Strange how death, stared at, sharpened the brain of a living man! He saw clearly why they wanted his uniform. It was for her. He went on smoothly and quickly. "As for me, I am honored if my poor garments will cover her. We admire her, too, though we are her enemies. A great spirit must be admired, though housed in a woman." He dropped his slightly grandiloquent tone.

"Hurry, whatever you are about to do," he said. "The prisoners are to be killed tomorrow morning."

The man with the dagger lowered his hand. No one spoke. But in a second they were gone, seeming not so much to go as to disappear into the moving shadows. Then Tani was left alone to bear as best he could the strain of his body bent and bound upon the tree.

Whether or not he dreamed in his agony, whether or not he saw what he saw, he never knew. But, hours after sunset, in the cold and glittering moonlight when he hung fainting and choking, he seemed to be in the midst of a crowd of the dark men. They swarmed about him in their strange silence. He was shivering in his own sweat, icy in the damp night air. Mist rose from the brook and hung about the willows. And in this mist he seemed to see the dark faces. Yet he was not sure. Perhaps they were only faces in his brain. All his body was a long spear of pain, bent against a tree. A Christian god had died once like this. He had heard the story as a child and had despised the god because he cried out in his pain. He would not cry out. That was because he was Japanese. He fainted at this moment. Pain and everything were gone.

From this faint he waked in icy sweat to see the faces dark in white mist. But directly in front of him the early morning sun was shining on the mist in a bright space. And in that space he could see plainly. Or he thought he could until he realized that what he saw stupidly was his own uniform. Then he looked again, remembering. A face looked at him, young and grave, a face he knew. Or did he know it?

"He is shivering," a low voice whispered. The face smiled a little in his uncertain gaze. "Let him go," the voice said.

And in that instant hands reached out and set him free.

He could not stand. His legs melted and let him down to the earth. The mists rushed upward and took everything away from him again. Or was that sound of horses galloping a fainting dream? From nowhere there were suddenly horses. He was to remember as long as he lived seeing a slender straight figure in his own uniform throw itself across a horse and, sweeping past him, bend low as circus riders do, to fasten something to his heart and sweep on again. Then he fainted down toward death.

But he did not die. He was found by two serving men who came out from the temple to throw waste into the flowing stream. They lifted him up and took him back. But he was not able to explain anything because he was still unconscious. He was therefore not aware of the confusion within the temple walls, or that no one had time to attend to him. The two servants laid him upon his bed and left him, merely going to the nearest sergeant to report having found him half-naked and unconscious beside the brook. They did not report the most important thing, because they did not see it.

But Tani himself was aware of it the moment he came swimming upward out of darkness toward light. He reached the small end of a funnel of light and was barely able to squeeze through it. But once through it, he was impelled toward the enlarging light of the other end of the funnel. When he was quite out of it he became conscious and he was aware that he was lying on his own bed. And in the mass of aches which was his body there was a small sharp pricking upon his left breast. It became intolerable and at last groaning he raised one numb hand and felt under the wet cotton vest he wore. His hand touched metal. He turned his blurry gaze downward. Something sharpened and focused that gaze. It was a small flower of gold whose metal points turned downward and pierced his flesh. He tore it off and held it hidden in his hand.

By the time the General sent someone to him he was able to drink a little hot sake. And soon he was able to listen to what they had to tell him. For in the excitement of what had happened in the temple the day before no one asked him any details of his own lowly adventure. It was to them merely a part of the whole miraculous day, though of course not to be understood either.

The real miracle was this. Last night after sunset, in the early moonlight, three hundred of the followers of the Golden Flower had come to the temple and surrendered themselves. Tani was still very weak. But these men, his comrades, crowded joyously into his room and he had to listen to them. Three hundred of the enemy, they said over and over, came of their own accord to surrender—all of them followers of Golden Flower.

"Where are they?" he asked.

"Waiting for General Seki," they said proudly. They had been in the prison for the night, pending examination this morning by the General. But there was no doubt of it. They had been there smiling this morning when the buckets of soft-cooked rice were taken in for their breakfast. And because of them, the General had postponed the executions which were to have taken place this morning, and had given all the prisoners a chance to surrender instead. All had surrendered. They had rushed out of the prison together in a happy body, shouting their surrender. Now they were in the courtyard waiting to see the General.

Tani's head was swimming with weakness. Voices hurled these

words at him and he was barely able to catch them. But he caught them, and his brain began to struggle.

"But who was the dead woman?" he muttered.

His tongue was so stiff no one understood what he said, and he could not repeat the words. It did not matter after all if the dead woman were now ashes. Golden Flower was alive. His uniform had saved her. He saw drowsily how it must have happened. She had slipped away when they all rushed out together this morning, her Japanese uniform hidden among them. And who would notice an extra Japanese in a camp too full of them for them to know each other? A moment later a young Japanese had followed a company straggling through the gates to the temple threshing floor to early morning drill. And horsemen had met her by the shadowy willow pool in the brook.

He held her emblem in his hand. He felt upon his breast the pricking of her wound. For a moment his imagination, never strong at best, fluttered and put forth weak wings. Suppose she had been a Japanese woman? But he could not imagine a Japanese woman leading bandit guerrillas, flying on horseback over hills, escaping from a prison—no, it was easier to imagine what it would be like if he were a Chinese too. But he was a Japanese.

His imagination died. Duty—he had a duty waiting. He struggled to clarify duty in his clouded brain. Her men—never surrender—the whole thing a plot—

"Tell the General," he said thickly, "I must see him—life and death—"

Back in the hills, Golden Flower stood upon the rock to which her feet clung by habit. She was talking to her men. She had slept a little, eaten, washed, and clothed herself in a fresh uniform of faded blue cotton. Her short black hair had been newly cut. She felt strong and herself again. Now that she had escaped, she felt she had known all along that she would escape. Her smile upon the Japanese had done no damage, after all. And she had pressed the tiny sharp points of her golden flower into the flesh of his breast. Now that she was free she regretted nothing, neither smile nor flower. He was a handsome man, that young Japanese—but still, a Japanese!

She put her hands on her cartridge belt and went on.

"I shall never rest until we have taken back our capital, and our province," she cried in a clear voice.

"Ammunition—we need more ammunition," they muttered. "What we have is still not enough."

She looked at them severely.

"Why do you think I left three hundred and fifty men behind me?" she inquired. "The Japanese have our ammunition."

She stood at ease before them while they took this in. Then she went on.

"When you have eaten, we will go back and attack the head-quarters of that old turtle Seki himself. We will attack from without and those who are waiting for us will attack from within —all those who have *surrendered!*"

Suddenly she smiled, and like a flame set to a forest, her smile lit their laughter. They burst into simple hearty laughter, that laughter which if Tani had heard it he would have so hated because he could never comprehend its meaning.

Thus began again the war.

X

THE FACE OF BUDDHA

THE FACE OF BUDDHA

Timothy Stayne could never tell anyone why he was living in an old temple outside the city of Tali, in the province of Yunnan in Southeast China. He had been living there for ten years, ever since he was twenty-five years old. When people did not know him it was easy enough simply to let his being a missionary explain anything. It did explain anything when one apparently belonged to a small sect called The Apostolic Mission of Life and Healing. But as soon as he let anyone come to know him, and sometimes even after all these years against his better judgment he did, there would come that question which he dreaded. It began in various ways. An Englishman would say, "Look here, old chap, I don't mean to be curious, but—" A Frenchman would say, "Without doubt you lead a life of ravishing interest, but if I may ask—" And Americans would say, "I don't mean to butt in, but—" The end of the question, however begun, was always the same. In effect it was this, why does Timothy Stayne, heir to the Stayne millions, live in an old temple in Tali?

Tim answered the question according to his mood on the day it was asked. He might point from the temple terrace in the direction of the lake and its snow-encircled mountains. According to his nationality his questioner would express disbelief. There are lakes in America, in Switzerland, almost anywhere, in fact. If Tim reminded them of the Apostolic Mission, the disbelief varied from polite English smiles to loud American laughter. Who could take the Apostolic Mission seriously when in the main hall of the temple, which Tim had made into his living room, there stood a large gold Buddha five times the size of a man?

"The old abbot made it the one requirement for renting the temple to me," Timothy explained. "He said the big Buddha must not be moved, or else bad luck would fall on Tali. I said if that were the case I would never move it."

What he could not explain, of course, was the feeling which had made him shape the decorations of the room around the handsome Buddha, so that whatever was said or done in the room seemed to be done in that powerful, inscrutable presence. For the Buddha was not gentle, though the huge golden face was smooth and amiable and one enormous hand lay palm upward upon the folded knee while the other was lifted as though in calm admonishment. The Buddha was too powerful for gentleness. Trivial persons in that room became uncomfortable sooner or later and disappeared from Tim's life without his having to trouble to dismiss them, and those who could continue themselves under that strong golden face he discovered were worth keeping as his friends. But this he found difficult to explain.

Difficult, too, to explain was the Buddhist chanting that floated through his rooms in the early morning and at sunset. Tim always said, and truthfully, that he had nothing to do with it. When he had first climbed the bamboo-draped hill upon which the temple was and had seen below him the blue lake and the black roofs of the city and then, lifting his eyes, had stood face to face with the snow-topped mountains, he had immediately offered the ragged abbot at his elbow a rent which would make him and the three old priests independent for life. For there were fashions in temples in Tali, and just now Tali ladies were going to a big new temple in the city where the priests were young and handsome and where besides one did not have to pay to be carried up a mountainside in a rickety bamboo chair tied with frayed ropes to two poles. The reason they gave was that the big gold Buddha had grown old and careless about answering their prayers, and so they were going somewhere else for a while.

The abbot had been grateful and had grasped at the young American's offer on condition, he said, that the big Buddha was not moved from the east end of the main temple, and that he and his brother priests could keep for themselves the farthest small courtyard. They had nowhere to go in the world, having renounced their families so long ago that they must be forgotten. Moreover, they were here for sanctuary, and it would be embarrassing to them as old worshipers of gods to return to men and be tried for murder and one thing and another.

Tim, his eyes always on the lake, had agreed to everything. His only bad moment had been when the head of the Apostolic Mission from Tennessee had come to inspect him.

"You can't live with an idol in your own home," the excellent man had exclaimed.

"I find it strengthens my faith," Tim said quite truly.

"And those heathen priests!" the good man cried.

"They respect my faith," Tim replied.

Since Tim took no salary from the mission, the Reverend Joseph Bram said no more. He might have asked, "Why did you join a mission in the first place if you were going to live in a heathen temple?" But being a thoroughly earnest man it did not occur to him to ask such a question. He went away merely saying to himself that God worked in mysterious ways, and that this rich young man was one of the most mysterious he had ever seen.

Tim had, however, already asked himself this question many times. Why, if he had wanted to live where he could see the lake of Tali, did he not simply come here and live since he was spending no one's money except his own? The answer to this was obscure and yet he had it. Marco Polo was the one who had first enticed him to Tali. At the bottom of the page upon which Marco Polo described a great city, in the second book and the fifty-ninth chapter, there had been a footnote saying that the city was Tali and the lake there of surpassing beauty. Tim had been eighteen the year he read it, the only child of a mother so gentle that she died when he was twelve, and a father so strong that it appeared he would live forever. Fred Stayne took it for granted that his son would go on with the munitions business.

The last thing Tim wanted to do was to manufacture anything, but he avoided saying so, because in a way of his own he was fond of his father. He found another escape, therefore.

Later in the same year he heard a white-haired missionary from China talk at chapel one Sunday evening. The man had lantern slides, but they were not very good and nobody had been much interested except himself, and he only because of Marco Polo. Then the man said something else to interest him.

"We believe in healing and in quiet persevering goodness."

The way he said it made Tim remember his mother, and afterwards he had gone up to talk, though none of the other boys did, and the old man had told him a little about China, and he remembered again that Tali was there. It occurred to Tim suddenly that if he said he wanted to be a missionary his father ought to understand his going to China to live, since his father was an elder in the church. His father had not understood as well as he had hoped, but by remaining quietly stubborn while his father expended his own stubbornness in fireworks of temper, Timothy had lived now ten years where he liked to live, troubled only by fits of feeling that maybe he ought to begin more definitely to be a missionary.

Otherwise the ten years had been satisfying. Nothing had happened for eight of them to make one different from another, and this was exactly what he wanted. He spent them in reading many books, in beautifying his home, and in coming to know desultorily the affairs and the people of Tali. Those people were also hopelessly confused by his living in the Bamboo Temple, and simply called him the White Priest.

The peace of those eight years ended sharply one night in late July in the year 1937. Tim had been spending the evening as he spent many of his evenings, in company with the old abbot, who had taught him to read and to write Chinese. They had been discussing astronomy since there was an unusual number of large and luminous falling stars in the pageant of sky before them.

"Falling stars," the old abbot was saying as they watched the elements, "are an evil omen of changing times. History tells us that every disaster to China has been presaged by great and brilliant falling stars." The abbot was an astrologist, as well.

At this moment one of the priests came to the round gate of the terrace on which they sat.

"What is it?" the abbot asked.

"The magistrate of Tali has come in haste up the mountain," the priest replied in agitation.

"Why, at this hour and after all these years?" the abbot inquired.

"He wishes to worship the big Buddha, because there is bad news from the northern capital," the priest replied.

"Will this disturb you?" the abbot asked Tim courteously.

"Not at all," Tim replied, without moving.

He had stayed where he was in the soft darkness and the magistrate had hastened in, his embroidered robes flying and his retinue trotting after him. He did not even see the American sitting quietly in the wicker chair near the edge of the terrace which seemed suspended against the sky. He went at once into the temple and ordered the red candles he had brought to be lit before the big Buddha and the incense also, and that the silk cushion be put on the floor so that he could knock his head on it. He had expected the usual tiles of the temple floors and he paused in his prayers to comment on the extraordinary thickness and softness of Tim's carpet. Then he went on praying loudly, and, Timothy's Chinese by this time being excellent, he understood the prayer.

"O blessed Buddha, drive the Japanese dwarfs from the northern capital, but if they are not to be driven out let them have it. If they come to Shanghai, drive them out, O Buddha, but if they are not to be driven out let them have it. But they are not to come to Tali, O Buddha! If they do not come here, I will promise that this temple will be the richest and the most famous in the world. I will compel my people to worship the great gold Buddha. But if you let the Japanese hurt us by so much as the whiskers of our dogs, I will raze the temple and return you to yellow dust, O Buddha!"

Having thus prayed, the magistrate rose, remarked the fact that there was no dirt on his knees as there usually was after he had prayed in temples, and went away again.

This was the first Tim had heard of the Japanese invasion of China. The next time he heard of it was from his father in Philadelphia.

"The Japanese are at the moment our best customers," his father wrote. "I'm told the fighting will be in north China mainly, so you had better stay where you are."

There was nothing to be done about either Japan or his father. Tim spent a good deal of time thinking about them both and some more time thinking about the extra millions he would one day inherit because so many Chinese were going to get killed by Stayne munitions. But there was nothing he could do about that either, though gradually he came to think about it night and day, and more and more. While he thought he sat in his living room looking at the big Buddha. His houseboy had not taken away the magistrate's red candles or the incense, and Tim had not spoken about it, so they were still there. It was just as well, for now a number of people in Tali began to remember the big Buddha who had not thought of him for years, and they climbed the bamboo-shaded hillside to kneel there in Tim's living room. The common people still went to newer temples, but Tim grew used to having to leave for a few moments while dignified old gentlemen in old-fashioned brocaded satin robes and white-haired ladies with their feet bound walked into his room, and ignoring him completely, lit the red candles before the Buddha and prayed always to the same end.

"Deliver us, O Lord of Heaven, from our enemies, the Japanese."

He heard these prayers and noticed their similarity and concluded that the Japanese must be winning the war. Mails, always slow to Tali, were now not to be depended upon at all, and when he saw a newspaper it was so old that it was not worth reading. This, which had always been one of the blessings of Tali, now became an inconvenience, and he began anxiously to wish that something could be done about the Japanese. He spent a good deal of time sitting in his comfortable chair beneath the golden eyes trying to think if there was anything he could do, and he could think of nothing.

It was while he was thus sitting one night that the abbot came in. After the formula of courtesy had been completed and Wang the houseboy had brought in tea, the abbot said calmly, merely as if it were common news:

"Have you heard we are to have a new road through Tali?"

"No," Tim said. There had been nothing new in five centuries near Tali.

"The old silk route to India is to be cleared and brought into use again," the abbot said. "The road our ancestors used to carry on their trade with Greece and Persia and Egypt. It has been forgotten for centuries. Now where camels once walked loaded with silks there will be trucks."

"Not for silk," Tim said.

"Not for silk," the abbot agreed.

By this time Japan was taking one port after another on the coast and stopping China up like a bottle.

"Then the bottom is knocked out of the bottle," Tim said.

"If you wish to put it so," the abbot agreed, "or you might say the back gate is opened, or a bridge let down, or a hole chopped through the Great Wall."

"Ah," Tim said, thinking.

He sat silently thoughtful for so long that the abbot saw that Tim wanted him to go and so he went, Tim following him to the edge of the terrace and begging him to stay. The abbot smiled and bowed.

"There is no doubt that in some earlier life you were one of us," he remarked. "The Buddha has merely reincarnated you as you are now for his own purposes."

But still Tim's thought led nowhere for the moment. The new road began to appear beyond the walls of Tali, a scar of raw earth in the midst of fields tended and made green by generations of human hands. It stung his imagination but brought him no inspiration.

And then late one afternoon, returning from a walk he had made to inspect the new road, he stopped on the threshold of the old temple. He heard a strong young voice crying out a new sort of prayer.

"O Buddha, give me ten thousand guns! American guns, not the old-fashioned long-handled ones, but the short strong ones that shoot quickly!"

Tim was astounded. What could even Buddha make of this? He looked through the wide doorway and saw before the image a young Chinese man in the short blue jacket and trousers of a peasant. He was unusually tall and strong, and he turned his head and returned Tim's look with bold black eyes.

"Don't let me interrupt you," Tim said apologetically.

"I have finished," the young man said. "If as Buddha's priest—"

"I am not Buddha's priest," Tim said hastily, "but I could not help hearing what you want. Who are you?"

"Men call me the Yellow Wolf," the young man said, as casually as though he were anyone.

Tim concealed his inward start. "I have heard of you," he said.

"Everyone has," the young man replied without pretense of modesty. "I have fifteen thousand good fighting men in my band, and five thousand rifles we have taken from government soldiers we have vanquished from time to time. Now we will fight the Japanese instead of the soldiers. But first we must have more rifles."

It was true that everyone in Tali knew the Yellow Wolf, but

few had seen him and no one knew who he was. At the head of any who cared to follow him he had marauded the countryside.

"Will it not be difficult for Buddha to find ten thousand American rifles?" Tim inquired delicately.

"Buddha has ways," the young man said as simply as ever.

Tim had come in as they talked, and now they stood directly beneath the gaze of the huge golden figure. That figure which could so dwarf an ordinary man did not diminish this one. The Yellow Wolf stood at ease, erect and careless and full of daring. Involuntarily Tim looked up to the golden face. He was not in the least superstitious, and he knew that Buddha was made of yellow Tali clay covered with gold leaf. That the huge statue was so beautiful was merely the chance of the yellow clay having fallen to the hands of an unknown great sculptor instead of to an ordinary idol maker. Nevertheless, as the young man had talked and he had listened, he had felt something pressing into his brain gently and firmly. It was an idea, and now as he looked into the eyes of the big Buddha this idea sprang suddenly clear and open like a lotus flower in the sun.

Tim resisted it steadily. "I couldn't possibly do it," he said aloud and in English to the golden face.

"What is that?" the young man inquired in Chinese.

"Your prayer can scarcely be answered," Tim said cautiously. "What if the guns were not used against the enemy but against the people of Tali?"

"Buddha knows my heart," the young man said after a minute's silence and without another word he went away. Tim, following out of pure curiosity, saw him stride through the courts as though he knew them all, and then pause at the last one to speak to some one. It was the old abbot. Through the vista of gates Tim saw the two take each other's hands familiarly and stand, hand holding hand, to talk. Then with a nod the young man was gone.

Accustomed as he was to live in surrounding mystery, this, Tim told himself, was mystery made more mysterious. But he did not go to the old abbot who stood in the distance, watching the Yellow Wolf go springing through the bamboos to the top of the mountain. It was evening, indeed, before Tim, having sat out the afternoon in thought, went to find the abbot in his cell. The old man was working out a horoscope.

"Can you," Tim said abruptly, "as the representative of Buddha, guarantee the Yellow Wolf?"

"In the matter of guns?" the abbot inquired.

"Exactly," Tim said.

The abbot peered at certain symbols he had been putting down on paper with his pointed camel's hair brush.

"It is clear here," he said, "that the Yellow Wolf will become a famous general, and he will be pardoned by the government for all his sins."

"And you?" Tim inquired.

"I will swear for him," the abbot said, and added, "for Buddha, of course."

"In that case," Tim said thoughtfully, "I will get my cane and go into the city. The snakes come out at night."

"Do," the abbot replied.

Tim, returning, paused for one second to look up at the golden face. There was no change upon it and he went on.

He went down the winding stone-paved mountain road. The moonlight was very fine, and he needed no lantern. When he reached the city wall, the gate was locked, but he pulled a string, and a little wicket opened and the watchman peered out.

"Ah, the White Priest," he said and drew back the great

wooden bar and swung the gate open enough to admit Tim's slender frame.

Tim gave him a coin and went down the quiet narrow city street to the small telegraph office and wrote a cable to his father.

"If I can get a contract from a friend will you sell at same price as to enemies stop Tim."

He waked the clerk who was asleep on the table, and the little man read the words loudly without understanding one of them, for he was proud of his high school English.

"Right," said Tim.

Two days later he had his father's reply.

"Why not stop Cash stop Love, Dad."

"Meet Brownell in Lashio," his father cabled two weeks later. "Send cash."

Tim had forgotten how Americans did things. He had been making chrysanthemum cuttings on the terrace and thinking about the Yellow Wolf when a panting coolie brought him the cable. He stuffed the cable in his pocket and planted the chrysanthemums at furious speed—he'd want them later—and then rushed down to the telegraph office.

"Personally responsible for cash," he cabled.

The next day he and Wang set out for Burma along the new road. That new road now swept over the countryside like the wake of a storm, missing Tali by a few miles. People had never seen such a road. It grew leagues, or so it seemed, in a few days. Actually there were thousands of small dust-colored creatures who worked upon it like mites, ragged men and women without machinery. Their hoes and little baskets on bamboo poles were no more than toys, but somehow they pushed the road open before them steadily and swiftly. It was finished enough, indeed, for trucks, Tim saw sharply from the old roadster he had bought at a blacksmith's shop in Tali, though it was dangerous too, new, untried, driven through rocks above cliffs and twisting and turning in horrible curves into valleys; still it was possible—that is, for four days. In the rumble sat Wang with the tin food box. Twenty times in an hour Tim caught in the mirror the picture of Wang's terrified face bouncing upward.

"Came down all right, didn't you?" he would call after a bump.

"All right," Wang always piped, resolutely.

But before they reached Burma they had to leave the car. The road stopped as abruptly as though there was its end, and ahead stretched a great bog across which Tim could not see, though he climbed up and stood on the car. Upon the bog the small creatures still worked, but now half naked and sick with heat. Even as he watched he saw one drop here and another there. They did not rise. He climbed down from the car and stood upon a crust of the black earth which shook under his feet. A sickly Chinese in uniform came slowly toward him. Under his muddied helmet his sunken eyes were shining with fever.

"Can I get through?" Tim asked.

"Not by car," the man replied. "Not yet. But you can go twenty miles by foot, and the road begins again."

"Can I go by foot easily?"

"Yes, but do not sleep. This is the tiger country of Shweli. If a man stops sickness falls on him and sleep kills him."

Tim went back to his car. "Come on, Wang," he said, "we'll have to leave the car and walk awhile."

Wang got out and tied the food box to his back with his long blue girdle and Tim pulled the car to the bank, locked it, and they set out. A footpath, barely to be seen, led toward the jungle beyond the bog.

. . . The dancing torrid heat clung like slime about his body. He saw or thought he saw snakes hanging from trees, snakes crawling under his feet, snakes writhing around rocks. But if there had not been so many snakes, he would have had to sleep even though he remembered that sleep was death. Now and then he remembered Wang and turned to look behind him.

"All right, Wang?"

"All right," Wang piped, his eyes popping and his face streaming with sweat.

The air was solid. It packed itself about them, wet, immobile. He had to force his way as though he were walking through water. It took them eleven hours to do the twenty miles. On the other side they bargained with the driver of a truck returning to Lashio, crawled into it, and slept on green watermelons. They were tossed for hours over a violent rough road and then in Lashio had to be shaken awake.

". . . Black malaria," Brownell told him in the small Lashio hotel. Brownell was his father's head man in Singapore and he had brought the shipment to Lashio, wondering if his chief in U. S. A. had gone crazy. This had been his state of mind while he waited for young Tim as his orders told him to do. Young Tim as everybody knew was certainly crazy. He'd been locked up in a Chinese temple for years. That he had locked himself up only made him more crazy. "You're lucky to have got through," he told Tim. "A mosquito so small you can't see it gives you a couple of bites, and in a little while, a day or two maybe, you drop dead."

"That so?" Tim replied. He was thinking of the bog upon which those listless creatures worked, dropping here and there to die. The road would never be finished if it were left only to them. Some of them had had no hoes or shovels. They had cleared the earth into baskets with their bare hands. Seven days, the overseer had said. Well, perhaps it might be seven days. The whole road had been a miracle so far, but another miracle would have to finish it.

"It'll be a few days anyway before that big hole is ready for trucks," he told Brownell.

"From what I hear from fellows waiting to get through it's been quite a few days already," Brownell retorted. "My orders are to deliver to you and get back."

"All right, then, deliver!" Tim replied.

He found himself immediately the owner of a fortune in American rifles for which he had to pay cash to Stayne and Company, U. S. A.

"Glad I'm the son and heir," he thought as he wrote his check. It was the first time in his life he had been glad. He spent ten days rounding up trucks and drivers and on the morning of the eleventh was ready to start. He was proud of the caravan of trucks, though the drivers looked like bandits. Lashio was full of old trucks and banditti drivers who owned them. To drive a truck along the Burma road was to make a fortune nowadays and was better than banditry. When the road went through finally, if it ever did, two trips would make a man rich for life. The drivers were in high spirits.

"Ready?" Tim shouted.

"Ready!" they shouted back in a chorus of many tones, and they left Lashio with tooting horns and yells.

This caravan now clattered behind Tim as he came to the bog and saw what had happened in those eleven days. The bog had moved on, that was all. Over the miles where he and Wang had staggered on foot there was a broad stretch of black mud, a bottomless swamp. A little man in a muddied white uniform came toward him. Under his helmet his eyes were shining with fever.

"How many days before we can get through?" Tim asked in Chinese.

The man answered in perfect English. "We say seven days. But we replace our men every few days because they die so quickly. Now they refuse to come, knowing that if they do they will die."

"You weren't here when I came through," Tim said.

"I replaced another, and another will replace me," the man said.

"Looks as though we'd have to wait," Tim said.

"There are many who wait," the man replied and went to his post, and Tim turned the caravan back to the last village inn.

The red candles and the incense were still before the big Buddha but they were dusty. The magistrate would not come back until it was clear the Japanese were not going to bomb Tali. It was certainly not clear yet, because they were bombing the capital of the province, which was no distance away. There had been some rumor of the Yellow Wolf's fighting them, but nothing had come of it. Indeed, the Yellow Wolf had merely been bolder than usual. There were those who had seen the band too near Tali for comfort.

"He knows I must keep my soldiers for my own protection," the magistrate groaned. Under the circumstances he had felt it was scarcely worth climbing the mountain again to remind Buddha of his threat, and gradually everyone stopped going, feeling now that what must happen would happen. And so the dust grew about the image.

The old abbot had the key to Tim's living room, and if he had been well he would have gone in himself to dust the Buddha; but he was ill, and he would give the key to none of the priests. Two of them had once been robbers who had taken sanctuary to escape having their heads cut off. As a mere murderer himself, he felt he could not trust them with Tim's possessions, when they wanted to know if they should not at least go in and dust off the big Buddha once in a while.

"Buddha will not care," he told them. "He knows that dust is the end of us all," and he kept the key in the folds of his dirty inner girdle.

But the old abbot upon his bed had been disturbed by bad dreams for several days. Usually he could cope with any trouble by smoking a little opium, but this time the dreams were stronger than the opium. He grew so annoyed by them finally that he got up and walked feebly about his room. The sun was shining so clearly through the paper lattices of the window that he went out into the courtyard. But he was still oppressed. The horoscope he had been working on would not come out to its proper end. He could not bring it past an obscure danger point, the cause for which he could not understand.

"I'll go and pray to the big Buddha," he told one of the old monks who sat in the sunshine hunting the lice out of his robe. "I am disturbed in my spirit."

"Pray for me," the monk replied absently, his mind on an insect that eluded him.

But the abbot did not pray for anyone. He went into Tim's living room and lit the candles and the incense before the big Buddha and then drew Tim's American leather chair quite close to the altar, and sat down in it to discover what was wrong. And after sitting there awhile his disturbance clarified itself. Tim was in trouble, and the Yellow Wolf's destiny depended on Tim. The more he thought about this the more his disturbance settled about it as a certainty. He felt relieved. If one could find the cause of a disturbance it could be cured. He must find Tim. Then, being economical, he pinched out the candles and the incense with his thumb and forefinger.

"*O mi to fu,*" he said to the Buddha. He felt much better. Besides, a trip would do him good.

He set out the next day with his begging bowl and his staff, and in his girdle Tim's last month's rent and the living room key. If the magistrate wanted to worship Buddha it would be impossible. But it was not likely. The Japanese had bombed Kunming again and their armies were advancing. Bombs could be avoided by crawling into the belly of the earth, but how could one escape armies? He set out on foot, walking with a limp he exaggerated slightly. As soon as he reached the new road a bus stopped, as he expected it would, since it is good luck to help a priest.

"A ride, Priest?" the driver inquired.

"Buddha provides," he replied gratefully, and got in.

"I could of course have sent my soul to you only," the abbot told Tim. "It would have been simpler. But I wanted a trip. I had never been on a bus."

They sat under a palm tree near the village just beyond the tiger country of Shweli. Tim had retreated to wonder whether the rest of his life would be spent here with his trucks. Meanwhile he had ordered two thousand shovels with bamboo handles from the local blacksmith, and the man and his apprentices were working day and night. At least these fragile swiftly-dropping men would not have to scrape the miles of earth with their bare hands.

"Anyway, I am glad you have come," Tim said. "How are my chrysanthemums?"

"I pinched the buds myself," the abbot replied. "When you return they should be at their best."

"If I don't return, they are yours," Tim said. "I need not tell you, who have just traveled the great bog on foot, that American trucks can cross it no more than as if it were an ocean. And men drop dead before they can remove ground enough for their own graves."

"Ah," said the abbot, "we need The Women."

"What women?" Tim asked.

But the abbot did not answer. He was thinking, and thought was deepening into trance. His eyes grew hazed and he turned in upon himself. Tim waited. He knew that mood when the abbot seemed to curl in toward his own soul, his hands curling, his feet, his head shrinking between his shoulders, all his body curling into itself. The abbot might stay thus for a few minutes or for hours. Tim waited half an hour and then he tiptoed away. He went to the village where his trucks were lined up just outside the inn where he had a dirty room, and examined them. Nothing, so far as he could see, was gone. He had drawn with whitewash upon the cases an intricate pattern of chrysanthemums, and as a touch of irony had made them the sacred imperial chrysanthemums of Japan, each with thirteen petals. The pattern was unbroken by theft. No one knew yet what was in the cases. He had lied simply when people asked him what was in the cases.

"Books," he had said.

When he went back to the palm tree the abbot was gone. Tim

looked for him now and again for two days, but he was not to be found. He gave up looking for him then because he had to give up everything to plan how to save the trucks. A new danger had come. On the afternoon of that hot September day he felt a rush of panic creep swiftly over the countryside like an instantaneous epidemic. The shops along the single street of the little village put up their shuttering boards, and one by one people closed their houses. By mid-afternoon the street and the alleys were bare, and everyone was shut into the dark steaming heat of his own court.

Tim, walking back from a hilltop from which in the distance he could see the stagnant road, was astonished at the blank and empty streets. He had left them full of lazy, contented people, selling a little, buying a little, and talking and laughing a great deal. Now he saw no one. When he entered the courtyard of the inn, the fat innkeeper was waiting for him.

"It will be better for you to move away from this miserable inn, sir," he said.

"Why?" Tim asked, surprised.

"Other guests are coming," the innkeeper said unhappily.

"I have been here a long time," Tim said gently. He understood that for some reason, sudden and strange, he was unwanted. But he had no intention of moving.

"I neglected to tell you," the innkeeper said, "but before you came your rooms were occupied by a man with the smallpox."

"I am not afraid of smallpox," Tim told him.

"It was leprosy," the innkeeper replied.

Wang, clutching the food box, made his face hideous with meaning and nodded toward the privacy of Tim's room. Tim went in, and Wang followed him.

"Sir, the truth is bandits are coming."

"Bandits?" Tim repeated. Bandits, of course, were everywhere, but why here and now?

"They think there is treasure in the cases," Wang said.

Tim nodded. Comprehensible, but his trucks were not for these bandits.

"I shall go out to meet them," he now told Wang. "I'm an American. They can't take my stuff."

Wang looked uncertain. "Ordinary bandits might listen to a white man," he said, "but these are The Women. They listen to no man."

"You mean women bandits?" Tim demanded. One reason why he kept on living in China was that no one knew what could happen next. He had seen so few Chinese women that they were almost a myth to him—peasants who ran when they saw him, a stout matron at a market place buying meat and vegetables, women beggars, pocked and blind, a young girl in a doorway who was gone when he looked at her.

"I mean The Women!" Wang said stubbornly.

Tim wanted to laugh. "If they are only women," he said, "then all this is nonsense. Go and tell the innkeeper that in my country we are not afraid of women."

Wang went but what he said was, "My master is the son of the chief governor who sits next to the King in America. He has a royal seal around his neck. It is magic. When The Women come he will walk out alone and talk with them and if they do not listen to him he will destroy them."

"Has he also magic guns?" the innkeeper asked.

"He wears two inside his shirt," Wang replied. He had discussed with Tim the advisability of a gun of his own when they set out on this absurd journey.

"I don't want a gun," Tim had said.

"Why, sir?" Wang inquired.

"Because I don't want ever to be put in the position of having to kill somebody," Tim had replied.

This, Wang knew, was insanity, and now he kept it secret.

"Since he has two guns, and if he has magic," the innkeeper said, "he may stay, though I am responsible for nothing."

But he went out and spread the word to the villagers to quiet them. They had been clamoring at him to strangle Tim quietly and to send word to The Women that the whole thing had been a fable, since there was no American and no treasure. When Tim was dead they could open the boxes themselves.

"It is well to let him try his magic," the innkeeper said, "since we have none strong enough for The Women."

. . . Tim, that night, creeping through moonlit jungle toward the edge of the bog, paused. There was little use, he thought to himself with a grin, in trying to be quiet when he smelled loudly enough for anybody to know he was around without even opening their eyes to see him. He had covered himself with a mixture of lard and eucalyptus oil; this was against the deadly mosquito bites. His sweat, struggling against the grease, made him feel he was encased in rubber. Now he crouched under a low-growing tree, having first searched the moss beneath it with his flashlight for snakes.

He believed not a word of this whole business, but he had given his promise and he had come out to meet these women. He could not believe in them. Women to him meant something gentle and childlike. He had not known many even in America and he had remained celibate under the eyes of Buddha. He was curious now but not afraid, and his only weapons were high boots and a stick against the snakes.

It was not quite midnight. Behind him the village was dead.

In his truck each driver lay curled into the seat, pretending sleep. Wang, faithful in all else, had refused to come with him now.

"It is better for a white man to be alone with The Women," he said, and when Tim was gone drew the wooden bar across the door of his room and sat on the food box. There was little enough in that food box now. A few tins of soup, one of beans, a can of dried milk and a little sugar—even a truck driver would not be tempted much. But duty had become habit.

Tim, crouching in that jungle midnight which is so full of evil noise, felt his skin stir and his hairs move. In the moonlight he saw at last people, gathering at the further edge of the bog. He saw a moving darkness broken by wavering and flickering light. He watched until it seemed to him the bog was half full of people. "Bandits," he thought, whether they were men or women, and slowly he grew very angry.

"Hell, my guns are to fight the Japs," he thought, watching them. "I'm simply going to march up to them and tell them. I shall put them on their honor as patriots."

He leaped up and, putting on his flashlight steadily, he struggled across a quarter of a mile of mire.

They saw him. He knew that because suddenly all movement ceased and every light went out. They drew together in a black mass, and he felt them there waiting. But he went on, dragging one leg and then the other out of the sucking black mud.

When he drew near enough to speak he stopped; then he lifted his flashlight. The circle of its light framed a face, a strong, handsome face. It was the face of a woman! He played the light upon one face after another. They were women, all of them.

"I'll be damned," he said clearly in English.

243

There was not a whisper, not a movement in the horde standing solidly together, blocked before him in the moonlight.

"Who are you?" he asked in Chinese.

No one answered. They stood in their silence.

He brought the light back to the one in the front. He studied her face again—granite, smooth, the great eyes black as onyx, comprehending nothing or everything, he could not tell which. And yet he had a curious knowledge of having seen it elsewhere. He turned his light over her huge body. She had no gun, no weapon indeed of any kind, for in her hands was a farm hoe.

"Where do you come from?" he asked. He put the light on her eyes as he did so, but there was not a flicker of response in them, only a vast, determined waiting. And he began in a sort of panic to back away from her. As the light swept across the bodies of the others he saw that each held a hoe or a shovel. He turned and ran floundering through the mud.

When he had reached the shadow of the trees he waited and watched. No one had pursued him, and after a while, as though they waited to make sure he was gone, he saw the mass begin to stir and move, and in the moonlight to scatter, and after a while there were flickering lights again. And then he saw what they were doing. They were working on the road, the road which had felled so many men. They had come for this and for nothing else. He stood watching them, their strong, oxlike figures moving steadily, swiftly. Yes, that was all they had come for, and all they were doing.

He turned away at last and went toward the village. It was not far from dawn when he pounded on the door Wang had barred.

"You are not dead?" Wang inquired when he saw him.

"No," Tim said shortly.

"And the bandits, sir?"

"They will not come here," Tim said, without thinking. He wanted to keep secret, somehow, that which he had seen. It was difficult to explain. But Wang darted under his arm as he leaned in the doorway. A moment later Tim heard him boasting everywhere in the inn.

"What did I say? The Women are not coming. My master forbade it."

He let him boast. What did it matter? He had seen a miracle.

It became known as a miracle, indeed, in that region, as the bog which had swallowed into itself the bodies of so many men grew within a few days to a strong belt of firm land. Stone was thrown into its depths, rocks and boulders crushed and smoothed over stone, and earth beaten into that. Men came back morning after morning to marvel at what the night had done. Or had they, they asked themselves, done more than they knew the day before? Undoubtedly there was a miracle somewhere. It was better not to ask, merely to accept it.

In five days and nights more the road was ready. Tim, at the head of the caravan, drove his truck cautiously, the first to pass. Was the whole thing a dream and a mirage? But the road was firm upon the quaking bog. It was safe. He drove on, and reached the farther side, and behind him came hundreds of other trucks and vehicles of every sort, carrying goods into the back door of China.

In the temple the boxes stood waiting to be claimed. Tim, bathed and fresh, came in from his bedroom and looked at them. He had not the slightest idea what to do next. At that moment he felt a touch on his arm. He turned and saw the abbot.

"I heard you were back," the abbot said.

"Only just," Tim said.

"You were successful?" the abbot inquired.

"Wholly," Tim replied. "And you—where did you go?"

"I?" the abbot said innocently. "Ah, I remember where I left you. Why, I returned to a region I once knew when I was young, where, in fact, I killed a man because of a woman. She was not my wife, for Buddha willed otherwise. Yet this time Buddha sent me to her again because in that region the people do not fear the tiger sickness. They do not die of it, especially the women."

"Immune at last, are they?" Tim asked. "They must have had centuries of it. I suppose you could call those mosquitoes tigers, at that."

"Buddha protects the people there," the abbot replied, "and I remembered and I went to find her, who in my youth was fearless of man or tiger."

The abbot paused, and went on, "She is a woman," he said, "and only I in all the universe could make her obey Buddha's will."

"A miracle?" Tim asked, smiling.

"Everything is a miracle," the abbot replied, "and this, also. I said to her, 'Our son has need of weapons against our enemy, and a white man has the weapons. But he waits for the road to be ready.'"

"Your son?" Tim repeated.

"Ah," the abbot said quietly.

"In that case," Tim said after a few seconds, "I suppose you can tell him the guns are here."

"They will be gone tomorrow morning when you rise," the abbot said peacefully.

Side by side they gazed out over Tali the beautiful, lying beyond the open door. It was exactly as it had always been for

246

centuries except for that new road lying flat and white beside it. Upon the road were moving shining sparks, weaving back and forth. They were cars and trucks of every sort. Tim watched them as each caught the sun for an instant and went on, between the mountains, east and west.

"It will be quite easy now to get anything in over the new road," Tim said.

"It will, truly," the abbot replied, and having said all he wanted to say, he went away.

So when the abbot was gone and Tim had finished his dinner he sauntered down the mountain once more to the dingy telegraph office and waked the clerk asleep on the table.

"Cable," he said and printed a few words on a bit of paper.

"Goods delivered," the little clerk read sleepily, scratching his head. "What is your best price for double last order. Rush. Tim."

"Right," Tim said.

He climbed the mountain again and found Wang in a long white robe waiting for him with tea and small sesame cakes. Under that perfection of calmness Tim discerned an enormous excitement but he paid no heed to it.

"I'm going to bed, Wang," he said cheerfully, "and I shall sleep soundly until morning."

"Yes, sir," Wang said, and added in a quiver of Chinese gratitude, "please, thank you, sir."

His hand was upon the lamp to turn it low. In the last flicker of its glow Tim, turning at his bedroom door, saw the golden face. Surely the golden eyelids lifted and surely the onyx eyes gazed at him, comprehending nothing or everything, he could not tell which.

"Don't thank me for a miracle," he said.

XI
GUERRILLA MOTHER

GUERRILLA MOTHER

ADAME CHIEN was fifty years old and full of secrets. To no one in her life had she ever opened this vast store. She had begun its accumulation as soon as she was able to think, which was many years before Japan invaded China. Thought had begun, perhaps, when Madame Chien discovered that she was a girl, and this was when she observed a difference in the love her parents bestowed upon her and that given to her brother. The difference was qualitative. The love her brother received, although he was younger than she, was weighted with deference; that given to her was delightful and indulgent, but full of demands upon her services and without regard to her wishes or to the needs of her mind. She brooded upon this until one day she felt compelled to put a question to her mother. This brought a sharp answer.

"You may as well learn early as late that you are a woman," her mother said, "and that, being a woman, you cannot expect to be treated as a man."

Madame Chien, then a child of nine, made no reply to this. But from then on she began the accumulation of her secrets, storing them behind the impregnable wall of her unusual beauty and great charm. Thus while her brother was tutored in much learning, she sat in the next room, embroidering endlessly, but so near the door that she heard everything. She stole his books so skillfully that he did not miss them or thought them merely misplaced, and from them she learned to read, not only Chinese, but a little English and some Japanese. This was another of her secrets. No one knew she understood any foreign language, and no one really knew how well she read her own, or that she found comfort in repeating to herself pages from the philosophies of the sages, written only for the comfort of men. Indeed, had she gone up for examination instead of her brother she would have passed higher than he. But at seventeen she was married.

She took with her into her husband's house all her secrets. One was that she had ceased to believe in gods. In a household where women were ignorant and therefore superstitious and devout attendants at temples, all would have been shocked and even terrified had they known that the beautiful calm young girl who spoke little and always gently had quietly put away all belief in gods. She had heard her brother's tutor explain too much science ever to believe in them again. But still she bowed her head decorously before the household gods in her husband's house as she had in her father's, believing not in them but in their usefulness as objects of worship necessary for those ignorant enough to need them.

Still another of her secrets was her profound though kindly contempt for the ignorant and the stupid. She discovered, almost immediately, that her husband was among these, not because he was poor, but because he was too rich, the son and grandson of rich men. This was a deep blow, for she had dreamed of the companionship of an intelligent man. But she accepted the truth as she found it, and in her husband's presence she was always amiable and smiling, using only so much of her thought as was needful to carry on a conversation as he liked it. The rest of her mind she occupied with much pondering and thinking upon the many books she continued to read in secret.

As years passed she became more and more intelligent and wise and as her wisdom grew, more beneficent, so that her husband depended upon her for everything, even the direction of his vast inheritance of land and tenants, and certainly her four sons and three daughters learned all they knew from her. Without revealing any of her secrets as they actually were, she instilled into them the love of knowledge so that they sought its sources for themselves. None of them penetrated behind the impregnable wall of her beauty and her charm, which she varied for each so that to her husband she seemed all wife and lover, and each child thought himself her favorite. She was fond of them all but she allowed none to enter behind her wall. There she lived with her secrets, her increasing stores of all sorts of knowledge, her pondering, her imaginations and conclusions about men and women and the universe.

Thus had passed her years. But there had been little of the peace she craved in her life. She was continually employed in the management of the great household and in settling the complaints and troubles it brought to her. Nor had the times into which she was born been peaceful. For she had experienced the threat of revolutions and the warfare between war lords that comes in times of change, and she had watched power taken from a single sovereign in the empire and bestowed upon many people in the newly made republic, though without hope. "For why," she thought, "should we expect many stupid persons to rule better than one?" So when taxes rose, when evils increased and quarrels were magnified, she was not cast down, being inwardly prepared and fortified from her secret stores.

There came a day when, bad having already gone to worse, it was evident to all that a foreign enemy had not only attacked the nation, but was winning a steady victory. Madame Chien had watched the advance of the Japanese from its first beginning in the far northern province of Manchuria to its present approach to her own home, which was in a small city near a southern sea coast. Now she knew that it was her duty to those remaining in her household to remove them to the inner country beyond the reach of the invaders. She made up her own mind on this, and then, as a dutiful wife, she asked her husband what he wished, skillfully revealing by her apparently humble questions what she herself thought best, and expressing her appreciation of his wisdom when a few moments later she said his wishes were her own.

It was when she was undertaking the organization of the huge household for flight that one day the greatest of her secrets took form in her mind. In the midst of confusion, terror, and noise, in the midst of the loud talking of carriers and servants, she thought of how peaceful the house would be when they were all gone, and the house would be empty.

"I have never felt peace," she thought, "I have never heard silence."

The more she imagined this peace and silence, the more she longed to experience it. At last she felt compelled, and she cast about in her mind for ways. Her household was very large by now. Her four sons were all married and had their wives and children under her roof. Two of her daughters had gone to houses of their husbands', but the youngest was still with her. It was this youngest daughter, she decided, who was the only real responsibility, and this the more because she was also the prettiest. It was for her sake that Madame Chien, after much thinking, called to her side her own faithful old woman servant the night before they were to leave.

"Li Ma," she said, "I have an especial charge to put upon you."

"I will take it, mistress," the sturdy old woman replied.

"It is no more than this—you are to stay always with your little third mistress, my youngest daughter," Madame Chien told her.

"That I will anyhow," Li Ma replied, "for I am always with you, mistress, and on this journey you will keep her with you."

Madame Chien smiled. She had now disposed of her two chief charges, for Li Ma would have insisted on remaining with her and she wanted no one.

"Good night, faithful one," she said.

They were to start when dawn broke. The Japanese by now were none too far away. Madame Chien slept well in the knowledge of her newest secret, waking only a little before dawn. The servants were already busy, and outside the compound wall three motor cars stood waiting. At the end of the good roads horses would be waiting to take them over the mountains, and from there they would go into inner China and be safe.

She rose, and Li Ma came in to dress her. Everything was ready and the family party came out of the courtyards, weeping as they came. There was little hope that this house could be again as it had been for five generations of life. All knew that some sort of end was come. Madame Chien was the last of the procession, "so that I may see that all is right," she had told them. She had asked her husband to lead the procession, and so he went into the first car, and with him were the two eldest sons, their wives, and children. Immediately behind him were the two younger sons, their wives and children, and some of the servants. The third car stayed for Madame Chien. In it already were the youngest daughter, Li Ma, and all the young bondmaids. The two cars started, and the driver of the third set his engine going. To this

driver Madame Chien had come out an hour ago and said in a
low voice when none was near:

"When I cry, 'Ready,' and when you hear the door of the car
slam, then go as fast as you can, and do not heed any clamoring
from my daughter or the women. Do not stop for any cause until
you are beyond the city gate."

This would have amazed him had she not first stupefied him
with the amount of silver she put into his hand as she spoke.
All he could do was to gasp:

"I will obey you, mistress."

He did obey, therefore. He heard her low voice say "Ready."
He heard the door slam, and he let the car leap forward. In all
the din he heard the screaming of women's voices behind him,
but, remembering he was not to hear them, he did not, and the
car rushed on to the city gate.

Madame Chien looked after it with quiet triumph. The city
gates had been locked for many days, and they would be opened
only a few moments at dawn for those who wished to flee. Then
they would be instantly closed and opened for no one. She was
safely left behind as she had secretly planned to be.

. . . The stillness about her was so intense that the world
seemed to have stopped. She went back into her own gate and
barred it that she might be utterly alone. There was no other
reason to bar it, for there was no longer anything of value to
anyone behind it except to herself. The jewels were in a pigskin
box in Li Ma's keeping. The family valuables and the finest of
carved blackwood furniture inlaid with Yunnan marble had been
sent to the country. All the pretty girls were gone. She had no
further responsibility toward anyone or for anything. Day and
night there had been those who had the right to make their
demands upon her, and, trained to outward submission, she had

fulfilled her duties. Now she had no duties. For the first time in her life, as long as she could remember, she was alone, and she had nothing to do. She smiled and sat down on a rock in the shade of a clump of bamboos in the main courtyard.

"I do not need to rise from this rock," she thought. "Not at least until I wish it."

So she continued to sit upon it quietly, enjoying the silence as she had dreamed she would. It was cool even as the sun rose higher. The shadows of the bamboos shrank but she was still within them. She did not even rise when in an hour or so the sound of a siren tore the silence apart to warn the city of approaching enemy planes again, as they did almost every fair day. There was a bomb shelter built under the peony court, but being alone she did not trouble to go to it. "Bombs will not pick out one old woman," she thought peacefully. She thirsted for more and more loneliness. "Besides," she thought, "perhaps death itself is only this empty quiet, but forever." She had never been afraid of death, but now it occurred to her that death might even be pleasant.

It was at this moment that the explosion occurred. She glanced at the sky and saw a solitary plane shine silver. Something dropped from it like thistledown, like an egg, then suddenly lightning was above her and thunder roared.

"It is to be death," she thought and closed her eyes and did not move.

But it was not quite death. The bomb struck the street outside her barred gate. She heard the clatter and crash of the falling wall. She rose then and went out. The wall was a ruin of dust and broken brick. She looked at it, and then up and down the street. So far as she could see, no one had been passing. It was a quiet street at all times and more than ever during these past days.

Yet even as she watched it, the street ceased to be empty. It began to be filled first with noise, and there was the noise of many feet running. Then around the far corner she saw a horde of men swirling in a mob. In an instant the street was full of these men, all in the uniform of the Chinese army. They swarmed around her and over the ruins of the wall. They passed her without seeing her. Every face was staring ahead, every mind intent on escape from some desperate danger.

"They are retreating," she thought and she knew that the enemy was at hand.

She had for many days expected the enemy, but she had reasoned that when they came, as of course they would come, they having the better arms, she would live somehow under their rule. So long as she could keep her secrets she could live under any rule, however alien. Besides, an old woman was valuable to no one, and then she marveled that life was still so sweet to her. Husband and children and duty had ceased to have meaning for her, but there were all her secrets whose meaning she had never had enough time to pursue, nor peace enough.

This peace she now gave up in the instant between one breath and another. While she drew one breath she stood upon her own ground, and when she drew the next she had stepped into the midst of the fleeing men as one steps into a rushing stream. The stream closed about her and carried her onward. There was no escape from it and no turning back. She gasped once or twice.

"I must remember I am not in retreat," she thought and recovered herself while she felt herself swept on. She laid her hand upon the arm of the man next to her.

"Why are you retreating?" she called into his ear.

He turned a dazed face to her and she saw he could understand nothing because of the panic in which he was engulfed with all the crowd.

"This is very stupid," Madame Chien thought as she ran. Her mother had bound her feet when she was a girl, but Madame Chien had allowed them to be gradually more free as she grew older, and long ago she had outgrown the pain both of their binding and their freeing. It was not therefore her feet which made her gradually slow her pace.

"You are all stupid!" she called loudly, and found a pleasure in saying aloud what she so often thought secretly of men. "You are stupid to run away from those little dwarfs—shame on you, sons of Han! Shame—shame—shame!"

And as she thus cried shame, she braced her body back, and in the center of that foolish rush of fear-crazed men, her body became a fixed and steady point.

"Shame—shame—shame," she chanted, bracing herself against them.

They seemed not to hear her. They seemed to slip about her and past her, leaving her behind. Then she turned so as to face those who still came, and, her back to retreat, she continued her chant of shame.

Imperceptibly they heard her, or perhaps they did not so much hear her as feel her in their midst as a force of some sort strong enough to oppose their flight. Certainly at last some stayed, and then many stopped. They stood packed together in the street about Madame Chien, their faces red and their eyes still wild, and they wiped their faces with torn and dusty sleeves. But in their faces she saw shyness because of the shame she had cried upon them. She saw, too, that they were very young and that they had as weapons only small light guns.

259

"Where are you going?" she asked them.

No one answered, and then a young man answered in a rough voice:

"Anywhere for escape! Why should we stay to be killed? The enemy has foreign cannon and all our captains gave us were these!" He held up his little gun to show her. She took it and examined it. It was the first time she had ever had a gun in her hand, but among her secrets there was one about modern weapons. She had found in the old shop she frequented, as other women frequent temples, a book in English entitled *The Science of Modern Warfare,* and there were many pictures in it. She had bought it, since it was then about the time of Japan's seizure of Manchuria.

"But this is a good enough gun," she remarked; "it is not too old in its fashion, and with it, if you crept close enough to a cannon, too close to be its target, you might kill the man behind it. Long-range cannon," she went on, "are more dangerous at a distance than near."

The men stared at her and the young man began to laugh. "Where did a lady learn this?" he asked.

Madame Chien looked at him with dignity. "Where is the enemy?" she inquired.

"They are advancing from the north," the young man replied, "and they are now less than three miles from the city."

"But that means they must cross the river," Madame Chien said.

"They are crossing now," a dozen voices shouted. "They have us in a trap!"

"Oh, you fools," Madame Chien cried, "it is you who have them in a trap. Does not the river circle the city except at the south and can you not circle the river and hold the south open like the neck of a bottle?"

"But when they cross the river to go on—" a voice began, but Madame Chien interrupted it.

"They will not cross it if they think they hold the city and do not know you are in ambush," she said.

They stared at her and at each other. This was only a woman, their eyes said, but certainly, they reflected behind their eyes, not one like other women.

"How do you know these things?" the young man asked boldly.

"I have my secrets," Madame Chien replied with her usual calmness. The sun was growing very hot. "We had better keep on moving as we are to the river," she said.

So they began to move again, but now there was no more of the flurry of retreat. They marched steadily as men do who have been given a direction, and Madame Chien walked with them. It was not too hard, for she had never been a slow-moving woman. She had by habit hastened her feet that her tasks might be finished quickly and her legs were strong and her graceful back was strong. It was an hour before she began to wish for rest. But an hour was long enough. By then they had reached the river and there they met the others, who, still in retreat, were bargaining for boats to cross the river.

"Stop," the young man said to them on every hand. "We have a better plan." He stepped forward and Madame Chien, though she still believed in no gods, thanked the clear heaven above her that among all these fools there had been this young man near her. For he, she now observed, was not a fool.

"Let us seem to retreat," he was saying. "Let us cross the river, and then we will encircle its loop. A fourth of us will go to the bottleneck at the south and there hide. The others will hide about the river. As we are able we will shoot one and another of the enemy if they pass through the city and make to go onward."

"But what if they stay in the city?" a man objected.

"All the better," Madame Chien murmured behind the young man. "Then how easy to mingle with farmers as they go to market and to mingle with crowds in teashops, to hear, to learn, to plan for attack—"

"All the better," the young man shouted loudly. "Then we can mingle among the people and we can listen and learn and when the moment comes we can attack."

Madame Chien, watching the listening faces, decided suddenly that these were not all fools. They were bewildered but not cowards.

"Brave men!" she cried suddenly.

They had forgotten her and many of them had never seen her, but now they all looked at her and laughed when they saw a delicate old lady had called so loudly.

"You are brave," they shouted and they spat on their hands and swore by their mothers, and one after the other said in one way or another the same thing, "We will all die one day anyway," they said, "so why not your way?"

And Madame Chien, watching them, thought, "If I leave them now, what will they do? They are strangers in this place."

She had chosen to remain in a city certain of beleaguerment because in the midst of that beleaguerment she might live alone and in peace. Now suddenly she foresaw the end of all peace.

"My wall is still fallen in dust and ruin, though," she thought, "and if I went back now, who would there be in all the confusion of the city able to build it up again?"

Without deciding to stay or return her attention was now di-

rected to the rapacity of a boatman. All boatmen on river or lake
are rapacious, but this man was so harsh in his demands that
Madame Chien grew angry.

"At a time like this," she remarked in her clear voice, "no one
should think of himself. Take his boat, you men, and man it
yourselves. Take all the boats you need, but see that they are returned, for they are a livelihood, even if there are some who do
not deserve to live."

"Seize the boats," the young man cried. "He who thinks of
his own profit now is a traitor."

In a moment the soldiers had seized the boats, and, being sons
of ordinary men and women, they rowed themselves across very
well. The young man waited for the last boat. Then he turned
to Madame Chien:

"Come with us, good mother," he said simply.

And as simply she rose from the grass where she had been resting and, putting her hand upon the arm he held out for her, she
stepped into the boat and knew as she did so that she left peace
behind her.

The attack itself did not take place for many days. Madame
Chien did not allow it.

"Let the bottle be filled," she told the young man. By now she
knew that his name was Tung Li. "Call me Lih-tse," he said.
"Everyone does."

But Madame Chien found herself unable to be so familiar and
so she called him by his full name or by nothing.

"When the bottle is filled we will put in the stopper," she continued.

There was a great deal to do before then. The men must be
disguised so that they could wander about the city freely and

see where the enemy was quartered and how many there were and what were their habits. The moment of attack must depend on knowledge. She lived now in a corner of a farmer's hut, cut off by a reed mat from his teeming family. A bamboo bed, an unpainted table, and a rough stool were its furniture. The bed she used very little. At the table she sat long with Tung Li, plotting every move of every day and she drew out of her stores one secret after another. Thus she said:

"I read a foreign book once, though translated into our own tongue, concerning war and peace. There was a great battle in it, and this was its progress."

With her long fingernail she traced in the dust of the table the moves of the campaign Napoleon had once made against Russia. "But first," she said, "we must send a spy into the city who can creep into the very headquarters of the enemy to listen to the plans as they are made. Common soldiers know nothing of what their captains plan for them."

"Alas, we understand nothing of their language," Tung Li said.

Madame Chien reflected upon this for the space of half a moment.

"Ah," she said then, "I must be the spy."

"Can you?" Tung Li asked. By now he was half frightened of her. He had begun seriously to wonder who this woman was whose face was still so delicately beautiful, and whose garments, though dust-stained, were so fine. Being the son of a peasant mother, he believed in gods and goddesses, in fairies and fox women, and he was now more than sure that Madame Chien came from among them, sent by heaven in man's need.

"I can understand a little Japanese," Madame Chien said shyly, "though it always seemed useless until now."

She was almost frightened herself. Had she all these years been shaped toward a destiny now near?

Thus she became a spy. In coarse clothing borrowed from the farmer's wife, with brown dust from the threshing floor rubbed into her skin, she took a basket and filled it with the lard cakes the farmer's wife made sometimes to sell, and put it on her arm as a vendor does. The farmer's wife examined her to see that all looked as it should. Madame Chien was an actress, having played for many years the part of a woman always amiable and never too clever for men's comfort. When she had roughened her hair and blackened her teeth, she also put on her face a look of stupidity clever enough to deceive all. Her own children would have passed her as a stranger.

"How nice you look now," the farmer's wife cried. "Exactly like one of us," she continued, and then she saw that the cakes were uncovered. "They will be full of dust," she exclaimed, and she snatched the family towel from a peg in the earthen wall of the hut.

But Madame Chien's gorge rose at the sight of this towel, though she knew unreasonably, for what did it matter what lay over cakes sold to the enemy? Nevertheless her instincts cried out beyond her control. The towel was black and filthy, and she had seen it used to wipe tables and bowls and children's faces and the farmer's sweat, and indeed for every necessity of family life.

"You will need your one towel," she said gracefully. "I can easily buy another at the city gate."

It was this fresh clean cloth that she bought a little later in the bazaar under the arch of the city gate which brought Madame Chien direct into the presence of the captain of the enemy. Thus Heaven arranges for those whom it loves. For though Madame Chien herself did not know it, the Japanese hated filth so much that in spite of hunger they would not eat cakes from under the dirty sweat-filled towels of the vendors. When she came to the teashop and they saw her basket covered with pure white, they clamored for her cakes, and she was obliged to raise the price of them lest they be sold before she wished them gone. Even so, this might have happened had not a young soldier pulled her sleeve and motioned to her to follow him.

"Do not buy any more," he commanded his fellows. "The captain will want these."

When she heard this she was frightened again by her seeming destiny. But she did not hesitate. She followed him along a familiar road until he brought her before the fallen wall of her own house. Then she perceived what had happened. Since hers was the best house in the small city, the captain had taken it for his own. She followed the soldier across her own threshhold into the courtyard where a few days before she had sat down to rest, dreaming of peace. She followed this stranger into her own house, and there in the main hall sat the captain, at ease in her husband's lounging chair. With him were his lesser officers.

The young man she had been following saluted.

"What is it?" the captain asked.

"I found an old woman selling clean cakes, sir," the soldier replied.

"Can it be?" the captain retorted. He wagged his head and laughed and motioned Madame Chien to come near. He lifted the white cloth and seized all the remaining cakes and began to eat them with great greediness. "If you had been a few years younger, old woman," he said with his mouth full, "I might have wanted more of you than cakes." His men, seeing this was a joke, laughed, and the captain was pleased with himself. "Come back tomorrow," he said loudly to Madame Chien. But she kept her

266

stupid look, and so he made motions until she seemed to understand and nodded and then she went away.

Thus day after day she returned to her own house and bit by bit she became a serving woman there where she had always been mistress. It was easy enough to begin by pouring tea into the bowls that were emptied as her cakes were eaten, and then she lit cigarettes and then she fetched food and then she tidied rooms and dusted their furniture. Her own room she found occupied by three young Japanese women, and she came gradually to wait upon them, and all the time she gave no sign of understanding any word spoken of all those she heard and did understand. She was careful to understand no command shouted at her, but continued to serve quietly as she saw need, as though she did not even know that it was she they commanded, and so at last they forgot her and spoke as though she were not there.

Then she learned everything about them, where their men were quartered and in what numbers, and how the campaigns to the north went and how many men must be sent to help in that campaign, and what ammunition was brought here to be stored and where it was stored.

Everything she knew she carried back at night to Tung Li who waited for her at the farmer's hut. "Let them eat and drink a few days longer, and grow softer and more weak," she advised him when he was impatient for attack. "In a few days half of the men are to be sent north. When that day comes, there will be left in the city only a garrison, but much ammunition where I have told you. We can attack easily, and with the ammunition and the stored cannon and guns we can pursue those marching to the north. Strengthen your men for that day."

So Tung Li obeyed her as he now did in everything. He built his men into a strong band, and they named themselves The

Black River Guerrillas, and one night some came to Madame Chien with a request from them all.

"We wish to call you our mother," they said, "because you have brought us good luck."

In their hearts they all now believed her faery, though she did not know it, being always modest. But she was touched by their childlike nature.

"I am proud to call you my sons," she replied.

Thereafter she gave her own response to them by small merciful deeds. She mended rents in their coarse garments with the exquisite skill she had once used in embroidering upon satin birds and butterflies and flowers. If a man were hurt she washed and bound his wounds. Of such things she knew much because she had once bought some large books of foreign medicine. A servant in the house of a foreign physician in another city had stolen them from his master to sell for a little money for himself, and they had drifted from hand to hand until she saw them. It occurred to her now that she should have these books by her, since there might be many wounded men in the days to come, and thereafter each day when she went back to her house she thrust one of these books under her peasant coat.

"We are now ready to take back the city," Tung Li told her one night. "But how shall we know which is the right and lucky day if you do not set it for us?"

"Two thirds of the enemy leave on the night of the full moon," she replied. "But whether that or the next day is the day, depends on a secret plan of mine."

"Keep your secrets," he replied hastily, a little afraid of her.

It was as though gods had put that word into his mouth.

"I will," she said calmly, not dreaming of his fear.

This secret was that she remembered where her husband kept his foreign wines. These wines he loved, but they spoiled easily until she devised a way to store them in an old well near his private courtyard. She had had a ladder hung against the side of this well and shelves built around its old brick walls and a thick cover made for its mouth.

"Foreigners put their wines in caverns under their houses," she had told him, for so she had once chanced to read, "but since our houses are built upon flat ground this is better."

Now in a moment left free she went to that well. Vines had grown over the cover and she could not lift it alone. But it meant also that none had discovered the place. So she went back and herself found the captain and pulled his sleeve and made motions that he was to come with her. He humored her now as they all did, and so he came. When she pointed to the old well he thought it was treasure and shouted for his aide to come and open it. That one put his shoulder to the cover and twisted it up against the vines and then the strong summer sunshine fell upon the dusty bottles.

The captain gave a roar of joy. "I thought it was only gold!" he cried. He reached his arm down and pulled up a bottle and cracked the head off on the stone curb and poured the foreign wine down his throat.

Madame Chien watched him. The men she had known, her father, her brother, her husband, her sons, drank this wine in sparing small porcelain bowls at meal times, but this man drank it down in gulps. She slipped away while he still tilted the bottle at his mouth. She crossed the courtyards and the fallen wall and hastened back to Tung Li, stopping only to bribe the watchman at the city gate.

"Prepare," she told Tung Li. "Tonight is the hour."

When he had hastened away she felt suddenly overcome with weariness. After all, she had never been a serving woman before, and busy though her life had been, it had been to command servants and not to serve. "After the enemy is driven from this city, my work will be done," she thought.

Time after time in that furious night she promised herself peace when it was over. The guerrillas crossed the river in the moonlit dark. She sat in the boat with Tung Li and she directed the men to the southern gate where the bribed watchman let them through, though his face was pallid when he did it, and when they were gone he leaped into his bed and pretended a sleep as sound as death. And Madame Chien led them to every secret place where the enemy was quartered. All that the men had not found out for themselves she knew, and at every place the men were stationed to wait for the attack. But Tung Li and his strongest men she led to her own house.

"Here is their captain," she said. And then to her own surprise her long loathing and disgust rose in her and cried out. She had so grown to hate that man, his brutal looks and ways, his coarse shouts and sudden rages that she had even come to pity the three women in her room because his lusts toward them were so vicious.

"Kill the captain first," she said.

"I will," Tung Li said.

"I shall wait beyond that gate," she said, pointing to a court.

"There I will bring you the news of victory," he promised her.

And she, while the attack was carried out in her house and in every house where the enemy was, went back to her courtyard and found that cool old rock and sat down upon it and waited for peace. When all this was over and the dead cleaned away she would go on with being alone. Loneliness in her house would be sweeter than ever. She sat waiting for it while the guns cracked in the darkness and men, surprised in sleep and drunkenness, swarmed and groaned and gave great sighing gusts of breath before they died. She sat in the darkness listening.

"Of all my secrets, when peace comes, this will be the strangest," she thought.

Quiet fell with dawn. Through the pale new light she saw Tung Li come wearily through the gate.

"They are dead," he said. "How they bleed!"

She did not answer this. She waited a moment and then rose.

"I will return to my own house," she said. She had told none of them from where she had come nor that this was it.

But before she could take a step Tung Li cried out at her, "Are you not going with us against the others?"

"What others?" she said as stupidly as if she had been anybody.

"The men who were sent against the cities to the north," he said.

And then to her amazement he dropped on his knees and knocked his head before her as men do before images in temples. "Do not leave us now," he said. "We must make greater battle than this if we are to drive out the enemy. What is a little town if they hold our great cities and our sea coasts and our northern provinces, and how can we prevail if you do not tell us the will of heaven?"

Then for the first time she understood that he thought her more than human and so he wanted her aid. She was about to deny her divinity and then she did not. He was a simple fellow and the simple, she thought with sad wisdom, must be given their gods. What did it matter if it were she or another?

She stood wavering. How lovely in her courts were loneliness

271

and peace! And did she not deserve them now and would it not be her only heaven, since she believed in no other?

And then suddenly loneliness was gone again and peace was scattered to nothing and heaven lost. Through the gate came a score or two of men who had been wounded. But they were gay with victory in spite of pain and bleeding. Their proud talk and laughter rent the last echoes of peace to shreds.

"I held a door against ten," one boasted, "and then a son of a Japanese turtle thrust his sword through a crack and gave me this."

"And I held two against a wall and killed them both," another said.

She had nothing with which to bind their wounds. "I will go and find some clean water and clean cloth somewhere," she said. They were so used to her doing what she would that they rested themselves and waited. And she went to her own room, passing without a look on the way the bodies of those dead. Her room was empty. The women had fled, for none of their things even were left behind. Yes, there was a clean robe, white cotton cloth with blue flowers, newly washed and hung to dry and so forgotten. She felt it, and now it was dry.

"It will do for their wounds," she thought. She stood for a moment in her room and sighed and took the garment and went back to the noisy court, stopping only to lift a wooden pail of water from a shallow well on the way.

"The enemy left you this to bind your wounds," she told the men. Her quick hands tore the robe to strips. Then she smiled and said playfully, "Good enemy, we must pursue you to thank you for this and all."

They laughed, and even those in pain were comforted, and Tung Li said, "It is you we thank."

None who thought they knew Madame Chien best ever saw her again or heard of her. The war went on so long that once her eldest son came back to search for her and to ask if any had seen or heard of his mother. But none had. He wandered through the empty house and saw no sign that she had been there after them. She must have been killed by the enemy, everyone said, staring into the house. He went away again, back to his father, and they all mourned for her as dead, wearing the white robes for twice the days they needed because she had been so dear to them, to each in his own way.

She herself forgot who she was. The war went on, and it seemed to her at last that all her life she had been nothing but what these young men called her, Guerrilla Mother. The soldiers were rough men and simple, and always too filthy for her wishes. Their torn garments she never could keep mended as she liked, and she must praise and scold and command and punish them by her displeasure when they did not do the right and be ready to comfort them when they died. But she stayed with them. She must lead and follow them, she knew now, until the war was over and peace come, or else until she made her own peace, after all, in a small bit of earth somewhere along the way.

XII
A MAN'S FOES

A MAN'S FOES

MARTIN LIU was bewildered as he stepped out of the train at the railroad station in Peking. Nothing was changed, it was exactly as he had remembered it for the seven years he had been abroad. But he had so long looked forward to this moment of homecoming that now it was come it was unreal.

He stood, looking about him, and at that instant saw Wang Ting, his father's chief secretary, and his own sister Siu-li. They were looking in the crowd for him and he now saw them first. He shouted and Siu-li saw him and waved a gay pink handkerchief. She came toward him eagerly, the elderly secretary following her. Martin had not seen this twin sister of his all these years. He had thought of her much and though he had seen many pictures of her he was not quite prepared for this extremely pretty and poised young woman who put out her hand.

"Elder Brother!" she cried in a soft voice. He was older than she by two hours.

"Is this you, Siu-li?" he inquired, unbelieving.

"It is no other, certainly," she replied, smiling. "But here's Wang Ting, too."

Wang Ting came bowing and Martin bowed. He remembered with affection this man who had stood as his father's deputy as long as he could remember. That Wang Ting was here now meant that his father was not. He was disappointed, though he

277

had known his father might not come to meet him. Still, after seven years, and he an only son—

"Is Father well?" he asked Siu-li.

He noticed the smallest of hesitations before she answered.

"Yes, he is well. Today it happens he has important business or he would have come."

Wang Ting cleared his throat. "Your father sent every message of welcome by me," he said solemnly. "And he says he hopes you will not delay. There are guests invited for a feast at seven, and it is now nearly half past five. You will want to rest and he will want a few moments at least with you alone."

Wang Ting stepped back, having done his duty.

"Thank you," Martin said courteously.

"Let's go home quickly," Siu-li said with an unexpected petulance. "Wang Ting, you see to his bags and trunks. We will go on."

Wang Ting bowed and took the checks that Martin handed to him. A few minutes later the brother and sister were sitting side by side in their father's car.

They said nothing for a short while. Each was shy of the other, now that they were alone. Though they were fully aware of their relation, still it remained true that they were a young man and a young woman, strange to each other. Then Martin forgot himself.

"I don't remember this road," he remarked. "I thought we used to go to the right."

"We always did until the Japanese came," Siu-li said. "Now we go this way so as to avoid their chief barracks."

"I see," Martin said. He knew that the Japanese had full possession of Peking. Even if his father and sister had not written him of it he would have known it from reading the newspapers in New York, where he had been a student. At first he had expected every letter to tell him that his family had moved away, but as time went on and this did not happen he began to believe that things had not changed so much as he had feared they would. Evidently it was still possible for proud Chinese like his father to live under a Japanese flag, although of course it would be only temporary. It was unthinkable that the Japanese would continue to rule in China. That was why he had come back to China with only a master's degree. His father had urged, indeed, had commanded him to remain abroad for two more years at least and if possible longer in order to get practical experience in his chosen field of metallurgy.

"China needs men of the highest training," his father had written.

But Martin, reading in the American newspapers about the way Japanese soldiers were behaving in his country, could not keep his blood calm enough to sit studying.

"I must come back and do what I can now against the enemy," he wrote his father. And without waiting for reply he had drawn his next term's expense money out of the bank and bought a ticket for China. He had expected questions and even trouble at the port; but when he had given his father's name there had been no trouble and the questions had ceased.

"Do the Japanese annoy you on the street?" he asked his sister now.

Again there was that faint but unmistakable hesitation in her answer. Then she said:

"Sometimes—no, not if they know who I am." Her face shadowed. "But I hate them!" she said in a low voice. "I want to avoid them!"

"Of course," he agreed. He was glad to avoid them, too, and

he said nothing when the chauffeur drove slowly through small winding alleys instead of the wide main streets of the city.

When the car drew up finally before the gate of his father's home, his throat tightened. He was really home at last!

"It looks just the same," he said, gazing at it.

It was just the same, the wide wooden gates painted vermillion red and set in the thick brick wall and over the wall the old twin pomegranate trees of the entrance court.

"How the trees have grown!" he said.

"Seven years," Siu-li said smiling. "I've grown, too, and so have you."

"Yes," he said.

Then he saw something was changed after all. Instead of the one watchman he had been used to see at his father's gate, he now saw two soldiers, uniformed, their bayonets fixed. They presented arms smartly as he stepped from the car and he was embarrassed.

"What's this?" he whispered to Siu-li when he had returned their salute.

"Father has to have a bodyguard just now," she said in a voice whose quality confounded him. It was angry with scorn.

But she led the way quickly into the gate and there was no time for questions. The first courtyard was full of eager servants, waiting to welcome home the son of the house. Firecrackers exploded and banners waved. He had to speak to all the old ones and to acknowledge the bows of the new. Even his old wet nurse was there, come in from the country for this day. His mother had died at the birth of the twins, and while Siu-li had her own nurse, Ling Ma had fed Martin and taken care of him when he was too big to suckle. Everyone had expected his father to take another wife but he had never done so.

"But where is Father?" he asked his sister when it was over at last.

"He seems not to have come home yet," she replied. She hesitated, then went on. "Why don't you go to your room and change your things? By then surely he will be back."

"I will," he replied.

They stood a moment, he feeling that she was about to speak of something. But she did not. She touched his hand merely.

"It is very good to have you home again," she said and left him.

His own room was not changed at all. Its wide paper-latticed window looked out into his own small courtyard. The bamboos, the pine, were the same. Bamboos attained their growth in a single year and seven years were nothing to the pine, already two centuries old.

"Japan and China," he thought, and was pleased with his comparison.

The door opened and Ling Ma came, her face all loving solicitude.

"Now, heart of my flesh, you are not to touch anything. I will unpack your garments and fold them away."

"Foreign suits must be hung, not folded, Ling Ma," he said.

"Then show me one and I will do the others," she said. "You must rest yourself, you must eat and sleep and play after all these years of study. You are too thin." She came close and searched his face. "You didn't take a foreign wife!"

Martin laughed at her. "No, no wife!"

She nodded her satisfaction. "Then we must see to it. I will talk with your father myself."

Martin sat down in his foreign easy chair. "I haven't seen my father yet," he said.

"Oh, he's busy—very busy—" Ling Ma said. She had her face deep in one of his trunks. He could only see her stout back.

"I never knew my father to be busy," he remarked. He could say things to Ling Ma that he could say to no one else.

"He's very busy now," Ling Ma's voice came out of the trunk. A sudden thought struck him. He put it away and then returned to it. After all, it was only Ling Ma.

"He's not getting married again, is he?" The thought was repulsive, but his father was only fifty years old and it was possible.

"Don't ask me!" Ling Ma's voice was suddenly snappish. She came out of the trunk and her face was very red from bending so long. "Don't ask me anything, Young Master! I don't know anything. If anybody asks me anything about this house, I don't know. I live in the country now with my son and I only came back to welcome you home, heart of my body."

He was used to outbursts from Ling Ma, for she was a woman of impetuous temper. Now he hardly knew whether there was truth in his suspicion or whether she was angry because she had been treated in some way she considered unfair. Ling Ma had quarreled often over his father's decrees during his childhood, and it might be her old jealousy against authority over the child in her care.

"Did my father treat you unjustly?" he inquired.

She laughed loudly. "Me, little heart? No, I left this house of my own accord. He even invited me to stay and await your coming. But no, I would not. No, it was nothing he did to *me!*"

Ling Ma pursed her lips and looked solemn. He was about to put another question to her. Then he decided against it. He did not wish to resume with Ling Ma the old affectionate childish relationship that gave her power over him. He was a man, now. So he said a little coldly:

282

"That is well, for if he had not given you your due, I should have felt I ought to make amends."

She felt the difference in him and gave way to it at once. "From you I expect only what is good," she said, and then spoke no more, but crept about with her silent solid tread, putting his things right. Then she went away and he was alone.

The house was very still. He had not in years heard such stillness. New York was full of noise, and in its own way, so was the ocean. But this was the stillness of centuries. He felt it around him a protection of strength. What could the enemy do against a great, silent old country?

"They are like swallows attacking a snow-capped mountain," he thought proudly.

At that moment to his astonishment the door opened abruptly, and his father came in.

"Father!" he cried with joy.

"My son," his father replied. He came forward and seized Martin's two hands and held them closely and gazed into his face.

And Martin, receiving that earnest, questioning gaze, felt suddenly shy. Why had his father done so strange a thing as to come to him in his own room? It was not like the austere man he remembered so to step aside from custom. He had been prepared to go to his father when summoned, to stand while his father sat, to answer when he was questioned. But instead here his father was, an eager, even importunate look upon his aging face. He had aged very much. Martin drew back. Instantly his father loosed his hands and the look disappeared.

"Are you well?" he inquired.

"Quite well," Martin replied. He hurried on, anxious for talk. "I hope you are not angry that I disobeyed you, my father. I felt

I must come home now—for two reasons. The first is that I want to be of what use I can against the enemy. The second is that I was honestly ashamed to be living abroad in ease and at study as though my country were not suffering."

His father stood looking at him. "I am not angry," he said, "It would be of little use if I were. This generation does what it pleases."

"No, Father, don't speak so," Martin cried. "It makes me feel you are angry!"

His father shook his head. "No, only certain of your misunderstanding," he said in a low voice.

"Father, how can you say that?" Martin demanded. "I am your son!"

But his father only gave him a melancholy smile. "We will see," he said gently. "Meanwhile, it is time for our guests." He glanced at his son's clothing. "What are you wearing?" he inquired.

"What do you wish?" Martin asked, surprised. He had imagined a dinner of old friends, informal and gay, and he had thought with pleasure of a soft silk robe, easy and cool, and which he had not been able to wear for a long time.

"Wear your formal foreign evening clothes," his father said. "And what badges have you? Put on the gold key they gave you, and any other thing you have."

He met his son's stare of astonishment. "I want to be proud of you before my—my friends," he said, and then looked at his watch. "It's late," he muttered and hurried away.

In his room alone Martin dressed himself carefully in his best, stiff shirt, silk vest, tailed coat. He had not worn them since the formal college banquet of his graduation day. He had thought then that he would never wear them again—certainly not in his father's home. More mystified than ever, he put on his Phi Beta Kappa key, and his gold signet ring, and his diamond-studded fraternity pins, one Greek letter and the other the honor society of his profession.

"I have nothing more," he thought. Then he remembered a small pin Siu-li had sent him once in play. It had been attached to the first page of a letter. It was made of silver and enameled in the design of the Chinese flag. Half in fun he took it from the box with his cuff links and pinned it to his lapel.

"Why not?" he thought. "I'm a good Chinese and I'll let the world know it."

He went out of his room, whistling an American tune under his breath. There was no one about, and he sauntered in the direction of the main hall. Then he heard voices and he hurried his steps slightly. It was half an hour beyond seven but he had not expected anyone before eight. If he knew his China no one came on time to a dinner. The noise now was that of many voices. It sounded as though everyone had come.

He drew aside the red satin curtain hanging in the door and looked. The room was large, but there were many there, between thirty and forty, his eye guessed. And then he saw something else. He could not believe it, but it was true. Three fourths of the guests were Japanese! Then his father saw him.

"Come in, my son," he said.

There was nothing for him to do except to obey.

"You should have warned me," he said to Siu-li.

He had come straight to her room after the interminable dinner was over.

"What do I know to tell you?" she retorted.

The years they had been parted were vanished. His anger and

dismay had demanded frankness between them, and she had expected him. When he went to her court the light was shining like moonbeams through the opaqueness of the rice paper lattice, and he saw the shadow of her head bent over a book.

"You should have told me what people are saying," he replied.

"What are people saying except what they, too, do not know?" she retorted again.

"At least you should have told me that my father has Japanese friends," he said.

"But he has always had friends among foreigners in Peking," she said stubbornly. "And some have always been Japanese. The Baron Muraki has been his lifelong friend and you know it."

Yes, he knew it. When he was a little boy Baron Muraki, even then a kindly, aging man, used to bring him miniature rickshas and animals and tiny fish of gold-washed silver. Nevertheless he said, "No one can have Japanese friends now."

"I have told Father that, too," Siu-li said quietly.

"What did he say?" Martin demanded.

"That he had seen too many wars to allow them to change his friendships," she replied.

They looked at each other with the tragic and absolute despair of the young.

"It is such men who will lose our country for us," Martin cried, "and I shall tell him so!"

"You will tell Father that?" she cried.

"I'm not afraid of him, any more, not after tonight," he told her. "If you could have seen him, Siu-li, bowing to those strutting little men, the gold on their uniforms like scabs! And calling them carefully by their titles, General This and General That! And pressing the best of everything on them and watching them grow drunk as though they were doing him a favor.

I could scarcely swallow, though I've been thinking for years of eating sharks fins again and spit-roasted duck!" His young face gloomed at her, and she cried:

"Ah, it is hateful, but how can you say anything to Father?"

"I can," he retorted. "These are not the times of Confucius."

He strode away on this strength to his father's court. But it was now very late. The rooms were dark around the large silent court where his father lived so much alone. He hesitated and knew he dared not knock in spite of his angry courage.

"I will wait until tomorrow," he thought, and tiptoed away. It would be all the better to wait, he told himself, back in his own room. He could speak calmly and reasonably in the morning. After all, his father was an old man and it was possible that he did not know what he was doing. It was hard to imagine that the keen eyes of his father did not see all that went on before them, but the time must come for him to fail as for all men. He sighed, tried to sleep, and could not until it was nearly dawn. Then he slept long and extravagantly, and it was noon when he was wakened by Wang Ting, standing by his bed.

"Your father commands your presence," Wang Ting said.

And out of old habit Martin leaped to his feet.

What he must remember, he told himself an hour later, in his father's study was that old bonds were broken between a man and his son. What the revolution had begun this war had finished. Everywhere young men and women were telling their parents that their country must come first. "Patriotism is higher than filial duty," they were telling old people who felt themselves deserted.

He struggled against the bonds still strong between himself and this tall, slender, silk-robed man. It was hard to believe so dignified a gentleman had been the one he had watched last night. When Martin thought of this his will hardened. His father had been that man, nevertheless.

"Sit down, my son," his father told him.

He sat down, not cornerwise as he had been taught to sit in an elder's presence but as one man sits in the presence of another. If his father noticed this, he made no sign of it.

"There are many things between us for talk," his father said. "And yesterday I was busy."

"Your time is no longer your own," Martin said boldly.

His father threw him a sharp look. "It is true I am busy," he said smoothly. Something crept over his face like a veil, leaving it expressionless. Against it Martin suddenly rebelled. The last seven years had been spent among frank and impulsive foreigners, and he would not return to careful speech.

"I shall speak plainly," he told his father. "I was surprised to see our enemies in this house."

"Baron Muraki—" his father began.

But Martin interrupted him. "The Baron was only one of nearly a score."

The look on his father's face grew closer.

"Do you accuse me?" he asked gently.

"I do," Martin said. His eyes were steady upon his father's face. But his father's eyes did not turn either.

"Does it occur to you that I may have my reasons?" he asked.

"There can be no reason, now," Martin declared. Small things he had forgotten were coming back to him. In New York a Chinese classmate had suddenly declined further friendship with him. When Martin pressed him one day with an invitation the young man had said curtly, before he turned away:

"My father does not know your father."

It had seemed foolish then to give as cause against friendship that a Chinese merchant in New York had not known a Chinese gentleman in Peking.

"That can scarcely be expected," Martin had said haughtily and thereafter had ignored the man. Now he understood.

And Ling Ma last night—now he understood her hints.

"Do you know, Father, what people are saying about you?" he demanded.

"I have never known what they say, because I have not cared," his father said calmly.

"You must care now—they are saying you are a friend of the Japanese." He watched his father's face. It did not change.

"I have always had my friends among the Japanese," he said.

"They are saying you are a traitor," Martin rose to his feet.

His father's face did not quiver. "Do you believe them?" he asked.

Martin saw curiosity in his look—nothing else. He was suddenly full of angry certainty. Nobody, he thought, had ever known his father well. He had come and gone in this house, a cold and dignified figure whom they had all feared.

"I do not know what to believe," he said.

There was a long pause, then his father spoke:

"You will believe what you want to believe," he said. "That is the habit of the young."

"And is that all you will say?" Martin demanded.

"That is all," his father replied.

They were both very angry, and Martin was the more angry because he was less able to control himself than his father.

"I cannot stay in a house where enemies are accepted as friends," he said proudly.

"Do you mean my house?" his father inquired.

His blandness drove Martin to his last step.

"Yes," he said.

He rushed from the room. He had exiled himself the day after he had come home. Where now could he go? Siu-li must know. She must help him. He went to find her. She was in her court-yard sprinkling small gray orchids in the rocks, her fingers dip-ping in and out of a pewter bowl she held.

"I have told Father I cannot stay," he said to her.

She turned, and the bowl dropped from her hand.

"You have quarreled with him!"

"Yes—forever," he said. "And you must come, too, Siu-li. Only traitors can live in this house. You must come!" he insisted when he saw her face. "I can't leave you if Japanese men are to be allowed to come and go here. But where shall we go?"

She stooped and picked up the bowl.

"I have it already long planned," she said softly. She glanced about the small courtyard. "Twice—I didn't know whether I could stay. There is an old general—did you see him last night? The one with the small white mustache?"

"Yes," he said, and his gorge rose.

"Well, that one—once he saw me, and he asked for me to be brought in." Disgust was dark upon her face.

"Did Father send for you?" Martin cried.

"Yes—I didn't know why, or I would not have gone. When I entered the main hall the old general was there."

"But—but—what did Father say?" Martin was bewildered. This was not like his father!

"He said he thought modern young women could take care of themselves," Siu-li said. A slight pink rose in her cheeks and she went on. "The truth is we had quarreled the day before, Father and I. He did not want me to go to a dance at the

Grand Hotel. I wanted to go and I went. So perhaps he was punishing me."

"It was not suitable punishment," Martin cried.

They stood full of a mutual anger.

"We must go," he repeated.

"It could be to the northwest," she said. "I have a friend who knows the way—a girl—soldier."

"Communist?" he asked.

"Guerrilla," she amended.

"Where?"

"I can send her a message for tonight. She comes and goes," Siu-li replied. "She is here now in the city. When she goes back we can go with her. She has ways."

He thought hard for a moment. Into the northwest! It was the birthplace of bandits and war lords in the old days, the stronghold of Communists in the new. He had seen men from the northwest, camel drivers and traveling merchants, soldiers and wandering priests. They spoke with a burr upon their tongues that was foreign to him and they were more foreign to him than the Americans among whom he had lived. And he was loath to leave this home to which he had looked with longing all his years away from it. Life in Peking was easy and beautiful.

"But not now," he thought; and aloud he said, "It may as well be there as anywhere."

Siu-li wavered one moment before she spoke, but only one.

"I also," she said firmly. She looked down and saw the pewter bowl in her hand and in a gesture of recklessness she lifted it up and threw it over the wall.

He was forever after to divide his life into two parts, that before he knew Meng-an, and all that which came to him afterwards. The question which he put to himself often was why he did not at once see her for what she was. But he did not. On the day on which he and Siu-li left their home with her, he saw his sister's friend as a small inconspicuous creature, so like a young boy in her peasant garb that it took faith to believe her a girl. He had seen plenty of girls in America, athletic girls, boyish girls, strongbodied and clear-eyed girls. But one always knew they were girls. Meng-an was without sex, he thought, looking at her again and again, even that first day.

"Though why did I look at her so often?" he inquired of memory.

She was not beautiful. An earnest face, a square, an unchanging mouth with small full lips, eyes very black and white, short shining black hair, skin as brown as a peasant's and a slim breastless body, carried like the soldier she was, though she wore no uniform now. He said for days of hard journeying, always westward, that there was no allure in this little creature. She seldom talked and when she did she seemed purposely brusque and plain. But though she was small, she was merciless in her strength. She could walk endlessly and ride anything of a beast. Once she leaped astride a farmer's ox as it pulled a wooden cart. And she had refused the motor car Siu-li had suggested bringing the day they started.

"Why trouble ourselves with a machine we can use only for a few miles?" she said scornfully.

He did not at that moment realize all that her words meant. They had left home quite openly one clear summer's day. Each carried a knapsack and no more. Their father never rose until noon, and Wang Ting meeting them at the gate smiled and bowed and said, as he hurried on:

"You have a lucky day for your holiday."

They had looked at each other and smiled behind his back.

"A long holiday," Martin had said.

They had not walked more than half a day before Siu-li was exhausted. The sun grew hot. Meng-an, springing along, her cloth shoes silent in the dust, was merciful.

"You will be able to walk more tomorrow," she said.

She kept watching for a vehicle and in a little while she stopped a farmer returning from market with his wheelbarrow empty and asked for a ride. He was willing enough, but when Meng-an bade Siu-li to seat herself he was less willing.

"I thought it was to be you, girl soldier," he complained.

"It is the same—she is my friend," Meng-an replied calmly, and so the farmer pushed Siu-li as far as he was going.

"Why was he willing for you?" Martin inquired, curious to know this small creature's power.

"He knows we work for them," Meng-an answered vaguely. "And I pass here often."

Everywhere it was the same. With an assurance that might have been impudent in another, Meng-an asked and was given. Village bakers gave her bread, at teashops she was given a pot of tea, and anywhere a small traveling restaurant keeper stirred up a bowl of noodles and vegetable oil and shook his head when she held out the cash.

"We all work for the country," he would say, a little pompously.

They depended on Meng-an for everything and the more as they came into the northwest where she knew all and they knew nothing. By now Siu-li wore man's clothing that she might walk more freely, and Martin wore peasant's garments, and Meng-an wore the ragged boy's clothing that she always put on when she entered land held by the enemy. They walked until noon, ate, slept by the roadside, and walked again until midnight. This they did day after day until it became the habit of their lives. Every other thing they had once done now grew dreamlike in their memories.

"I wonder if Father minds that we are gone?" Siu-li said one day as they rested for a moment.

"He knows why we went," Martin replied.

Meng-an's eyes were upon the bare and distant hills.

"I have not seen my parents for six years," she said suddenly.

"Do you long for them?" Siu-li asked.

"Sometimes," Meng-an said. "Then I remember that if I return to them I return to all the old life—marriage to a man I do not know, a courtyard with the gates locked. And then I get up and go on."

She had never said so much. There was a flicker in her eyes as she spoke but no more. But Martin thought to himself that this small creature had felt things that he did not know.

"Were you early betrothed?" he asked.

She nodded, but did not speak, and he could not for decency ask again.

All these days they had been walking through enemy-held country. Had they been without Meng-an they would have been stopped before this by enemy soldiers. But Meng-an knew how to come and go as a mouse does in a crowded house. Everywhere she was told by someone, a beggar, a farmer, a priest, if there were enemy soldiers near, and then she led them differently, by secret devious ways of her own. Never once did they meet the enemy face to face.

"Though sometimes I do," she told them.

"What then?" Martin asked. He watched her while she answered. Upon that small inscrutable face he was beginning to discern changes, slight to an unseeing eye but vivid to him. This girl could feel.

"I always pretend to be a fool," she said. "Like this—"

By some trick she threw her lower jaw crooked and crossed her eyes and looked an idiot. She straightened herself again.

"Then they let me pass."

"I should think so," Siu-li said laughing.

But Martin said nothing. At this moment he was not sure whether a girl should be like this Meng-an. There she sat, on a side of the dusty road where they had stopped for a rest. Her hair was brown with dust, and dust lay in shadows on her face.

"She is not beautiful," he thought, "though brave."

And then that night they passed out of enemy-held country and into their own. He could feel the difference, or thought he could, even in the twilight air. Certainly people were more free in their talk and their laughter at the inn where they lodged, and there was much boasting of how this one and that had crept in and out of the enemy line. But Meng-an was the most changed of all. When they reached the inn she went into one room a while. A little later she came out for the evening meal. Martin had washed himself and changed his garments. But he was not prepared for what he now saw. A slim young soldier came out of the room Siu-li and Meng-an shared, a soldier in a clean khaki uniform, belted and buttoned and with a small pistol at the waist. It was Meng-an. When she saw him she saluted and gave him the smallest of smiles. It was the first she had ever given him.

"You must go to our general," Meng-an told him. Three days more had brought them to the stronghold of this Chinese army to which she belonged. For three days they had walked among a tranquil people, tilling and working the land as though war were in another world. Night brought them to the camp itself, where he would go to the men's division and Siu-li and Meng-an to the women's. They halted at the gate of the temple compound where guards stood. Once inside they must part. Thus Meng-an had paused to speak.

"I will see him tonight," she went on, "and when I have given him my secret messages from the old city, I will tell him of you. He will be glad, for he needs men like you."

Now Martin did not want to part from her.

"When shall we see each other?" he said boldly.

The flicker in her eyes he could discern but not its meaning. Was it feeling for him or against him? He did not know.

"There are many meetings for us all," she said, and whether it was promise or evasion he still did not know. And she gave him no time to think. She led the way inside the gate and they were parted. He was given food and a bed and by dark he slept as all slept, because light at night meant oil and oil was money, and money must be spent on bullets for the enemy.

At dawn he rose, called by a bugle, and after food Martin was summoned by a young man so carelessly clothed as a soldier that on the upper part of him he wore a farmer's coat.

"Are you the son of Liu Ming Chen?" he inquired abruptly of Martin.

"How do you know my father's name?" Martin asked.

"We all know it," the man replied.

Martin was silenced by fear. Why should all here know the name of his quiet scholar father in Peking except now as a traitor? He said nothing.

"The general calls you," the man said. "Follow me."

Without hesitation Martin followed and found himself in the

doorway of the cave house where the general lived at the back of the temple as many did here, among these high barren mountains. But this room was comfortable with furniture and the floor was rock swept clean. The general was not a fat old man but a young thin-bodied man in faded uniform. No one could have said he was anything more than another, except agile and clever, relentless if he were an enemy.

"One tells me you know metals," he said to Martin without greeting.

That one, Martin knew, was Meng-an. He wondered jealously if she knew this man well and if they were friends. He had missed her already, for when he woke he wondered if today he would see her and how and when.

"It is true," he replied.

The young general looked at him shrewdly.

"You left your father," he said.

"Yes," Martin said. The man knew that!

"Many leave their parents these days," the general said gravely. "Once when I was a child I was sent to a Christian school. In their sacred book I found one day by chance words like this: 'And a man's foes shall be they of his own household.' I who had been taught the doctrine of Wu Wei, I thought, 'How evil are these Christians not to know filial duty!' But the days are come." He paused a second. "I, too, left my parents. We must seek a new foundation for the state, lest we be lost."

The general's accent was not that of a peasant.

"Did you go abroad?" Martin asked.

"Yes—who told you?" the general replied.

"No one—but where?" Martin asked again.

"To Harvard and to Leipzig," the general said.

"And you are here," Martin said. It was wonder enough.

"I would be nowhere else," the general said. He hesitated a moment, and then went on. "Out of these inner regions will come those who will take back the land."

"But do these people know they are being attacked?" Martin asked. "They are so calm and they work in their fields as they always have."

"By day," the general broke in. "By night they put down their hoes and take their guns. But by what good luck you came I cannot say. We lack iron, and there is ore in these hills. The rocks shine when they are split. Is that iron? If it is, I will set about mining it out. It may be silver—and it is not so quickly useful. Do you see your task?"

"Yes," Martin said. He was looking at the seamed side of the cave as he answered. In the rocks was his task. He must find iron to make bullets for the enemy.

"Have you any message for your father?" the general asked abruptly. "Meng-an will start for Peking tonight."

"She goes back?" Martin cried.

"It is her work—to slip between the enemy armies and find out everything and bring me word."

"She told you of my father," Martin said.

The general nodded.

"No, I have no message for him," Martin said.

The general nodded again. "Then you may go," he told him.

He did not see Meng-an again. When he reached his tent six men were waiting. When they saw him they saluted.

"We are to go with you into the hills," they said.

By some means they had with them the few tools he needed—pickaxes, baskets for rock fragments, materials for mapping, and rolls of bedding.

"At once?" he asked.

"It is so ordered," they replied.

"But I must see someone before I go," he protested.

"We will wait a few minutes," a soldier said, "at your command."

"Let it not be longer, sir," another said. "The general does not like delay."

No, he would not, Martin knew, thinking of that firm young figure. He had turned away and at the door of the women's barracks he asked the girl soldier on guard for Siu-li, and was told to wait.

She came a few moments later and quickly he told her his orders.

"And you?" he asked.

"I am to go into training, merely," she said.

"And Meng-an?" he asked, wanting only to hear of her and knowing very well that he knew more than Siu-li did.

"I have not seen her," Siu-li replied.

He knew he should tell nothing he had been told and yet he wanted some communication with that small creature slipping her lonely way among the enemy. He said in a low voice, too low for the waiting guard to hear:

"If you see her today, tell her I said to take care for herself as she goes." And then when he saw the astonishment in Siu-li's eyes he added quickly, "She is more valuable than you know —to the cause, I mean."

But Siu-li was shrewd with the shrewdness of a woman.

"I was about to ask you now that we are here if you regret coming, but I think I need not," she said.

He laughed sheepishly, feeling himself grow red.

"No, you need not," he agreed. "I am not sorry."

Weeks passed him, and he spent them day upon day in searching the barren hills. They were not barren, he was beginning to discover. Under their sandy tawny surfaces there was rock and in the seams of the rock minerals. He walked up the steep beds of mountain streams, his eyes upon every glint and glitter. The men with him were well chosen, for they were men who belonged to the hills, who had spent their youth washing the streams for silver.

"But is there iron?" he asked them as he asked the hills themselves.

"That we don't know, for we never looked for it when there was silver," they said.

In their fashion they had mined some parts of the hills, and they led him to shallow pits they had dug. These he tapped and examined and tested the fragments he chose. There was silver everywhere, but he could not find iron.

"We may have to make our bullets of silver," he thought grimly.

The strange hills surrounded him, and silence was their atmosphere. There seemed no life in them, and yet sometimes he came upon a monastery built out of sandy rock and seeming in its shape and color so like a cliff that only a gate told the difference. Inside the priests lived, silent so long that they could scarcely speak when he spoke, men whom the mountain winds had dried and beaten upon and bleached until they too were sand-colored. And yet everyone of them when he told them his task, were eager to help him and to show him certain dark ledges they had seen. Everyone of them knew that they had an enemy.

Everywhere they knew. In the night under the endlessly clear skies and beneath the sharp stars he thought of those who were farmers by day and soldiers by night, and he thought of priests who wanted no peace, and of his sister, who had been so tenderly reared, learning to march long hours and to fire a gun, and most of all and longest he thought of Meng-an making her lonely way in and out among the enemy.

"She has the hardest and most dangerous work of us all," he thought. When he thought of this his bitterness against his father heaped itself up with gall. "He betrays every one of us," he thought.

The filial piety he had been taught he put from him forever, that ancient teaching which had tied together the generations of his people.

"I am no more his son," he thought. And he thought, "We must build a new country, and every generation must be its own lawmaker."

"There is no iron," he told the general.

"There must be," the general said. "Go back."

The hills were bitterly cold now with autumn. The foolish silver was rich everywhere. But the hills held nothing more. He had stayed a month, and then the cold rain had driven him down from the summit. And then it had seemed he must make report of having found nothing. And he knew, too—the long silent nights and the hot noons had told him—that he longed to see Meng-an. Had she come and gone safely? He must know or thought he must. And so he had come down. He had gone at once to Siu-li. But Siu-li was not there. She had been sent the day before with her regiment to a village to the east to make forays by night against an enemy garrison. He was sick with alarm when he heard it, and then dismayed because since she was gone there was no one he could ask of Meng-an. Everyone went about his business here, and it was no one's business to speak of Meng-an. And he had had to go then to the general.

"Go back," the general said now.

And against his look there was no hope of refusal. Besides how could he say, "I cannot, until I have seen a certain woman," and how could he even say, "I must hear first if Meng-an is safe?"

The general saw his hesitation. "We are still at war," he said. "Why do you delay?"

"I do not," Martin said doggedly.

He went back that same day.

He had lived in the hills so long now that when he thought of cities and of people they were words and nothing more. Had he once seen ships and trains and traveled upon them? Even his memories of them were gone. He had for companions these men as dogged as himself and for his strength his own determination that if there was iron in these hills he would find it. And if he had needed a spur to prod him he had it. One day when in an October as cold as winter where he was, he sat on a rock near a summit eating his bread and salt fish, at noon, he saw even there an airplane. It flew well above the mountain top and yet close enough for him to see it. It was an enemy plane! He could see its markings clearly above him as he looked up at it. It sank a little as though it saw him, then rose and sped on. An enemy plane over these far, inner mountains! He swallowed his food quickly and called his men. They were eating fifty feet below him in a shallow valley. He had climbed out of it to see the hills while he ate.

"Come on!" he cried, and when they were come he said, "We must make haste if the enemy has flown as far as this."

They had worked longer after that, and every day they searched the skies. There were no planes for ten days more, and then eleven planes flew over them like wild geese.

That was the day he found iron. He found it early in the morning, low, near the base of the peak upon which he had spent uselessly nearly fifteen days. He had gone too high. The iron was old, and aeons had driven the deposits deep into the bowels of the mountains.

"Have I been looking too high, everywhere?" he asked himself.

He was so excited by this possible thing that he went no higher. He covered half the base of the mountain by noon and in seven places he found signs of iron, whether it was seven different places or all one great rich vein he did not know. But when he sat down at noon, he ate his bread in such excitement that he could scarcely swallow.

Then it was he heard the planes, and looking up he saw their geeselike passage. The sight might only yesterday have filled him with despair. But today he shook his fist at them and with his mouth filled with bread he shouted:

"We have our bullets for you!"

Now he could go back with good news. He was even glad that he had found iron in autumn instead of spring. Soon it would be too cold for the enemy planes to fly over the inland, and during the winter months the mines could be planned and made ready. He had long talks about machinery with his men. When he thought of machinery for mines he was troubled. How could they construct and haul and place those great masses? But these men had been miners without such aid. Bamboo and ropes and wooden buckets were their utensils, and Martin listened to them. "A little more than they have had and it will be much," he thought as they went on.

Everywhere through the countryside there were signs of autumn. The harvests were good, and the farmers grew bold to reap them, because few airplanes came now to bomb.

"In the summer we spend half the day in our bomb huts," they told Martin. "Well, it's cool there!" they said, grinning with mischief. "Well, we have had bandits of many kinds," another said. Wherever he went there was no talk of hardship or surrender, only of how work could be done, whether the enemy came or not.

"I wish my father could be here," he thought. "If he saw these people, could he still betray them?"

The thought of his father was like a sore in his heart. Whatever he did, he thought, it would not be enough to atone for his father. And when he thought of Meng-an he asked himself what right he had, the son of a traitor, to think of her.

In this mood he walked the miles back to the encampment and, without asking of his sister or Meng-an, he went, dusty as he was, to report to the general. In his hand he carried the fragments of rock and he laid them upon the table.

"I have found iron," he said simply, "and plenty of it." The news was enough of itself.

The general took up the rocks as though they were gold.

"Better than gold," he said. And then when he had examined them he looked up at Martin. "When can you go back?" he asked.

"Today, if you bid me," Martin replied steadily.

But the general laughed. "Now you are taught," he said. "It is the answer I wanted. But you shall not go today. We must make our plans."

"There is not much time before winter comes down," Martin said doggedly.

"Not much, but a day or two," the general said, "and that is long enough for everything. I have news for you. Do you remember my little spy?"

"Meng-an?" Her name flew out of Martin's mouth like a bird from a cage.

The general nodded. "How did you know her name?" he asked, surprised.

"She brought my sister and me here," Martin said.

"Do you have a sister?" the general demanded of him. "And if you have, why did you not tell me?"

"There was no need," Martin said.

But the general struck a bell on his table. "She must come here, too," he said. "This news is for both of your father's children."

A soldier appeared.

"Go and fetch—what is her name?"

"Siu-li," Martin said. "Of the Third Regiment."

"Surname Liu, name Siu-li, of the Third Regiment," the general ordered. "And tell Meng-an to come also."

"So!" the soldier cried as he had been taught, and saluting he hurried away.

At the mention of his father Martin was afraid. What would the general call good news except that a traitor had been killed? If this was the news he must warn Siu-li first. They must show no grief. He thought quickly.

"Sir," he asked, "may I speak first with my sister? If something has befallen our father, it will be better to prepare her for it."

"Nothing has befallen him," the general replied. He was turning the fragments of rocks over in his hands, dreaming of the precious stuff they held.

So there was nothing to do except to wait.

"Sit down," the general said and he sat down. It was very hard to wait. The general was looking at the rock now through a small hand microscope.

Then in a while they heard the light quick tread of feet trained to march, the feet of girl soldiers. The general put down his microscope and looked up. The door curtains opened. Two straight slender girls in uniform stood there. They saluted and stood at attention, Meng-an and Siu-li. Martin smiled at Siu-li and looked at Meng-an. His heart rose on a great wave of pride. These two girls in the old days would have been sheltered, helpless creatures behind a courtyard wall; Siu-li even a few months ago had been in her way useless.

"Is this your sister?" the general asked of Martin, but gazing at Siu-li.

"It is she," Martin said, rising to his feet.

"Be at ease, all of you," the general said. He seemed to have forgotten why he had called Meng-an here. "Be seated," he told Siu-li, without taking his eyes from her face. "I have not seen you before," he said.

Siu-li blushed a little. The uniform, her straight-cut hair, the pistol at her belt, her feet in hard leather shoes, none of these could hide what she was, a soft-eyed girl. Those large soft eyes she now turned upon the young general as full of coquetry as though she wore a silk robe and had jewels in her hair.

"I did not know you wished it," she said demurely.

"But I do," the general said.

Meng-an looked at Martin. In her eyes he saw that flickering —it was laughter, surely. He smiled to answer it. It was pleasant to communicate thus with her over those other two. Then Meng-an coughed a small dry cough, and the general glanced at her and remembered.

"Ah, you also," he said, but his voice was very different to her. "Yes, and now repeat what you told me. Who told you that the enemy is about to march southward and how we can surprise that march?"

"Wang Ting," Meng-an replied.

"Wang Ting!" Siu-li cried. "But he is my father's secretary!"

Meng-an did not turn her head. She continued to make report, her eyes upon the general's face. "He is sent by his master. Of himself he knows nothing, but his master is in a position to know much and will be as long as his life is spared by the enemy. If they find out he will die. But until that time, I go to a certain small teashop and there I can be told."

All this Meng-an said in her even voice as though what she said was nothing.

"If I had known there was also you," the general said to Siu-li as though she were the only one in the room, "I would have told you at once what your father was. He has been for us since the city fell. Why do you think this little spy comes and goes except to bring me news from your father?"

Now Siu-li turned upon Meng-an. "And you did not tell me!"

"How did I know what you thought of your father?" Meng-an retorted. "And I have my orders against talk about him with anyone," she added.

"And you," the general said to Martin, "you I wanted to try, to see if you were fit to be your father's son. When you did not give up until you found the iron we need, I said, 'He is fit.'"

"You knew I doubted my father?" Martin asked slowly.

"Your father begged me in a letter to tell you what he was, when I saw the time was right," the general replied.

They sat, these impetuous two, the modern son and daughter of an old Confucian scholar, and humbled themselves in their knowledge. Then suddenly Siu-li began to weep. She turned to Martin.

"We—we were very unjust!" she whispered.

"Yes," Martin said in a daze, "yes, we were." He thought of his old father in the midst of the comings and goings of the enemy in his house, holding his life as lightly as a toy in his hands, and he cleared his throat. "I wish we could tell him so," he said.

"I will tell him," Meng-an said calmly.

"Don't cry!" the general said suddenly to Siu-li.

She looked at him, her great eyes dewy with tears and very beautiful.

"How can I help it?" she said piteously. "I have been a wicked daughter. I ought to have known my father couldn't—be what we thought he was!"

"I say you are not to weep any more!" the general shouted. "I cannot bear it," he added in a gentler voice.

And then Martin felt his own eyes caught by someone's gaze, and looked up, and there were Meng-an's eyes, holding his, and this time it was as though their hands clasped. And suddenly his heart inquired, "Is there any reason now?" and then answered itself, "There is no reason."

"Now this is all settled," the general said hastily, "and it is time we went back to our work." His eyes took leave of Siu-li's soft black ones, though unwillingly. "Let us proceed," he said sharply. "Soldiers, attention!"

Martin rose, Siu-li and Meng-an leaped to their feet, saluted, wheeled, and marched out.

The general stared after them and sighed. Then he smiled at Martin.

"You are in love with that little spy of mine," he said.

"How—who—?" Martin stammered.

"Ah, I saw it," the general said calmly. "Well, why not? Everything must go on the same in wartime. Well, you may have my little spy. Tell her so. But she must go on working. We must all go on working."

"Yes, sir," Martin said. He was dazed with the general's calmness over the most enormous thing in the world. Then even as he looked at the general he saw a strange thing happening. Over that firm stern young face he saw a soft sheepish smile appear that turned the general at once into an ordinary young man such as may be seen any spring day in any country.

"Your sister has very fine eyes," he said abruptly.

"They have been so considered," Martin replied.

The general looked startled. "I suppose so," he said unwillingly. He reflected a moment, still staring at Martin without seeing him.

"Why not?" he demanded after a moment.

"Why not, indeed?" Martin replied. "As you said, sir, even in war everything must go on as usual."

They looked at each other for the least part of a moment longer and suddenly they laughed, and then, sharing this laughter in their youth like a cup of wine between them, they laughed again for pure pleasure.

XIII
THE OLD DEMON

THE OLD DEMON

O LD Mrs. Wang knew of course that there was a war. Everybody had known for a long time that there was war going on and that Japanese were killing Chinese. But still it was not real and no more than hearsay since none of the Wangs had been killed. The Village of Three Mile Wangs on the flat banks of the Yellow River, which was old Mrs. Wang's clan village, had never even seen a Japanese. This was how they came to be talking about Japanese at all.

It was evening and early summer, and after her supper Mrs. Wang had climbed the dike steps, as she did every day, to see how high the river had risen. She was much more afraid of the river than of the Japanese. She knew what the river would do. And one by one the villagers had followed her up the dike, and now they stood staring down at the malicious yellow water, curling along like a lot of snakes, and biting at the high dike banks.

"I never saw it as high as this so early," Mrs. Wang said. She sat down on a bamboo stool that her grandson, Little Pig, had brought for her, and spat into the water.

"It's worse than the Japanese, this old devil of a river," Little Pig said recklessly.

"Fool!" Mrs. Wang said quickly. "The river god will hear you. Talk about something else."

So they had gone on talking about the Japanese. . . . How, for instance, asked Wang, the baker, who was old Mrs. Wang's nephew twice removed, would they know the Japanese when they saw them?

Mrs. Wang at this point said positively, "You'll know them. I once saw a foreigner. He was taller than the eaves of my house and he had mud-colored hair and eyes the color of a fish's eyes. Anyone who does not look like us—that is a Japanese."

Everybody listened to her since she was the oldest woman in the village and whatever she said settled something.

Then Little Pig spoke up in his disconcerting way. "You can't see them, Grandmother. They hide up in the sky in airplanes."

Mrs. Wang did not answer immediately. Once she would have said positively, "I shall not believe in an airplane until I see it." But so many things had been true which she had not believed—the Empress, for instance, whom she had not believed dead, was dead. The Republic, again, she had not believed in because she did not know what it was. She still did not know, but they had said for a long time there had been one. So now she merely stared quietly about the dike where they all sat around her. It was very pleasant and cool, and she felt nothing mattered if the river did not rise to flood.

"I don't believe in the Japanese," she said flatly.

They laughed at her a little, but no one spoke. Someone lit her pipe—it was Little Pig's wife, who was her favorite, and she smoked it.

"Sing, Little Pig!" someone called.

So Little Pig began to sing an old song in a high quavering voice, and old Mrs. Wang listened and forgot the Japanese. The evening was beautiful, the sky so clear and still that the willows overhanging the dike were reflected even in the muddy water. Everything was at peace. The thirty-odd houses which made up the village straggled along beneath them. Nothing could break this peace. After all, the Japanese were only human beings.

"I doubt those airplanes," she said mildly to Little Pig when he stopped singing.

But without answering her, he went on to another song.

Year in and year out she had spent the summer evenings like this on the dike. The first time she was seventeen and a bride, and her husband had shouted to her to come out of the house and up the dike, and she had come, blushing and twisting her hands together, to hide among the women while the men roared at her and made jokes about her. All the same, they had liked her. "A pretty piece of meat in your bowl," they had said to her husband. "Feet a trifle big," he had answered deprecatingly. But she could see he was pleased, and so gradually her shyness went away.

He, poor man, had been drowned in a flood when he was still young. And it had taken her years to get him prayed out of Buddhist purgatory. Finally she had grown tired of it, what with the child and the land all on her back, and so when the priest said coaxingly, "Another ten pieces of silver and he'll be out entirely," she asked, "What's he got in there yet?"

"Only his right hand," the priest said, encouraging her.

Well, then, her patience broke. Ten dollars! It would feed them for the winter. Besides, she had had to hire labor for her share of repairing the dike, too, so there would be no more floods.

"If it's only one hand, he can pull himself out," she said firmly.

She often wondered if he had, poor silly fellow. As like as not, she had often thought gloomily in the night, he was still lying there, waiting for her to do something about it. That was the sort of man he was. Well, some day, perhaps, when Little Pig's wife had had the first baby safely and she had a little extra, she might go back to finish him out of purgatory. There was no real hurry, though. . . .

"Grandmother, you must go in," Little Pig's wife's soft voice said. "There is a mist rising from the river now that the sun is gone."

"Yes, I suppose I must," old Mrs. Wang agreed. She gazed at the river a moment. That river—it was full of good and evil together. It would water the fields when it was curbed and checked, but then if an inch were allowed it, it crashed through like a roaring dragon. That was how her husband had been swept away—careless, he was, about his bit of the dike. He was always going to mend it, always going to pile more earth on top of it, and then in a night the river rose and broke through. He had run out of the house, and she had climbed on the roof with the child and had saved herself and it while he was drowned. Well, they had pushed the river back again behind its dikes, and it had stayed there this time. Every day she herself walked up and down the length of the dike for which the village was responsible and examined it. The men laughed and said, "If anything is wrong with the dikes, Granny will tell us."

It had never occurred to any of them to move the village away from the river. The Wangs had lived there for generations, and some had always escaped the floods and had fought the river more fiercely than ever afterward.

Little Pig suddenly stopped singing.

"The moon is coming up!" he cried. "That's not good. Airplanes come out on moonlight nights."

"Where do you learn all this about airplanes?" old Mrs. Wang exclaimed. "It is tiresome to me," she added, so severely that no one spoke. In this silence, leaning upon the arm of Little Pig's wife, she descended slowly the earthen steps which led down into the village, using her long pipe in the other hand as a walking stick. Behind her the villagers came down, one by one, to bed. No one moved before she did, but none stayed long after her.

And in her own bed at last, behind the blue cotton mosquito curtains which Little Pig's wife fastened securely, she fell peacefully asleep. She had lain awake a little while thinking about the Japanese and wondering why they wanted to fight. Only very coarse persons wanted wars. In her mind she saw large coarse persons. If they came one must wheedle them, she thought, invite them to drink tea, and explain to them, reasonably—only why should they come to a peaceful farming village . . . ?

So she was not in the least prepared for Little Pig's wife screaming at her that the Japanese had come. She sat up in bed muttering, "The tea bowls—the tea—"

"Grandmother, there's no time!" Little Pig's wife screamed. "They're here—they're here!"

"Where?" old Mrs. Wang cried, now awake.

"In the sky!" Little Pig's wife wailed.

They had all run out at that, into the clear early dawn, and gazed up. There, like wild geese flying in autumn, were great birdlike shapes.

"But what are they?" old Mrs. Wang cried.

And then, like a silver egg dropping, something drifted straight down and fell at the far end of the village in a field. A fountain of earth flew up, and they all ran to see it. There was a hole thirty feet across, as big as a pond. They were so astonished they could not speak, and then, before anyone could say anything, another and another egg began to fall and everybody was running, running . . .

Everybody, that is, but Mrs. Wang. When Little Pig's wife seized her hand to drag her along, old Mrs. Wang pulled away and sat down against the bank of the dike.

"I can't run," she remarked. "I haven't run in seventy years, since before my feet were bound. You go on. Where's Little Pig?" She looked around. Little Pig was already gone. "Like his grandfather," she remarked, "always the first to run."

But Little Pig's wife would not leave her, not, that is, until old Mrs. Wang reminded her that it was her duty.

"If Little Pig is dead," she said, "then it is necessary that his son be born alive." And when the girl still hesitated, she struck at her gently with her pipe. "Go on—go on," she exclaimed.

So unwillingly, because now they could scarcely hear each other speak for the roar of the dipping planes, Little Pig's wife went on with the others.

By now, although only a few minutes had passed, the village was in ruins and the straw roofs and wooden beams were blazing. Everybody was gone. As they passed they had shrieked at old Mrs. Wang to come on, and she had called back pleasantly:

"I'm coming—I'm coming!"

But she did not go. She sat quite alone watching now what was an extraordinary spectacle. For soon other planes came, from where she did not know, but they attacked the first ones. The sun came up over the fields of ripening wheat, and in the clear summery air the planes wheeled and darted and spat at each other. When this was over, she thought, she would go back into the village and see if anything was left. Here and there a wall stood, supporting a roof. She could not see her own house from here. But she was not unused to war. Once bandits had looted their village, and houses had been burned then, too. Well, now it had happened again. Burning houses one could see often, but not this darting silvery shining battle in the air. She understood none of it—not what those things were, nor how they stayed up in the sky. She simply sat, growing hungry, and watching.

"I'd like to see one close," she said aloud. And at that moment, as though in answer, one of them pointed suddenly downward, and, wheeling and twisting as though it were wounded, it fell head down in a field which Little Pig had ploughed only yesterday for soybeans. And in an instant the sky was empty again, and there was only this wounded thing on the ground and herself.

She hoisted herself carefully from the earth. At her age she need be afraid of nothing. She could, she decided, go and see what it was. So, leaning on her bamboo pipe, she made her way slowly across the fields. Behind her in the sudden stillness two or three village dogs appeared and followed, creeping close to her in their terror. When they drew near to the fallen plane, they barked furiously. Then she hit them with her pipe.

"Be quiet," she scolded, "there's already been noise enough to split my ears!"

She tapped the airplane.

"Metal," she told the dogs. "Silver, doubtless," she added. Melted up, it would make them all rich.

She walked around it, examining it closely. What made it fly? It seemed dead. Nothing moved or made a sound within it. Then, coming to the side to which it tipped, she saw a young man in it, slumped into a heap in a little seat. The dogs growled, but she struck at them again and they fell back.

"Are you dead?" she inquired politely.

The young man moved a little at her voice, but did not speak.

She drew nearer and peered into the hole in which he sat. His side was bleeding.

"Wounded!" she exclaimed. She took his wrist. It was warm, but inert, and when she let it go, it dropped against the side of the hole. She stared at him. He had black hair and a dark skin like a Chinese and still he did not look like a Chinese.

"He must be a Southerner," she thought. Well, the chief thing was, he was alive.

"You had better come out," she remarked. "I'll put some herb plaster on your side."

The young man muttered something dully.

"What did you say?" she asked. But he did not say it again.

"I am still quite strong," she decided after a moment. So she reached in and seized him about the waist and pulled him out slowly, panting a good deal. Fortunately he was rather a little fellow and very light. When she had him on the ground, he seemed to find his feet; and he stood shakily and clung to her, and she held him up.

"Now if you can walk to my house," she said, "I'll see if it is there."

Then he said something, quite clearly. She listened and could not understand a word of it. She pulled away from him and stared.

"What's that?" she asked.

He pointed at the dogs. They were standing growling, their ruffs up. Then he spoke again, and as he spoke he crumpled to the ground. The dogs fell on him, so that she had to beat them off with her hands.

"Get away!" she shouted. "Who told *you* to kill him?"

And then, when they had slunk back, she heaved him somehow onto her back; and, trembling, half carrying, half pulling him, she dragged him to the ruined village and laid him in the street while she went to find her house, taking the dogs with her.

Her house was quite gone. She found the place easily enough. This was where it should be, opposite the water gate into the dike. She had always watched that gate herself. Miraculously it was not injured now, nor was the dike broken. It would be easy enough to rebuild the house. Only, for the present, it was gone.

So she went back to the young man. He was lying as she had left him, propped against the dike, panting and very pale. He had opened his coat and he had a little bag from which he was taking out strips of cloth and a bottle of something. And again he spoke, and again she understood nothing. Then he made signs and she saw it was water he wanted, so she took up a broken pot from one of many blown about the street, and, going up the dike, she filled it with river water and brought it down again and washed his wound, and she tore off the strips he made from the rolls of bandaging. He knew how to put the cloth over the gaping wound and he made signs to her, and she followed these signs. All the time he was trying to tell her something, but she could understand nothing.

"You must be from the South, sir," she said. It was easy to see that he had education. He looked very clever. "I have heard your language is different from ours." She laughed a little to put him at his ease, but he only stared at her somberly with dull eyes. So she said brightly, "Now if I could find something for us to eat, it would be nice."

He did not answer. Indeed he lay back, panting still more heavily, and stared into space as though she had not spoken.

"You would be better with food," she went on. "And so would I," she added. She was beginning to feel unbearably hungry.

It occurred to her that in Wang, the baker's, shop there might be some bread. Even if it were dusty with fallen mortar, it would still be bread. She would go and see. But before she went she moved the soldier a little so that he lay in the edge of shadow cast by a willow tree that grew in the bank of the dike. Then she went to the baker's shop. The dogs were gone.

The baker's shop was, like everything else, in ruins. No one was there. At first she saw nothing but the mass of crumpled earthen walls. But then she remembered that the oven was just inside the door, and the door frame still stood erect, supporting one end of the roof. She stood in this frame, and, running her hand in underneath the fallen roof inside, she felt the wooden cover of the iron caldron. Under this there might be steamed bread. She worked her arm delicately and carefully in. It took quite a long time, but, even so, clouds of lime and dust almost choked her. Nevertheless she was right. She squeezed her hand under the cover and felt the firm smooth skin of the big steamed bread rolls, and one by one she drew out four.

"It's hard to kill an old thing like me," she remarked cheerfully to no one, and she began to eat one of the rolls as she walked back. If she had a bit of garlic and a bowl of tea—but one couldn't have everything in these times.

It was at this moment that she heard voices. When she came in sight of the soldier, she saw surrounding him a crowd of other soldiers, who had apparently come from nowhere. They were staring down at the wounded soldier, whose eyes were now closed.

"Where did you get this Japanese, Old Mother?" they shouted at her.

"What Japanese?" she asked, coming to them.

"This one!" they shouted.

"Is he a Japanese?" she cried in the greatest astonishment. "But he looks like us—his eyes are black, his skin—"

"Japanese!" one of them shouted at her.

"Well," she said quietly, "he dropped out of the sky."

"Give me that bread!" another shouted.

"Take it," she said, "all except this one for him."

"A Japanese monkey eat good bread?" the soldier shouted.

"I suppose he is hungry also," old Mrs. Wang replied. She began to dislike these men. But then, she had always disliked soldiers.

"I wish you would go away," she said. "What are you doing here? Our village has always been peaceful."

"It certainly looks very peaceful now," one of the men said, grinning, "as peaceful as a grave. Do you know who did that, Old Mother? The Japanese!"

"I suppose so," she agreed. Then she asked, "Why? That's what I don't understand."

"Why? Because they want our land, that's why!"

"Our land!" she repeated. "Why, they can't have our land!"

"Never!" they shouted.

But all this time while they were talking and chewing the bread they had divided among themselves, they were watching the eastern horizon.

"Why do you keep looking east?" old Mrs. Wang now asked.

"The Japanese are coming from there," the man replied who had taken the bread.

"Are you running away from them?" she asked, surprised.

"There are only a handful of us," he said apologetically. "We were left to guard a village—Pao An, in the county of—"

"I know that village," old Mrs. Wang interrupted. "You needn't tell me. I was a girl there. How is the old Pao who keeps the teashop in the main street? He's my brother."

"Everybody is dead there," the man replied. "The Japanese

have taken it—a great army of men came with their foreign guns and tanks, so what could we do?"

"Of course, only run," she agreed. Nevertheless she felt dazed and sick. So he was dead, that one brother she had left! She was now the last of her father's family.

But the soldiers were straggling away again leaving her alone. "They'll be coming, those little black dwarfs," they were saying. "We'd best go on."

Nevertheless, one lingered a moment, the one who had taken the bread, to stare down at the young wounded man, who lay with his eyes shut, not having moved at all.

"Is he dead?" he inquired. Then, before Mrs. Wang could answer, he pulled a short knife out of his belt. "Dead or not, I'll give him a punch or two with this—"

But old Mrs. Wang pushed his arm away.

"No, you won't," she said with authority. "If he is dead, then there is no use in sending him into purgatory all in pieces. I am a good Buddhist myself."

The man laughed. "Oh well, he is dead," he answered; and then, seeing his comrades already at a distance, he ran after them.

A Japanese, was he? Old Mrs. Wang, left alone with this inert figure, looked at him tentatively. He was very young, she could see, now that his eyes were closed. His hand, limp in unconsciousness, looked like a boy's hand, unformed and still growing. She felt his wrist but could discern no pulse. She leaned over him and held to his lips the half of her roll which she had not eaten.

"Eat," she said very loudly and distinctly. "Bread!"

But there was no answer. Evidently he was dead. He must have died while she was getting the bread out of the oven.

There was nothing to do then but to finish the bread herself.

And when that was done, she wondered if she ought not to follow after Little Pig and his wife and all the villagers. The sun was mounting and it was growing hot. If she were going, she had better go. But first she would climb the dike and see what the direction was. They had gone straight west, and as far as eye could look westward was a great plain. She might even see a good-sized crowd miles away. Anyway, she could see the next village, and they might all be there.

So she climbed the dike slowly, getting very hot. There was a slight breeze on top of the dike and it felt good. She was shocked to see the river very near the top of the dike. Why, it had risen in the last hour!

"You old demon!" she said severely. Let the river god hear it if he liked. He was evil, that he was—so to threaten flood when there had been all this other trouble.

She stooped and bathed her cheeks and her wrists. The water was quite cold, as though with fresh rains somewhere. Then she stood up and gazed around her. To the west there was nothing except in the far distance the soldiers still half-running, and beyond them the blur of the next village, which stood on a long rise of ground. She had better set out for that village. Doubtless Little Pig and his wife were there waiting for her.

Just as she was about to climb down and start out, she saw something on the eastern horizon. It was at first only an immense cloud of dust. But, as she stared at it, very quickly it became a lot of black dots and shining spots. Then she saw what it was. It was a lot of men—an army. Instantly she knew what army.

"That's the Japanese," she thought. Yes, above them were the buzzing silver planes. They circled about, seeming to search for someone.

"I don't know who you're looking for," she muttered, "unless it's me and Little Pig and his wife. We're the only ones left. You've already killed my brother Pao."

She had almost forgotten that Pao was dead. Now she remembered it acutely. He had such a nice shop—always clean, and the tea good and the best meat dumplings to be had and the price always the same. Pao was a good man. Besides, what about his wife and his seven children? Doubtless they were all killed, too. Now these Japanese were looking for her. It occurred to her that on the dike she could easily be seen. So she clambered hastily down.

It was when she was about halfway down that she thought of the water gate. This old river—it had been a curse to them since time began. Why should it not make up a little now for all the wickedness it had done? It was plotting wickedness again, trying to steal over its banks. Well, why not? She wavered a moment. It was a pity, of course, that the young dead Japanese would be swept into the flood. He was a nice-looking boy, and she had saved him from being stabbed. It was not quite the same as saving his life, of course, but still it was a little the same. If he had been alive, he would have been saved. She went over to him and tugged at him until he lay well near the top of the bank. Then she went down again.

She knew perfectly how to open the water gate. Any child knew how to open the sluice for crops. But she knew also how to swing open the whole gate. The question was, could she open it quickly enough to get out of the way?

"I'm only one old woman," she muttered. She hesitated a second more. Well, it would be a pity not to see what sort of a baby Little Pig's wife would have, but one could not see everything.

She had seen a great deal in this life. There was an end to what one could see, anyway.

She glanced again to the east. There were the Japanese coming across the plain. They were a long clear line of black, dotted with thousands of glittering points. If she opened this gate, the impetuous water would roar toward them, rushing into the plains, rolling into a wide lake, drowning them, maybe. Certainly they could not keep on marching nearer and nearer to her and to Little Pig and his wife who were waiting for her. Well, Little Pig and his wife—they would wonder about her—but they would never dream of this. It would make a good story—she would have enjoyed telling it.

She turned resolutely to the gate. Well, some people fought with airplanes and some with guns, but you could fight with a river, too, if it were a wicked one like this one. She wrenched out a huge wooden pin. It was slippery with silvery green moss. The rill of water burst into a strong jet. When she wrenched one more pin, the rest would give way themselves. She began pulling at it, and felt it slip a little from its hole.

"I might be able to get myself out of purgatory with this," she thought, "and maybe they'll let me have that old man of mine, too. What's a hand of his to all this? Then we'll—"

The pin slipped away suddenly, and the gate burst flat against her and knocked her breath away. She had only time to gasp, to the river:

"Come on, you old demon!"

Then she felt it seize her and lift her up to the sky. It was beneath her and around her. It rolled her joyfully hither and thither, and then, holding her close and enfolded, it went rushing against the enemy.